COLD TRAIL

ELLIE KLINE SERIES: BOOK EIGHT

MARY STONE
DONNA BERDEL

Mary Stone

To my husband.

Thank you for taking care of our home and its many inhabitants while I follow this dream of mine.

Donna Berdel

First, a big thank you to Mary Stone for taking a chance on me by collaborating on this story. I'm honored and indebted!And, of course, to my husband. Thank you for being you. You're my rock.

DESCRIPTION

The cold trail offers no place to hide...

On New Year's Eve, Charleston Cold Case Detective Ellie Kline vows this will be the year she finally brings Dr. Lawrence Kingsley to justice. Not only did the elusive serial killer force her to play his twisted games as a teen, but his reign of terror has killed countless other victims and traumatized the few who survived.

When her boss hands her the files containing dozens of trafficked children, she's instructed to close as many as possible. Drawn by the case of a twelve-year-old boy who disappeared sixteen years ago, Ellie decides that Kingsley—who also vanished without a trace—will have to wait.

Before long, the autistic boy isn't the only missing person Ellie must follow the clues to find. One by one, those who once escaped Kingsley's snare begin to disappear. It's only a matter of time before Ellie's next.

Each shocking twist and turn of Cold Trail, the eighth book of Mary Stone and Donna Berdel's Ellie Kline series, leads to a wild goose chase where the hunter becomes the hunted in a thriller that will convince you of one thing...safety is only an illusion.

1

———

Luke Harrison flipped the page of *The Backwoodsman* magazine and scrunched lower in the back seat of the beat-up Toyota Corolla to avoid the torn spot in the cushion near the top. He hated that spot. He hated the way the stiff, uneven fabric scraped his bare neck.

His mom yelled at him all the time to quit fussing over the seat, but she didn't understand. The scratchy feeling didn't just stay on his neck. It spread all over, not stopping until it felt like the bumpy material was rubbing every inch of his body at once.

The other seat was even worse, with stuffing puffing out of the long gash. The white stuff had yellowed and then turned so brown and nasty that he couldn't bear to look at it. If he'd been forced to touch it, he thought he might go mad.

Luke gazed longingly at the empty spot in the front. The passenger seat didn't have any rips or cracks, but his mom said she couldn't focus on driving when he sat next to her. That left slouching into the back seat as his only option.

Ripped spot avoided, Luke returned to the article, immersing himself in the latest technology on how to purify water without a purification system. Luke had read five other articles on this same topic just that week. He liked learning about anything that had to do with surviving in the wild. He never got bored of the subject, not even when he read about the same topic over and over again.

Honk!

The driver of the silver van on their left blasted his horn, and the sound was like a physical assault. Luke didn't like loud noises. They made him too hot, like his ears were on fire.

"Watch where you're going, asshole!"

At his mom's scream, Luke scrunched even lower in the seat, keeping his eyes firmly on the page, focusing on the bright orange leaf of a tree. He wished he was there right then. The forest looked so pretty, and he wished he could blink and disappear from here to there. He'd camp and build a fire in which to cook the fish he'd catch for his dinner. He'd purify his water and live on the land.

The woods were quiet. No cars. No horns. No constant hum of voices from the TV.

"Fuck off!"

No yelling mothers would ever be allowed at his camp. No bad words, either.

He'd sing the songs that wrote themselves in his head to the rhythm of the stream flowing not far away. He'd make instruments from the trees and learn to play them while crickets and frogs joined along.

My feet are in my shoes...my toes wiggling all around...

His mom yelled again, but Luke tried to close his ears to the sound as he focused on the leaf and the song in his head. He also forced his hands to remain still. Mom didn't like it when he flapped his hands, even though it always made him feel better.

Nothing had been making him feel better lately, not since she got that one phone call a few days ago.

She'd cried at first, then she pulled one of the brown bottles from the top shelf. She drank straight from the bottle, which made her too busy to cry. For a while. When the bottle was empty, though, she ended up crying even louder, this time banging cabinets in the kitchen. She'd even thrown a plate at the floor. On purpose.

If Luke broke a glass on accident, he got in big trouble. He guessed that rule didn't apply to adults. Stupid, if you asked him.

The shattering noise of the plate breaking into little pieces combined with his mom's sobbing had made Luke remember the time he'd tripped onto a fire ant hill. Her crying and screaming and banging had felt the same.

When the pain turned overwhelming, Luke had yelled at his mom. "Stop-stop-stop."

She'd slapped him hard across the face and cried even harder, which only made the awful stinging itch more painful.

She yelled so much more since Aaron left. Luke hated all the yelling, but the constant crying since the phone call was worse. His mom had even stopped showering and cooking or going to the grocery store. All Luke could find to eat this morning was a piece of bread. The last slice, and a butt at that. He didn't like the butts, but his stomach growled so much that he ate it anyway.

When he asked his mom about lunch, she'd smacked him across the face so hard his cheek stung. Then she'd started crying again.

Don't think about that. Think about nice things that make all the hurting go away.

Luke refocused on the article, managing another paragraph before a little gasp from the front seat dampened his palms.

Oh no. Not again.

He read faster, trying to block out his surroundings. That never worked, though. Not without his headphones. Mom told him they didn't have money for a new pair when his last ones broke.

Her cries were soft at first, then grew louder and louder. The sound upset him, so Luke jerked up in the seat. The jagged strip of fabric clawed at his neck.

Flames began to burn the world around him. Brighter. Hotter.

Stop, stop, stop!

He wanted to flap his hands so badly, to lose himself in the soothing movement, but that only made his mom cry harder. Or yell. So, Luke did the next best thing and stroked his watch band. The smooth material beneath his fingertips helped a little, so he kept rubbing it. Again and again, until his body stopped stinging inside and out.

His mom's sobs continued, and the car drifted to the right. *Bump!* Luke bounced in the seat as the front tire veered onto the shoulder. His mom yanked the steering wheel, jerking the car back into their lane.

Luke stared at the back of his mom's head and wished he knew what to say to make her happy again. He wasn't so good with words, though. Somehow, he always managed to say the wrong thing. Which was usually whatever thing was in Luke's mind at the time. His teachers said he was missing a filter. Like the white paper cup that Aaron used to pour coffee grounds in to make coffee.

Apparently, there were rules about when you could share your thoughts and why. Luke liked rules, but he didn't understand these rules. No one had ever explained them to him or why they were important. He just knew that all his teachers told him that he didn't need to share every one of his thoughts.

Like the time in second grade when Sally Meyers asked him if he thought her horse drawing was any good. Luke had taken one look at the stick figure picture with bulging eyes and no ears and told the truth. "No. That doesn't look like a horse at all."

Instead of appreciating his honesty, Sally had cried to Mrs. Wilkins, and Luke had gotten in trouble for being mean.

He hadn't wanted to be mean. Just honest. But even at twelve, Luke was starting to realize that, to a lot of people, honesty was the same thing as unkind. That didn't make sense to him. Why would someone want you to lie to them? But then, most people didn't make sense to Luke. And they didn't understand him.

Except for Aaron.

If Aaron was here, Luke could talk to him. Aaron always knew what to do. But his stepdad was stationed in Iraq, doing important things to help their country.

That left him with Jimmy Hoffa.

"Hey, Jimmy Hoffa. Did you know that if you're camping, you can purify water even without iodine tablets or chlorine tablets or a filter?"

Luke paused, even though he understood Jimmy Hoffa couldn't reply. He wasn't stupid. Jimmy Hoffa was his imaginary friend. Imaginary meant not real. In Luke's experience, real people got mad when he talked too much about camping. Luke didn't know why. He loved camping and learning how to survive in the wild, and anything related to living outdoors.

That was why Jimmy Hoffa was so great. No matter how long Luke talked, Jimmy Hoffa listened. Without rolling his eyes at Luke or making fun of him like the kids at school did.

"You can purify water with fire. First, you have to find water from the cleanest source possible. The higher up in the mountains you are, the cleaner the water will be. And moving water, like a stream, is better than still water. Once you find water, you have to build a really hot fire, and then you fill a metal pot halfway. Only halfway, because if you fill the pot too full, it can boil over onto your fire. That's bad because water on your fire makes the temperature less hot, and your water might stop boiling, and then you have to start all over again."

Jimmy Hoffa pointed at Luke's watch. He didn't talk much, but that was okay. Luke talked enough for both of them.

Luke nodded. "Good question. It takes ten minutes total to purify the water, but you only boil it for five. When that whole five minutes is up, you take the pot off the fire and set it somewhere safe to cool. Once it's cool enough not to burn your mouth, you can drink it. You can also drink rainwater if you're camping, but that's not purifying water because it's already clean enough to drink. You just have to set up a container to collect the rain in."

"Jesus, Lucas Richard Harrison, can you shut up already?" Mom's words were their own kind of slap. "No wonder you don't have any friends. No one gives two shits about how to purify water. And how many times have I told you to quit talking to your imaginary friend? It's creepy."

His mom made that scrunched up face at him in the rearview mirror, and though he could only see her eyes right then, he knew her lip was curled up too. Almost like a dog snarl.

Luke's fingers returned to the watch band. "Jimmy Hoffa likes camping too."

So did Aaron. Aaron was the one who'd given Luke the special watch. The coolest watch ever. It had a compass, and a fire starter, and even a little multi-tool. He'd even had Luke's name engraved on the inside.

"How the hell would you know what Jimmy Hoffa likes? He's been dead for years."

That painful prickling sensation returned, like the fire ants were biting him again. Luke stroked the watch with more force. "Jimmy Hoffa is my friend."

His mom made a noise deep in her throat, just like she did when she got snot caught there and had to hack it out. "If I'd known the drugs I took when I was pregnant would give you such a weak mind, I never would have touched them. And that goes double for your real father, the piece of shit. That rat didn't even stick around long enough for me to see the two pink lines on the pregnancy test. God!"

She slammed her hands on the steering wheel, making the car jerk.

Luke rubbed his fingers over the watch band again. What had he done wrong this time? Why did his mom care if he talked to Jimmy Hoffa or that he liked talking about camping? Lately, she'd been upset all the time. Ever since that stupid phone call.

Not that things had been great before then, but Luke would take the late-night dancing to loud music after too much wine any day over this. The music was better than the screaming or crying.

And everything had been better before Aaron left.

Luke sighed. He hadn't needed Jimmy Hoffa much then. Not when Aaron was around. Aaron was the person who'd taught Luke about camping. About how to set up a tent, catch and clean a fish, build a fire, make a mat out of branches, and so much more.

Once Aaron got back from overseas, he'd take Luke camping again. And his mom would stop crying.

Luke brightened. Mrs. Hawkins, his teacher last year,

had told the class that focusing on the good in life helped people to feel happier. Maybe all his mom needed was a reminder.

"Remember when Aaron was here all the time? That was nice. When is he coming home?"

His mom sucked in a loud breath but didn't answer. Instead, she swerved the car into a gas station and pulled up in front of the little store. Luke liked the little stores. They almost always had Slurpee machines. Luke liked cherry Slurpees best, and then cola ones. The other kinds were gross and made him gag.

But he only liked them when the cup wasn't filled all the way to the top so that it wouldn't leak over the lid, because Slurpees were sticky, and sticky things on his skin made Luke feel almost as bad as the time his mom and Aaron tried to take him to a concert where the outdoor arena was so loud and crowded that Luke had felt like he was under attack.

"Stay put." His mom slammed the car door and entered the store before Luke could protest.

"I'm thirsty," Luke said to her retreating back on the far side of the glass. "I want to go inside too."

In the seat next to him, Jimmy Hoffa shook his head. *Don't go in. Something's wrong.*

Luke wanted to argue, but he sensed the wrongness too. An itch crawled over his neck, so he turned back to the article on water purification and began rereading from the beginning. The familiar information soothed him, like wrapping him in his favorite blanket. The furry one Aaron gave him, not the itchy old blanket his mom had picked up at a flea market.

Camping made sense. Tools made sense. Luke found things that followed rules to be calming.

The front door opened, and the car rocked as his mother

climbed into the driver's seat. She pulled a cherry cola out of a plastic sack and popped the top.

Luke perked up. Not as good as a cherry Slurpee, but he liked cherry anything. He leaned forward and reached for the can, but she whisked it away.

"Hold your horses."

Luke frowned. His mom said that expression enough that he knew what she meant, but he still thought it was silly. He didn't have any horses.

She moved the can to where he couldn't see it and dug through the purse sitting on her lap. He played with his watch and waited...waited...waited...

"Here you go."

Luke grabbed the cold can from his mom's hand before she could change her mind and guzzled two giant gulps, enjoying the way the syrupy sweetness fizzed down his throat.

"Make sure you drink every drop."

He paused with the can halfway to his lips. That was weird. His mom never said that about soda.

Even as he stared at her in surprise, she did something even weirder...she smiled at him. He froze. It was the first smile she'd given Luke in a long time. Then he remembered. Luke had reminded her of a good thing in their life—Aaron. His old teacher's advice had worked!

Luke smiled back and drank a few more sips.

His mom drove them back to the highway while Luke sipped his drink and went back to reading about camping. Before long, the words started to blur, and his eyelids grew heavy. They were drifting shut when the car jerked to a stop.

Luke blinked and looked up and around, trying to focus his blurry gaze on his surroundings. They were parked outside a plain beige building he'd never seen before. After shutting off the engine, his mom twisted in her seat. She grabbed the soda from the drink holder and shook the can, sending the remaining liquid sloshing against the metal.

"I thought I told you to finish the whole thing. Can't you do anything right?"

Her cheeks flushed bright red, and her eyes turned scary. Luke dropped his gaze to his lap. He didn't like the itchy sensation of looking people in the eye anyway, but he especially disliked it when his mom's pupils changed to tiny black dots. That was when she got the meanest.

Luke realized he might be different than other kids, but he wasn't stupid. He knew that his mom took drugs.

She slammed the can back into the plastic holder and started swearing, beating the steering wheel with her fists and calling Luke names before finally calming down.

Luke curled up, waiting for the fire ants to strike. But they didn't. Instead of the burning, his body felt like...almost like he could float away.

"At least I'm almost done with you."

This time, when she turned to Luke, her face was different. She reminded Luke of a monster. Which was weird enough that Luke shivered.

Something's very wrong, Jimmy Hoffa whispered. *Run.*

Luke trusted Jimmy Hoffa and reached for the door handle. Or tried to. Though his inside voice told his arm to move, it didn't. It felt too heavy to lift. Except that didn't make any sense. He lifted his arms all the time.

He shook his head, and the car spun. That's bad, right?

Very bad, Jimmy Hoffa agreed. *Run, Luke. Now.*

Luke gritted his teeth and reached for the door again. His arm only twitched in response.

Pressure built inside Luke, the same way it did when he was stuck in a small room with too many people talking at once. He was trapped. He hated feeling trapped.

"I want Aaron. When is Aaron coming home?"

His mom climbed between the space in the front seats, not stopping until she was beside him. Her face still like a monster, she grabbed his cheeks with her hands. "Never." She shook him. "You hear me, you worthless little brat? Aaron is never coming back."

Never?

Why?

Before Luke could ask the question or beg her to stop touching him, his mom's hand whipped out and covered his mouth and nose.

Luke didn't know that a monster could become even more monsterish, but he knew now.

Her hand pressed harder. "And neither are you."

2

C harleston Cold Case Detective Ellie Kline slid another discrete glance at her phone while the animated discussion of which Swiss chateau was the best for an intimate spring getaway raged on around her.

The numbers blinked up at her without mercy. Eleven twenty-nine in the evening. Fourteen whole minutes had passed since the last time she'd checked the time.

With a sigh, Ellie slipped her phone back into the black satin Gucci clutch—a gift from her mother—and pasted a smile on her face, in case her mom was watching her now. Helen Kline's high society parties had never been Ellie's favorite, even before she'd shocked her parents by announcing she planned to become a cop.

This particular party, hosted within the walls of her mom and dad's elegant Charleston mansion, was no different. The expansive living room where Ellie grew up was oozing with men in tuxedos and expensive dark suits while women draped themselves in diamonds and gemstones. Most of the latter group wore shimmering dresses to match, with their hair twisted into chic updos or falling in perfect waves around their shoulders from a fresh salon blowout. A far cry from Ellie's untamed mane, which exploded around her face in a riot of red, untamed curls. Her default look when she couldn't be bothered to style it.

Ellie glanced down at her sleeveless black sheath and silver heels—the first items she'd pulled from her closet—and mentally shrugged. At least she was here in an outfit more suitable than the fleece pajamas she'd rather be wearing.

In her own home.

While she tried to hunt down the madman who appeared to be more ghost than human.

Don't think about him.

Mentally berating herself for letting her thoughts return to the evasive Lawrence Kingsley, Ellie swirled the champagne in the flute she'd been carrying around like a prop since arriving. The amber liquid looked about as flat as she felt, the optimism she'd mustered for the Christmas holidays having faded over the past week.

If today wasn't New Year's Eve, Ellie would have made her excuses and stayed home. In deference to the holiday, she'd stick it out for another half hour and make her escape once the clock struck midnight.

"Oh, we donated one-hundred thousand to that group this year." A middle-aged brunette preened while the other women gasped and complimented the large number. She waved a *it was nothing* hand. "We needed the tax write-off. I swear, that husband of mine spends more time looking for tax write-offs and shelters than he does working."

Two of the other women chimed in with agreements while a third raised a crystal flute in her manicured hand. "And amen to that, unless you ladies want your hard-earned money to go to Uncle Sam while you're forced to start shopping at the mall."

"Eww!" The other three women said it at the same time before all of them broke into peals of laughter.

Ellie scowled. Eww was right. Just not for the reason they thought.

Before she said something her mom would regret, Ellie pivoted and stalked her way through the people to a less-crowded spot by the archway that led into the dining room.

She probably looked like a wallflower, but she didn't care.

Helen Kline had outdone herself with the decorations, so Ellie distracted herself with those. Strategically placed garlands draped along the arches and over doors while fairy lights twinkled throughout the rooms and outside. The air held the combined scent of cinnamon-spice and the delicacies splayed along the massive dining room table.

Ellie's favorite were the giant silver and red candles ensconced in glass scattered through the rooms. As if it was bowing its thanks, the candle nearest her flickered like a tiny orange dancer. As Ellie stared, the small flame grew until she was no longer staring at a candle but into a giant wall of fire.

Orange flames licking high at the sky.

The acrid smell of smoke.

Screams coming from the car trapped on the other side until they died off.

Choking on the reek of burnt hair while clawing at the dirt until her fingernails bled.

Ellie dug her nails into her palms, utilizing the sting to yank herself back from the nightmare scene. She'd been half out of her mind that night. So desperate to smother the flames and rescue the man trapped in the trunk that she'd kept digging at the dirt long past the point of hopelessness.

Afterward, her guilt over the sight of the burned remains assembled on the autopsy table had almost overwhelmed her. Ellie remembered her fervent, desperate pleas to the universe for the bones to belong to someone else. She'd clung to that hope, right up until the dental records confirmed the dead man's identity, leaving no room for doubt.

The poor soul screaming in fear and agony from behind a wall of flames had belonged to Gabe Fisher.

And now he was dead. Burned to death. One more victim of the monster known as Dr. Kingsley.

Despite the crush of people and the thermostat her mom set at a comfortable seventy-two, a chill streaked across Ellie's bare arms. She distracted herself by people-watching, but that only soured her mood even more.

Look at them.

Dressed in ensembles that cost thousands of dollars, enjoying a spread of alcohol and food that cost even more. Pretending to be here because of their altruism, but really, they were only in attendance to flaunt their wealth and rub elbows with others in their income bracket while simultaneously discussing tax shelters.

"Hey, you okay? What's wrong?"

Ellie started at the light touch on her shoulder. Her coworker, roommate, and best friend frowned up at her, still diminutive next to Ellie despite her gravity-defying red heels. Unlike Ellie, Jillian Reed had spent time on her appearance. A red halter dress made the most of her friend's curves, and the mass of soft blonde curls piled on top of her head flattered her gamine face.

Jacob Garcia didn't say anything, but she knew her ex-partner well enough to read the concern in his furrowed brow as he studied her over a pint of beer.

Ellie sipped from her glass and then pulled a face at the tepid, bubble-free liquid. "I'm fine. Nothing's wrong. Nothing new, anyway."

Jillian and Jacob did that couple's trick where they read each other's minds just by exchanging a glance.

Jillian squeezed Ellie's arm. "Gabe?"

The sound of his name pierced through her like a knife, and she didn't even try to deny it. "Yeah."

Ellie didn't need to explain. Besides being her best friends, Jillian and Jacob both worked with her at the Charleston Police Department. They knew all about Gabe Fisher, the young man who'd once worked as Dr. Kingsley's assistant until he risked his life to save Jillian from his sadistic boss.

When Gabe had entered the federal witness security program known as WITSEC, Ellie had been happy for him to get a fresh start. That happiness hadn't lasted long.

Defying all odds, Kingsley had somehow managed to track him down. After sending him a dead bird in the mail, the once renowned psychiatrist had kidnapped Gabe and whisked him off to a warehouse where he'd tortured him on camera.

Ellie clenched the flute tight. So close. With the help of Gabe's federal marshal and others, they'd tracked Kingsley's hideaway down and rushed a federal SWAT team there to save him.

Except Kingsley had outsmarted them again, disappearing with Gabe minutes before they arrived.

Just a few miles from where she'd come so close to finding them, he'd burned Gabe to death in a car he abandoned on the side of the road.

Gabe's screams were cut off by Jillian's soft voice. "That's understandable, but it's New Year's Eve." Jillian clinked her champagne glass against the one still in Ellie's hand. "You're allowed to spend quality time with your family and not think about anything, especially work, for a little bit."

Ellie snorted and looked around to make sure the sound hadn't offended one of her mother's guests' sensitive ears. "Quality time with my family plus two hundred of their wealthiest friends, you mean."

Jillian pressed a dainty hand to her chest. "Why, Eleanor Elizabeth Francis Kline, are you turning into a reverse snob?"

Ellie's lips twitched at her friend's antics, making her love her even more. "Maybe, but don't tell my parents, okay? Winning Helen over to the idea of me being a cop was tough enough. She might disown me over this." The weight resettled across her shoulders. "Seriously, though, why am I here, hanging out with these people," she waved her hand at the crowd, "while Kingsley is still at large, undoubtedly plotting his next kill?"

"Oh, I don't know." Jillian gave her a look that rivaled her mother's. "Maybe because it's not healthy to hang out at home or work all day and think about murderers?"

When Ellie turned to Jacob for support, he shrugged. "Don't look at me. I'm just here to act as arm candy."

Jillian rolled her eyes before leaning in to give him a peck on the cheek.

Ellie faked gagged. "Ah, so sweet."

As her friends laughed, a tall, attractive man wearing an exquisite black suit materialized to Ellie's right. She felt him before she noticed his approach.

"Ellie, fancy seeing you here." The blond man winked, triggering a rush of nostalgic warmth in Ellie's chest.

"Nick. Nice to see you."

Nick Greene looked good. Not that Ellie's ex-boyfriend ever looked bad, but there was a new quality to him that she couldn't quite put her finger on, one that injected an extra sparkle into his already handsome face.

Jillian exchanged a quick greeting with Nick before wiggling her fingers at Ellie. "I'm dragging Jacob to the dance floor now. See you in a bit."

Jacob yelped, his dark eyes wide. "Wait, you're doing what? Arm candy, remember?"

Ellie and Nick waited until Jillian tugged her reluctant

partner out of sight before facing each other. When Ellie gazed into his eyes, she steeled herself for an onslaught of pain over their breakup, or at the very least, regret.

To her surprise, neither emotion surfaced, and she found herself grinning in response to his larger than life smile.

"I'd ask what you've been up to lately, but I think I can guess. Still chasing bad guys and making the world a safer place?"

Ellie stiffened. Was that a dig?

After studying his expression and discovering nothing but warmth, she relaxed. "Lots of the first part, not enough of the second. What about you? What are you working on these days? It's been a while since I've seen you around."

His lips curved into a smile, a once-familiar sight that pierced her heart. The pang she felt wasn't over their breakup, though. It was over the loss of Nick as a friend. It was hard not to mourn the man she'd counted on for years.

For so long, the pair of them had been attached at the hip, serving as each other's plus-one to everything from galas to family events. On paper, they'd made perfect sense as a couple. Their parents moved in the same social circles. They knew all the same people.

For a long time, nothing had thrilled the hard-to-impress Helen Kline more than the notion of a Kline-Greene wedding.

Even Ellie started believing she and her lifelong friend had a real shot. Until her career came between them.

"Still not paying attention to your mom's events, I see. Some things never change."

Ellie wrinkled her nose, baffled. What did her mom's events have to do with him? "I'm sorry?"

He grinned and tugged at one of her stray curls. "This," he swept his arm to encompass the partygoers, "is what I've been doing. Well, sort of. The part I'm actually doing is building low-income retirement housing. That's what this fundraiser is for, to raise money for my project. Which you'd know if you ever read the invitations your mom sent you closely. Or at all."

Valid point, but whatever. Ellie was far more interested in his project. She reached out and clasped his hand. "That's so wonderful, Nick. Really. Thank you for helping our community. Can you tell me more?"

His cheeks flushed pink at her compliment. "You're too kind, and I predict that you're going to regret asking me that in a few minutes. There's nothing I like to talk about more."

True to his word, Nick dove right into an animated discussion of his project. As he filled Ellie in on the details of his nonprofit venture, she experienced a bittersweet pang beneath her ribs.

Nick truly was one of the good ones. If only she had been able to love him the way everyone told her she should. Ellie had cared about him a great deal. Just not in the way that he deserved to be loved.

Once Nick realized that she never would, he'd broken up with her. Ellie's heart hurt at the time, but even then, she'd realized his decision was for the best. Nick could never figure out why her job was so important to her.

Unlike Special Agent Clay Lockwood.

Ellie's mind drifted to the dedicated, soft-spoken FBI agent who understood Ellie on a level that Nick, in his charmed life, would never be able to touch. Both she and Clay had demons in their past that drew them to police work in the first place. Ellie never had to pretend to be someone else around Clay or make excuses for who she was.

Still, things between Ellie and Clay were...complicated. She traced the rim of her crystal glass and pretended to listen to Nick talk about the land he was buying.

Where was Clay tonight? Out with friends? Or was he

doing what Ellie wished she were doing...sitting at home, figuring out how to reel Kingsley in, once and for all. Or were his thoughts wound up in all those missing kid cases they'd uncovered on their recent trip to Florida?

The specifics of the few files they'd read still haunted Ellie...but not nearly as much as she bet Clay's missing sister haunted him. Caraleigh.

"Uh oh, I know that look." Nick's hand waved in front of her face. "You're thinking of all the people you might be helping if only you weren't stuck at this dreadful party."

Ellie blinked up into Nick's amused eyes and blushed. "I'm so sorry. I've been distracted lately. Don't be mad, please?"

He shook his head. "I'm not mad. That's why we broke up, so I wouldn't have to be mad at your work anymore." Nick softened the words with a smile, easing Ellie's discomfort.

"Right. Good call on your part, I might add." She saluted him with her sad drink before taking a gulp. She grimaced at the taste. Nope. Not any better this time around.

Nick slid his hands into his pockets and tilted his head, gestures that Ellie knew meant he had an uncomfortable observation to share.

Uh oh. She eyed him warily over her crystal flute.

"Look, I know we don't talk as much anymore, but I... would you like some friendly advice?"

Was there a tactful way to say no to that question? If so, Ellie had never learned the trick. She squared her shoulders and summoned a wan smile.

"Friendly sure sounds better than unfriendly advice." She winced at the forced cheerfulness in her voice, took a deep breath, and tried again. "I mean, of course. Who better to give me advice than the person who was my best friend for so many years?" She touched his arm. "We're still friends, aren't we?"

Nick glanced at where her fingers rested on his suit, pale against the black fabric, before covering them with his own and giving a quick squeeze. "We are. Always."

Relief whooshed through her veins. A second passed, then two, before they both disentangled their hands at the same time.

Ellie stepped back. "So, about that friendly advice?"

"Right. I was just going to say that doing meaningful work is very fulfilling. So is helping people. But that doesn't mean it isn't work." He speared her with a knowing look. "You need balance, Ellie. At the end of the day, if you do nothing but pour your time and energy and heart into your work, you'll burn out."

The observation caught Ellie off guard, like a car side-swiping her on the highway. Hadn't she just gotten a variation of this same lecture from Jillian?

She didn't recover in time to form a coherent response because a dark-haired woman sidled up to Nick and curled red-tipped fingers around his shoulder. The newcomer flashed Ellie a perfect, white-toothed grin before turning to Nick.

"Sorry to intrude, but the ball is going to drop soon."

Nick's entire being lit up as he gazed down into the woman's upturned face. "We can't miss that, can we?" He grazed his lips over her cheek and wrapped an arm around her waist.

The pair made a beautiful couple. Far better than she and Nick ever had. The woman looked perfectly at home at the event, the epitome of flirty yet sophisticated in a black dress with a frothy skirt that shimmered in the light from scattered beadwork. Her dark hair was twisted into an elegant style on top of her head, and her skin held the same golden gleam as Nick's, suggesting that they'd both just returned from the same tropical vacation.

A life that could have been Ellie's. One that she'd traded for criminals and cold cases.

"Well, it was nice seeing you, Ellie. I hope you have a wonderful year. Oh, and consider what I said, will you?"

Ellie nodded. As the dark-haired beauty led him away, she felt the final nail sink into the coffin of their relationship. Good for Nick. She hoped they'd be happy together.

The noise level in the house ratcheted up as excitement over the impending countdown rose. Ellie weaved her way to the French doors, trading the warmth of her parents' living room for the fresh air on their patio. This time, her shiver was due to the temperature.

Charleston tended to be mild weather-wise, but on this particular night, the air held a brisk chill. She hugged herself and gazed out across the massive expanse of her parents' backyard, lit from the glow of the fairy lights twined around the wrought iron railing.

When heels clicked across the patio behind her, Ellie knew without looking who it was. Jillian leaned on the wrought iron railing beside her while Jacob wrapped his arms around his girlfriend's waist.

Ellie shook her head. "Can you believe this year is almost over?"

"Only if you can believe everything that happened this year." Jillian cupped her hands to her mouth. "In case anyone out there is listening, I hereby put in my request for a calm, uneventful new year."

"Your request for an unexciting year is duly noted."

As a reward for his humor, Jillian jabbed an elbow into Jacob's ribs. "Not you, doofus. You can give me all the excitement you want. I meant…" She bit her lip and stole a glance at Ellie.

Jacob rubbed his side. "She meant it'd be great if we could catch Kingsley so we aren't constantly chasing him down and cleaning up his messes. Oh, and maybe a little less Katarina Volkov drama too."

At the mention of Katarina, Ellie's teeth clamped together, while at the same time, her heart softened just a little. She waged this internal war, fluctuating between anger and empathy, every time she thought of the woman Kingsley had groomed as both victim and protégé.

"It's New Year's Eve, though, so instead of dwelling on that, I'd like to take this moment to thank you both for being such good friends to me during this batshit year. You have no idea how much having friends who understand me and who I can trust makes my life so much better. I won't lie and say that I don't worry about Kingsley taking one of you away from me because we all know he'd do it with a song in his heart if he thought he could."

"Ten…nine…"

A chorus of voices erupted from the house, interrupting Ellie and leaving her mind free to flash with images from the past.

"Eight…"

There was the girl who sat across from her in Kingsley's warehouse, back when Ellie was only fifteen. The girl she'd sentenced to death by uttering the phrase, "Die, Bitch! Die."

"Six…"

Gabe's pretty face appeared next, making Ellie's abdomen clench with grief. What might the softhearted man have accomplished with his life had he not gotten tangled up in Kingsley's web?

"Four…"

The images blinked faster. Clay and his missing sister, Caraleigh. Katarina and the daughter she'd just been reunited with.

"One! Happy New Year!"

Jacob pulled Jillian in for a kiss while noisemakers rattled in the New Year from inside the house. Before Ellie had a chance to feel too awkward, the couple broke apart and flung their arms around her, drawing her into a three-person hug.

"Happy New Year, guys," Jacob said from within their little circle. "Here's to a great year for all of us."

As love and friendship washed over her, Ellie made herself a promise. She wanted to turn the possibility of a great year into reality, which meant one thing.

This would be the year she finally dragged Dr. Lawrence Kingsley to justice.

3

Katarina Volkov ran her fingers through her short, jet-black hair and assessed the new style in the mirror that hung inside the guest bathroom at Clayne Miller's house. The image reflected back showed a woman dressed to kill in a sleek red dress glimmering beneath the light fixture. The fabric hugged her breasts and skimmed her hips before ending halfway to her knees in a frothy little skirt that bounced when she walked, leaving a long expanse of her muscled thighs bare.

She leaned over the marbled countertop and bared her teeth in a feral smile. Combined with the red stiletto heels and the knife attached to her upper thigh, the new haircut made her feel like a badass. The spiky black layers emitted a very don't-screw-with-me vibe.

Perfect.

She unscrewed a tube of red lipstick and swept more color onto her lips. The bold hue suited her new look. Katarina had changed her style so many times over the past year, she could barely keep up. So many new masks on the outside that she often struggled to recognize who she was on the inside. Even now, as she admired the brazen, tough haircut, she wondered how much of the woman in the mirror was truly Katarina, and how much was a Kingsley creation?

Wait. Not Katarina. *Katrina.* She flinched. Katrina Cook. That was her new WITSEC identity, not Katarina Volkov. The sooner she erased the old name from her consciousness, the better.

"Shouldn't be that tough," she murmured to the stranger in the mirror. "Not like Volkov was your real name to begin with." No, Katarina Volkov had only been one of many names she'd acquired as a little girl when being juggled between illegal adoptive homes.

Katarina fluffed her short strands before tossing her head and staring deep into her own brown eyes.

"Who are you, really?"

The reflection didn't answer.

"Mama?"

The tentative, high-pitched voice triggered a visceral reaction in Katarina. Like her heart might burst at the seams from excess love while at the same time her abdomen clenched with a fierce, protective urge.

Her daughter, Harmony—*Bethany* now—stood in the doorway, one hand kneading the material of her *Wonder Woman* nightshirt while the other rubbed her eye.

Katarina's lips twitched at the sight of the nightshirt. Her daughter was just now getting into superheroes with all the enthusiasm at an eight-year-old's disposal. That shirt had been a Christmas present, and ever since squealing when she'd unwrapped it, Bethany had resisted taking the garment off. Katarina had to sneak the stupid shirt into the washer while Bethany bathed. She wouldn't be surprised if her daughter had watched the movie fifty times by now.

The beautiful superhero smirked at Katarina from the

white fabric, dressed in her traditional red and blue outfit. The jet-black hair that cascaded over the do-gooder's shoulders was so dark, it held a blue tinge.

Jet-black hair. *Oh.*

Katarina's gaze swung back to her own ebony hair. Huh. Maybe her color choice hadn't been so random, after all. Wouldn't be the first time she'd changed her appearance for someone else.

This time, though, the idea of switching up her looks to please someone else sparked joy in Katarina's chest. Not distaste.

Not when the person Katarina wanted to make happy was her daughter.

She tapped the little girl on the nose. "What are you doing still up?"

"It's too loud here, and I can't sleep." Bethany yawned, sounding miserable. "And I thought I saw a monster outside my window."

Katarina's heart twinged. "It is loud, I'm sorry. We'll be going home before too long, okay?" She made the promise with a confidence she didn't feel. As a general rule, drug parties tended to drag on into the wee hours of the morning. Throw in the fact that it was New Year's Eve, and there was no telling when the partiers would finally quit. "Want Mama to take you back to bed and make sure there are no monsters?"

Bethany nodded and lifted her arms. Katarina scooped up the eight-year-old and carried her back to the guest bedroom that her boyfriend, Clayne Miller, had set aside for her.

"Are we going to stay in Wyoming a long time?"

Katarina kicked the door to the guest bedroom shut behind them. "No, I don't think so. I'm hoping we'll be leaving soon. Why do you ask?"

"Does Clayne have to come with us when we go?" The little girl buried her head in Katarina's neck, hiding her face.

Katarina sighed as she lowered her daughter to the rumpled bed. Bethany had met Clayne for the first time less than a week ago, when Katarina had finally decided to let the drug dealer she was dating in on the secret of Bethany's existence. Not that she'd wanted to, even then. But the town was too small. Sooner or later, Clayne would have discovered Bethany anyway, and if Katarina didn't tell him herself, he'd wonder what else she was hiding from him.

Turned out, the answer to that last question was *a hell of a lot*. Katarina had secrets. Lots of them. So, the practical thing to do was for Katarina to introduce her daughter to the man she was dating before that option was taken out of her hands.

What Katarina hadn't counted on was sunny-natured Bethany taking an immediate dislike to Clayne.

Although, when the ancient threadbare blanket scratched her hands and emitted a sour reek as she pulled it up to cover the little girl, Katarina wasn't convinced that Clayne was trying all that hard to win Bethany over, either.

She perched on the edge of the double bed and resisted the urge to drop her face into her hands. This wasn't the life she'd ever pictured for her daughter…sleeping in strange houses while her new boyfriend tried to wow big names in the drug business at his holiday party.

Katarina would have to make some adjustments to rectify that soon.

"You forgot to check for monsters."

"Oops, silly mama!" Katarina slapped her forehead, sending Bethany into a peal of giggles. "I'll do that right now."

She rose and began prowling the room, making a big production of searching for any beasts that might be lurking.

"Here, monster, monster. Come out so I can send you back to monsterland with my magic blade."

Bethany clapped her hands when Katarina plucked the knife from her thigh holster. She was pretty sure other moms didn't have magic blades, but so what? The idea of a monster-removal knife both delighted her daughter and helped her fall asleep.

Plus, it was never too early to teach a girl the value of a good weapon.

After peering under the bed, in the closet, and out the window, Katarina declared the room to be monster-free. She sank back down on the bed but hesitated before kissing her daughter goodnight. "If you could pick the perfect place to live, where would we go?"

The little girl's eyes lit up. She forgot all about Clayne and monsters, the way Katarina had hoped. "I want us to live on Themyscira. That's *Wonder Woman's* homeland." Bethany explained this fact solemnly, as if she hadn't made Katarina watch the movie with her enough times to memorize the entire script.

Katarina stroked Bethany's soft blonde hair. "That sounds wonderful, sweetie, but Themyscira is a made-up place."

The sparkle in the little girl's eyes dimmed. Her mouth drooped. The expression tugged at Katarina's newly discovered mom-heart, compelling her to try to ease her daughter's sadness. "But you know what does exist? Greece."

Bethany tilted her head. "What's Greece?"

Katarina described the image in her head. "Greece is a country in Europe that's partly made up of a bunch of small islands. One of the most stunning islands is Santorini. It has white sand beaches and the bluest water you've ever seen, but the city itself is built up into the cliffs."

"Ooh, that sounds so beautiful! Like somewhere that mermaids would live." Bethany fidgeted beneath the covers.

In her book, mermaids were only second best to her favorite superhero.

"I bet mermaids would love it there. The buildings are a bright white that sparkles in the sunlight, and lots of the roofs are tiled in the same blue color as the sea. There are little shops and restaurants everywhere, so you can just walk around, tasting food and shopping. And that's just one of many islands, each one as beautiful as the next."

Bethany beamed up at Katarina. "That's where I want to live! On a teeny tiny island. Just me and you. Can we do that, Mama? Move to a little island in Greece one day?"

Katarina leaned in and squeezed her daughter's shoulders, inhaling the sweet scent of her strawberry shampoo while her heart overflowed with a love so deep it hurt. More than anything, she wanted that too. To escape with Bethany to a faraway place where Katarina could leave her old life behind, once and for all.

"We can, sweetie. And we will, if that's what you really want."

"I do."

Bethany yawned again, so Katarina tucked the ratty old blanket around her shoulders, even knowing that the little girl would wrestle the covers off not fifteen minutes after she fell asleep. She pressed a kiss to her daughter's cheek, still plump with baby fat. "Sweet dreams."

"Night night, Mama."

Katarina rose, and after one last glance at her daughter, locked the door and pulled it shut behind her. She gave the knob a hard jiggle to make sure it wouldn't open before she went in search of Clayne.

A couple staggered down the hallway toward her. The brunette—whose skin-tight black dress was cut so low in the front that Katarina could see the indent of her navel—

giggled when she stepped on Katarina's toe before stumbling back. "Whoopsies, guess I forgot how to walk."

That comment sent the bearded man she was with into howls of laughter. Katarina bared her teeth at them and slammed her shoulder into the other woman's as she shoved her way past. Already off-balance, the brunette crashed into the man, and both of them tumbled to the floor.

"Whoopsies, guess I forgot how to walk too."

Ignoring their shrieks, Katarina continued down the hall until she entered the large, open living room. The space was still crammed full of party guests in various stages of inebriation, who'd grown so loud that even the high ceilings couldn't help mute the din.

She darted around a solo woman writhing to a beat that had nothing to do with the hip hop song pumping out from the speakers and hurried by a younger man as he hurled into a copper urn in front of the oversized fireplace. The whiff of bile mixed with whiskey churned her stomach.

Greece sounded better and better every second.

Why was she here? Submitting herself and her daughter to the vileness of these people?

Oh yeah...money. The one thing she needed to make her and her daughter's dream come true.

As Katarina continued hunting for Clayne, she allowed the idea of island life to wash over her. The warm sun beating down on her skin. Cooling off in the crystal blue water and digging her toes into the white, pristine sand.

She pictured Bethany splashing in the waves and the two of them snorkeling. When their fingers were pruny from the water, they'd hit up a little café and eat fruit and yogurt sweetened with honey. Just the two of them in a wash of sunlight and warmth.

The complete opposite of the frigid winters in Podunk, Wyoming.

A crash yanked her back to the party, a depressing contrast to the peaceful waves in her imagination. Katarina frowned. In her daydream, Clayne didn't even exist, so she asked herself again...what exactly was she doing here? Why was she wasting time with Clayne at all?

Her frown deepened. Was she really willing to sacrifice everything, including her life with Bethany, just to experience the transient thrill of being back in the game?

Kingsley's game. The one he'd taught her in the first place.

Katarina rubbed her arms as she wound her way through the room. She hated herself for allowing boredom to propel her down the path Kingsley had revealed to her. Giving in to her hunger for risk and violence was a weakness. Especially now that she had Bethany to consider.

If she could just get out of this small town, Katarina knew things would be easier.

She finally spotted Clayne near the kitchen. He was speaking faster than normal, waving his hands around and slurring his words. She gritted her teeth. Great. Drunk, and probably on some kind of upper.

Why was she here again?

Katarina sidled up to him without a word as he blabbed away to the other three men. She had only met Lance Martinez before tonight. Clayne had pointed the other two out earlier, so she knew their names—Mick Fortner and Eddie Taylor. All three of them were part of a drug ring that Clayne salivated over the chance to impress.

"I'm your guy. Lay it on me. I can handle any size deal you're running." Clayne puffed out his chest, and Katarina held back a snicker at her boyfriend's attempt to put off alpha vibes. Too bad all she could think of were pigeons on the Animal Planet show she'd watched with Bethany last week.

Lance Martinez rubbed his goatee. "Maybe you could help us with a big run that's coming through soon, out of Savannah and headed to the Canadian border." He slid a glance at Katarina and dismissed her just as quickly.

Katarina's hackles rose. Idiot. He probably assumed that she had no idea what a run even was. She bit her tongue to keep from spouting off her knowledge of the motorcycle gangs that moved large amounts of drugs and illegal weapons across the country.

"Then tell them to head here. I can keep the haul safe overnight." In his eagerness, Clayne flailed his hands in the air and whacked Katarina on the arm. "Hey, where'd you come from, you sneaky little thing?" He narrowed his eyes as if she hadn't been standing there for the last two minutes, then roared with laughter.

Her cheeks ached from the effort of holding a fake smile. How much longer until she could scoop up Bethany and drive back to their own little house? "Just got back from freshening up a little."

"Yeah? What took you so long? I was getting ready to send a search party out for you."

Since the last thing Katarina wanted to do was discuss putting her daughter back to bed or share their dreams about Greece, she puckered her lips. "What? You don't like my new lipstick?"

The distraction worked. Clayne's gaze lowered to her mouth, so she leaned forward and pressed her lips to his. The entire time his tongue twisted with hers, she lamented how predictable he'd turned out to be and how bored she was.

That first kiss they'd shared back in the bar where they'd met had sent a thrill through Katarina. Especially when she'd grabbed Clayne's balls and he hadn't even flinched.

Since then, the shine had worn off.

"Damn, boy. I'd say get a room, but hey, this here's a room, so knock yourself out."

Katarina wasn't sure which man made the comment, but he was loud enough that Clayne finally came up for air, sporting a shit-eating grin. "Aw, come on now. Can I help it if my girl is too hot to resist? She can get a little pissy if I don't give her enough attention, you know how it is."

He winked at the threesome before wrapping his arm around Katarina's waist and tugging her off to the side. An arm she was half-tempted to stab with the knife strapped to her thigh.

Attention? Please.

Right now, she'd pay someone to steal Clayne's attention away from her. Especially once he started blathering on about his ideas on running drugs.

She nodded and smiled at all the right moments while, inside, her distaste for the drunk cowboy grew. Clayne Miller might think he was top dog but that was sheer geographical luck on his part. Pluck him out of this tiny little nowhere town and drop him into a city and Katarina gave him a week, tops, before he was offed by a drug runner who actually knew how to run a business.

Take her, for example. If she were in charge here, she could grow Clayne's business tenfold within six months. That reality ate at her and fed her growing contempt, until every day, Katarina found herself hating him a little more.

"Well? What do you think of my idea?" Clayne bounced on his heels and puffed out his chest again. Any second now, she expected him to coo and peck at her for a breadcrumb.

She hadn't been paying attention, but with Clayne, that was okay. A good ego stroke was all the redneck wannabe kingpin required. "Sounds great, just like always."

He slapped a quick, sloppy kiss on Katarina before

returning back to the group. "So, tell me more about this haul? I need details."

The conversation kicked off again. Katarina tried to interject once, only to have all the men talk over her like she didn't exist. Bored, she passed the time by assessing each man in turn. First Lance Martinez: arrogant, with a cruel glint to his brown eyes that belied his ready grin and elegant clothes. Then Eddie Taylor. His calloused palms suggested that he'd done manual labor at one time or another, and Katarina hadn't missed the pistol tucked under his shirt.

Her gaze settled on Mick Fortner. From what Clayne had told her, the tall, sandy-haired man was the enforcer of the bunch. Odd, because Katarina didn't see it. Not macho enough by far. All the enforcers she'd come into contact with over the years were bottom dwellers. Neanderthal types on the low rung of the ladder who didn't think much beyond making money to beat people down. Neither particularly smart nor observant.

Mick Fortner, on the other hand, held himself with the air of a person who checked both of those boxes. An anomaly that rang alarm bells in her head.

While the other three gabbed away, she studied him, noticing the way that every few minutes, he scanned the room. Assessing. This time, when he completed his survey, those blue eyes landed on her, catching her interest. A flicker of surprise crossed his face before he leveled a slow grin at Katarina. Hooking his thumbs in his pockets, he cocked his head and gave her a thorough once-over, followed by licking his lips.

Katarina could have told him not to waste the effort. Enough men had flirted with her over the years for her to spot the difference between genuine interest and faking.

The question was, why bother pretending?

She examined him with renewed curiosity, determined to

uncover what Mick was hiding. Before she had a chance, Lance whistled. "Uh oh, looks like you might have a fight on your hands for that girl of yours."

Clayne stiffened while Katarina perked up, her blood thrumming predictably over the promise of violence. *Finally.* Something interesting at this party full of sweaty drug abusers.

Katarina scooted forward, not wanting to miss a testosterone-infused second. No way Clayne would allow Lance's challenge to go unmet.

True to form, her boyfriend yanked back his shoulders and flexed his biceps. "That true, Mick? You making eyes at my girl? You best stick your tongue back in your mouth if you know what's good for you."

Clayne punctuated the threat by lunging forward and slamming his hands into the other man's chest.

Electricity crackled along Katarina's skin as she held her breath in anticipation of what might happen next.

The reality was a letdown.

Mick showed Clayne his palms and flashed him an easy smile. "My bad. I didn't mean any harm. I'm a dumbass when I start drinking. Won't happen again."

His ego assuaged, Clayne clapped the other man on the shoulder. "No harm, no foul. Now, speaking of drinking... who's up for another round of whiskey?"

Fortner didn't so much as glance in Katarina's direction as the four men headed for the bar. Didn't matter. She had seen enough.

She watched the man's easy, catlike strides as he tailed the others and smiled.

Not only had the enforcer skirted the fight Clayne had all but dropped at his feet, but the other man had lied about being drunk too, and Katarina was pretty sure she knew why.

Mick Fortner was only posing as an enforcer for a local drug runner. He wasn't a criminal at all.

No, Katarina would bet ten kilos that the watchful, too-calm man was a cop.

As the certainty of his true identity crystalized, a plan began to form in Katarina's head.

4

The party inside the large, sprawling ranch-style house showed no signs of dying, which delighted Milos Velky to no end. Noise and chemically altered guests made his job that much easier.

Habit dictated that he proceed with caution, so he'd crept his way up to the front window, to his current position behind a wild bush. As far as he could tell, though, the majority of people who'd streamed in and out of the house were incapable of noticing danger at this stage in their intoxication, even if he jumped out in front of them wearing a bloody hockey mask.

Usually, New Year's Eve parties meant glamorous people all prettied up in their cocktail attire. The type of party where Milos, with his gaunt, ghoulish appearance, tended to stand out like a sore thumb.

From his hiding spot, Milos sneered at the two men staggering out of the house and down the walkway, with their shirts rumpled and stained, their hair disheveled, and one of them sporting a nosebleed. Milos would fit right in with the late-night druggie crowd. An unexpected blessing that meant, for once, he didn't have to worry that his skeletal form would out him as an intruder.

"Whoa, did you see that? When I move my hand, it makes colors in the sky." The shorter of the two men waved his hand all around his face, while the taller one watched with his mouth slack.

And in the event that any of these idiots did happen to spot Milos, they were far too blitzed to care.

He turned his attention back to the window. Inside, lit by a dim lamp in the corner, a little girl slept on a bed. A worn beige blanket pooled around her waist, revealing a white shirt with a picture of some television character.

As his gaze roved over the sweet young thing, Milos's palms dampened and his breathing quickened. He liked the way her young, innocent body looked in the nightshirt. So tender and sweet. Ripe, and oh-so-breakable.

She laid on her back with her little arms flung over her blonde hair. Like sleeping beauty. But instead of a kiss, Milos wanted to wake her from slumber with a knife cutting through her tender flesh.

Desire stabbed his groin at the thought. He remembered the two little children he'd snatched not long ago. The melody of their cries as they'd sobbed for their mother. He wished he could have spent more time playing with them before he'd launched all of them over the edge of that cliff and into a ravine.

Children were so precious. They still believed in fairy tales and happy endings and that a hero would swoop in to save the day. There was nothing in the world that Milos enjoyed more than slowly stripping that innocence away, piece by piece. No sound more nourishing to his soul than the high-pitched music of a little girl's screams.

He studied the girl, and his hands clenched and unclenched with thwarted longing. A child's fear was like oxygen, and over the years, he'd become a master at extracting the emotion. The trick was to play with them a little first. Give them time to allow the terror and suspense to build.

Milos hoped that, once he completed this job, Mr. del Rey would reward him with the opportunity to indulge in his little hobby. Before he had to kill her off.

He lifted the phone to the glass pane and began snapping pictures of the sleeping girl. He sidled along the window, getting shots from different angles. His shutter clicked and clicked, many more times than it had when he'd snapped a few shots of the girl's mom earlier.

That was because grown women didn't interest him. Not in the same way.

There'd been a moment when Milos had feared the woman would spot him when she approached the window. He'd ducked behind the bush, waiting there until enough time had passed.

When he'd peeked again, she was closing the door, leaving Milos and the girl alone.

As he watched, the girl rolled onto the side facing away from the window, and her nightshirt hiked up, tantalizing Milos with a glimpse of pink cotton underwear. Saliva flooded his mouth, and his fingers curled. Forget the pictures. He could slip into the house right now, sneak past all the wasted partiers, grab the girl and climb out the window before anyone batted an eye.

While he considered his new plan, the phone buzzed. Milos didn't need to look at the screen to know who was texting his unknown number at this hour.

He sighed, and after casting one last longing glance at the front door, Milos returned to snapping photos.

His boss, Abel del Rey, wasn't a man Milos wanted to anger. Besides, del Rey had a plan. Once Milos completed the tasks he'd been assigned and the plan played out, Mr. Abel would reward Milos's loyalty by giving him Bethany.

And then, think of all the fun we'll have playing together.

He took one final picture before blowing the sleeping girl a kiss. Not allowing himself to linger, he slipped back the way he'd come, driving off into the night without any of the New Year's Eve revelers being the wiser.

5

Early Monday morning following the holiday, Ellie shouldered through the front doors of the Charleston Police Department and burst into a lower level already bustling with employees. Lots of eager workers, all determined to kick off their New Year's resolutions on a good note.

Ellie scurried by, giving most of them a week, maybe a month tops, before the majority defaulted to their old ways and started straggling in again.

She climbed the stairs two at a time to the second floor, where the homicide detectives were housed, and made her way to her desk in the middle of the pen. Unlike the first level, this space was empty, save for one other person.

Detective Fernando Valdez. Of course.

Ellie pretended to read a text, hoping she could pass him by without having to exchange forced pleasantries. Valdez dismantled that plan by lumbering over and blocking her path.

She gritted her teeth. So far, this year wasn't off to a great start. "Detective Valdez. You need something?"

The taller man folded his arms across his chest and stared down at her. The cocky smile he sported didn't reach his flat brown eyes. "You could say that. I need to know why you got assigned to the Kingsley task force when I'm the one working his case. What gives you that kind of pull?"

The skepticism in the other detective's voice raised Ellie's hackles. She exhaled slowly, telling herself Valdez had a legitimate reason to ask. Even if a big part of her wanted to stomp on his foot rather than explain. "Since I was one of Kingsley's victims, I have personal experience with him that other detectives don't. I guess the powers-that-be think that gives me some kind of special insight."

Valdez drummed his fingers on his biceps while he studied her. "Funny, because as far as I can tell, most of Kingsley's surviving victims turn out to be killers."

Ellie's mouth fell open. *Surely he hadn't meant that to sound as bad as it did.*

The narrowed brown eyes itemized her every little reaction and suggested that, oh yes, he most certainly had.

Her hands balled into fists, itching to connect with his nose. But as satisfying as that urge would be, Ellie didn't want to kick off the new year by landing on probation for punching a fellow officer.

She counted to five in her head. "Do you have a point you're trying to make, Detective Valdez? If so, have the balls to spell it out instead of throwing around vague accusations. Otherwise, get out of my way. I have work to do."

Valdez gave a curt nod of his head. "All right, how's this? I think you get a lot more leeway than the other cops around here, an observation that makes me suspicious. The party line is it's because you're such a great cop, but if that's the case, why is Kingsley always slipping through your extremely talented hands?"

Wow.

Ellie had taken an instant dislike to Valdez when the detective joined Charleston PD last year, but that had nothing on the depth of her animosity now. From their very first meeting, she hadn't trusted the interloper. Now, those initial instincts were proving correct.

Just what was Valdez playing at with these wild insinuations? Did he truly believe for a second that Ellie was in league with Kingsley, the man who'd kidnapped her as a teen and inflicted lifelong trauma by forcing her to play the starring role in one of his deadly games?

Or, most likely in Ellie's book, was Valdez one more in a line of bad cops planted in the Charleston office, like Detective Jones before him? Was he deflecting his own association with Kingsley by pointing at Ellie?

Between all the moles and her past, Ellie's circle of trust in the department remained very small. Jillian, Jacob, and Clay. Those were the only three people she trusted implicitly. So, more of a triangle than a circle. Even her boss, Detective Fortis, made her pause and squint upon occasion.

As for Valdez? Ellie's gut insisted the arrogant detective was hiding something.

"What, cat got your tongue? Go ahead, I'll wait while you dream up an excuse."

Ellie's nostrils flared, and her hands shook from fury. "I'm sorry, why would I need to dream up an excuse. As you just pointed out, *you're* the one assigned to Kingsley's case, not me." She scoffed. "If Kingsley's slipping out of anyone's hands, it's yours, not mine. Seriously, where's the headway you've made, Detective Valdez? Or is there something we don't know that's keeping you from bringing Kingsley in?"

Valdez's ruddy cheeks flushed red. He stepped closer to her, and Ellie mirrored his move. The two of them glared at each other from only a foot apart, close enough that Ellie smelled the remnants of bacon on his breath, with both of them curling their lips up like feral animals.

Valdez lifted a finger. "If you think you can—"

"Don't you two knuckleheads have any real work to do around here? If not, I promise I can find something to occupy your time."

At the boom of Lead Detective Harold Fortis's voice, Ellie and Valdez sprang apart like guilty children.

"Morning, sir." Ellie gulped when she peeked at her boss. The lead detective always emitted a formidable aura, with a sharp tongue and dark curls sprinkled with silver earned from years on the job. A glowering Harold Fortis was even more intimidating than usual, though. Especially when that muscle twitched near his right eye.

"Morning, boss," Valdez mumbled his own greeting.

"And a good morning to you too. I'd ask how your New Year went, but I don't care. Oh, and speaking of finding something to occupy your time, Kline..." Fortis shoved a bulging case file box into Ellie's hands.

She stared at the offering. "What's this?"

"Burton's files. You're being assigned the older children."

Hope flared in Ellie's chest. "But...what about the task force? Shouldn't they be handling these cases?"

Fortis stared down at her, arching a dark eyebrow. "I remember how upset you were over that William Warren kid and pulled some strings. Are you saying you've had a change of heart since then? If so, I'm sure I can give them back."

He extended his hands for the box, which Ellie whisked out of reach. "No, sir. I haven't had a change of heart. Thank you!"

Her earlier encounter with Valdez all but forgotten, Ellie's body buzzed with excitement while the assignment sank in. She remembered when she'd first come across the files on the trafficked kids back in that shady Miami law office.

At first, Neil Burton, the owner of that law practice, had feigned ignorance of any illegal adoptions, but Ellie and Clay had refused to let the rat scuttle away. Under threat of a long prison sentence, he'd caved. Burton had opened a huge legal tome that lined his bookshelf to reveal hidden files. Multiple tomes that secreted hundreds of files, spanning over twenty years of trafficked children.

Once Ellie had returned to Charleston, she'd started going through the files and found William Warren. The boy had been twelve when his parents took him to Neil Burton. The lawyer promised to send their son, who was on the autism spectrum and proving difficult for them to handle, to a special boarding school. The Warrens thought they were helping their child, but as it turned out, they were scammed.

They never saw Will again.

William Warren's case had prompted Ellie to look at the other kids in a new light. What if all of the older children in the illegal adoption ring they'd unearthed that day had developmental issues? That would explain why they'd made easy targets.

She studied the box that Fortis handed her, a lump building in her throat. Every one of those cases represented heartache and pain. Digging into these would dredge up horrors, and Ellie wouldn't delude herself otherwise.

Odds were that at least some of the kids documented in the pages within the box had been used in sickening ways, but if Ellie could locate them and reunite them with their families, then her pain didn't matter.

The kids. They were what mattered.

"I assigned you about fifteen percent, which ends up being thirty-seven cases in total. I want you to go through each and every one of them with the goal of closing as many as you possibly can."

"Yes, sir." She hesitated, nibbling her lower lip. As much as the missing kids pulled at her, what about Kingsley? Shouldn't she be working on his case? She'd made herself a promise on New Year's Eve to bring that bastard in. One she was determined to keep.

Fortis read her expression and scowled, his bushy brows knitting together. "Those kids deserve your attention, Detective Kline."

Her boss's rebuke mentally propelled Ellie back to Burton's law office, reminding her of how she'd placed her hand on one of the law books that held the children's files and made a silent pledge.

I'll find you. I promise.

Two different vows. Both pulling Ellie in different directions.

Images of the innocent, frightened faces from Burton's files flashed through Ellie's head, and she nodded. Her boss was right. Those kids deserved attention and so much more. "I know."

Kingsley would have to wait.

After a satisfied grunt, Fortis turned to glare at Valdez. "As for you...do I need to remind you that you two are on the same team? In this building, we work together to solve crimes. We do not get into scuffles like barnyard cats fighting over who gets dibs on the nicest stall."

Once again, Fortis had a point. But even though Ellie recognized that fact, her temper still flared when she glanced at Valdez. Territorial dispute or not, the other detective was hiding something, and sooner or later, Ellie was going to find out what.

After glowering at each of them once more for good measure, Fortis slapped the nearest desk with a beefy hand. "Now, get to work. Let's start this year off right by closing some cases."

Dismissed, Ellie lugged the overflowing box to her station

and began sorting through the files. Each folder held a different little face, and each face had to be compared to hundreds of missing children files.

She cracked her knuckles, fired up the computer, and jumped into the monotonous work of updating each file into the system. Before she'd gotten even halfway through the stack, her inbox pinged with emails from other precincts in the east and south, burying her with an avalanche of hard copies of files where the cases of missing children were still open. Unsolved, and until now, likely to remain that way.

Once she completed the update, Ellie turned to the whiteboard. She attached a picture of each child in neat little rows, then used a dry erase marker to print their name, age, and information on where they were last seen below.

"Hey, stranger."

Ellie's pen clattered to the floor. She whirled to find FBI Special Agent Clay Lockwood leaning his hip against her desk, dangling a cardboard carrier with two coffees and a bag bearing the name of her favorite local sandwich shop in his hands.

She blinked at the logo on the bag, then checked the time on her phone. It was a little after one. First day back, and she'd already worked straight through lunch.

Not only that, but Clay knew her well enough to predict as much.

Her heart warmed a little at the thought. "Hello."

She accepted the coffee and sandwich, inhaling the familiar woodsy scent of his soap along with the rich aroma of dark roast, allowing her mind to imagine how easy it would be to fall into a routine. It wasn't a stretch to picture the two of them bringing each other coffee and food every day and then heading home together at night to Ellie's apartment. Especially since Clay had already been staying in her guest room for months now to help ensure her safety. With him, there would be no need to explain the ups and downs of her workday because he already understood. In the way that only another LEO could.

As she blew at the steam wafting from the lid, Ellie felt herself weakening. Would it really be so bad to close the distance between them? To give a relationship another try?

But as usual, her mind shied away from that idea. *Remember Nick?*

Her shoulders sagged. Right. Nick. Ellie had thought their relationship was easy too. After all, they'd known each other since childhood. Yet, look at how badly she'd managed to mess that one up.

No, nothing had changed since the last time she'd waged this internal debate. Her career came first. She needed to focus on that and saving lives. And ultimately, on bringing Kingsley down. Anything else was a distraction.

Ellie scooted over to the far side of her desk. "Thanks for the food. First day back, and I'm already swamped."

If Clay noticed her ploy to put more space between them, he didn't comment. "I can see that." He gestured with his coffee cup at the files strewn across her desk. "What are you working on?"

"The Burton files."

Clay's rugged features softened. He'd been the agent with Ellie when they'd interviewed Burton and persuaded him to turn over everything regarding his illegal adoptions, so he understood what was at stake. "Based on the state of your desk, looks like Fortis assigned you more than a few of those kids."

"You think?" Ellie gazed at the enormous stack of files that dominated almost every surface. "And that's not counting all of the digital files that started flooding my inbox already. Everyone wants to know if their missing kids could have been adopted out through this ring. By updating the files, it's like I triggered a wave of false hope."

Beneath the brim of his cowboy hat, Clay's eyes were unreadable. "Maybe it's not false hope."

"I wish that were true. But you and I both know the reality is that the chance of finding a missing child gets lower every hour after they disappear, and those odds approach zero by the time a week has passed, let alone a month. These kids have been missing for years."

Pain flashed across Clay's features, and Ellie wanted to kick herself. Here was a man whose younger sister was still out there, missing since she disappeared at a county fair as a kid. Yet there went Ellie and her big mouth, babbling on about how most missing children cases were hopeless once too much time passed.

Idiot.

"I'm sorry, Clay. I wasn't thinking. That's what I get for skipping my caffeine this morning." To punctuate her point, Ellie gulped down half her coffee. The hot liquid burned her tongue, but that was no more than she deserved.

"It's fine."

From his gruff tone, Ellie knew it wasn't fine at all. She touched his arm. "You know that there's always hope, right? Statistics aren't everything."

Clay shrugged her off and approached the whiteboard. He pointed at a photo in the center. "Who's that?"

Ellie sighed but let the subject of his sister drop. "Lucas Harrison. Originally from Miami. He was twelve when he went missing. On the autism spectrum."

"Twelve? Isn't that a little older than usual?"

"Exactly what I was thinking. Even in legal adoptions, most parents want to adopt babies or little kids, not the older ones. And healthy kids at that. It seems really odd that someone snatched an autistic twelve-year-old for an illegal adoption ring."

Clay tilted his head, studying Lucas's photo. "Being autistic doesn't make you unhealthy."

Ellie winced at her flub. "You're right. I meant special needs. It's a lot harder to find parents willing to take in a child who might require extra attention or work." She shook her head. "My gut says if he was taken at twelve, that it likely wasn't related to adoption."

Not wanting to rub more salt into Clay's wound, Ellie left the rest unsaid. No need to remind him that older kids were often trafficked for sex work.

After another long glance at Lucas's picture, Clay stepped back, shoving his hands into his pockets. "Why him?"

Ellie searched the mess on her desk for Lucas's file, showing Clay when she found it. Unlike the files on the other missing children, Lucas's was anemic, containing a single sheet of paper.

Clay saw the nearly empty folder and went still. No notes, no extra information, no follow- up. Nothing beyond the initial intake form.

They both understood what that meant.

A muscle twitched in Clay's jaw. "No one ever cared enough to look for him?"

Ellie stared at the sad page, wondering yet again how a parent could give up on finding their child so quickly.

She glanced over at the boy's photo on her whiteboard. Her heart twisted while her resolve hardened. Ellie lifted her chin.

"Someone cares enough to look now."

6

The diners in the upscale restaurant chatted over their filets and grilled salmon, unaware that one of the criminals who occupied a top spot on the FBI's Most Wanted list was seated a scant few feet away from where they consumed their overpriced meals.

In the time leading up to my surgery, I'd almost forgotten how delightful anonymity was. All of these succulent little lambs, so blissfully ignorant of my true wolfish identity. Ripe for the plucking, if I were feeling so inclined.

The silverware was crooked, so I adjusted the utensils until they lined up the way they should, allowing my gaze to rove over the other patrons once more. My hands stilled when I noticed a new diner being seated across the way.

Tall, slender, and oh so pretty. The dark-haired man possessed the type of features that would keep him looking young, even once he hit fifty.

He reminded me of Gabe.

Metal bit into my ring finger and thumb. I dropped the fork I'd been squeezing too hard and took a sip of my water, but it did nothing to erase the bitter coating on my tongue.

Gabe and I had been robbed of our final moments together, my elaborate plans for my traitorous assistant cut infuriatingly short. Instead of savoring the memory of carving away pieces of Gabe until he regretted his choice to turn on me, one slow cut at a time, I'd been forced to flee and end his suffering far too soon to avoid capture.

All because of that bitch, Ellie Kline. Once again, the redheaded detective who'd escaped me as a teen had showed up to ruin my fun.

My hands trembled with impotent rage, rattling the silverware and glasses on the table. A few seconds later, and I was back in control, smoothing the tablecloth and straightening the silverware once again.

No need to get upset. Ellie would pay for her little stunts, and so would everyone else who'd ever dared to cross me.

The server who came to refill my water glass had a lithe grace that reminded me of Katarina. My lip curled. Ah, yes, the lovely Katarina. Yet another woman who topped my revenge list. Unlike the others, her betrayal had come as a surprise.

My bloody angel. The little girl I'd rescued from abusive adoptive parents, albeit the illegal kind, and raised as a daughter. All those years I'd spent teaching her to follow in my footsteps, only for her to turn on me the second I was laid low. Stealing my business while I was holed up in Costa Rica, recovering from my injuries out of sight.

My fury flared again, so I pulled out my phone to go through the photos Milos had sent. Control returned as I scrolled through dozens of shots of both Katarina and her whelp.

I paused on a photo of Harmony, now Bethany, where the little girl faced the photographer, asleep with a hand tucked beneath her cheek, her nightgown rumpled around her thighs.

A mini Katarina. So innocent.

The perfect vessel to deliver my revenge.

"You gave up everything for her, Katarina," I murmured, stroking the screen with a fingertip. "All for nothing. I wonder how long it will take for a strong woman like you to beg for death?"

After studying the photo for another several seconds, I scrolled again until my screen filled with the image of a well-muscled man wearing a cowboy hat over his dark hair.

I sneered into his unconcerned eyes. "As for you, Clay Lockwood, for the life of me, I don't know what our flame-haired detective sees in you. You're like a dog that trots along to do her bidding, but you know what happens to dogs, right?" The thought made me giggle. "They get put down. Except I like to play with my dogs a little first before they gasp their last breath."

Keeping the picture of Clay open on my phone, I fished my wallet out of my pocket and flipped to a small photo nestled inside. The young girl who smiled up at me was pretty, her dark curls wild around a cherubic, pink-cheeked face.

Not a carbon copy of her older brother, but the resemblance was obvious to anyone who looked.

It was a small world after all.

The thought made me giggle again.

Pleased with my trot down memory lane, I tucked my wallet away and scanned the restaurant again. This time, I spotted the woman I was seeking, sitting alone at a table near the bar. She bit her lip and fiddled with her hair, glancing at the diners around her before checking her phone with a frown.

I checked the time. Five minutes past the hour, which made me fashionably late. Even with my new face, I wasn't taking any chances, so I'd procured the booth early enough to scout the rendezvous spot for hidden threats. No sense rolling the dice. Especially after my own dear mother had somehow managed to recognize me when I'd visited her in the plush Florida assisted living center...moments before I'd injected air into her IV to hasten her departure from this world.

The woman glanced up when I approached the table, her hands fluttering like nervous little birds.

"Good evening." I smiled to put her mind at ease, noting how the smattering of freckles across her nose hadn't changed. Nor had she lost any of her beauty. Her brunette hair was styled in becoming waves that framed a heart-shaped face, and a tasteful navy pants suit flattered her fit figure. Classy, despite the ordeal she'd been through.

Really, I'd expected nothing less of Valerie Price. Or Pryor, according to the new identity WITSEC had provided for her. The same information Milos had procured from a secretary within the U.S. Marshal's office before pushing her and her two kids off a cliff.

Children made for handy bargaining chips.

"Hello." Valerie's tone was uncertain, as nervous as her hands. A warning for me to proceed with caution so as not to frighten her away.

"May I?" I gestured to the chair across from her, and after a brief hesitation, she nodded, her gaze glued to my face. Searching, I was certain, for any hint of familiarity.

The good doctor's work from Costa Rica held up, though. After several seconds, she reached for the napkin on the table in front of her and spread it across her lap. "I'm sorry." She gave a rueful laugh. "This is my first time ever using a dating site, and I'm sure it shows. I probably wouldn't have even tried it this time, except, well, my roommate kind of set up a profile for me."

"Ah, well, I hope that I serve as a good ambassador for

online dating programs then."

Of course, I already knew all of that information about her roommate. When Milos first stumbled across Valerie on the dating site, I'd been shocked and more than a little suspicious of a trap. Witnesses under federal protection didn't just toss their information onto the web for anyone to see.

I was convinced that her profile was courtesy of the FBI attempting to set me up when Valerie's roommate messaged back, confessing that she'd created the profile on the sly, on behalf of her hermit friend who needed to get out of their apartment.

Ah, sweet providence. Smiling down on me once again.

Even so, I'd remained skeptical that Valerie would show for our date, right up until I'd spotted her at the table. I smiled. The risks a woman would take in order to achieve the elusive fairy-tale ending never ceased to amaze me. A charming quality, if utterly delusional.

"If you're uncomfortable, though, I can leave. As much as I'd enjoy getting to know you, I don't want you to feel trapped here with me."

I half-rose from my chair, and either that action or my offer eased the remainder of the tension from Valerie's posture. She waved me back into my seat. "No, please stay. This will be good for me."

I did as she asked, unsurprised that my little plot worked. Women could be so very predictable.

Victory tasted sweet, the harbinger of many to come.

Just wait until you see what I have in store next for you, Ellie, and Katarina.

"Now that I know I'm staying, allow me to introduce myself properly." I reached out my hand. "I'm Abel del Rey."

Valerie's smile reached her eyes this time as her cool palm pressed against mine.

"Hi, Abel, it's nice to meet you. I'm Valerie. Valerie Pryor."

7

E llie laced up her Nikes and stepped outside, shivering despite dressing in running tights and a sweatshirt when the brisk air nipped at her bare cheeks and hands. Sunrise was still two hours away, so she flipped on her headlamp before heading out into the darkened streets. She loved this time of day, when most of the city still slumbered. The empty streets and the sidewalks free of pedestrian traffic. Perfect for clearing her sluggish mind.

The first mile dragged, her fault for falling out of the routine over the past few weeks. Tossing and turning last night hadn't helped. Slowly, though, her body and lungs warmed up, allowing her muscles to fall back into a familiar rhythm.

She jogged down quiet residential streets, the historic homes shadowy shapes that hovered outside the circular glow of her headlamp. The steady slap-slap of her bodyguard's shoes pounded the sidewalk behind her, an auditory reminder of his presence that kept her on edge. Ellie gritted her teeth. Just because she understood the logic behind having private security didn't mean she enjoyed the intrusion.

After shaking out her arms, Ellie picked up the pace. The increased exertion did the trick. By the next block, the bodyguard had faded from Ellie's consciousness, allowing her mind to focus on the missing kids.

Images of their faces filled her head as she veered right to race down a side street, her exhalations forming puffy white clouds in the air. The age range of the Burton files she'd been assigned nagged at her. Eight years to almost eighteen.

Nothing about those ages made sense. Not for an illegal adoption ring. Ellie's gut insisted that there was something different about these cases, which had led to nights full of tossing and turning. But Ellie suspecting an anomaly did zilch to help find those kids. Especially when she didn't even have a working theory to explain the purpose of rounding up older children.

Ellie kicked up the tempo yet again, pumping her legs faster and faster until her mind cleared of everything else. She ran until her quads burned, and her breathing turned to ragged gasps, pushing her body until a side-stitch knifed her lungs and black spots danced in front of her eyes. Only then did she slow the pace, from a sprint to a jog to a walk, two blocks away from where she'd started. A glance at her smartwatch confirmed the distance. Four point two miles. Not a bad start after a hiatus.

A second set of harsh gasps trailed her on the walk back to her apartment building, but unlike earlier, this time the reminder of her bodyguard's existence made Ellie smile. At least she wasn't the only one huffing and puffing. "Good job, Shane."

A grunt was his only reply. Probably cranky from the surprise exertion. Ellie's smile widened. That settled it. Now, she was practically obligated to jog even more often, if only to help her bodyguard improve his lung capacity. Shane would be thrilled.

Chilled now that the sweat had dried, Ellie hurried the rest of the way to her front door. She waved over her shoulder at the disgruntled guard before heading inside, pulling up short when a savory-sweet aroma greeted her. She gave an appreciative sniff. *Bacon?* "That you, Jillian?"

The click-clack of dog nails answered Ellie's question. Sam, Jillian's black lab mix, trotted into the entryway, nuzzling her head under Ellie's hand for an ear scratch.

"Nope, it's your friendly neighborhood thief, who got a little hungry mid-burgle and decided to whip up some breakfast before taking off with your fine china."

Ellie rolled her eyes at her friend's smartass reply. She kicked off her shoes, finished rubbing the dog's head, and padded into the kitchen to find Jillian scraping scrambled eggs out of a skillet and onto a plate.

"What are you doing here?" Lately, Ellie's roommate had been spending the majority of nights at Jacob's place, so a morning Jillian sighting was a rarity. "Not that I'm complaining about eating something that doesn't come wrapped in plastic or in a Styrofoam takeout box for once." Stomach growling, Ellie settled at one of the stools behind the counter.

Jillian slid a plate full of eggs, bacon, and toast to Ellie before plopping onto the stool next to her. "Jacob and Duke got called in a couple hours ago on a drug raid. I couldn't fall back asleep so I figured I'd head back here and whip us up some real food for a change."

Ellie's fork froze midair over the eggs. Jillian made the statement so casually, like Jacob disappearing in the middle of the night was no big deal, but Ellie wasn't sure she bought her friend's nonchalant attitude.

After inhaling a few bites of fluffy eggs and crunching on

a piece of bacon, Ellie decided to press. "Does that happen very often?"

Jillian finished chewing a bite of toast. "Does what happen?"

Ellie waved her fork. "You know. Getting interrupted by Jacob's job and having to reschedule things?"

"Sometimes."

Her roommate's expression was serene as she sipped her coffee, but Ellie remained unconvinced. "So, you don't get upset by him getting called into work at the last minute? His job isn't having a negative impact on your relationship?" Ellie toyed with her napkin while she waited, pretending like the answer wasn't important to her at all.

"This wouldn't have anything to do with the photo I saw of Nick in one of those fancy magazines your mom insists on sending us, would it? The one where he has his arm around a beautiful brunette? And the article mentioned something about an engagement?"

Drat. Ellie should have known Jillian would see right through this line of questioning. Her best friend knew her far too well. After flashing a sheepish grin, Ellie shrugged. "Busted."

"You doing okay with all of that?"

"I am." Ellie laughed when Jillian raised her eyebrows. "No, really. I'm truly happy that Nick found the right partner for him, because that person was never going to be me."

Jillian scrutinized Ellie's expression for a good ten seconds before nodding. "Okay, I believe you, although I'm sure it still has to feel a little weird."

Ellie snapped a piece of bacon in two. "I guess."

Her roommate smiled, understanding in her eyes. "But you were asking about Jacob and me, though."

Ellie relaxed, glad to have the spotlight turn away from

her. "Yeah. I was just wondering if his job made it hard for you to be with him."

Jillian leaned back in her seat. "I think some people need a partner who's by their side every possible moment without fail, which is totally okay as long as both of them are on the same page. But I don't need that. Heck, I don't even think I'd want that. I love Jacob, and he loves me, but we don't have to live in each other's pockets to feel secure in our relationship, you know? As long as he leaves me a goodnight message when he gets in late, or we meet up when we both have the time, then I'm okay. We support and respect each other, and that's the most important thing, if you ask me."

As Ellie sipped her coffee, she fought to ignore the sharp pinch beneath her ribs because…no. Uh-uh. She refused to feel envious of what Jillian and Jacob had found together. If anyone deserved happiness, it was those two. They'd stuck by her side while Kingsley terrorized her, and by extension, them.

She sighed. The loneliness got to her sometimes. That was all. "That sounds really wonderful."

"I won't lie, it's been pretty great. But I think partly because we make a concerted effort to focus on quality versus quantity when it comes to time." Jillian paused, blue eyes twinkling. "Besides, when Jacob is gone, there's always your host of hunky bodyguards to ogle."

Ellie snorted. "I'm glad at least someone appreciates them." After Kingsley planted a bomb in Ellie's Audi, Ellie's boss had put his foot down and insisted on assigning her round-the-clock security.

Since Ellie didn't feel right having the Charleston PD footing the bill, she'd relented and hired them on her own. Begrudgingly. Rules weren't always her strong suit, and more often than not, she resented the intrusion.

She blew out a noisy breath. Not that either of the above was the fault of the guards who followed her around.

No, Ellie knew exactly who to blame.

Kingsley.

Jillian shot Ellie a sympathetic look, misinterpreting the reason for her loud exhale. "Honestly, the reason for our success isn't that complicated. We know what we need from each other and try our best to deliver." She nudged Ellie's ankle with her toe. "So, the first step really is to ask yourself, what do you need? And then figure out what you think Clay needs, and if those two things are compatible."

Cheeks burning, Ellie grabbed her cup on the pretense of a refill and bolted across the kitchen to the relative safety of the coffee maker, relaxing once her back was to Jillian. Sometimes, her friend read way too much on Ellie's face.

"The only thing I need right now is to find out what happened to Lucas Harrison." She lifted the coffee pot and topped off what little she could. Talking to Jillian was usually so easy. Except when it came to this particular topic.

"All right, I'll allow the subject change—very obvious, I might add—and quit bugging you about Clay. For the moment, anyway. Now, go ahead and tell me about Lucas Harrison, starting with who he is."

Ellie sagged against the counter, weakened by relief over the reprieve. Even if her friend had made it clear that the reprieve was only temporary. "Lucas Harrison is one of the kids from the Burton caseload."

"Okay. I'm listening."

Ellie returned to her seat and updated her roommate on the files in between bites of food. "I've potentially closed three cases this week and provided the DNA matches, which should feel great."

Jillian tilted her head, frowning. "You're right, closing three cases already should feel great, so why doesn't it?"

A fresh wave of frustration swelled in Ellie's chest. "There's just something off about several of these cases that's nagging at me, especially Harrison's."

"How so?"

"For starters, he's one of a handful of kids who only had a single page in their file. One page for a missing kid. Do you know how rare that is?" Ellie scowled at the leftover flecks of yolk on her plate. "Why didn't the parents follow up? And why didn't the police department? Standard operating procedure in most places is to revisit a child disappearance case at least every six months initially, and then every three years once the case turns cold."

"But that didn't happen for Lucas Harrison."

"No! Which makes me suspicious that the reasons behind his skimpy file are linked to his disappearance."

Jillian nodded, and her eyes narrowed. "Understandable. Start from the top and tell me everything."

Ellie filled her friend in on the details, warmed by a surge of gratitude. They'd performed this routine multiple times now, and more than once, the act of talking Jillian through a conundrum had helped puzzle pieces click together in Ellie's head. Jillian made a perfect sounding board. She was silent when Ellie needed her to be while also managing to prod Ellie in all the right places.

By the time Ellie finished sharing Lucas's story, Jillian was frowning too. "You're right, that is weird. Especially the part where Lucas is an older kid and on the spectrum. Like you said, those don't seem like traits that would net an illegal adoption ring much money."

"Exactly. Just another reason why I can't get this case out of my head." Ellie hopped off the stool, groaning when her legs trembled.

"Sore already?"

"A little, but mostly just tight. I'll feel better after a hot shower." After shaking out each leg in turn, Ellie headed to the coffee pot for an actual refill. Caffeine might not be the solution to all her problems, but it sure didn't hurt.

Ellie was wiping coffee drips off the counter when her phone rang. She checked the caller ID and the sponge slipped from her grasp.

Clay Lockwood

Only one kind of news would compel the FBI agent to call Ellie at home this early in the morning...the bad kind.

After sucking a calming breath in through her nose, Ellie accepted the call. "Clay, what's wrong?"

Her pulse thudded in her ears while her mind whirled, sifting through possibilities.

She needn't have bothered. Despite all her mental conjectures, the news shared in Clay's deep baritone came as a complete shock.

"It's Valerie Price. She's gone missing."

8

Clay Lockwood's plane taxied to an on-time arrival in front of the gate at the Hilton Head/Savannah International Airport. Before the wheels on the plane stopped spinning, the FBI agent popped out of his seat, slung a duffle bag over one shoulder, and strode up the narrow aisle toward the exit.

The bald flight attendant surged forward to block Clay's path just as he reached the first row. A tight-lipped smile signaled his irritation. "Sir, I'm going to need you to return to your seat until the fasten-your-seat-belt sign turns off."

Clay flashed his FBI credentials. "I'm usually a firm believer in the seat belt rule, but I'm here on a time sensitive matter."

The flight attendant's hazel eyes rounded before his entire demeanor flipped like a switch. "Oh yes, of course," he peered at the badge, "Agent Lockwood. My apologies. Let me see if we can't get you off this plane any faster."

"Appreciate it, thank you." After tipping his cowboy hat at the man, Clay checked the time as he deplaned and headed for the rental car desk. Twelve twenty-two. Roughly four hours had passed since the alert announcing Valerie Price's—now Pryor's—disappearance had popped up on his phone.

Months ago, Clay had created a list of people who'd come into contact with Lawrence Kingsley, rigging his system to send a notification any time there was news relating to one of them. The moment he saw Valerie's name, Clay dropped the Dallas case he'd been working and rushed straight to the airport to hop the earliest flight to Savannah.

Clay flipped on the turn signal of his rental and shifted into the fast lane, passing a black Highlander that was crawling along. Most days, he was fine cruising along with the flow of traffic.

His mouth tightened. Today was not most days, though.

After checking the speedometer, Clay pressed harder with his right foot, edging the Ford's speed to a little over eighty as a sense of urgency flooded him. He hated this. Another woman missing on his watch. Didn't matter that the federal marshals were the ones tasked with keeping Valerie safe in their WITSEC program. Not when Clay was partly responsible for getting her into the program in the first place. He'd assured Valerie that she'd be safe.

And now she was missing.

Just like Caraleigh.

As the GPS navigated him off the highway and down the city streets that led to Valerie's apartment building, Clay's mind flashed to another girl who'd disappeared years ago. That girl had been much younger than Valerie, only eleven at the time, and just the thought of her triggered a sharp, twisting pain in Clay's gut.

No matter how much time passed, Clay would never forget the day he lost his little sister at the county fair.

Nor would he ever stop dreaming that one day, he might find her again.

Clay followed the directions on autopilot while the memory of that day washed over him.

Clay remembered biting back a whoop when his parents finally caved in front of the Ferris wheel, granting permission for him and his sister to explore the fair together. Caraleigh had beamed at him with her big blue eyes while his dad issued a single warning.

Don't let your sister out of your sight.

And Clay hadn't. At first. Until he'd run into Jana Danielson. Once he'd caught sight of his long-time crush and the way her legs looked wrapped in those tight black jeans, Clay hadn't been able to focus on much else.

Not the cheerful carnival music that played as he, Jana, and Caraleigh weaved through the crowds at the fair, or even the sugary scent that wafted from the cotton candy vendors. And he definitely hadn't paid much attention to Caraleigh's insistent tugs at his hand as she pleaded with him to take her to the petting zoo so she could see the pigs.

Pigs. Pigs and math. Those were Caraleigh's things, and boy, could she rattle on about both topics. All day long, if he gave her half a chance.

Clay remembered the spinning lights. The exact maroon of Jana's sweatshirt. The way she'd smiled at him in the pretzel line had spun his head faster than the Tilt-A-Whirl.

What he couldn't remember was the exact moment when Caraleigh stopped tugging on his hand. But by the time Clay realized his sister wasn't in line with them, it was already too late.

Too late.

Too late.

Clay shook off the rest of the memory and the foreboding that came with it when he pulled into a parking spot in front of Valerie's building. He climbed out of the rental car, not paying much attention to the Ford Explorer parked two spaces down until he hopped onto the sidewalk and spotted the woman leaning against the front bumper, her head topped by a mass of wild red curls.

"Ellie? What are you doing here?"

Ellie sprang off the hood. "Waiting for you. I drove down as soon as I heard the news, to help you look for Valerie. The drive from Charleston is only two hours."

Her expressive green eyes conveyed all the same worry that ate away at Clay's gut. Even with the tension vibrating between them over the past few months, Clay was damn glad she was here. Ellie understood what was at stake without him uttering a single word. "Fortis let you off to help out?"

Ellie lifted her shoulders and feigned a sudden interest in the landscaping. "He didn't have to. I'm on my own time."

Clay groaned, filled with the sudden certainty that Ellie had jumped into the car to race to Savannah without a word to her boss first. Not that he'd expect any less. Despite the years Helen Kline spent attempting to smooth her daughter into a polished, high-society lady, Ellie had somehow managed to retain her raw edges.

She was impatient, impulsive as hell, and unlike her poised mother, often ended up with a size nine foot in her mouth. Clay found those traits endearing. More importantly, though, Ellie's heart was huge. She bled a little piece of her soul into every case and loved those closest to her with a fierceness that matched her red hair.

All reasons why Clay wasn't ashamed to admit that he'd give a lot to have Ellie aim some of that love his way. Or that he'd fallen for her. Hard. But after a promising start to their romance, Ellie had built a wall between them that Clay had yet to figure out how to scale.

"I could tell you to go home." A bluff on his part. Clay would only send Ellie away if he suspected her presence in

Savannah placed her in imminent danger. "I'd hate for you to get behind on your own cases."

"I won't. I've already got some people trying to track down Lucas's birth parents for me while I'm here." Her green eyes flashed. "Besides, Valerie is more my prerogative than yours. If you send me away, I'll just wait until you're gone and investigate on my own."

The uplifted chin signaled her intent to do just that. Clay conceded defeat with a rueful smile. "I figured as much, but I had to try." He waited until her posture relaxed to add, "To be honest, there's no one I'd rather have by my side."

On this case.

In the interest of keeping their interactions professional, those were the words Clay should have tacked onto the end, but what was the point? They both recognized that he'd prefer Ellie as his partner. Both on and off the field.

Emotion flared in Ellie's eyes before her lashes swept down, hiding her expression from view. "Glad to hear it. You ready?"

She quickened her pace down the brick-lined path. Clay trailed a few steps and released a silent, disappointed breath, then chided himself for acting like an idiot. What did he expect? That, after pushing him away, Ellie would fling her arms around his neck and blurt a declaration of her undying love right here in the parking lot?

He must have watched one too many sappy movies lately.

His long strides closed the distance between them, until he navigated the path by her side once more. They wound their way through the brick and wooden buildings, counting numbers every so often to ensure they were headed in the right direction.

"Why is Valerie living in Savannah now? Did something happen before this?"

Right. Clay had forgotten that Ellie probably wasn't up to

date on all the latest details in Valerie's life. WITSEC worked hard to ensure only a select few people knew the whereabouts of the witnesses in protective custody. Another reason why this case was so troubling.

"Something happened, but not in the way you're probably thinking. The marshals moved her to Savannah under the new name of Valerie Pryor after she broke up with Flynn."

Ellie gasped, her hand moving to her mouth to cover the sound. "Oh no. I really thought the two of them could make it work. What a shame."

Her shocked reaction made Clay snort. "I think Keanu said it best in *Speed*. 'I have to warn you, I've heard relationships based on intense experiences never work.'"

His mirth faded. If romance born from a single shared stressful experience had no chance of a happy ending, then how could he hope for one with Ellie when they'd lived through numerous fraught situations together?

Great. Now, he was letting a cheesy action flick from the nineties mess with his head. Time to cut back on the late-night TV and find a new hobby.

He focused back on the business at hand. "Anyway, Valerie's been taking night classes in accounting, and she has a day job working as a receptionist in a chiropractor's office. From what I understand, the breakup was hard, but you've got to hand it to her, she's been getting on with her life. Tough thing for a lot of victims to do. Takes a lot of inner strength."

A quality the woman next to him possessed in bucketloads. Ellie was one of the strong ones. A victim who'd lived through a terrifying experience as a teen and emerged on the other side as a survivor. The inner fire that blazed in Ellie as a result of that trauma was one of the qualities that Clay admired most.

He studied her profile, his tongue burning with the

desire to tell her. Self-preservation kicked in first and saved his infatuated ass. He was all but sure Ellie would not appreciate him blurting his admiration out like a lovesick teen on the way to an interview, so he left the words unsaid.

Along with the rest of his feelings.

"Do they know who saw Valerie last?"

Clay moved to the side to allow a young woman walking a tiny dog to pass. "Not yet, that's why I flew out. When I called, Valerie's marshal didn't even realize she was missing."

"Then who filed the report?"

"Valerie's roommate. Since she's unaware that Valerie is in WITSEC, she went to the local PD. The marshal is meeting me at her apartment so we can talk to the room-mate. And looks like this is it." Clay nodded at the 71 before rapping three times on the door. "James L. Wallace, you in there? It's Special Agent Clay Lockwood."

"Come on in," a deep voice called. "Door's unlocked."

Clay twisted the knob and the door squeaked open.

A man unfolded himself from the white and blue striped couch and ventured across the room to greet them, slow despite a pair of legs so long and lanky they made Clay think of stilts. A white scar traced the edge of his hairline on the left side, from ear to chin, and the tie he'd paired with his gray sport coat was a startling shade of purple.

He extended his hand. "Like you said, I'm James Wallace of the USMS."

Clay shook before motioning to Ellie. "This is Detective Ellie Kline from the Charleston PD. She was involved in rescuing Valerie from the trafficking ring, so when she heard the news, she hopped in her car and drove here to meet us. Ellie, this is Valerie's marshal."

The marshal dipped his head. "Nice to meet you, Detective Kline."

Ellie inclined her chin, but other than that, didn't return the marshal's greeting.

Wallace gestured to the couch and armchairs arranged around a glass coffee table. "Might as well take a seat, make yourselves comfortable. We've got another half hour yet before the roommate gets back from work. Luckily, the apartment manager let me in after I showed my badge and gave him the abridged version."

"I'm good. Between the drive to and from airports and the two-and-a-half-hour flight, I've been sitting all morning."

Clay wandered farther into the apartment, inspecting the colorful prints on the walls. Beach scenes and cityscapes and sunsets, all of them bursting with warmth and life. Made sense. Valerie had lived through so much darkness, it was only natural that she chose to surround herself with joy and light.

Clay shifted the cowboy hat farther back on his head as he studied a picture of a tropical landscape painted in neon colors. He was so absorbed at first, that he didn't pay much attention when Ellie started talking.

"I was wondering, Marshal Wallace—"

"James, call me James."

"Okay. James, I was wondering if you could explain to me how you, as Valerie's marshal, didn't realize that your charge was missing until Clay called and told you?"

Clay winced. Hell. He'd only been distracted for a few seconds, but by the time he turned, he found Ellie scowling down at the marshal. Her hands were clenched into fists, ire flushing both cheeks.

The poor marshal blinked up at Ellie from the couch, a deep line forming between his eyebrows. "I'm sorry?"

"You should be." Ellie unclenched her hands long enough to prop them on her hips. "According to the missing persons report, Valerie was last seen on Friday. Her roommate reported her missing on Monday evening. Today is Tuesday. Maybe you're unaware, but every hour a person is missing, our window of recovery shrinks a little more."

She stopped short of accusing Wallace directly, but one glance at his tight face was enough to tell Clay the other man was pissed.

The marshal stood and straightened to his full height, towering over Ellie by a good six or seven inches. A lot of women would find that disadvantage intimidating and retreat a few feet. Not Ellie. His eyes widened in disbelief as she stalked forward, closing the gap between herself and the fuming marshal and tipping her chin up to meet his glare dead-on.

James Wallace crossed his wiry arms. "I'm well aware of that fact, ma'am. Just like I'm sure you're aware that my job as a marshal isn't to babysit my witnesses twenty-four-seven. Especially when no one thought to inform me that my witness might be in immediate danger."

After a silent battle, Ellie's shoulders sagged. "You're right, and I'm sorry. I have no right to take my worries out on you. I'm just really stressed." She bit her lip. "If anything, Valerie's disappearance is my fault."

The groove in the marshal's forehead deepened. "Come again?"

"I stumbled onto Valerie's case after my boss dropped a file with a dead John Doe in my lap. It was supposed to be an open-and-shut case, a hunting accident. Only it turned out that the shooter was hunting humans. He'd buy them via dark-web auctions, feed them and give them a head start, and then track them down and murder them for sport."

"I know. A real life *The Most Dangerous Game*. You were the detective who saved her?"

Ellie nodded. "Valerie and her boyfriend Ben, the John Doe, were kidnapped together and were unwilling participants in the same auction. Ben drew the short straw. He was purchased by the hunter, who killed him the next day. Valerie lucked out, if you can call any of this lucky," Ellie's mouth twisted, "because the man who bought her had a little girl fetish."

Wallace ran a hand through his hair. "I'm not seeing the luck at all here."

Clay felt sure the marshal already knew every bit of Valerie's story, but he also felt sure that Ellie was intent on reminding the man of everything the woman had been through.

"Well, the way his fetish played out was pretty tame, all things considered. Valerie spent every day locked in a room decorated for a little girl, dressed in frilly underwear and a skimpy t-shirt. The man was a voyeur, he never touched her. But when I started breathing down his neck, he panicked, and handed her off to a crooked cop in our department to dispose of."

"Jones," Clay added, in case Wallace didn't know that part.

"Yes, Roy Jones." Ellie spit the dead cop's name out like it was a stray bug. "Jones, in turn, handed her off to the hunter. I barely made it in time."

She shuddered at the memory while Wallace rocked back on his heels. "Damn. That's some wild shit. They should make a movie out of that one day."

Ellie blanched. "Yeah, no thanks, that sounds terrible. Anyway, after that, I had some trust issues with the police and who should guard Valerie, and we bonded a little. Which brought her to the attention of a very bad man. Lawrence Kingsley enjoys hurting the people I care about. Like another person in WITSEC…"

Ellie bowed her head, a pained motion that scraped the outer layer from Clay's heart. When she didn't speak up to finish, he filled in the remainder of the story. "Gabe Fisher.

He worked as Kingsley's assistant for years, up until he intervened to save Ellie's best friend and roommate from Kingsley's torture. We got him into WITSEC and moved him to the Portland area, but somehow, Kingsley tracked him down and grabbed him." An image of the burning car flickered behind Clay's eyelids and his jaw tightened. "It didn't end well for Gabe."

The marshal sighed. "That's a tough break for everyone involved. Remember, though, the Marshals have never lost anyone who followed their rules. And as of now, there's zero proof that this Kingsley creep has anything to do with Valerie's disappearance. Although…"

The marshal's frown set off alarm bells in Clay's head. "Although, what?"

"Valerie did break the rules, in a big way. She joined a dating app and posted her picture."

Wallace shook his head, like he still couldn't believe it, while Clay and Ellie gaped at each other. The thought of a WITSEC participant blasting their photo all over a dating site was hard enough to swallow, but Valerie? That seemed so out of character as to border on the absurd.

"Are you absolutely sure?" Ellie asked. "Because that makes no sense at all."

Without a word, Wallace pulled out his phone. A few moments later, Valerie's face appeared on the screen, complete with her new WITSEC name typed beside the photo.

Ellie studied the picture for a long time before breaking the silence. "I don't like it. My gut says Kingsley is linked to all of this somehow."

James Wallace snorted. "Good luck getting your gut to testify to that on the stand."

Clay followed their exchange, his own gut tingling over the wrongness. None of this added up. "On the flight over, I searched for Valerie on social media but didn't find her anywhere else online. Why bother hiding from those sites, just to turn around and join a dating app?"

"Hell if I know." Wallace scratched his neck. "It's also kind of weird that she's got a roommate, but the pair of them work opposite shifts, so they hardly see each other."

Clay agreed, although weird didn't begin to cover the anomalies.

The knock came out of nowhere, jerking Clay's attention to the door. "Expecting anyone?" He kept his voice low.

"Just the roommate." Tension laced the marshal's words.

Beside him, Ellie's hand drifted to her gun, and Clay knew all of them were thinking the same thing.

Why would Valerie's roommate knock on her own front door?

Clay pulled out his own gun as he approached the door with Ellie on his heels. One glance out the peephole was enough to have him re-holster the weapon. Even distorted, the woman standing on the porch in a navy pantsuit screamed *law enforcement.*

The moment he swung open the door, the stranger confirmed his hunch by sizing him up with a suspicious once-over. "Who are you?" Without giving Clay a chance to answer, she squeezed her way past him into the apartment, stopping short when she spied Ellie, then Wallace. The woman subjected them to the same clinical scrutiny she'd bestowed upon Clay. When his turn came back around, her eyes were narrowed. "I repeat, who the hell are you? All of you?"

Like they'd choreographed the motion ahead of time, Clay, Ellie, and Wallace whipped out their respective badges in unison. When the woman read his badge, Clay caught her mouth a single word—*what?*—but only because he'd been watching her expression, waiting for a crack in that cool façade. Even anticipating her surprise, she recovered her composure so quickly that Clay almost second-guessed himself.

"Thank you, Special Agent Lockwood." She nodded stiffly before moving on to Ellie's badge. "You too, Detective Kline, who, might I add, is over a hundred miles or so out of jurisdiction."

She read Wallace's badge last. "And Federal Marshal Wallace. Wow. Lucky me, stumbling into quite the LEO trifecta. I'm Detective Charlotte Cross. Now that we've gotten the formalities over with, can one of you please tell me what the heck is going on? Unless something I ate last night made me sleep-dial, I'm pretty sure I didn't ask for the Feds." She arched a well-shaped eyebrow at him before whirling to Wallace. "Or the Marshals. Or a detective from a precinct that's a good two hours away."

Once Charlotte Cross finished addressing all of them in turn, she tapped a sensible black shoe on the floor and waited. When Clay and James only glanced at each other, drawing mental straws over who would speak first, the petite detective growled deep in her throat. A sound completely at odds with her girl-next-door looks.

"Okay, let me try to simplify this a little. What I'm asking is, why are you," she pointed at Wallace before whipping the finger at Clay, "and you involved in my local missing persons case?"

An odd choked noise from Ellie snagged his attention. Incredulous, Clay turned to stare. "You okay there?"

"Sorry, something caught in my throat." She coughed into her hand as if to demonstrate.

No doubt to cover up another snicker.

After shaking his head, Clay launched into a recap of Valerie's history, starting with the events that led to her entering into the WITSEC program. Wallace piped in with additional information every now and then.

By the time they finished, Charlotte Cross's hands were curled, her eyebrows merged together, and the entirety of her five-foot frame vibrated while standing terrifyingly still. Like a bobcat, Clay decided. Just before it pounced. "So, what I'm hearing is that we've had a witness under federal protection here in our jurisdiction for months now, and not a single person bothered to fill in anyone at the Savannah PD? How am I supposed to do my job when I don't have the information I need?"

She directed the entire diatribe at Wallace, who tried—and in Clay's opinion, failed—to appear unruffled. The marshal squirmed but held his ground. "Uh, there's no provision that requires me to make local cops aware of WITSEC participants...mostly because the local police departments have leaks bigger than Niagara Falls."

The detective's scowl deepened. She opened her mouth as if she wanted to argue, then sighed before snapping her lips closed. Instead, she granted Wallace a curt nod to acknowledge the truth in his words.

In that moment, Clay's respect for the newcomer flourished. Most cops suffered from an overzealous tendency to jump in to defend fellow officers of wrongdoing regardless of the merits of the accusations. Even generally speaking. An officer who acknowledged the problems with the badge was a rare bird.

Ellie stepped forward. "Valerie was just trying to live her life, so there was no real reason to think she was under any current threat. The untrustworthy component I'm concerned about right now has nothing to do with crooked cops. I'm worried about keeping Valerie safe from a serial killer."

Charlotte seemed to process this information for several seconds before nodding. "Thank you, I appreciate the information. Now, can I suggest that we all take a seat? My neck is cramping from staring up at all of you tall people."

Once again, the Savannah detective didn't wait for any of them to acknowledge her request before tromping over to the closest chair and plunking herself down. Ellie was the first to follow the other woman's lead by perching on one end of the couch. The marshal took the other chair, which left Clay with the open spot on the couch beside Ellie.

When they were all seated, Charlotte released a pent-up sigh. "Much better. Now, I need to lay down some ground rules before Barbara shows up and you three," she motioned at each of them in turn, "do something to mess up *my* case with the interview *I* set up. Did you miss the emphasis I put on *my*? No? Good. Because I'm going to do you a solid and let you hang out while I talk to the roommate, but I need you to know that the invitation is extended out of the goodness of my heart and can be retracted just as quickly. Understood?"

Wallace leaned forward. "But—"

Charlotte Cross held up a hand. "That was a rhetorical question. And if you don't like it, please refer to the part of my speech where I mentioned invitation retractions."

The expression of outrage on Wallace's face was so comical, Clay had to avert his gaze or else risk bursting into laughter. He half-expected Ellie to exhibit similar signs of temper, given how she hated being bossed around, but she dug her elbows into her thighs and leaned forward, like she was hanging on Cross's every word.

Clay swallowed a rueful groan. Of course. He should have guessed that Ellie would admire the feisty detective. As Clay's gaze swiveled back and forth between the two women, he pictured the kind of trouble they'd stir up if they worked cases together and winced. Poor Fortis. They'd likely send the crotchety lead detective into an early retirement.

Clay checked his watch and frowned. Based on the timing Wallace had given, Barbara was running a few minutes late. Worry pinched his gut, prompting him to issue a silent plea.

Please, don't let Valerie's roommate disappear too.

The doorknob rattled a quick warning before the door flew open and Barbara Vanhousen strolled in. She crossed half the entryway, glanced up from her phone, and let loose with a high-pitched shriek.

"Anyone else fighting off a weird urge to yell *surprise?*" Charlotte Cross muttered before springing to her feet and crossing the distance over to Barbara with a speed that defied her short legs. "Sorry for the startle, Ms. Vanhousen. I'm Charlotte Cross, we spoke on the phone."

With her hand still pressed to her chest, Barbara checked the badge the detective held up. "Right. Sorry, I just didn't expect y'all to be waiting inside my apartment." The woman peeked at Clay, then the others. "Or that there'd be so many of you."

Wallace rose, a string bean in a purple tie. "Sorry, Ms. Vanhousen, that's my—"

The glare Detective Cross shot the marshal from over her shoulder could have cut glass. He clammed up—wise move, in Clay's opinion—and when Cross turned back to Barbara, she'd traded the glower for a smile soothing enough to make the Madonna proud. "What my colleague was going to say was that it's his fault for not scheduling with me ahead of time."

And then, in front of Clay's eyes, Detective Cross completely shifted, shedding the hard-boiled cop demeanor and slipping into a softer, more inviting presence as if it were a second skin. "You must be beat from work. Why don't you come sit down, take a load off, before we get started."

"That sounds good, thanks."

Smooth as a spin doctor, Cross led Valerie's roommate

over to the one empty chair and gestured for the woman to sit. Once Barbara was seated, Cross spun to shoot Wallace a pointed look. "You don't mind, do you, Marshal?" This voice was new too. As sugary as sweet tea.

Clay's admiration grew. *Nicely played, Detective Cross.* Without any good way to refuse, Wallace lumbered to his feet, muttering something unintelligible under his breath before slinking away.

In a flash, Cross claimed the vacant spot. "If you don't mind, why don't we start with you telling us how Valerie was acting the last time you saw her? And when was that, exactly?"

"It was Friday, a couple of hours before her date. I was here for a little bit while she was getting ready." Barbara paused, then shrugged. "And she seemed antsy and nervous, like usual. But also a little excited? I was really hoping this would be a good thing for her, you know?"

Cross made a sympathetic noise. "I do know. Now, could you share some background information about Valerie from your perspective? Real simple stuff, like, do you all spend a lot of time together? Any friends you know by name that she'd hang out with? That sort of thing."

Barbara filled her cheeks with air, puffing them out like a chipmunk's before blowing it back out. "Okay, let's see. Valerie and I work opposite shifts, so we don't really spend a lot of time together, especially not once she started night classes. We're friendly enough but calling us friends would be a stretch. I just haven't had a chance to get to know her that well, you know? She's the kind of person that's hard to get close to. Kinda closed off, the type who doesn't like to talk about themselves. Jumpy too, almost like she had skeletons in the closet. If she has other friends, I've never seen them, and she's never told me about them."

Cross stared at her notepad for a long moment. "So, in

your opinion, Valerie was secretive and very cautious, am I understanding that correctly?"

Barbara nodded. "Yes! Exactly. She didn't even have social media accounts like Twitter or Facebook."

"All right, that's very helpful. You're doing great so far, Barbara." The detective tilted her head, tapping a pen against the page. "Except, hmm, that doesn't seem to gel with the type of woman who'd upload personal information on a dating app and meet a perfect stranger for a blind date. What do you make of that?"

Barbara's face fell. "Um..." She fidgeted in the chair, looking anywhere but at Detective Cross. "I'm not sure..."

Cross leaned forward and patted Barbara's hand. When she spoke, her voice flowed like warm honey. "I know how scary this must feel, Barbara, but trust me when I say you're not in any trouble here, okay? All of us in this room are working toward the same goal: finding Valerie before anything truly terrible can happen to her. The thing is..." The detective bridged her fingers across her nose and heaved a sad sigh.

"What? What's the thing?" Barbara leaned in, snagged by the Savannah detective's dangling hook. Clay made a mental note to add that trick to his repertoire.

"The thing is, the longer Valerie goes missing without a lead, the worse our chances of finding her. That's why it's so important that all the people we talk to in a missing persons case tell us everything they know, from the very start. Not to pressure you, but even the most insignificant detail can make all the difference."

When Cross finished, she nudged Barbara with a soft, encouraging smile. Valerie's roommate chewed a thumbnail, then hunched her neck into her shoulders. "I'm the one who downloaded the dating app for Valerie and set up her profile."

Cross's serene expression remained unchanged, but Clay spied the clenched fist in her lap. "See, that wasn't so hard, was it? I can't begin to tell you how helpful all of this is. Now, tell me more about this dating profile. Valerie asked you to create one for her?"

Barbara slipped her feet onto the chair and hugged her knees to her chest. "Not exactly." She grimaced. "I mean, not at all. I made the profile without asking. I even took the photos of her for the site when she wasn't looking."

"Ah," was all Cross said this time.

Barbara's eyes pleaded with the detective. "I thought that if she found a boyfriend or at least got laid, Valerie might lighten up a little, have some fun."

"I understand. Valerie was wound tight as a tennis ball. You were just trying to be a good roommate and help her out."

Barbara grabbed the excuse with both hands. "Yes! Thank you, that's exactly what I was doing."

"Okay. Walk me through what happened next."

"I published her profile and started sorting through the guys who replied. The one I picked seemed perfect. His messages were smart, respectful. He seemed like a real gentleman, the kind of guy I figured Valerie would like. So I set up the date between them and then showed Valerie. She was upset at first, but I kept pushing her to go. Telling her that she was too young to stay holed up in the apartment all the time." Barbara's face crumpled. "What if my pushing got Valerie into trouble?"

Barbara's lower lip wobbled before she broke into sobs. Cross rose and disappeared into the hallway, returning with a box of tissues that she set on the other woman's lap. Then the detective stared back down at her notepad, jabbing the pen at the paper so hard she poked holes all over like polka dots.

Sensing that the detective could use a break, Clay tapped her on the arm. When she glanced up, he jerked his head toward Barbara, then pointed at his chest. The detective hesitated before granting her permission with a nod. Her eyes narrowed with a clear message.

Don't mess this up.

Clay waited until the sobs subsided before squatting next to Barbara. He plucked a tissue from the box and offered it to her. "Sorry, this must be overwhelming."

Barbara accepted the thin paper with a hiccup. "It really is."

"Well, you're doing great so far. You mentioned that you set up the date. You wouldn't happen to know where Valerie went to meet this man, would you?"

"They were supposed to meet at this fancy restaurant about fifteen miles from where we live. That's another reason I thought he'd be a good match for Valerie. He seemed like a fancy man, and she always acted so classy."

"Good, that's good."

"Do you have a description?" Ellie burst out, earning her a head swivel from Cross which she pretended not to notice. "Of the man, not the restaurant."

Clay held his breath, worried the interruption might overwhelm Valerie's roommate, but the woman perked up. "Better than a description. I have a photo."

This time when Charlotte Cross craned her neck toward Ellie, she graced the other detective with an approving nod. Anticipation crackled in the air like electricity before a lightning storm while they all waited for Barbara to pull up the picture on her phone.

"Here he is."

When Barbara turned the screen to face them, Clay's shoulders fell. Right away, it was plain that the person in the photo bore little resemblance to Lawrence Kingsley. The man staring into the camera was brown-skinned, attractive, and looked a good fifteen years younger than the murderous doctor.

He checked on Ellie's reaction. She stared hard at the picture before shaking her head, disappointment evident in her drooping mouth. "That's not Kingsley. Although," she paused, tapping an index finger against her chin, "he could be like ninety-nine percent of the other online daters who alter their image with filters or hijack someone else's photo. Even people who aren't cold-blooded killers catfish at times, so why not him? Plus, we don't know for sure what Kingsley even looks like now."

"Or maybe this Kingsley guy isn't involved at all." For the first time in a while, Wallace piped in, only to be shut down when both detectives whirled to glare him back into silence in unison.

Ellie's phone pinged. "Excuse me, I'd better check this." When she stood and headed for the front door, Clay followed. He wanted to get her take on the case so far, plus his quads had started to cramp.

But Clay knew the talk would have to wait the moment she looked up from her screen. "They tracked down Lucas Harrison's mom. If I hurry and hit the road now, I can make it to Jacksonville before it gets too late."

She didn't move, though. She remained rooted to the same spot, twirling a red curl and glancing at Valerie's door. Torn.

Clay dropped a hand on her shoulder. He'd planned on a quick squeeze, to offer reassurance, and once there, he couldn't bring himself to let go right away. The touch lingered too long to be construed as professional, but the connection felt too good to relinquish so easily. "Go ahead, go. I've got it covered here, and I promise to pull out every stop to find Valerie."

Beneath his fingers, Ellie's deltoids contracted. Other than that, she remained still. Debating the options, Clay guessed. Seconds ticked by, each one causing the pressure in Clay's chest to build while he fretted over the verdict.

Either she trusted him, or she didn't. Clay squirmed, knowing the latter option had delivered the death blow on her relationship with Nick.

Emerald eyes locked with his brown ones, dragging the suspense on until Clay's ribs ached. Finally, Ellie nodded. "If Valerie's case can't be in my hands, at least I can feel reassured knowing that it's in yours."

Before Clay could react with anything other than a slack jaw, she patted his cheek and headed down the path that led to the parking lot. "See you back in Charleston."

Clay stared at the swish of her retreating red ponytail long after his surprise wore off. Then, with a new lightness to his feet, he headed back inside the apartment to make good on his promise.

9

W ater splashed Katarina's hands as she rinsed the suds from the dishes, and the warmth transported her away from the snow-covered Grand Tetons looming outside the kitchen window to sun-washed beaches on another continent. The mountains were replaced by Bethany, twirling in a *Wonder Woman* swimsuit, kicking up white sand while turquoise waves lapped at her feet.

A plate slipped from Katarina's hands, clattering as glass hit glass. She flinched and checked for damage. No broken pieces, but the interruption whisked the daydream away.

With a sigh, Katarina grabbed the top plate off the stack and began drying it with the red-and-white checked towel. She strategized as the dishes piled up. First, she and Bethany could learn Greek, but the most crucial aspect of the plan centered on obtaining papers, which required a boatload of cash and the right connections. Katarina already had a plan for that, though.

She was drying the last two plates from her and Bethany's breakfast that morning when a door squeaked from down the hall. A loud yawn that sounded more bear than human followed. Clayne shuffled into the kitchen a few moments later, squinting at the daylight that spilled in through the window.

"Look at you, being all industrious this morning." He squinted at the window. "Wait, afternoon. I'm guessing your head is feeling a little better than mine." Clayne came up behind her and slid his arms around her waist, rocking his pelvis against her ass. He leaned over to nip her ear. "Then again, you feel better than me in general. How about we head back to bed and see if we can't sweat this hangover off?"

Sour fumes from last night's drinkathon rolled off his breath and slapped Katarina in the face. So potent, she could probably catch a buzz off the smell alone. She wrinkled her nose and finished with the last plate. "I have a bunch of stuff I need to get done this morning."

Clayne only squeezed harder, letting his teeth travel to her neck. "And that stuff will still be there waiting this afternoon. C'mon, you know you want to. Got to take advantage while the kid is at school."

Actually, Katarina didn't want to, and hadn't for quite a while now. A disappointing turn of events, when the only reason she'd hooked up with Clayne in the first place was to prevent the onset of severe boredom.

She clenched the granite counter as Clayne rubbed up against her, waiting for a spark. Nothing happened, because Clayne now bored her too. Same exact problem that always plagued Katarina in terms of men. The second the initial thrill died off, Katarina had one foot out the door.

"We could do it right here, against the counter." He rocked into her again, as if to demonstrate.

"We can't." She searched for an excuse. "A neighbor might see."

"Then I suggest you get your sweet ass back to the bedroom before that happens."

Katarina's eyes narrowed until the mountain range reduced to a white sliver. A piece of her would love nothing more than to pivot and knee him right in the nuts, but logic prevailed. Yeah, she'd grown tired of Clayne, but she couldn't afford for him to get sick of her. She still needed him on the hook. For now. But if she shot him down, odds were he'd get pissy about it, and pissy didn't work for Katarina. For her plan to succeed, she needed his unwavering devotion and trust.

She dug her nails into the kitchen counter before forcing her arms to relax. That meant playing along and fulfilling his sexual urges.

Even if mopping the kitchen floor sounded more enjoyable these days.

"You really think my ass is sweet?"

Katarina wiggled the body part in question, and Clayne responded with an appreciative groan.

"Baby, your ass is sweeter than anything else in the entire state of Wyoming."

He flipped her around and dipped his head to kiss her, but Katarina swatted him away with a playful pout. "Only Wyoming, and not the entire continental United States?"

"That too, baby. That's what I meant to say."

Once again, he reached for her, and once again, Katarina dodged his greedy hands. "I'm sorry, that's not good enough. Now, I'm going to have to punish you by making you wait."

His groan was louder this time, but the gleam in his eyes told Katarina he enjoyed this new game. "Yes, ma'am. Whatever you say. I've been bad, so I'll take my punishment."

His eagerness made Katarina want to roll her eyes. "Good boy. While I make you wait as penance, why don't you tell me if that big deal is going to go through with...uh, those three guys from the party on New Year's Eve. Whatever their names were."

When Clayne's forehead wrinkled at the unexpected demand, Katarina shook out her hair before trailing a hand between her breasts. "I can't help it if hearing you talk business turns me on. It's your fault, you know. For being such a badass."

The instant Clayne puffed out his chest, Katarina relaxed. Ego strokes worked like a charm as a distraction every damn time.

"You bet that sweet ass the deal went through. Reckon my business will be expanding real soon. And don't you worry about their names, that's not important."

"You're right." Mostly because Katarina had already memorized the drug dealers' names. Clayne didn't need to know that. "Will the job be dangerous?"

A silly question since any sizeable drug deal carried high risk. But Katarina thrived on risk. Danger was the main component necessary to rev her engine, so she figured she might as well attempt to make the next hour as enjoyable as possible.

A slow grin spread across Clayne's face. One good thing about the small-town criminal was his willingness to feed that dark need in her. "Oh, it's going to be real dangerous. We're gonna have so many bricks that we could build a house entirely out of cocaine if we wanted to."

He sidled closer and slipped his hands onto her hips. This time, Katarina allowed the touch, even pushed into it as her pulse drummed a quicker tempo. "A house? That much coke must be worth a lot of money." She licked his neck, hiding her face while she waited on the information.

"Damn right it is. Thirty-two million, babe. That's how much cocaine is gonna be parked out in my shed overnight. Now, have I suffered enough yet?"

Katarina's thighs clenched. Thirty-two million dollars of coke? Hot damn.

"Yes," she murmured against his skin, "I think you've learned your lesson."

At the announcement, Clayne whooped and practically dragged her down the hall to the bedroom. In under a minute, he had them both undressed and naked on the bed. While Clayne thrust and panted on top of her, Katarina plotted.

Two nights from now, the drugs would arrive at Clayne's warehouse, transported there by a group of bikers. All those bikers would be armed with guns. Perfect, because Katarina wanted extra guns to keep her and Bethany safe. She also needed enough coke to fund new identities for both of them and matching black market passports. Plus, a little extra for living expenses. If she played it smart, a couple of bricks should be enough to set her and Bethany up to live out the rest of their days comfortably.

After a few more frantic pumps of his hips, Clayne shuddered and moaned before rolling off to sprawl next to her. "Damn, baby, that was hot."

Katarina murmured an agreement. Even though the only hot thing for her had been the literal sweat dripping off his chin, and already, she was planning to wash his sour sweat off the sheets and her body the moment he drove off.

Her smile was genuine, though, because Clayne was satisfied, and Katarina knew that a satisfied man was a complacent man.

Ten minutes later, they rolled out of bed for the second time that day. Katarina collected the clothes Clayne had scattered along the floor and slipped them back on while he did the same. "You sure you have to leave so soon?" She injected a pout into the question, even as she rejoiced inside.

"I'm sure. Got that big deal to prepare for, but I promise

not to neglect you. Or this sweet thing." He finished pulling down his shirt, then patted her ass. "Walk me out?"

Katarina trailed him down the hall to the front door. After he shrugged into his jacket, Clayne turned and planted a hard kiss on her mouth. "Think about me while I'm gone."

"Oh, I will." Him, and the way his drug deal was going to pave the way for her and Bethany's new lives in paradise.

Icy air gusted in when he swung open the front door. Katarina shivered and wished she'd grabbed a sweatshirt.

"You got something here. It was hanging on the porch."

She frowned at the object dangling from his hand. A white envelope. Innocuous enough, and yet a chill separate from the weather streaked across her skin.

Who the hell would leave Katarina a letter? She didn't know anyone in Wyoming.

An impulse urged her to dart forward and snatch the envelope from his hand, but Katarina was smarter than that. "Thanks, probably another neighbor inviting me to one of those stupid MLM home parties where they try to sell you stuff." She accepted the envelope while pushing up onto her toes and pecking him on his cheek. "Good luck with work this afternoon."

"Thanks, babe. See you tonight."

Despite the freezing air, Katarina shivered on the porch until Clayne's car roared to life. She waved as he raced away, only fleeing inside and slamming the door when his bumper disappeared around a bend.

With fingers shaking from a combination of cold and nerves, she ripped open the envelope. All the while chanting in her head, *please actually be a stupid MLM home party.*

The moment she unfolded the single page inside, her heart froze in her chest. Oh, god.

Not a letter at all, but a printout of a photo.

"Dammit, no!" Katarina cursed, then screamed, then

whirled and pounded the door with her fists. Once the initial surge of enraged horror abated, she gathered her wits and smoothed the crumpled page back open, revealing an image of Bethany sitting in the back of a strange car.

Dressed in the clothes she'd worn to school that morning.

10

Weariness settled into Ellie's shoulders during the last half hour of the drive to Jacksonville. After two hours on the road from Charleston to Savannah and the interview with Valerie's roommate, Ellie had jumped into her Explorer and headed off on the two-and-a-half-hour trip to Florida. That left her with a four-and-a-half-hour ride back home, and there was no telling when she'd get on the road. The timing of her return departure depended on what Lucas Harrison's mother had to say.

Ellie rolled her neck before sipping from the iced latte stashed in the center console. Hopefully, the caffeine would trigger a second wind. If not, she might end up booking a hotel room for the night.

The idea of decompressing in a hot bath as soon as the interview with Lucas's mom concluded was almost too tempting to resist. Ellie felt like a battery that had run out of juice too soon. She wasn't sure why she felt so drained. Only that her body could use a chance to recharge.

At the prompt of the robotic navigator, Ellie merged into the right lane and exited the highway, stopping at a red light at the end of the off ramp. She sipped more of the latte, then stifled a yawn. Maybe she'd treat herself to an overnight stay, regardless of what time the interview ended.

After following the GPS for another five miles, Ellie turned left into a trailer park. Palm trees flanked an entry-way, leading to streets lined with neat little rows of mobile homes. Ellie steered straight, then veered right at the first stop sign, crawling along at fifteen miles per hour until she pulled in front of a blue single-wide.

After double checking the address, Ellie climbed out of the Explorer. As she reached the three stairs that led to a small porch covered by a green awning, the trailer's front door swung open. A blonde woman appeared. Head glued to her phone, the woman crossed the porch before she noticed Ellie. She stopped short and squinted at Ellie, her feet poised at the top of the steps.

"You need something?"

Ellie offered the woman a friendly smile while assessing her features. She looked younger than expected, but the resemblance between her wide-spaced eyes and defined cheekbones and Lucas Harrison's photo was unmistakable. She had a blue apron slung over one shoulder, like she was on the way to work, and reeked so strongly of cigarettes that even standing several feet away, Ellie's eyes threatened to water.

"I do. I'm looking for Lisa Harrison. Does that happen to be you?"

The woman twitched like a spooked rabbit. Her gaze darted over her shoulder to the trailer's front door, and for a tense second, Ellie feared she was about to flee back inside and hide until Ellie gave up. Instead, she balled a handful of the apron in her fist and jutted her chin out. "Who's asking?"

"I'm Detective Ellie Kline from the Charleston Police Department."

Ellie caught the alarm that widened the woman's eyes before her expression hardened, adding ten years to her age in a flash. She shoved a hand onto a bony hip. "So maybe I am Lisa Harrison, so what? I'd like to know what's a Charleston cop doing showing up on my porch at seven-thirty at night."

"Mind if I come up there and join you? Then I'll fill you in on why I'm here."

Lisa Harrison's lips thinned before she grunted and stepped to the side. "Suit yourself, but I haven't got all day to chitchat. I'm on the clock soon."

Ellie bounded up the stairs and onto the small patio lined with artificial turf before the woman could have a change of heart. "Thank you, and I'll try not to take up too much of your time. Over the course of a recent interview with a lawyer named Burton, our department, in conjunction with the FBI, uncovered an illegal adoption trafficking ring. Some of those children's cases fell into my lap. That's why I'm here, because one of the kids in Burton's adoption files matched the description of your missing son, Lucas."

Lisa stared at Ellie like she'd appeared out of thin air, then swayed on her feet. "I need to sit down." She plunked into the sun-weathered plastic chair behind her and yanked a pack of cigarettes from her purse. After a flick of a purple lighter and a deep puff, Lucas's mom released a shaky sigh in a cloud of smoke, her nicotine-stained fingers trembling. "Are you saying that you think Lucas ended up being adopted by someone else? Okay, but I still don't get why you're here. That was years ago."

Ellie's radar chirped as she examined the top of the woman's head. Seemed like an odd reaction for a mother to have regarding information about her missing child. No matter how much time had passed.

"I'm sorry if this has come as a shock. My job is working

cold cases, so all of them are old. If you could see fit to go over a few items with me, I'd really appreciate it."

Lisa Harrison frowned and took another puff of the cigarette. She exhaled and jerked her chin down. "Yeah. Okay. But only for a few minutes."

Up close, Lucas's mother appeared older than at first glance, with deep-set wrinkles slashing her forehead and grooves on either side of her mouth. "Thank you. Lucas's file is pretty slim, so I was hoping you could give me more information on what happened the day he disappeared."

Smoke curled from the glowing tip of the cigarette while Lisa shrugged. "I was up late the night before, partying a little by myself. I overslept the next morning. When I woke up, I went to check on Lucas, but he was gone."

Ellie waited for Lisa to fill in the details, but the woman didn't venture any additional information. She just sat there, sucking more nicotine into her lungs.

A headache gathered behind Ellie's temples. The woman's brief story matched what Ellie had read in the file almost verbatim. Almost like it had been rehearsed. "Is there anything else you can remember?"

Lisa cocked her head as if considering, then shrugged again. "Nope, that's pretty much it. Once I realized he was gone, I drove down to the local police department and filed a report, but I could tell none of those bozos took me seriously."

"Do you have any ideas as to why that might be?"

The woman barked a sandpaper-rough laugh, the sound hoarse from years of self-inflicted throat damage. "Sure did. They could tell I was all drugged up and didn't think it was worth going to all that trouble just to try to find some little retard."

Ellie flinched at that last word and counted out several deep breaths before trusting herself to reply. "Did they come right out and tell you that, and if so, do you remember which officers said those words?"

Lisa fidgeted in the chair, making the plastic squeak. "Sorry, don't recall their names, and I'm not sure if those were their exact words. Pretty sure they said something like that, although, come to think of it, maybe I was reading too much into things. I was still pretty high at the time."

The woman turned her attention back to smoking while the anger flaring in Ellie's chest grew more challenging to hide. She fought a rising urge to grab the cigarette and crush it beneath the heel of her shoe. "I understand." An utter lie. Ellie would never comprehend this woman's nonchalant attitude toward her missing child. "How about what the officers looked like. Can you tell me that?"

Lisa Harrison turned her head and stared into the night. "Like I said before, I was high. I don't give a rat's ass what some dickhead cops look like when I'm feeling good, you get me?"

The burger Ellie had scarfed down on the drive there churned in her stomach. Feeling good? When her son had just gone missing? No, Ellie did not get this woman at all.

"Okay. What other details can you remember? Was Lucas unhappy? Did he talk about running away? Or did you have any suspicions over who might have taken him?"

A strange expression distorted Lisa's features. The kind of face someone might make if they'd just stepped in dog crap. "Only thing that kid ever talked about was camping. Camping, and Aaron. Doubt he was smart enough to run away, but who knows?"

Ellie turned and fake coughed into her hand. She needed a second to calm herself. Ellie always strived for empathy, but Lisa Harrison had to be one of the more distasteful humans she'd ever had the misfortune to interview. The woman's clear disregard for her own son was close to pushing Ellie over the edge.

After picturing her peaceful place and counting to ten, Ellie resumed questioning. "Tell me about Aaron. What was his relationship with Lucas like?"

To Ellie's surprise, genuine emotion flared in Lisa's eyes. Her lower lip trembled. "Aaron was the glue that held our family together. By the way he acted, no one would have ever guessed that Lucas wasn't his birth son." She released a long sigh, and her face softened. "Aaron was great with that kid. He always knew the right thing to say to calm Lucas down when he was in one of his freak-outs, or how to stop him from banging his head on the wall. They used to go camping together. But then Aaron was sent overseas. He didn't make it back alive."

Despite disliking the woman, Ellie's heart softened a little. Losing your partner to war had to be awful. If nothing else, Lisa Harrison had truly cared for her husband.

Too bad she hadn't seemed able to muster that type of heartfelt emotion for her own son.

"Sounds like losing Aaron was rough on both of you."

"Yeah. I dabbled a little in drugs here and there beforehand, but nothing too major. When I got the phone call that he'd died in combat, though, I went off the deep end. Like a ten-day bender. Lucky I survived, tell you the truth."

"And you woke up one morning, and Lucas was gone."

Lisa's face turned stony again. "Yup. He just up and disappeared."

Ellie doubted that very much, but she moved on. "What about now? Are you still using drugs now?"

The head shake was definitive. "Been sober for three years. Apart from the cancer sticks, that is."

"Good for you. So, now that you're sober, can I ask what's stopping you from looking for Lucas?"

Lisa scoffed. "You think I don't know what it's like out there?" She circled her hand toward the street. "The world's a shithole, even for folks who aren't slow. Ain't no way Lucas survived out there, but if he did somehow manage to last this long, he probably wishes he were dead, because the only way he's alive is if some creep took a liking to him. You and me both know, Detective Kline, that the world chews up boys like Lucas and spits them out in pieces once it's through with them." She checked the time and swore. "Now, I've gotta go before I lose my job."

After a last suck on the cigarette, Lisa flicked the butt into an old coffee can littered with other remnants and jumped to her feet. Ellie followed the woman down the steps, watching as she headed to an ancient gold Chevy that looked as broken down as she was. The engine turned over three times before catching with a death rattle.

Not once did Lisa Harrison look back as she drove away. Nor had she asked Ellie to keep her updated on any new developments in Lucas's case.

Ellie climbed into the driver's seat and sat there for several minutes without moving. With a heavy exhale, she reached into the back seat and grabbed Lucas Harrison's file. As she stared at the signature of the detective who'd signed off on the case, her mind shifted to Roy Jones. He'd been the cold case detective in the Charleston PD before Ellie, and the crooked cop had left a shocking number of similarly thin reports behind him when he'd retired.

Turned out, the shoddy notetaking had been deliberate. Roy Jones had taken bribes to help cover up crimes for someone else.

She focused on Lucas's page as the wheels in her head gathered momentum. Based on the crappy file, Ellie bet that the local police department had a crooked detective of their own to root out.

11

W hen Luke Coleman entered the group therapy room, most of the other participants were already there, waiting on the session to begin. Three of them were already sitting in the plastic chairs arranged in a circle formation, while the rest stood around. Luke thought they always acted like they didn't know they were supposed to sit until instructed, even though the routine never varied, three times a week.

The pretty, older woman seated in the chair at the top of the circle smiled at Luke before addressing everyone in the room. "I think we're all here now, so please take a seat so we can get started."

Luke claimed the chair directly opposite the woman. The same place he always sat. Even though the seats weren't assigned, all the patients in the Elysium Psychiatric Center group sat in the same spot for every session. Luke frowned. Well, except for that one time when Cade showed up early and snatched Amanda's chair just to make her mad.

Group ended up getting canceled that day after Amanda threw a different chair at Cade, which led to a fistfight with lots and lots of screaming. Neither of them had returned to group since.

Luke hated screaming, but he didn't usually mind these sessions. The psychiatrist was one of the nicer employees at the hospital, and he liked hearing other people's stories. But today, he couldn't seem to sit still. His leg bounced, and he kept plucking at a loose thread on his pants. He tucked his hands under his thighs, to remind himself not to bite his nails. Dr. Eddington didn't like it when Luke bit his nails. She thought that the act held some important meaning, when really, it was just a nervous habit.

But Luke wasn't going to argue with her, not today. Not when he needed to show Dr. Eddington that he was okay.

Like always, the session began with each participant introducing themselves. Some of the other patients rolled their eyes and groaned. They thought introductions were stupid because it was usually the same people over and over again. Luke liked the introductions, though. The routine was comforting. Although this time, there was even a new person.

"Hi, I'm Eddie Spencer, this is my first group session."

Luke glanced at the soft-spoken newcomer, who was small with delicate features, wavy red hair, and freckles on his pale skin. Luke guessed his age to be around twenty.

He reminded Luke of someone he'd met years ago. William Warren.

When his turn came to introduce himself, Luke mumbled. "I'm Luke Coleman. I've been here lots."

It was a lie, so Luke ducked his head so nobody could see his face. He hadn't always been Coleman. His name had been Harrison at one time, but that was a long, long time ago.

Back when he'd met that other boy. *William.*

The voices of the other patients in the circle faded away

as Luke's mind took him back in time, to that awful, noisy room he'd been trapped in after his mom disappeared.

In a back corner, Luke flapped his hands near his lap, trying to fight off the fire ant sensation stinging its way through his body.

Too much. There was too much going on in this room, and all of it felt like an attack. Tiny babies screamed in cribs up front, and to his right, two little kids shoved each other and argued over a dirty yellow blanket. The girl directly in front of Luke hadn't stopped whimpering since they'd dragged her in earlier.

"Hey, weirdo, why you flapping your hands like that? Think you're gonna fly away?" A boy about five inches shorter than Luke with buzzed blond hair and cruel eyes pointed at him and sneered.

Luke ignored the comment, the way he always did. Even though he was the oldest kid in the room, some of the other kids picked on him anyway. And none of them talked to him. They all agreed he was weird.

One of the babies let out a particularly shrill wail, and the crawling sensation along Luke's skin grew close to unbearable. He hated this place, with all the noises and screams and mean kids and the cramped room that smelled like baby poop and armpits and dirty socks. He wanted his magazines. A quiet place to read.

"Aaron, where are you?" he whispered. "Please, get me out of here and take me camping. I promise not to make Mom mad anymore."

But enough days had passed now that Luke understood. Aaron wasn't coming back for him. Neither was his mom.

The truth mixed with the screams that bounced off the walls, ambushing Luke and electrocuting him all over. Even worse than when he used to rub his old blanket too much in the winter. The racket pumped Luke so full of terrible feelings that he worried his skin could burst. He squeezed his eyes shut, flapped his hands harder, and repeated the same sentence, over and over in his head.

Make it stop make it stop make it stop.

Like magic, the noise stopped.

Except Luke didn't believe in magic. Not anymore.

Still curled into a protective ball, he opened one eye, then the other. A man wearing a gray suit, who Luke had never seen before, had entered the room.

The gray-suit man's gaze traveled over the area until it landed on where Luke sat huddled in the back corner. He nodded. "You. Luke. Come with me."

Murmurs started up as the other kids whispered to each other and turned to stare at Luke, but for once, Luke didn't care about being singled out. He got to leave the horrible, smelly noise room!

He sprang out of the chair, tripping over his own feet as he hurried to follow the man before he changed his mind.

"Klutz," a kid said as Luke stumbled past, but Luke didn't care. Because the other boy was right—Luke was clumsy. But that didn't matter anymore because today, Luke got to leave!

The noise kicked up again when Luke reached the hall, but then gray-suit man shut the door, sealing the racket in on the other side. Away from Luke. The fire ants were still crawling because, once they came out, they didn't disappear right away. But the quiet helped the burning sensation to fade, and at least Luke no longer felt like he might explode.

He followed the gray-suit man down the short hall to another door, where the man stopped and gestured for Luke to enter. Inside the small room, a man and woman sat behind a desk. Luke skimmed their faces quickly—the woman's smiling lips were bright red, the color of a fire truck, while the man's lips made a straight line— before he dropped his gaze to the safer territory of their clothes. He lingered on the woman's outfit. She wore a pretty green dress under a big fur jacket. The man wore a collared shirt and slacks, both gray.

Going-out clothes, his mom used to say.

The thought hurt his belly.

Luke wiggled his hands down by his sides. He didn't understand why they were all in this room together.

"Oh my gosh, you must be Lucas! Aren't you a doll? Bless your heart, you're gonna be just perfect."

Luke froze. Wait. She couldn't mean him? No one ever said Luke was perfect. Maybe there was another Luke nearby.

The woman squealed again, so Luke braved another glance at her face, sure he must be mistaken. But no, those blue eyes stared right at him, and her red lips were spread wide in a grin.

The eyes traveled up and down Luke in a way that made him squirm a little, although he didn't know why, because her words were so nice. She smelled nice too. Like flowers and sugar water. "Yes, we're going to take you home and show you all kinds of love, just you wait."

When he heard the words "take you home," Luke forgot everything else. He could feel his heart beat harder in his chest. Was it possible? This woman might rescue him from the noisy place? He might really get to leave?

"Luke? Luke, time to wake up from your daydream, group is over."

Luke blinked to find himself back in the group room of the Elysium Psychiatric Center, with its sharp lemon smell and plain white walls. Chairs scraped back as the other patients stood and left the circle. All except for Dr. Eddington, who studied him with her pen and notebook in hand.

"You seemed really out of it today. Did you have a tough time sleeping last night?"

Luke plucked at the loose thread. "Not really." The last thing Luke wanted was the doctor to increase the nighttime meds that already made him feel like he was underwater. "Was just thinking about some stuff. Sorry, I promise to talk more next time."

The doctor smiled. "I'm going to hold you to that. See you next time."

Luke nodded and then slipped away to wander the hallways of the facility, taking comfort in the familiar white walls and faces, and predictable routines.

The daydream had reminded Luke that the hospital was his home now, which was a good thing.

He walked the halls until he stopped shivering, and the memory faded away.

Except for his cabin and the woods, the world outside wasn't a good place. Luke needed to stay at the hospital. At least inside these walls, he was safe.

12

I hummed a jaunty little ditty to myself as I arranged the cutlery around the cherry-wood table in front of five of the chairs, stepping back once I finished to double-check that I'd displayed the utensils just right. Both sterling silver forks lined up atop the cream linen napkin to the left of the plate, with the dinner knife and soup spoon resting on the right. After straightening the butter knife that bisected the bread plate and making sure I'd remembered the dessert spoon, I nodded, pleasure curling inside me like a Christmas ribbon as I admired my handiwork.

The real gold flecks in the Hermès plates glittered beneath the chandelier, and the Baccarat crystal sparkled as well. "See, Mom? All those hours you spent instructing me on the fine art of setting the perfect table for a dinner party paid off."

Not that my mother could answer, unless ghosts really did exist.

I sighed when my chest pinged with the slightest twinge of regret. Nostalgia over returning to one of my childhood homes, no doubt. To be expected. Even if the sentiment over my drunk of a mother was misplaced.

My gaze wandered the vaulted, wood-beamed ceilings, the plantation shutters. The original wooden floors, sanded and stained to restore their former glory. This house hadn't even been our yearly home, merely my family's winter retreat. After the estate was sold off and passed between several buyers throughout the years, I decided to purchase the place myself around twelve months ago. Through a fake name and layer upon layer of shell companies and corporate structures, of course, to shield my identity from prying eyes.

And now, I was shielding my houseguest from prying eyes too.

I smiled, drinking in the elegant dining room, tickled by how well my interior design aesthetic suited the space. The antique wooden pieces and classic lines of the understated cream and blue upholstery created a much more refined atmosphere than the overwrought Tuscan furniture my mother had favored. Especially when combined with that hideous gold-orange paint she'd chosen for the walls.

I shuddered at the horrid memory, then snickered as I adjusted one of the wine glasses so that its position matched the others. Unlike Mother's decorating, mine wouldn't include half-empty thousand-dollar bottles of wine strewn throughout the house like a baby's toys.

"But you did teach me the importance of planning every event down to the smallest detail to ensure things run smoothly, and for that, I can be grateful."

After one last reassuring scan of the place settings, I picked up a pen in preparation of writing names on the little white cards that would inform each guest of where to sit. The anticipation that had danced beneath my skin since this morning intensified, until my pulse fluttered as I formed an elegant, cursive V for the first name.

Oh, Valerie, I have to give you credit. You've proven far more successful than most at making my life difficult.

I finished her name with a flourish, clucking my tongue. "And yet, you still fell for my infatuated admirer act over dinner, and practically stumbled all over yourself to share details of your life, like how excited you were about your night classes, while I had to sit there and pretend to care. Tragic, really, how you lapped up my attention like a starving mongrel does a bowl of milk." I clucked my tongue. "So eager to share a five-course meal with an attractive man that you didn't even think about the drink you left unattended during your trip to the ladies' room."

Once Valerie's card was set in the correct spot, I allowed myself to return to that night.

After I paid the bill, I watched with secret delight as Valerie stood up and wobbled, grabbing at her chair for support. "Whoops, guess that wine hit me harder than I expected."

I arranged my expression to simulate concern. "Perhaps I should drive you home? I'd hate to risk anything happening to you."

Valerie giggled, her cheeks flushed pink from the effects of the drug. "That might be for the best, thank you."

"No need for thanks, it's my pleasure." The complete, unvarnished truth.

I moved around the table and extended my arm, which she clung to gratefully. Her legs shook like a newborn foal's, offering me the opportunity to pull her even closer and drink in the vanilla-cinnamon scent of her perfume, the faint musk of her own skin beneath. As we walked out of the restaurant toward my car, her words started to slur, and her tongue loosened.

The drug again. Working its magic.

"This evening was so nice. I wasn't sure I'd ever date again, after what happened to Ben."

She stumbled, but I held her steady. "Easy does it, we're almost there."

"I'm so sorry, I don't know what happened. I promise, I never drink this much. Thank you for helping me. You're so sweet."

She gave me a glassy-eyed smile before muttering some more about Ben. How they'd met, how long they'd been together before he was taken from her, blah blah blah. All information that I knew already, but she didn't know that. I shook my head. Would a real date want to hear the details of a new flame's murdered ex the first time they ventured out together? I suspected not.

No wonder women had such a hard time nabbing and holding on to a man.

When the car I'd parked deep in the shadows of a towering oak was only a few feet away, I clicked the remote to unlock the doors and pop the trunk. The drugs had continued to spread through Valerie's bloodstream, rendering her weak and clumsy. Delectably vulnerable. Over those last few steps, her legs began to fail completely, and were it not for the arm I'd wrapped around her waist for support, she would have crumpled to the ground.

After a quick scan of the street to ensure no one was watching, I scooped her limp body up and took the last step toward the car with her cradled in my arms.

Her eyelids were drifting shut when I smiled down into her face. "Your coach awaits, Valerie Price."

Three entire seconds passed before she reacted to my use of her real name. Her eyes flew open. "Hey, how did..."

They drifted closed again before she finished verbalizing the question she'd been about to ask, and didn't open again, not even when I deposited her into the empty trunk and slammed the lid shut.

A timer dinged, returning me to the dining room in my family's old winter home. I finished the other four cards, displayed one at each place setting, and then headed to the kitchen to pull the frozen meal out of the microwave. Once the plastic container was on the serving tray, I carried it down the drafty stairs that led to the wine cellar, humming again.

Valerie was in the same place where I'd left her after carrying her in from the trunk. Not that she could have moved, since I'd chained her to a bed that, in turn, was bolted to the floor. The room was dank, as befitting a cellar, and musty from disuse despite the exorbitant amount of money my parents had spent to build lower-level wine storage. Every so often, rat pellets dotted the grimy stone floor. The perfect little dungeon for my guest.

The drugs had worn off because Valerie was awake now, chains clinking as she huddled as far from the door as they would allow on the sad little mattress. Her navy pantsuit, so sharp at the beginning of our date, now sported a multitude of wrinkles, and Valerie's eyes were red, smudged black beneath from smeared mascara and other remnants of the tools a woman used to snare a man.

Despite the signs of trauma, the annoying bitch summoned a glare when I entered, peering down her nose like she was royalty. "Who are you?"

I threw back my head and roared with laughter until tears sprang to my eyes and the tray shook in my hands. "Oh, sweet Valerie, you know who I am." I approached the bed, setting the meal where she could reach.

Valerie scrutinized my face. "Do you work for Kingsley?" She shook her head and muttered to herself. "Don't be stupid, Valerie, who else would do something like this? Why snatch me again, though? What does he want?"

As I savored the play of emotions across her face, I was tempted. So very tempted. I could already predict her reactions to my unwelcome news, and how very sweet the sight of her disbelief, followed by rejection, and then eventually acceptance and terror would taste.

Not yet, though.

"Eat your food before it gets cold and even less palatable. You'll have answers to all of your questions soon enough."

After which, she'd get to participate in a new round of my favorite game.

Crooning once more, I bounded up the stairs, my legs bursting with energy at the prospect of the fun that awaited.

13

On Wednesday morning, Ellie was clutching her third cup of coffee when she dragged her exhausted body to the entrance of the Charleston Police Department. Last night's interview with Lisa Harrison had left Ellie feeling antsy, so instead of grabbing a hotel near Jacksonville, she'd jumped behind the wheel of the Explorer and tackled the long drive back to her apartment.

When she'd arrived home in the wee hours of the morning, Ellie's mind buzzed like a radio talk show that refused to turn off, bombarding her with facts from Lucas Harrison's case and those of the other missing kids. Too wired to sleep, she'd harnessed the excess energy and poured over files again, hoping a piece of the puzzle might snap into place.

Not that she had anything to show for her efforts, unless dark circles and a stiff back from hunching over her dining room table counted.

Ellie squinted at the bright lights as she entered the station, ducking her head to allow her sleep-deprived eyes time to adjust.

"Rough night?"

The smooth voice penetrated Ellie's brain fog. She pulled a face at the floor. Valdez. Great. Figured the first person she'd run into would be her least favorite.

Ellie glanced up at the smirking detective, noting with a stab of petty satisfaction the missed dab of shaving cream that marred his brown skin. "Late one."

She quickened her pace toward the stairs in hopes of avoiding any further communication with her cocky coworker, but his next comment stopped her short.

"That's too bad, because I think it's about to be a rough morning."

Just what was that supposed to mean? Ellie whirled, ready to demand that Valdez supply an answer to that very question when music blasted from her blazer pocket.

She pulled the phone out and checked the screen. *Captain Browning.*

Shit. This couldn't be good.

Turning her back on Valdez's widening smirk, Ellie summoned the most cheerful voice she could muster. Maybe her cheerful greeting would garner one in return. "Good morning, Captain Browning. What can I do for you?"

"*Kline*! In my office, *now!*"

So much for that idea. Ellie winced as too many decibels entered her left ear.

This morning just kept getting better.

Valdez's gaze tracking her the entire retreat was the only thing that kept Ellie from slinking off like a shamed dog. Annoying jerk. She'd rather forfeit coffee for a month than give him the satisfaction. With her chin held high, she marched into the stairwell, not allowing her shoulders to sag until the door slammed shut behind her, blocking her from view.

Her legs behaved like someone replaced the muscle tissue with lead, stiff and heavy as they carried her up the stairs.

Once she exited on the second floor, she cast a longing glance at the bull pen that housed the Violent Crimes Unit before heading toward Browning's office just down the hall.

When she reached the open door, her stomach sank. Captain Browning waited behind his gleaming desk, and he wasn't alone. Fortis sat in one of the two chairs facing the captain. From her boss's stiff spine and jutting jaw, Ellie guessed the two of them hadn't been discussing their golf game.

Ellie stifled a groan and rapped on the wall. "You wanted to see me, Captain?"

"Get in here and shut the door already!"

After doing as she was told, Ellie hovered a few paces behind the empty chair. Unsure of what to do next.

"Well, don't just stand there, Kline, sit down!"

Ellie scrambled over to the seat and parked her butt on the unforgiving wood. Beneath the thick braid that skimmed her neck, her skin grew damp.

Browning placed his palms flat on the desk and leaned forward, his brown eyes narrowed. "What exactly did you think you were doing in Savannah yesterday?"

Crap! Browning already knew about her off-duty trip?

Ellie tilted the travel cup to her lips, to give her foggy brain a chance to process. From the subtle eye roll Fortis directed her way, though, her stall tactics weren't fooling anyone.

She swallowed, deciding to stick to the tried-and-true evasion tactic of answering a question with a question. "How do you know I was in Savannah?"

Captain Browning's nostrils flared. "That's not an answer."

So much for that tactic. Now what?

Ellie grimaced at a tiny pool of coffee trapped in the cup's lid. She was pretty sure sharing the absolute truth—that the news of Valerie's disappearance had prompted Ellie to act without thinking, in large part because she related to Valerie on a personal level as a fellow survivor—wouldn't help to cool anyone's temper.

A half-truth it was, then.

"Clay Lockwood asked for my opinion on Valerie's case, and what I think might have happened." Ellie kept her gaze glued to the lid when she spoke, worried that Fortis or Browning might read too much in her eyes. Not that she'd lied, technically speaking. Clay *had* asked for Ellie's opinion.

No need to share that she'd already made the trip to Savannah and was waiting for the FBI agent outside of Valerie's apartment complex before that happened.

She made a mental note to shoot Clay a text as soon as she escaped the current interrogation, asking him to back her up in case Browning asked.

"Oh, well, I guess if Clay Lockwood asked, then no big deal, right?"

Uh oh. Browning's sarcastic reply advised Ellie that to him, it was a very big deal indeed.

Ellie turned to Fortis for help, but the lead detective ignored her in favor of staring a hole in the wall behind Browning's back.

She clenched the cup to her chest. "Uh, wrong, I take it?"

"That's right, Kline. I don't care if God himself asked you to go to Savannah, you should still have found the time to inform me before leaving on that trip! Is that understood?"

"Yes, sir."

"Good. Now, did you go anywhere else during your little unauthorized out-of-state jaunt?"

Oh boy. He had to go and ask that question, didn't he? Ellie licked her dry lips. "Yes, sir, I did. After I left Savannah, I drove to Florida to interview a witness in one of the missing children cases that Detective Fortis just assigned me."

"You. Drove. To. Florida." Browning's words were slow and deliberate. Like he couldn't believe what he was hearing. "Let me guess, you failed to inform anyone in the department about this segment of your trip too?"

Ellie considered dropping Clay's name again but decided a second mention of the FBI agent would only piss the captain off more. "No, I didn't tell anyone in the department about the trip. It was last minute."

Captain Browning scowled. "In case you hadn't noticed, we're living in the twenty-first century, Kline. There is no such thing as too last minute to shoot off a call or a text."

Since he wasn't wrong, Ellie did the smart thing for once and nodded her agreement while zipping her mouth shut.

The captain glared at her for another ten seconds before leaping from his chair and pacing back and forth behind the desk. "What will it take to get through that thick skull of yours that we need you to keep us in the loop? This cannot keep happening, Kline. Your family brings a lot of extra attention to the department. Can you imagine how embarrassing it is for me to have you running around half-assed on your own? Or God forbid, if something bad were to happen to you while sneaking around doing off-the-record investigations on my watch?"

Browning shuddered and smoothed his hands over his hair, and for a second, Ellie's attention diverted to its inky black hue. The unnatural color was the result of Browning's attempt to dye away his gray.

Browning shook a finger at her. "I don't care how important your family is or how much positive attention you bring to our department, this type of reckless behavior needs to stop. Is that understood?"

"Yes, sir." Why wasn't Fortis jumping in to defend her? Ellie snuck another peek at her boss, but apart from the twitch by his right eye, her boss might as well have been crafted of stone.

"And for God's sake, please tell me you at least had your bodyguard with you?"

Ellie crossed her fingers. "Yes, sir." She figured her best bet at defusing Browning's temper was to agree in as few words as possible. The more she talked, the more likely she landed herself in hot water.

"That's something, I guess. But not nearly enough." Browning stopped pacing and crossed his arms, seething. "If you think your leash was short before, then brace yourself, because it's about to get a whole lot shorter."

What? No! Surely now Fortis would interject, but her boss said nothing. Not one word in her defense. He might as well have been a stuffed animal, for all the help he was.

Coward.

"Sir, with all due respect, I don't think—"

"That's your problem in a nutshell, Kline. You don't think." Browning pounded his fist into his palm to emphasize his point. "There are hundreds of kids in those Burton files. If you waste a week on each and every case, do you know how much time that would take you to finish? Too damn long, that's how much!"

Ellie flinched. Her stomach bloated painfully. Churning and bubbling, like a pressure cooker ready to burst. She slipped her hands beneath her thighs, digging her nails into the wood where no one else could see. A week was too much to spend investigating those poor kids' cases? Those families deserved as much time as it took. But as hot as the time constraint made Ellie, she had to admit that Browning had a point.

Ellie needed to pick up the pace. "I understand."

"Good. Now, both of you, get out of my office and stop wasting resources."

Captain Browning ended the conversation by presenting Ellie with his back. Fine by her. She fled out the door before he could find some new infraction to rip her a new one over. Fortis followed close behind, closing Browning's door behind him.

Ellie stomped down the hall, waiting until they were out of the captain's earshot to whirl and glare at her boss, her hands on her hips. "No, really, thanks for all your help back there. I love the way you sat there so stoically while Browning handed me my ass. I feel very supported."

"That's because I was too busy juggling my own ass after Browning lit into me before you showed up to worry about yours." Fortis dragged a hand down his weathered face and sighed. "Look, I've been there, Kline. I've gotten too close to cases before too, and I know how hard it is to back off. But you're not assigned to Kingsley's case right now. Valerie Price's disappearance is a federal case, and Browning is right, we've got a box bursting with missing kids to find. Speaking of, how's Lucas Harrison's case coming along?"

"Slowly, but I'm working on it." Ellie didn't elaborate, and for once, Fortis didn't push.

"Good. Make sure you keep me in the loop."

After a curt nod, Fortis strode the rest of the hall and entered the detective bull pen. Ellie trailed a few paces behind. She rounded the corner in time to watch him enter his glass-walled office at the rear of the open space and flip the door shut before heading over to her station near the window. Once parked in her chair, she plucked the files from the box she'd stashed beneath her desk and prepped herself to start making phone calls.

Several hours later, Ellie's chin sagged into her hands as she stared at the pile of files she'd slogged through. Compared to the folders that had yet to be touched, the height of the completed stack was unimpressive. Even after hours of talking to strangers on the phone. Each file contained so many names. Not just the name of the kids who'd disappeared, but pseudonyms for the people who bought them. Burton had been crafty in that respect, using fake names and nicknames for the buyers.

A craftiness that made Ellie despise the crooked lawyer even more.

She was staring at a photo of Lucas Harrison when Jillian walked up and leaned on the desk.

"Making any progress?"

Instead of replying, Ellie flicked the photo with her finger. "Look at this picture."

Jillian peered at the image of Lucas. "Okay. What am I looking for, exactly?"

"Does he seem pretty to you?"

Jillian lifted her tawny brows at the unexpected question. "Wow, okay. Just to be clear, he's a good ten to fifteen years on the young side for me...but sure, he's a good-looking kid." Jillian studied the photo again, pursing her red lips. "I have a bad feeling I'm going to regret this, but why do you ask?"

"Hang on." Ellie tapped the keyboard and a few moments later, a printer whirred to life. She rose and snatched the pages from the machine, returning to spread them across her desk. "This is another case, for a kid that Burton called Dumb Adonis."

Jillian leaned over to examine the photo that Ellie had just printed. A preteen, blond, blue-eyed boy with soft pink cheeks and a guileless expression stared up from the page. "Okay, I guess I can see how he got saddled with that godawful nickname. And?"

"And Dumb Adonis was purchased by the Bird and the Brute." Ellie tapped her nail on one of the pages from Burton's records, below where the contract listed the couple's names.

"Yikes. I take it that's going to make finding these people a real pain in the butt?"

"Pretty much." Ellie's fingers twitched as she glared at the typed names on the contract, wishing she could reach through the page and wrap her hands around Burton's neck. "But that's not the worst part."

She yanked a stack of files toward her and opened the top one, scanning the lines until she found what she was seeking. She jabbed the section with her pen. "Look here."

Jillian's lips moved as she read. Ellie recognized the instant her roommate reached the punch line because her hand flew to cover her mouth. "The Bird and the Brute bought this child too?" When Ellie gave a curt nod, Jillian winced. "And the rest of the kids in that stack too?"

Pain flashed through Ellie's jaw. She inhaled a deep breath through her nose and unclenched her teeth. "Yeah, them too. Twelve kids total."

"And I'm guessing the odds that this couple bought twelve kids on the illegal adoption market out of the goodness of their hearts are slim to none?"

"Probably closer to none than slim. Which means we really need to figure out the Bird and the Brute's real names."

"Okay, but how do we do that?"

Ellie stroked a finger along the edge of the blond boy's photo before reaching for her keyboard, her spine rigid. "We hunt."

Clicking followed. Her fingers flew along the keys as she typed her search parameters into VICAP, the FBI created database that collected information and analyzed crimes nationwide. "And hope these predators had other brushes with the law involving children. Which is pretty likely, given the statistics."

Jillian grabbed a stack of folders. "Come downstairs where it's quieter, and I'll help you."

Ellie practically jumped to her feet, not willing to miss out on the opportunity to have both the privacy of the basement as well as her good friend's eagle eye.

Downstairs, Ellie grabbed an empty chair and dragged it over to sit beside Jillian before typing in her credentials and pulling up the database. Together, they glued their eyes to her monitor and began scanning the data that appeared.

Over the next hour, they sifted through a good fifty cases without coming across so much as a breadcrumb. Ellie made a notation in her spreadsheet, recording yet another case that failed to yield results. Her way of ensuring that she didn't get stuck reviewing the same crimes more than once.

She rubbed her neck, growing more and more convinced that she was deluding herself as the seconds ticked by. How could they possibly hope to track down people based on a couple of ridiculous, fictitious first names? The only outcome this line of investigation would likely yield was a massive waste of energy and time. At this rate, Ellie would end up solving zero cases by the end of the month. She'd be better off focusing her attention in a new direction.

Ellie massaged her cramped muscles again and sighed. One more. She'd open one more and then take a caffeine break.

She clicked on the next case, her mouth already watering from the sugary latte that she was five minutes away from downing. Halfway through skimming the info that popped up on the screen, Ellie froze. She rubbed her eyes while her heart gave an excited little gallop.

"Jillian? Come look at this, tell me what you see."

Her roommate set down the hard file she'd been examining and peered at the monitor. "Robyn and Adam Barlow," she read before studying the images of the Caucasian man and woman. A couple beats passed before Jillian shot up in her chair. "Well, he certainly could be the brute from that bulging forehead, and how tall does it say he is, six-five? Wait, isn't that eighty-eight tattoo on his neck a Hitler reference?"

"Yeah, it's a neo-Nazi thing. The eights correspond numerically to h's in the alphabet for 'Heil Hitler.' The 6MWE one is another Hitler reference. It stands for six million wasn't enough."

Jillian's mouth fell open. "As in six million Jews?" she whispered.

"Yes."

Jillian jerked away from the screen, like she was afraid of contamination. "That's disgusting." She wrinkled her nose. "He could definitely be the brute, but I'm not really getting bird vibes from the woman, are you?"

Ellie toyed with a curl that had sprung free from her French braid and waited, knowing it wouldn't take her friend long to make the connection.

She was right. Within seconds, Jillian was slapping her forehead. "Oh my god, *Robyn*. Like the bird. Wait, what were they arrested for?"

"Mass creation and distribution of pedophilic material, right here in Charleston. Robyn got forty years at Leath Correctional while Adam is serving out a sixty-seven-year sentence at FCL, Estill." Ellie rattled off the name of the local federal correctional institute that housed men who got slapped with longer sentences.

"Ew." Jillian shuddered. "I'm glad they caught the creeps, but why the different length sentences for the same crimes?"

"Because Robyn's well-paid lawyer managed to convince people that she never took any of the pictures, never touched the kids, was never even in the same room when those activities were taking place, and the prosecutor couldn't produce a single witness to say otherwise. Her lawyer also managed to get his client a separate trial and claimed that Adam

Barlow pressured his smaller, mentally ill wife into helping out, but even so, said that Robyn only agreed to assist with the business-side of things."

Jillian shuddered again. "Excuse me while I go take a five-hour shower."

Ellie could relate. Her own skin crawled just from staring at the couple's mug shots. No telling how grimy she'd feel if she executed the plan that had already started to form in her head.

Because as loathsome as Robyn and Adam Barlow were, as of now, the pair of them were the only lead Ellie had. In order to follow up on her hunch, she'd need to interrogate them.

In person.

After one last look at the sinister tattoos inked across Adam Barlow's neck and the gleam in his wife's eyes, Ellie hunted down the phone numbers for the prisons.

She had meetings to arrange.

L eath Correctional Institution, 2809 Airport Road.

The blue sign on the corner of the greenbelt cued Ellie to turn left down a long, curved drive. From the street view, the cluster of sun-bleached buildings embedded in a blanket of grass could have been mistaken for a youth sports complex if not for the sign warning that visitors must consent to searches, or the barbed wire that coiled like snakes along the fence tops.

After parking next to a red Ford Taurus, Ellie removed her car key from the ring and slipped her smartwatch into her purse before storing it, her phone, and gun beneath the seat. She locked up and walked across the cracked asphalt lot to the self-proclaimed Visitor Center.

As she approached, the South Carolina and United States flags fluttered in the breeze, and the steady electrical hum that emitted from the fence blocking off the prison grew louder. An audible warning for Ellie not to touch, since frying herself into human barbecue wasn't on today's agenda. To the right, one sign gave notice that tobacco products were prohibited beyond that point. Another forbade visitors to carry cell phones.

Ellie pushed the call button. A bell sounded, and then a disembodied female voice replied. "Can I help you?"

Ellie confirmed her identity and relayed the number assigned to Robyn Harlow by the South Carolina Department of Corrections. The gate buzzed open, allowing her to head down the short path to the door, where she entered a small, empty waiting area that smelled of chlorine and fake lemon.

After signing in at the front desk, an unsmiling middle-aged woman with severe brown bangs gave Ellie a once-over. "No guns or weapons, cell phones, tobacco or other drug products, no money of any kind. No keys. Do you have one you need me to store?"

"Yes, please."

Ellie slid the key to the woman, who slipped it into a cubby along with a slip of paper before turning back and pushing a computer-generated visitor pass across the counter. "Take a seat."

Ellie perched on the edge of one of the uncomfortable plastic chairs, wondering how long she'd have to wait to meet Robyn. Her throat burned with acid as she recalled what she'd uncovered during her research with Jillian yesterday.

Robyn and Adam Harlow bought kids and took them home, but instead of tucking them in at night and helping them with their homework, the couple forced them into child pornography. They'd provide their illegal adoptees with scripts, film them, and then sell the videos and photographs online via the dark web.

The acid burned its way up to Ellie's mouth, coating her tongue with a foul taste. Those poor kids. How many of them had sparked with hope at the prospect of going home with a new family, only for that excitement to turn to ash when reality sank in? How much trauma had the Harlows inflicted over the years with their vile, depraved acts?

Ellie swallowed hard, wishing she had a soda to wash away the lingering sourness. She found it odd that once the Harlows were caught, Adam never said a single word in his own defense, whereas Robyn couldn't blab enough in her eagerness to toss all the blame for the crimes at Adam's feet.

The door buzzed, and a correctional officer entered the waiting area. The heavy-set woman with a crooked nose and a surprisingly sunny smile scanned Ellie's pass. "You've read all the rules and understand that guns, weapons of any kind, tobacco, drugs, cell phones or other devices that connect to the internet, or metal of any kind is strictly prohibited by the state of South Carolina and violation of those rules will result in you being banned from this facility and may result in criminal charges?"

"I do."

The woman jerked her head toward the door. "This way."

Ellie walked through the metal detector without incident. On the other side, she lifted her arms as instructed while the guard patted her down. The woman scanned the photos in Ellie's pocket, handing them back with a grunt. "You're clear. Follow me."

Ellie trailed the woman down a dingy hallway to a room that resembled a high-school cafeteria, complete with the same uncomfortable plastic chairs and crappy fluorescent lighting. The guard pointed to the closest one. "Have a seat, they'll bring her in shortly."

Ellie did as requested, jiggling her leg while she performed a quick scan of her surroundings. On the other side of the room, a harried-looking Latina in her fifties sat across from a sullen, twenty-something woman wearing teal scrubs with SCCD emblazoned across the back in white letters. The prisoner slouched in her chair, scowling at the scarred table that separated them. The only other pair was a gray-haired, apple-cheeked woman in the Leath colors, nodding and laughing at whatever the blond man across from her was saying.

The door buzzed. Ellie sat up as a different guard led a petite woman into the room. Despite the prison uniform, thinning hair, and smudged coral lipstick that made her pale skin appear sallow, Robyn Harlow sauntered up to Ellie like she knew she was something special. She draped herself into the chair opposite Ellie before flashing a coquettish smile. "Detective Kline, I've spent all day so far wondering about your request to visit me, so don't keep me in suspense. What could the police possibly want with me now?"

Given her knowledge of Robyn's crimes, the woman's flirty mannerisms sent Ellie's blood pressure skyrocketing. Best to dive right in and get this interview over with as quickly as possible. "Ms. Harlow. I was recently assigned some missing children cases that we discovered while arresting Noah Burton, and I have a few questions."

Robyn's upper lip curled before she released a low, grating laugh. "And they call me slime. That man was a real piece of work, let me tell you."

You should know.

"I'm glad you feel that way, because I've been trying to locate some of the missing children from his files, and I was hoping you could help me."

The woman fluffed her hair. "Yeah? What's in it for me?" Her blue eyes narrowed, like she was already calculating the potential payoffs.

To mask her disgust, Ellie dropped her gaze to her folded hands, shrugging with forced carelessness. "I can't promise anything yet, but I'm sure we can work something out. What do you want?"

With her ring finger, Robyn traced lazy circles on the plastic table. She paused, peering up at Ellie from beneath her lashes. "I could do with a few years off my sentence."

Ellie's hackles rose, but she managed to keep her tone pleasant. *Play nice.* "As I'm sure you know, sentencing isn't up to me."

Robyn's finger stopped circling but continued to twitch, like someone else was controlling the movements. "Too bad, guess we don't have anything to discuss after all."

She shoved her chair back from the table, then started to rise while peering over her shoulder, as if ready to signal the guard to leave.

Witch.

Ellie balled her hands into fists and blurted, "I'm here about Lucas Harrison."

The other woman stilled before sinking back into the chair. When she turned her head to face Ellie, the motion wasn't continuous and smooth, but jerky. The coral lips no longer smiled. "There were a whole lot of kids back then, and we didn't use names much."

Ellie pulled the photo print out from her pocket and slid it onto the table. The mere sight of the image twisted her gut all over again. The picture was a still from one of the Harlows' movies, featuring Lucas and a younger boy gazing directly into the camera. Although both of them were clothed, the framing of the photo made Ellie's skin crawl. Too much focus on their young bodies and the intimate way they posed, so close together, rather than centering on their faces.

Robyn's gaze flickered to the photo and bounced right back off. She hugged her arms across her chest and leaned all the way back in her chair, as if seeking to physically distance herself from the two boys. "People always get mad at the folks who take the pictures, but the real criminals are the pedophiles. They're the problem. If there wasn't any demand for kids, then the supply would die out too, right? But there's always demand, because our country is full of slimebags who get off on the idea of diddling kids. And someone's gonna make money filling that need. If it's not us, it's someone else. Lots of someones."

Robyn drummed her fingers on her arm, nodding along as she rationalized her role. "We're just the business part, the middleman, trying to make ends meet like everyone else, but they throw the book at us, while the scum who do the real crimes hardly ever get caught. Does that seem fair to you?"

Ellie bit the inside of her cheek until she tasted copper and made an *uh-uh* noise in her throat. She didn't trust that any words she could form at the present moment would be civil.

Lucky for her, having a captive audience for her self-serving rant was all the encouragement Robyn needed. "Right? I never touched those kids! I wasn't even in the room when the videos were filmed. But look at me!" She tugged at the shapeless prison top. "Here I am, serving forty years for running a business while the men we sold the movies to get two years, three tops. Where's the justice in that?"

The other woman's pale cheeks were flushed now, and her chest lifted and lowered from the increased force of her breaths. The sight sent shock coursing through Ellie's veins. Holy shit. Defying all laws of logic or common decency, Robyn Harlow had somehow managed to convince herself that she was the injured party here. This woman actually believed her own propaganda.

An arsenal of scathing rebuttals raced to Ellie's lips, but she wasn't here to school Robyn on the fallacies of her thinking. "Okay, but I'm not here to talk about pedophiles in the justice system, I'm here to see what you know about Lucas Harrison."

Robyn huffed loudly before pretending to study her fingernails. "And I'm still waiting to hear what I get for talking. Maybe that will trigger my memory, cuz right now I'm drawing a blank."

As she spoke, her left shoulder spasmed up toward her ear, three times in rapid succession. The unnerving part was the way Robyn carried on like she didn't even notice. She started picking at her left thumb, tearing at the skin until she drew blood.

Ellie frowned. A neurological condition that resulted in a tic disorder could explain the involuntary movements, but that wouldn't explain the skin picking, or the woman's flushed cheeks. Especially since this room held a damp chill.

Tearing her attention away from Robyn's mutilated thumb, Ellie gave her brain a mental shake. Whatever weirdness was happening with Robyn, the purpose for her visit remained the same. "Lucas was a special kid."

"That's what they say about all kids." Robyn's shoulders jerked up and down. "Like I told you before, we had a lot of them, so it was hard to keep track. 'Sides, Adam's the one who catered to the truly special ones. There was a real market for that type, you know. Some buyers will pay extra for the kind of kid who's never gonna grow out of that kid phase."

"Why is that?" Ellie braced herself for an unpleasant answer.

"Extra security, mostly. They figure even if a kid like that tattles about what's going on, who's gonna take them seriously?"

"A kid like that?"

Robyn circled her hands near her head. "You know what I mean. Retards. Clients paid extra for retards. Maybe we had this Lucas kid, maybe we didn't. I need a little something to shake my memory."

When Ellie imagined shaking this woman, her memory was the last thing that popped to mind. Everything about Robyn sickened her. The idea of giving this child abuser even a whiff of satisfaction made Ellie feel slimy. But she needed Robyn to find Lucas, so she'd play the game. If dangling a carrot made the woman talk, then that was all that mattered.

"I can talk to the district attorney's office about knocking a couple of years off, but they have final approval."

Triumph flashed in Robyn's blue eyes. "Put that in writing and we have a deal."

Borrowing a pad and stubby pencil from a guard, Ellie spelled out what she could and couldn't do. Once the woman read her words over, she nodded. "Okay. So, what can I say? Lucas was a cute kid, a real pretty boy type. Problem was, he didn't like to play. Honestly, he didn't like to do much of anything except read his stupid camping magazines and talk about camping, and man, could that kid talk. I swear, once he got started on his favorite topic, you couldn't shut him up to save your life. He never let up. All day long it was, 'this is how you build a survival shelter in the wild,' or 'do you know you can purify water without a special tool?'" She made a disgusted sound in the back of her throat. "I even tried to take him camping once, figured maybe once we were out there he'd open up a little, talk about something else, but nope, not Lucas."

Ellie's heart ached for the boy. "It sounds like things didn't work out with Lucas the way you'd hoped."

Robyn's top lip curled. "You can say that again. Kid with an angel face like that, who could be rewarded with a cheap five-dollar camping magazine, or a new flashlight. Or the promise that you'd throw up a tent in a pile of dirt and let him sleep there overnight? He should've been worth his weight in gold. Instead, he turned out to be a real dud."

A dud. Ellie's breath hissed between her clenched teeth, but Robyn was too enraptured by her own story to notice.

"Even the perverts want to see real emotion. They want the kids to laugh, cry, scream. Maybe be curious, depending on their specific kink. But Lucas, he just stared blankly at the camera, like no one was home beneath that pretty face. No emotion, no nothing, and trust me, we tried. Encouragement, rewards, punishment. None of it worked. And then the little brat had the nerve to up and bite me." She broke off, scowling.

"He bit you?" Ellie prompted, trying to inject her expression with faux outrage.

"Yeah! Little shit. All I was trying to do was help him out, give him a little nudge in the right direction. The first time he shows any reaction on camera, and it's to sink his teeth into my arm." She extended her left arm toward Ellie, pointing at a spot halfway between her wrist and elbow. "See?"

A pale scar in the shape of a semi-circle peeked up at Ellie. "Ouch," is what she said out loud. In her head, though, Ellie uttered a silent cheer. *Good for you, Lucas.*

"That's when we realized Lucas just wasn't going to work out. What were we supposed to do with a biter? So, we took him back to Burton." Robyn said that last bit like returning a kid to a vendor was an everyday occurrence.

Ellie hadn't thought it possible to hate this woman any more than she already did, but she'd been wrong. "And how did that go over?"

"Bout as well as you'd expect. Burton was pissed. Yelled that he wasn't a damn discount store with some money-back return policy. Adam even got all up in his face, but Burton wouldn't budge, not on the refund, anyway. He did finally agree to take the kid back, but on the condition that we paid his room and board until Burton found a replacement family." Robyn sneered. "Except, get this, that crook kept our money and still made *us* find the replacement family! Can you believe the nerve of that guy?"

Robyn shook her head. Her anger seemed to intensify the twitching, but for once, Ellie didn't care. She scooted forward, planting her palms on the table while her own muscles trembled with eagerness. "Who? What were the names of the replacement couple you found?"

In her excitement, the question came out sharper than intended. The guard by the door frowned over at them before looking away. Robyn reared back. Then—*twitch, twitch* —cocked her head and studied Ellie from beneath her lashes.

That annoying, flirty smile returned. "My my, Detective Kline, sounds like you're very impassioned about finding this kid. Surely that's worth a few more years off my sentence?"

The batted eyelashes were the last straw. To this hateful woman, Lucas's life was nothing but a bargaining chip. To Robyn Harlow, children existed to serve her needs. And she expected Ellie to reward her for doing the bare minimum to help locate a child? A teen boy who she'd once bought to perform for pedophiles in exchange for money that would line Robyn's pockets?

Fury pulsed through Ellie, coiling muscles so tight that she felt spring-loaded, like the tiniest provocation might trigger her to snap. A growl built in her throat. She yanked the signed plea agreement off the table and positioned her hands in the middle of the page.

If that hateful woman batted one more eyelash or flashed another cutesy smile, Ellie swore she would rip the document to shreds and blow the pieces in her face. "I'm done playing, Mrs. Harlow. Tell me what you know or you can kiss our deal goodbye."

Ellie flexed her fingers. A tiny tear appeared on the white page. The knowledge that Lucas was depending on her was the only thing that held Ellie in check from turning the agreement into confetti.

Robyn's eyes rounded. "Whoa, hold up! No need to freak out, geez."

"Then quit messing around and tell me what you know."

"Fine!" Robyn slouched into the chair, chin tucked to her chest like a sulky child. "I don't remember their name, but pretty sure it was something Irish or Scottish. They were old, though, I do remember that. Real old. And they lived out in Summerville."

The weight in Ellie's chest lifted a little at the last bit. Not having a name would make tracking the couple down tough, but a location meant the search wasn't impossible. "Anything else?"

Robyn appeared transfixed by a nick on the table, stroking her thumb back and forth over the blemish.

What the hell? "Robyn?"

The woman jumped. "What?"

"I said, do you remember anything else? About the couple who took Lucas?"

Twitch. Twitch. "Oh, right. No, that's all I've got."

Probably for the best. In her current state, Ellie doubted the woman could be of further use even if she wanted to.

Time to get the hell out of here.

Ellie shoved the plastic chair back with a squeal and sprang to her feet, slipping the photo of Lucas and the other boy into her pocket. Now that the interview was over, she couldn't wait to escape Robyn Harlow. Merely breathing the same air as the remorseless child abuser made Ellie's lungs feel unclean, worse than if she'd been sucking down factory exhaust. "Thank you for your cooperation."

She strode past the woman without another glance, motioning to the guard that the session was over.

"Wait, that's it? When am I gonna hear from the D.A.?"

Robyn's screech followed Ellie to the door. Her shoulders tensed, but she didn't bother to respond, or turn around. She followed a guard back to the visitor's office, the blood rushing in her ears all but drowning out the click of their shoes along the hard floor. After reclaiming her key from the front desk and relinquishing the visitor's pass, Ellie burst through the doors, gulping down huge lungfuls of fresh air like she'd been oxygen deprived.

A shower, she promised herself on the short walk to her car. A long, hot one to wash away the last half-hour's grime, followed by a generous pour of wine.

When Ellie slumped into the driver's seat, her entire body began to shake. Those poor kids. Never in a thousand lifetimes would she comprehend how adults could commit such heartless crimes against children.

Ellie rested her forehead on the steering wheel and focused on what she could control...her breathing. Once the tremors died down, she chugged sweet tea from her travel cup. After the last swallow, she dug her phone out of her purse and punched in a number.

"You'd better be calling to update me on progress and not to tell me you hopped a flight to Timbuktu on some wild goose chase."

Fortis's grumpy bark prompted Ellie's lips to curve into a weak smile. Cranky or not, she drew an odd kind of comfort from his predictability. "I'm just getting ready to leave Leath now. I'm calling because I promised Robyn Harlow that we'd talk to the D.A. about knocking a couple of years off her sentence."

"You did *what*?"

Wincing at her boss's roar, Ellie yanked the phone away from her ear and hit the speaker button. Okay. Maybe not so comforting after all. Fortis could really use a few lessons in volume control. "I know, but trust me, it was the only way to get her to talk. Also, is there someone you can call to request a drug test? She was all jittery and twitchy, like she was on something."

Fortis swore. "Christ. Yeah, I'll put a call in, see what I can do."

"Thanks. Also, I think we should have someone check the trial transcript and depositions, to go over Robyn's exact statements under oath. I'm pretty sure I remember reading that the reason she got forty years instead of sixty like Adam was because she claimed she was never in the room when the kids were being abused."

A pause. "Are you saying you have reason to believe she lied?"

Through Ellie's window, the barbed wire glinted in the winter sun. "I know she did. Because just a few minutes ago, she admitted to an officer of the law that she wasn't only in the room with Lucas Harrison, but that she also touched him."

15

C lay relaxed his shoulders into the padded polyester of the booth, sipping coffee from a chipped green mug and watching the petite detective across the table inhale a Frisbee-sized burger like a linebacker trying to bulk up. The diner they'd stopped at for dinner was half-full but not too noisy yet, despite the steady parade of fifties hits playing in the background. At the moment, Elvis whined about hound dogs, while servers decked in pink ruffled dresses or bow ties scurried around to black vinyl booths, balancing trays full of burgers and cherry-topped shakes on their upturned hands.

When Charlotte Cross finally came up for air, she patted her mouth with the paper napkin in her lap and frowned at his plate. "Did you just remember you have a beef allergy or something?"

Clay nudged the untouched burger in her direction. "Just not very hungry right now. Feel free to dig in."

Charlotte pushed the plate back before rolling her eyes. "Let me guess, you're not hungry because all you can think about is being out on the street, looking for Valerie Price, aka Pryor."

At her astute assessment, surprise flickered in Clay's chest. He set the mug on the table and offered her a reluctant smile. "Am I that easy to read?"

Charlotte Cross didn't smile back. Her blue eyes skimmed over him in a clinical way, as if she were a doctor examining a patient. "I don't know you well enough to answer that question in a general sense, but as it pertains to this specific instance? Yes. If you don't want people to know you're anxious to be anywhere but where you are, I suggest you quit looking out the window or checking your phone for updates every thirty seconds."

Ouch. Apart from Ellie, Charlotte Cross might be the most direct woman he'd ever met. Clay jerked his body in an exaggerated wince. "That bad, huh?"

"I can't answer that. Bad is a subjective assessment that varies based on personal criteria. What I can say is that your actions and body language suggest that you're eager to leave, and I drew the logical conclusion that the reason was related to our case."

At the mention of body language, Clay sat up straighter.

She dragged a French fry through a puddle of catsup and wolfed it down before continuing. "But you also look tired. The deep kind of tired that makes me wonder when you last had a day off, and how long before you burn out or crash. So I suggest for both of our sakes and for the benefit of the case we're working that you quit acting like you're a second away from making a run for it, stay put, eat your damn burger, and tell me everything you know about Valerie and this case. The last thing I need tonight is to coddle an FBI agent who starts feeling faint from lack of caloric intake."

She nodded, like that was that, and returned to annihilating the last of her fries, while Clay fought to keep his jaw from gaping open. In the short time he'd known Charlotte Cross, she'd yet to fail to impress him. She'd nailed him, right down to the part where Clay had been seconds away from leaping to his feet and driving off to go search for Valerie on his own.

And she also hit the mark about his lack of time off and needing to eat. This was their first real meal all day, and all the coffee on an empty stomach wasn't helping his jitters. But sitting still knowing that Valerie was out there, in desperate need of their help, was near impossible. Especially given the sinister thought that slithered through his head.

First Gabe, now Valerie.

Kingsley was obviously hunting down the people who'd escaped or betrayed him. It was only a matter of time until Ellie was next.

"Seriously, eat. Your brain will thank you." Charlotte pushed his plate even closer, then leaned back and brushed her knuckles over her blazer. "Besides, if you pass out, don't think for one second that I'm going to break your fall. I like this jacket too much to risk ruining it over some stubborn FBI agent with a savior complex."

Her blunt summation made Clay blink before his chest began to rumble with laughter. "And here I thought you said you didn't know me that well yet."

Under her watchful eye, he lifted the burger and took a bite. A little lukewarm at this point, but still pretty darn good. Before he knew it, he'd scarfed down half, and the twitchy sensation eased. He washed the burger down with ice water and swiped his napkin over his mouth. "There. Now your jacket is safe from ruin, Charlotte Cross."

She nodded as she slurped chocolate shake through a straw. "Call me Charli, and good. Now, fill me in about Valerie."

Clay leaned back. "You already heard most of the story back in her apartment. The part you didn't hear was that when the dirty cop panicked and turned her over to the man who liked to hunt people, Ellie almost lost her own life trying to save her."

With a napkin, Charli dabbed the faint milkshake mustache from her top lip. "What about this Kingsley guy, what can you tell me about him?"

"The most important thing to know about Dr. Lawrence Kingsley is that he's pure evil."

"Pure evil? Wow, that's quite an introduction." She fiddled with her straw. "Doctor? As in medical?"

Clay nodded. "Yeah. Psychiatrist." Goose bumps fluttered across his neck. "A real arrogant, twisted son-of-a-bitch. He had one of his associates work at the Charleston PD for a while as their on-staff psychiatrist just so he could mess with Ellie's head."

Charli's eyes widened. "That is…wow. And this is the guy you think has Valerie?" At Clay's grim nod, Charli folded her hands on the table. "Okay, tell me everything you know about this guy."

Clay did. He started with Kingsley's kidnapping of Ellie when she was fifteen. Of how he'd forced her to play the sick game that he'd christened with the name, *Die, Bitch! Die*, where he tortured one prisoner until the other one shouted the magic words that would end the suffering.

He told Charli that Kingsley had been the reason his and Ellie's paths crossed in the first place, when they'd investigated a long-haul trucker for serial murders and the search led them to Kingsley's dark web auction enterprise.

Her blue eyes rounded at times, and her lips parted in surprise, but the Savannah detective never interrupted once. Not when he explained how Kingsley had kidnapped Ellie's roommate and best friend. Almost blown her up with a car bomb meant for Ellie. How Ellie had maimed him while rescuing Jillian, forcing the murderer into hibernation…only to have him emerge with a brand-new face.

Charli's mouth tightened in sympathy as he talked about Gabe again. How they'd been so close to finding him in time, but Kingsley had managed to stay two steps ahead.

He even found himself telling Charli how Kingsley, with the help of his old protégé Katarina, had caused Ellie to suspect her old boyfriend, Nick, of being involved in a plot to kidnap Valerie. Solely for Kingsley's amusement.

When Clay finished, Charli was frowning into the dregs of her silver shake cup, stabbing the bottom with her straw. "You know that's highly unusual, right? Serial killers rarely hire out their dirty work because they get off on having complete control. Same with that game he plays. Serial killers almost never delegate the choice over who dies to someone else. That's part of the thrill for them, the notion that they get to decide which life they snuff out."

Clay's eyebrows shot up. "You seem extremely well informed on serial killers, any particular reason for that?"

He noted that Charli's hands went still. "Just an interest of mine since I was in high school. Other kids read romances, or Stephen King, or YA books...I read about serial killers, and never really stopped." She shrugged.

"You know, that specialized interest could nab you a spot in the FBI's Behavioral Sciences department. They're always looking for qualified people with sharp minds."

Charli's head shake was emphatic. Her expression grew shuttered. "Not interested. I'd much rather be here at home, out in the field where I can do some good, rather than stuck behind a desk writing up endless papers."

There was more to that story, Clay would bet money on it, but despite the curiosity that urged him to press for details, he let the topic go. For now. Like she'd said before, they barely knew each other. Maybe once they'd worked together longer, the enigmatic detective would feel more comfortable sharing stories from her past.

He lifted the mug to his lips right as Charli asked a question. "So, is there something personal between you and Valerie?"

Clay choked on the coffee, sputtering as the mug clattered to the table and he fumbled for his napkin. Once he finished coughing, he stared at Charli. "No, there's nothing personal between Valerie and me, not in the sense you're meaning. I've spoken and met with her multiple times, though, and know her case inside and out. The only personal thing between us is the responsibility I feel toward a woman who already survived one traumatic kidnapping and was promised that she'd be safe afterward, once we put her into protective custody. She *should* have been safe."

Charli yanked a fresh napkin from the metal dispenser at the far edge of the table and slid it over to him. That was when Clay noticed that his old one lay shredded into little pieces beside his plate. He grimaced and grabbed the white square. "Thanks."

"No problem. And I'm sorry if the question was out of line. In my experience, it's just very rare to find a cop who cares that much about the actual people in their cases. I know a big portion of our country still buys into the mythology around the police, how they're all these altruistic heroes who care so much about the people they serve and wouldn't hesitate to sacrifice themselves for the greater good, but that's all it is. A myth."

Her blue gaze remained steady, but Clay got the impression that she was no longer seeing him or the diner and had retreated to some old memory. He polished off a few fries, reluctant to intrude.

He was eating his last fry when she gave a little shake and blinked.

"I won't ask where you went just now, but I will say that

it's unusual for a cop to speak so plainly about other cops like that," Clay said.

Charli shrugged. "Maybe other cops are too stuck believing in their own mythology to grasp reality."

"But not you?"

She snorted, but to Clay's ears the sharp noise sounded more bitter than amused. "No. Not me."

Clay braced his forearms on the table and leaned in. His curiosity piqued, he considered how to prod her to elaborate in a tactful way.

"So, what about the redheaded detective? Anything going on with you there?"

"Uh…"

Where had that come from?

Caught off guard, Clay fumbled to come up with a quick, believable denial.

He'd hate to be on the receiving end of a real interrogation by this woman.

Charli pounced. "*Uh?* I don't know, that sounds pretty serious."

Clay's first instinct was to fake a laugh and tell the irritatingly astute detective that she was way off base, but one glance into her shrewd eyes convinced him that he might as well save his breath.

Dammit. Clay tugged at his shirt collar and decided, *what the hell?* "To be honest, I have no idea what's going on with us, but I sure wish I did. There's something there, but I couldn't tell you exactly what. I think Ellie needs to catch Kingsley and put him away before she can move on."

Charli nodded. "Makes sense. And what about you? What's your story? The damage in your past that made you want to become an agent and save the world?"

Yeah, no. Talking about his feelings for Ellie was one thing. Digging into his past and how he'd failed Caraleigh and his entire family wasn't a topic Clay was prepared to dredge up now. Especially not when Valerie was out there. Probably in trouble and counting on them to find her.

"We're done refueling, so I think it's time we got back to work." Clay scooted over to the edge of the booth and pushed to his feet.

Charli studied him for an uncomfortable moment before pulling her wallet from her purse. "All right, then, back to work we go."

16

"Here's your order, have a nice day." The teenage boy with angry red pimples sprinkled across his forehead stifled a yawn as he opened the drive-through window and handed Milos the white paper bag and a Styrofoam cup.

"Thanks." Milos plunked the bag onto his lap and peered inside to check the contents. Satisfied that his order was correct, he snuck one last glimpse at the teen to ensure that his visit hadn't drawn the employee's curiosity. The bleary-eyed boy had already turned away from the window, dismissing Milos as just another customer in a long line of them. Another faceless person grabbing a quick meal near the South Carolina state border.

Exactly the way Milos had planned. He'd taken great care to ensure nothing about him stood out. Not the plain gray baseball cap on his head, or the nondescript navy-blue sweatshirt. Definitely not the boring beige Nissan Altima.

Milos rolled the window up, once again sealing out the chilly air. The scent of grease and coffee permeated the car's interior. He pulled away from the restaurant, exiting the drive-through at a leisurely speed. To the employees at the fast-food grease trap and anyone else who cared to look, Milos was one of the thousands of early risers out there. Driving along the highway and stopping for a quick breakfast sandwich, behind the wheel of one of the most popular cars in the country. Not one detail about him suggested he was worth a second glance.

He flipped through the radio stations until a familiar tune spilled from the speakers. "Dreams," by Fleetwood Mac. Whistling along to Stevie Nick's raspy croon, Milos steered the Altima back toward the highway, his fingers drumming the steering wheel in time to the beat. Headlights from other early commuters beamed out, waiting for the sun to rise. Milos loved this time of morning the best. Still dark enough to provide a layer of anonymity but holding all the promise of a brand-new day.

He flipped on his signal before changing lanes. Checking the speedometer, he saw that he was still two miles under the speed limit. Perfect. And he intended to keep it that way.

This time, everything was going to work out just right. For once in his life.

With his eyes glued to the road, Milos rummaged in the bag and found the breakfast sandwich. He loved the way the thin paper rustled when he unwrapped it. A sound he'd never heard once as a child because his mother believed fast-food was bad.

He lifted the sausage and egg biscuit to his nose and inhaled the spicy-sweet scent. No, worse than bad. Fake. Toxic. Poison. Full of unpronounceable chemicals created in a lab. And if God didn't make the ingredients, then why would she allow her son to put them into his God-given body?

Milos's mother had been a severe woman, with a stern, thin mouth that spit scripture far more than it ever smiled. No makeup or hair dye covered her premature gray streaks, and she'd covered her body in drab colors. Always long dresses or house coats that reached well below her knees, and Milos couldn't remember ever seeing her bare shoulders.

After each lecture, she'd pinch his cheek or his arm. Twist and pull until the sharp pain brought tears to his eyes. Just before she let him go, she'd lean into his face until their noses almost touched and he all but choked on the stench of the garlic she added to her green smoothies, hissing that if she ever caught him listening to devil music in a car that reeked of fast-food, she'd beat him until her hands turned bloody.

Milos sank his teeth into the sandwich and savored the flavors as he chewed. Fried egg and sausage and flaky biscuit. All full of delicious, wicked chemicals. Washed down with a swig of the devil's caffeine and Stevie's sultry voice.

He hadn't understood at the time, but his mother had given him a gift. She'd taught Milos one of the most important lessons of his entire life. She'd instructed him on the value of pain. At first, he'd fought the knowledge. As a young child, Milos had been too stupid to realize that the love he yearned for was inconsequential compared to the power of pain.

Hugs and kisses were fleeting, whereas the taste of salt on a split lip lingered on. Like the purple and black tenderness of a bruise, or the sharp ache of a fractured rib. But Milos's mother was a persistent teacher, and under her cruel, insistent hands, he learned. Through all the bruises, scrapes, and scars. Beneath the terrible statue of her bleeding god, where she forced him to pray, until the skin on his knees rubbed raw.

Yes, over time, Milos learned. Not to believe in his mother's god, but to realize that the only reliable higher being in his life was pain. Pain was constant, unavoidable. Real. His mother wanted to teach Milos about her god, but he saw the light, and it wasn't held within the fantasy of some man who died centuries ago, as much as Milos admired the creative manner in which the Christian deity had been killed.

No, Milos's faith centered on a different entity. One that held more value than any teacher or lover the world could possibly offer.

Milos worshipped at the altar of pain, because pain was truth. Pain was stronger than every other emotion or feeling combined, and stripped people down to their most basic, pure beings.

The music ended, and the DJ filled the silence with a quick spiel, announcing the next song. The Altima cruised down the highway as sunlight began to spill across the sky and chase the darkness away. Milos chewed another bite of sandwich, smiling as he reminisced. Over time, he'd accepted that his calling was to bring the truth to others. But they didn't always listen or understand. Not at first, anyway. And sometimes, never. Especially not adults.

Although, by the end, everyone came at least a little closer to enlightenment, because pain refused to be denied.

Milos savored every remaining bite of his sandwich, licking his fingers one by one once he finished, delighting in the thought of his mother's rage if she could see him now. Once Milos had outgrown her in height and strength, he'd fought back. He'd bestowed upon her the same pain that she'd gifted to him.

The old bat had fought the gift hard, and Milos wasn't sure she'd ever fully accepted. In doing so, she'd taught him yet another valuable lesson...adults made less than optimal students in the art of pain and punishment.

Milos turned down the volume on the radio, sipped his coffee, and listened. He didn't have to wait long. By his third sip, a girl's voice drifted to his ears. Soft and muffled, only just audible. Pleading for someone to let her out. To Milos, the sound was sweeter than any singer's voice by far.

He whistled again as the highway spilled out before him.

While adults made for disappointing subjects, children, well, they were the best.

Children were much more open to the truth of pain, and nothing in the world was more beautiful than enlightening them.

Milos merged into the slow lane, smiling.

He couldn't wait to enlighten the whimpering girl trapped in the trunk.

17

E llie was camped behind her desk the next morning, doodling on a yellow legal pad while a synthesized rock ballad crackled into her ear. As she scratched another mini tornado onto the page, waiting for a live person to answer her call, Valdez approached with a file tucked beneath his arm.

What game was Valdez playing at now?

She eyed the thick folder he slid onto her desk warily, like the offering might double as a hell portal. Was this his idea of a peace gesture? Some kind of test? An extra case that he figured he'd pawn off on her?

Ellie ended the call, her nerves stretched too thin to stomach another second of bad Muzak remakes. She snagged the file with the tip of her pen and dragged it closer. "You know, I can't keep doing all of your groundwork for you, Valdez."

At her snide remark, the other detective's lips twitched. Ellie hid her surprise. Up until now, she'd been convinced that Valdez only laughed at other people's expense.

He leaned his hip on her desk. "Heard you paid a visit to the kiddy porn dealer out at Leath."

Apparently, someone was keeping tabs on her. "Your point?"

"Also heard that not too long ago, you raided a meth house without proper protection, and somehow managed to avoid getting your ass handed to you on a plate."

Ellie bristled at his mocking tone. "I fail to see how that's any of your business, but even if it was, so what? Put yourself in my shoes. What would you have done if you were in that situation? Hide in your car like a scared rabbit while a possible victim was trapped inside or a kidnapper got away?"

Valdez rubbed his chin, clean-shaven as usual. Not one dark hair was out of place. As always, his button-down was immaculate and crisp, his trousers perfectly creased.

Ellie smoothed a hand down her own blouse. No matter how long she ironed, her shirts appeared rumpled well before lunch time. Maybe the Marines had taught Valdez wrinkle-prevention secrets. If the guy wasn't such a prick most of the time, Ellie would be tempted to ask.

"Tell me again, how many kidnapping victims and perps did you find inside the trailer that day?"

Ugh. Valdez knew exactly how many. The arrogant little shit.

Ellie wrapped her fingers back around the pen and squeezed. "Zero, but since I don't have x-ray vision and can't see through walls, I had no way of knowing that until after I went inside."

Valdez stepped forward as if to argue, before stopping and shaking his head. "Look, I didn't come here to fight, okay?"

"You have a funny way of showing it," Ellie grumbled, then regretted her childish outburst. She sighed. "Fine. Why are you here?"

"To let you know that a friend of mine was part of the task force that brought the Harlows down. It's the kind of case that sticks." He rapped the file once with his knuckles before turning and walking away without another word.

Ellie frowned at his departing, wrinkle-free back. The kind of case that sticks? What was that even supposed to mean? Maybe she'd had it right the first time, and Valdez was messing with her.

Nibbling on the pen cap, she opened the folder, half expecting the contents to reveal some stupid prank. Like a photo of a horse's ass, or her face attached to a ridiculous meme.

Instead, she found a social services report.

Weird.

Frowning, she leaned back in her chair and began to read. The report covered a short internal investigation of a small retirement community in Summerville that was suspected of buying children to serve as in-home help for the residents, a strategy to save the facility money by providing a steady supply of reduced cost maintenance workers.

Ellie paused, heart pounding. *Buying children. Could this be the link she needed?* She glanced around the office in search of Valdez, but the other detective was gone. Figured that the one time she actually wanted to see his cocky face, the man was nowhere to be found.

Snorting, she returned to the report. After scouring the report for any employee names that sounded Irish or Scottish and coming up short, Ellie deflated a little and jotted down a note for future research before flipping along to the next pages.

Tenants.

To get an idea of how many names were listed, Ellie flipped through the next pages, groaning when the entries seemed to continue on forever.

She continued turning pages until she found the next section of the report.

Summerville residents applying for in-home help by date.

Bingo.

Using her finger to mark her place, Ellie skimmed through the pages until she located the date range that covered when the Harlows returned Lucas Harrison to Burton. She sped past name after name until she spotted one near the bottom of the page.

O'Rierdon, Pat and Dena

Her breath caught. Last names didn't come more Irish than that.

She read on, learning that the O'Rierdons had once lived in a Summerville retirement community called Winding Oak. Sixteen years ago, but it was still a lead. The most promising one she'd stumbled across since visiting Robyn Harlow in Leath.

Except, Ellie hadn't discovered the O'Rierdons. They'd been dropped into her lap.

This time, when she looked up from the file, she caught a glimpse of Valdez out in the hall. The chair shot back with a squeal of metal on concrete as she lunged to her feet and raced after him.

She caught Valdez en route to the elevator. "Hey, hold up!"

The detective turned, dark eyebrows raised. "Kline? Three interactions in one day? To what do I owe the pleasure?"

For once, Ellie ignored his irritating smirk. "Where did you get that file?"

Valdez tucked his hands into his pockets, his amusement disappearing. "A friend."

"Great, thanks. That's very informative." Ellie huffed as annoyance cranked up her internal thermostat. "You know, you're acting awfully cagey for someone who's supposed to be on my team."

He lifted his shoulders, his dark eyes hooded. "See, that's where we have our wires crossed, because I'm not on your team. I'm on the victims' team."

Heat crawled up Ellie's neck. Valdez couldn't seriously be implying that Ellie wasn't working on behalf of the victims? She dug her nails into her palms, glad that they were in the hallway, where she was safe from the temptation to chuck something at his arrogant head.

"I shouldn't have to tell you this, but my team and the victims' team are one and the same. By the way, since you're so focused on victims, tell me, any updates on Gabe's murder yet? By my count it's been over three weeks since he was burned to death in the back of a sociopath's car."

Valdez's mouth flattened at the mention of Gabe's name. Ellie probably should have stopped right then, but she couldn't seem to help herself. Adrenaline must have flooded her receptors, shorting out common sense. "Surely someone as concerned with victims as you are has made some kind of progress by now?"

Something about Valdez didn't sit right with her. Ellie wasn't sure why, but her gut insisted the detective was keeping secrets.

In Ellie's experience, the only cops who kept secrets were dirty ones.

The detective glared at her. "Trust me, I'm working Gabe's case every chance I get."

Except, that was the crux of the problem right there. Ellie didn't trust Valdez. Not at all. In large part because he refused to update her on the Kingsley case. A snub that never failed to piss her off.

Ellie folded her arms across her chest. "You know, I'm a law enforcement officer, not a member of the victim's family or general public. That means there's nothing preventing you from telling me what Kingsley is up to."

"From what I've gathered, the people who are wrapped up in Kingsley fall into one of two camps." He held up a finger. "The ones who can't be trusted, or the ones who end up dead. Like Roy Jones, for example."

Ellie's eyes widened as a loud ringing filled her ears. "I'm sorry, did you just compare me to *Roy Jones*? A dirty cop who ended up killing himself to escape being caught and facing punishment for his crimes? What, is that some kind of threat or something?"

"You're the one who made the comparison, not me. Although, doesn't it strike you as a little odd, the way so many of Kingsley's victims turn out to be his accomplices?"

"You arrogant son-of-a-bitch," she breathed before closing her eyes and forcing herself to slow down and calm her thundering heart, her nails cutting into her palms until she felt a sting.

Focus. Breathe. Whatever you do, don't let this asshole provoke you into doing something that will end up in your permanent file.

When Ellie was confident she could speak without lunging at the man, she opened her eyes. "Whatever your problem is with me, nothing I've done makes it okay to victim-blame. Not me, or any of those other women whose only crime was being unfortunate enough to fall across Kingsley's path. What happened to me, to them, wasn't our fault. Do you hear me? That. Wasn't. Our. Fault." Her body began to tremble.

"I—"

"Do you know how long it took me to believe that? Do you?" Ellie cut him off as pain seared her chest. "How many years I suffered before I understood that lying to my parents about meeting a boy and going to a party didn't somehow make me culpable for my own kidnapping? Do you know how hard I fight every day? To help other survivors like me, or at least give their families closure, which deep down, is probably a way of penance for my one stupid mistake back when I was fifteen? Don't bother answering because I can tell you right now…you don't. No one can understand unless they've experienced that type of horror firsthand. Because only survivors understand that escaping the abuse is just the first part of the nightmare. The second part is overcoming the guilt and shame."

By the end, Ellie's throat had tightened up, and her voice wobbled, but she was beyond caring. How dare he insinuate that she was culpable? That was an insult to victims and survivors everywhere.

When seconds passed without so much as a peep from Valdez, Ellie looked up. The detective stood rooted in the same spot. As soon as her gaze locked with his, he held up his hands as if to surrender and backed up a step. All remnants of humor and arrogance disappeared from his face, leaving his eyes and mouth looking uncharacteristically soft.

"You're right, that was a low blow. I'm sorry, Kline. I guess this case is getting to me. Seems as if Kingsley can worm his way under your skin and into your head, even from a distance. I've been working on tracking him down, but the man is hard to find. I might have a lead on a nurse who took part in some plastic surgery on a man matching his description down in Costa Rica, but it's not confirmed yet."

The rock in Ellie's throat shrank as she studied Valdez. Still wary, she was willing to give the detective another chance. Though his insinuations still hurt, Ellie understood better than anyone how working Kingsley's case could chip away at your trust, cranking up your suspicions of the people around you.

How could she judge Valdez for treating her like a suspect? At least they were only coworkers. Unlike poor

Nick, when she'd questioned his potential involvement with Kingsley's circle.

The memory made her flinch. A timely warning that no one who came into contact with Kingsley was immune from his head games.

"Yeah, that's the problem with Kingsley. When it comes to that bastard, it's impossible to be sure of anything."

18

W hen Ellie steered the Explorer into the bumpy entrance of the Winding Oak Retirement Center, she gazed at the surroundings in surprise. The name Winding Oak conjured images of peaceful, scenic luxury, full of elegant brick buildings intermixed with towering green oak trees and meandering nature paths.

The reality was nothing like that. Perhaps sixteen years ago, the cluster of weathered, paint-cracked apartments and overgrown crab grass had been nice, but passing time had stamped the complex with a patina of neglect.

Ellie spotted a sign on a squat little building to the left that read *Management Office*. After parking the Explorer, she approached a dented front door and twisted the knob. Locked. Pounding on the peeling brown wood elicited no response, so she peered into the long, grimy window on the left. Between the slits of plastic blinds, she spotted a vacant desk with a couple of chairs in front, and a doorway that appeared to lead to another office in the back, but no signs of life.

From the far side of the glass, a phone began to ring. Ellie waited, but no one came to answer. Six rings later, the silence resumed.

She stepped back, brushed her hands off on her pants, and blew out an annoyed breath. So much for talking to the manager. Now what?

Hands on her hips, Ellie spun a slow circle and spotted a sign across the hall. *Maintenance.* Couldn't hurt. She crossed the leaf-covered walkway and knocked three times.

"Coming, hang on!"

The door flew open. A skinny teenager in faded jeans and a stained yellow SpongeBob t-shirt stood in the opening, his brown hair mussed and curling around his ears.

The boy looked young. Probably too young to be working here as maintenance. Did he live with a parent?

"Hey, I haven't seen you before, I'm Henry. Sorry if you need something fixed, but I'm the only maintenance guy for this entire complex, and I've got to go take a look at the fridge in Mrs. Livingston's place first. Stupid thing is leaking again."

Well, that answered her question about Henry working here. Whether he was of legal age or not to live alone was another matter entirely. Ellie fought to keep a frown off her face and showed him her badge. "I'm Detective Kline from the Charleston PD, and that's okay, we can talk while you work."

The boy hesitated, scratching his arm and shifting his weight between his feet. "I'm not in any trouble, am I?"

Henry sounded uncertain, so Ellie smiled to ease his fears. "No, you're not in trouble. I'm here investigating a case that happened long before you were here."

He scratched his arm again. Nodded. "Okay, then, sure. Let me just grab my toolkit, hang on."

Henry disappeared inside, leaving the door open wide enough for Ellie to snatch a glimpse of a sagging brown couch in a cramped living area, a flipped plastic container doubling as a coffee table, and empty soda cans everywhere. When the stomp of work boots announced his return, she turned away from the door, pretending to study the landscaping.

Not that the overgrown, brown bushes and dirt patches left much to admire.

"I'm ready."

Ellie was happy to note that Henry locked the door before he hopped off the concrete porch and onto the nearest path, carrying a battered red toolbox that appeared so ancient, it could have passed for a World War II relic. Dried brown leaves crackled beneath their feet as he steered them farther into the interior of the complex.

"So, how long have you worked here?" Ellie kept her voice light.

"Like a couple months, not long."

"How's the pay?"

"Eleven dollars an hour, plus I get to live in the apartment for almost free."

"Nice." They walked a few more steps, their progress accompanied by the steady *crunch-crunch* of the leaves. "Don't take this the wrong way, but you strike me as a little young for this type of job."

Henry's loose-limbed, easy gait turned stiff and choppy. "My dad was a handyman, and so was my uncle. My grandma helped fix planes for the military. I'm good at figuring out the mechanics of things and how parts work together, always have been. Probably better than lots of guys older than me."

Ellie wanted to press for more information, but Henry stopped in front of a first-floor apartment near the back parking area. "Here we are."

A gray-haired woman answered the door in a wheelchair,

wearing a faded purple robe with a ripped neckline and a cannula in her nose that attached to a metal oxygen tank. She spotted Henry and grunted, "S'about time," in lieu of a greeting, before spinning her chair in a one-eighty and rolling away.

Henry released a tiny sigh. "Sorry, Mrs. Livingston. I just finished fixing Mr. Jaccard's toilet."

He followed in the old woman's wake, and Ellie took up the rear, entering a shabby, dimly lit space cluttered with miscellaneous junk and papers and books across every available surface. The apartment smelled like tuna fish and overripe fruit.

"Don't mind my mess, and if you do, you know where the door is, use it. Oh, and on your way out, go ahead and complain to Medicare. Maybe then they'll start paying for me to hire a decent live-in maid." She laughed at her own joke, a sound that turned into a harsh, rattling cough.

Ellie noted dirt tracks from the wheelchair streaking across the linoleum and wondered when someone had last cleaned the floor. "I thought Medicare was supposed to cover in-home help if it's medically necessary? Surely they could provide some assistance for you?"

"Pffsh. You've been drinking the Kool-Aid. They don't pay those people near enough to attract decent workers. Most of the ones willing to work for barely above minimum wage are terrible, and none of them last long. It's too much of a hassle having to teach a parade of new people what needs to be done every week or two, so I've just decided I'd rather live with the mess."

They entered a kitchen, the chipped counters piled high with unwashed cups and plates. Henry jumped directly to work, pulling the fridge away from the wall so he could climb behind and investigate.

Ellie leaned against the oven. "It sounds like you've lived

here awhile, Mrs. Livingston? Do you know anything about the investigation that happened a few years back, regarding children working here?"

Mrs. Livingston pivoted her chair to face Ellie. "You mean that complete waste of our tax dollars?" She paused, plucking a tissue from the box on her lap and hacking into it before continuing. "Course I remember. That program was great. They paired orphans up with elderly tenants. The kids got a home and food, us old folks got free help. A win-win, up until some snooty social worker stuck her nose into our business and ruined everything."

Ellie's skin tingled. "A social worker? Did something happen here with one of the kids that made them come investigate?" The report Valdez had given her had told her as much, but if Mrs. Livingston knew about the incident, she might have even more information to share.

Banging erupted from behind the refrigerator, causing both of their heads to turn. "I think I know what's wrong, Mrs. L." Henry's voice was muffled.

"I sure hope so." Mrs. Livingston waited until the banging started up again before frowning at Ellie. "What were you saying again?"

"I was asking if something happened to one of the kids that prompted social services to come out?"

The woman smacked her armrest. "That's right! And yeah, something stupid. Just a broken arm! Kids get them all the time doing all kinds of things. Skateboarding, climbing trees. My nephew even broke his wrist once just falling on the playground at school." She shook her head. "Weird kid. The one who lived here in the complex and broke his arm, not my nephew. Come to think of it, that boy did belong to Pat, I suppose, so maybe the broken arm wasn't all his fault. Pat tended to get a little too rough sometimes."

At the mention of the name Pat, Ellie's pulse spiked. She

forced her posture to remain relaxed, aware that too much eagerness could scare people off. "Pat O'Rierdon?"

Mrs. Livingston snapped her pale, liver-spotted fingers. "That's him. Mean as a snake, that man. Never knew when to quit. The two of them had five kids and still managed to end up in a shithole like this. Only way that happens is if you're a bad parent."

The woman stared up at Ellie as if waiting for her to agree, so she nodded. "You're probably right."

Satisfied, Mrs. Livingston prattled on. "Meanwhile, I had the opposite problem. I married a man who couldn't knock me up. No kids, no help, so now I'm the state's problem, and let's face it, we all know they don't give a damn."

The woman readjusted the cannula to prevent the tubes from slipping out of her nostrils, hitting Ellie with a whiff of body odor when she raised her arm. Did she have anyone to help her shower? Ellie bet not.

"I'd only just moved in when that stupid investigation started up. Saw that boy just a few times but that was enough to know he was a pretty kid, but strange. Didn't act the way other kids did, and Pat, well...he had no idea how to handle him."

Mrs. Livingston's mouth drooped. Ellie wasn't sure if the woman was feeling remorse about the way Lucas had been treated, or was mostly sad because Pat's behavior cost her free help. Not that Ellie could judge her too harshly. If she were stuck here alone at that age, with those health conditions and mobility issues, she'd probably leap at the offer of no cost reliable aid too. "Do you know where I can find the O'Rierdons now?"

The woman clucked her tongue. "Let me think. Mrs. O'Rierdon died a few years back, and Pat moved into another facility, can't recall which one, though."

Ellie wanted to groan. She'd hoped that Mrs. Livingston

would have that information, but she should have known better. The way this case was going, Ellie would probably end up interviewing over a hundred tenants before one of them recalled what happened to Pat O'Rierdon.

If anyone ever did, period.

Ellie allowed herself a moment to experience the disappointment that weighted her limbs before steeling her shoulders. Time to start knocking on doors. "Well, thanks for talking to me, I appreciate it, and nice to meet you both. I'm going to head back out."

After leaving her business card on the counter, Ellie began to retrace her steps to the front door when in the kitchen, a tool clattered to the floor.

"Hold up!"

She whirled as Henry popped out from behind the fridge and jogged over, his heavy-soled boots loud against the floor. He shoved his hands into his back pockets and cleared his throat. "I, um, think I might know where Mr. O'Rierdon is."

19

In the long, quiet hallway outside of Dr. Eddington's office, Luke sat bouncing his leg while he stared at the closed door and waited for his session.

Bounce. Bounce. Bounce.

The motion caused the ugly brown chair to vibrate and squeak, but Luke couldn't stop himself. Just like he couldn't stop from chewing on his lower lip.

He ran his tongue over the rough skin, all cracked and peeling from the cold, and shivered. The texture bothered him. A lot. Not as bad as too many loud noises, but still bad.

Luke raked his teeth over his lip until he caught pieces of loose skin between them. Starting on the left and working his way right, he ripped each strip off.

He'd been remembering the old man and his cane a lot lately, from back when he was Lucas Harrison. Whenever he did that, his insides felt squirmy, like he had worms for guts.

Luke jiggled his leg faster. If he thought about the old man too much, Dr. Eddington might not let him visit the cabin this year.

"Hello, Luke. Come on in." Dr. Eddington appeared in the

doorway, dressed in the white lab coat she always wore, smiling and motioning for him to follow her inside, the way she did every week.

Luke liked that, for the same reason he liked the ugly brown plastic chair in the hall and the blue fabric chair behind her desk—the routine. Knowing what to expect made him feel safe. He sat in the blue chair now, making sure to scoot back far enough that his feet couldn't reach the desk. Sometimes, he kicked things without noticing. That made people mad.

"Would you like anything to drink?"

He shook his head. She always asked and he always said no. Dr. Eddington grabbed a water bottle for herself from the tiny refrigerator near the door. Luke scanned the familiar room while she settled herself behind the big black desk. Not really looking, just checking to make sure that none of the family photos or colorful sunset paintings or green plants on the wooden bookshelf had been moved or replaced.

Dr. Eddington folded her hands on the desk and watched him without speaking. That was one of the things Luke liked about her. She never tried to rush him or told him his habits were silly. Sunlight from the window behind her turned the gray streaks in her dark hair a shiny silver. Luke enjoyed watching them shimmer but staring at people's hair was weird.

He drew in a deep breath and made eye contact because she'd told him doing so let other people know you were listening. After a few seconds, though, staring at her hazel eyes made his leg bounce again, so he stared at a beach painting behind her left shoulder instead.

"How have you been feeling these past few days, Luke? I know this tends to be a difficult time of year for you."

Luke scuffed his shoe on the floor. He hated these questions about feelings. Dr. Eddington always tried to tell him there were no right answers, but Luke was pretty sure there were wrong ones.

If he said the wrong thing, he might not get to go to the cabin. "I've been okay."

"I see. Do you think you could be more specific?" Dr. Eddington checked the red notebook in front of her. "Last session, you started to talk a little about how you feel angry sometimes. Is that still happening?" At his reluctant nod, she smiled. "Okay. Will you tell me more about that? Do you have any clues as to what triggers your anger?"

Luke wished he could say no. Talking about it made him feel all squirmy and stupid. He doubted other people his age got upset by such dumb stuff. But for some reason, Dr. Eddington seemed happier when Luke shared, and he really wanted to make her happy.

He really wanted to go to the cabin.

Luke kicked the chair leg with his heel, fumbling for the right words. *He* knew why he got so angry, but explaining those reasons in a way that made sense to anyone but him was hard. "A lot of times, it's because the world gets to be too much."

"Too much, how?"

"Too many people and too much noise and too many bright colors or things moving, everything." Just the thought of it made Luke's skin start to itch.

"So, you find yourself getting upset when there's too much stimulation around you?"

Luke had never thought in terms of the problem being too much stimulation before, but that sounded right. "Yes."

"Okay. And what happens inside you when there's all that noise or chaos?"

"It feels like I'm being attacked and I can't get away, and my skin burns." He didn't mention the fire ants, because that sounded stupid. Like something a little kid would say. "And then I freak out and get mad. Sometimes..." He trailed off and kicked the chair leg again. Ashamed to admit the next part.

Dr. Eddington adjusted her glasses. "Go ahead, finish what you were going to say. Remember, this is a safe place, Luke. I'm not here to judge you, I'm here to help."

When Luke glanced up, she offered him an encouraging smile. A no-teeth one, which was good. Wild animals showed their teeth to warn other animals away. That made more sense to Luke since teeth were for biting.

"Sometimes when you get mad...?" Dr. Eddington prompted.

Luke curled his hands around the edges of the blue chair and tried again. "Sometimes, when I get mad, I...I hurt people." His voice dropped to a whisper on that last part, and he ducked his head while misery flooded his stomach.

Dr. Eddington would hate him now. Maybe even stop seeing him. He didn't want that to happen because he liked Dr. Eddington. She was nice. Luke knew she was doing her best, trying to help him.

Not everyone wanted to help. Some people only wanted to hurt others.

Luke rubbed his arm and tried not to think about those people.

"Anger is an understandable reaction when you feel like you're being attacked. Would you like to talk about that more? The people you've hurt when you were mad?"

No. He didn't like talking about those people. Or even thinking about them. He didn't want to be Lucas anymore. Or Luke, even though that was what Aaron used to call him.

He stared at the white floor without saying anything.

"I know it can be tough reliving difficult or ugly events from our past, but I really do believe that talking about it is often the best way to heal. Keeping traumatic memories bottled up inside you can make you sick. You've never told me everything about that night, but I'm guessing it's on your mind today."

Luke fidgeted and began plucking at his dry lip again with his teeth. *Suck, pull, chew.* Already raw, his lip bled right away this time, filling his mouth with copper and salt.

He shivered. The taste reminded him of that night.

The idea of telling Dr. Eddington what happened scared him. But what if she was right, about the talking? Luke hadn't thought of himself as being sick until Dr. Eddington brought it up, but the label felt right. The ugliness he kept locked up inside him felt way worse than that one time he'd caught the flu.

"Grandpa hit me."

He stopped. No more words would come.

When they'd found him at the hospital, they'd asked who he was. Where he was from. His birthdate. He had refused to tell them, even though he remembered. Instead, he told them that his name was Coleman, just like his favorite camping gear.

He'd clung to his new name all these years as well as the knowledge of those long, ugly nights in that dark room. The room where, every morning, the old man woke him up by screaming into his ear and slapping his shoulder. Demanding that, "Lucas, boy, you haul that lazy ass out of bed and take care of us."

The first time, Luke had corrected him. "This is a couch, not a bed." He'd said it because facts mattered to Luke. Not to be a smartass, like the old man had screamed right before he smacked Lucas across the face.

The couple hadn't given him his own bedroom. He slept in an open space, on a couch covered with a clear plastic sheet. The crinkle the material made hurt Luke's ears every time he moved or rolled over.

But he'd take that over helping the old man to the bathroom every morning. Washing him after he used the toilet. The foul smell turned Luke's stomach.

At least he could do those chores. The man's wife slept most of the time, with tubes stuck in her throat. When she woke up, Grandpa expected Luke to help her. There was just one problem, he had no idea how.

Didn't matter. Grandpa's face would turn all red anyway, and he'd start screaming swear words at Luke.

"Can you tell me more about Grandpa, Luke? I know this is difficult, but you haven't said much in our meetings yet."

Luke flinched at the memory of Grandpa's cane slamming into his back. He shook his head. Dr. Eddington seemed nice, but that didn't mean he could trust her.

He wasn't sure he could trust anyone.

The tiny sigh that Dr. Eddington released made Luke tug harder at his lip.

"Okay. How about the hospital, can we talk about that? You didn't do very well there, did you?"

He shook his head, frowning. "The hospital made me stay inside all the time. I like it here because I can go outside. I even get to go to the cabin on my birthday."

"Right. And I see that your birthday is coming up. Do you still want to go this year? You've been pretty anxious lately, going on a long field trip to the cabin might make that worse. Maybe we should postpone the trip. What do you think?"

This time, Luke shook his head so hard, wind whipped in his ears. "No! We can't postpone! She might be there this time!"

Luke knew better than to mention the girl, but the words were out before he could stop them. *Stupid*, he told himself as he rocked in the chair. *Stupid, stupid, stupid.* Now they'd really try to keep him from visiting the cabin.

He gulped and peeked at Dr. Eddington. She set her pen aside and peered at him from over the top of her glasses.

"Luke, we've been over this, remember?"

Her voice was gentle but that didn't matter. Luke had messed up. He stared into his lap. Waiting for his doctor to tell him the same thing she always told him.

"There was no girl. She was only a figment of your imagination. You created her in your head to help you get through a difficult time in your life. There's no shame in that, lots of people do the same."

I'm not ashamed! he wanted to shout. Why would he be? He'd had an actual imaginary friend once, and he wasn't ashamed of him. He didn't care who knew about Jimmy Hoffa. But he understood that wasn't the answer Dr. Eddington wanted.

Or the answer that would get him permission to visit the cabin.

So, though he disliked pretending, Lucas nodded. Even as memories of the girl played through his mind like a video.

Her blue eyes and wide smile, and how she'd throw back her head and laugh until her entire body shook.

The way she'd wake up with her hair all big and tangled on the mornings when she forgot to braid it the night before. Bed head, she'd called it.

How she actually listened to him when he talked about camping and survival, and even asked for his opinion before making big decisions. The girl never yelled at him or seemed to care that Lucas didn't act normal. Never made fun of him if he got frustrated and flapped his hands, or asked him why, even when he talked about sad things, he didn't cry.

No, the girl had just been his companion all that time, without complaint. Not only that, but she'd acted like she enjoyed living with Lucas.

No one else had ever done that before. But that didn't

make the girl *a figment of his imagination*. He might be weird, but he understood the difference between real life and pretend.

Jimmy Hoffa had been pretend.

The girl was not.

Familiar frustration swelled in his chest, along with the same dull ache he always felt when he thought about the girl. He missed her so much. Why couldn't Dr. Eddington understand? Lucas had thought that by explaining about Jimmy Hoffa, his doctor would see. He'd been wrong. Telling Dr. Eddington about Jimmy Hoffa had only convinced her even more that the girl was imaginary too.

That was part of the reason why Lucas didn't like to share.

Dr. Eddington finished scribbling in her notebook, then folded her hands on the desk. "Let's try again. What can you tell me about the night you ran away from the hospital?"

20

I stepped inside the enormous closet, reaching out a hand and letting fabric flutter across my fingertips as I walked a slow path along the perimeter and savored the luxury. The garments were arranged by color, with enough space between each hanger to make each piece more accessible and prevent wrinkles. The built-in shelves hosted folded items, arranged in tidy rows.

Fine wool skimmed my fingers. Silks and cottons. A black leather jacket so soft the fabric practically melted to the touch.

At the far end of the closet, a rough texture stopped me. A khaki green uniform hung in the corner. The garish color glared back at me, an eyesore compared to everything else.

A boy's uniform, not a man's.

The outfit whisked me back in time, to the days when I'd been forced to don that hideous material every day.

My feet dragged as I headed down the hallway that led to the headmaster's office, the leather strap heavy in my hand. The gleaming hardwood floor smelled like lemon and beeswax, two scents that usually didn't bother me, but on this trip, soured my stomach. Portraits of former headmasters frowned down on me from gilded, fancy frames, like they knew why I'd been summoned and disapproved.

"I'm glad someone knows," I mumbled.

Because I had no idea why the old psychophant was mad at me this time. Had I walked too fast on my way to class? Eaten my cafeteria dinner too quickly, or forgotten to put my napkin in my lap? Laughed too loud in the halls?

Not that the reason mattered. If the headmaster didn't have a legitimate excuse to punish the boys at my boarding school, he'd make one up. The pretty boys always got targeted the most.

I rubbed the back of my thigh and winced. It was still bruised from the last time I'd faced the strap only three days ago.

Glancing at my watch, I cringed and quickened my pace, my regulation brown dress boots clattering along the empty floor as I scurried. Tardiness resulted in additional swats.

As I hurried, I wondered, not for the first time, if the headmaster got hard from hitting boys. That would explain why he grabbed any excuse to discipline us, no matter how stupid.

This time, maybe I'd make sure to take a good, long look at the front of his pants. If our esteemed leader was getting a woody over beating on the unwanted teenage sons from wealthy families, surely there was a way for me to trade on that information?

I skidded to a stop before the forbidding brown door with the gold Headmaster Wiggins *nameplate across the top, swallowing hard before knocking twice.*

"Come in."

At the sound of the voice, my hand froze on the old-fashioned, curved door handle, before I squeezed. The door swung open, allowing my eyes to confirm what my ears had already told me.

The person seated behind the antique desk wasn't the headmaster at all, but someone far more concerning...his wife.

I hesitated, unsure what to make of this new development. My heart flipped, either from fear or lust or a combination of both. The headmaster's wife was a knockout. The kind of woman you'd expect to find stuck inside the pages of the magazines some student was always stealing from his father's closet and smuggling in.

She had fiery red hair that fell in thick waves halfway down her back, and a curvy, perfect figure that made it hard to breathe. Even when her body was hidden beneath an outfit like the one she wore tonight, a high-necked, shapeless dress in a severe shade of navy blue, it was hard to think straight when she was around.

With all her feminine beauty, Mrs. Wiggins looked out of place sitting in the headmaster's brown leather chair, behind that giant wooden desk, with her husband's framed degrees hanging over her red head. The entire office was decorated in shades of brown with manly furniture and a huge, stone fireplace dominating one wall. The type of room I could picture Sherlock Holmes inhabiting, only much neater. It even smelled like the cigars Headmaster Wiggins liked to smoke when he thought no one else was watching.

The leather creaked as Mrs. Wiggins shifted positions to face me. Light from one of the bronze wall sconces caught her hair, painting the color a bright copper, and my nose caught a new scent. Sweet, like vanilla, but also musky.

My mouth dried out, like I'd been sucking on sand. "Ma'am?"

The headmaster's wife regarded me with catlike greenish gold eyes that missed nothing. When she set the fragile white teacup she'd just sipped from on a silver tray next to a set of matching cloches, a red smudge remained near the top. Lipstick.

I stared at that red smear, jealous, with an uncomfortable tightening in my groin. Her lips had touched that exact spot. I wet my lips before jerking my attention back to her face, shoving the trembling hand holding the strap behind my back. Her slow smile eased the worst of my nerves. "Why, hello there. You must be Mr. Kingsley."

Her voice flowed over me, warm and sweet as the strawberry jam they served with our biscuits at breakfast. The other boys must have been messing with me, when they'd whispered warnings in my *ear about how she was far worse than the headmaster. And stupid me, I'd fallen for their prank. This woman wasn't just beautiful, but warm. Small, too. I doubted her head reached much higher than my chin.*

"Yes, ma'am."

"Good, I'm glad you're here. We have some work to do."

Someone whimpered. I jumped, unaware until that moment that anyone else was in the office with us. A quick room scan revealed another student, cowering near the wall opposite the head-master's desk.

My mouth fell open. I recognized the other kid, Nick something or other. He was a younger boy, a grade below me, but the thing that caught my attention was his uniform. Someone had stuffed his pudgy body into a khaki shirt and pants that were a good two sizes too small for him. The fit was so snug, he looked a little like a sausage about to burst free from its wrapper.

Then I remembered that Nick had been absent from classes for several days. When I'd passed by a table at lunch, I'd overheard some of the other boys gossiping about how he must have been sent home.

As I studied the quivering boy, the hairs on the back of my neck lifted. Had Nick been in the headmaster's office this entire time, and if so, why?

Mrs. Wiggins stood up, bringing my attention back toward the desk. "Thank you for bringing me the strap."

The strap. Right. I'd almost forgotten.

The pain in my bruised legs flared up as I crossed the polished hardwood floor, but I worked to keep my bearing erect, like the teachers here taught us. That musky-sweet scent grew stronger as I approached, almost choking me by the time I stopped a few feet away.

I moved to hand her the strap before hesitating, wondering if I could wipe it off on my pants first. No. That would only draw more attention to the pathetic state of my sweaty palms.

Just pray she doesn't notice.

Clenching my teeth, I offered her the strap, praying to the gods of embarrassed schoolboys or whoever might be listening.

My plea must have worked because Mrs. Wiggins shook her head, her smile widening.

"No, you keep that. I need your help. Nickolas here has been sneaking candy at night." *She wagged a pink-tipped finger at the boy, who refused to meet her eyes.* "For the good of his health, he's been staying in the Blue Room."

A chill shivered across my back. I'd never visited the infamous Blue Room myself, but rumors were always flying around the school about our headmaster's secret punishment spot, none of them good.

"The Blue Room?" *I echoed, for lack of anything better to say.*

"That's right. We needed to provide Nickolas with a private place where he could have time to consider his actions, somewhere without access to food. At this school, it's our job to teach him the importance of healthy eating habits. Just because you feel hungry doesn't mean you need to eat. Especially not garbage food. Isn't that right, Nickolas?"

Nickolas made a noise like a scared mouse. "Y-yes, Mrs. Wi-Wiggins."

"Good." *The headmaster's wife moved to the silver tray and lifted the first cloche. A delicious aroma enveloped us, meaty and rich with garlic and other spices. The large black tureen held what appeared to be beef stew. A perfect, round loaf of homemade bread with golden crust sat on the white plate beside it.*

With a flair, the headmistress's wife plucked the second cloche from the tray, revealing a silver stand. A two-tier cake sat on top, the entire thing drenched in thick, creamy white icing and chocolate swirls.

Wow. Even my mouth watered, and I'd already eaten dinner that night. Not like Nick. From what Mrs. Wiggins had said, it sounded like he hadn't eaten in almost two days.

I risked another peek at him, wanting to see his reaction. Nick's eyes were glued to the tray, his round cheeks and pudgy chin trembling.

"Doesn't it smell divine?" The headmistress's wife waved the steam toward her face and inhaled deeply through her nose. "But it's important that young men learn control. Unfortunately, I think Nickolas needs another day of fasting to master that skill, so I'm afraid he won't be allowed to eat."

"Ma'am?" Surely I must have misunderstood.

"Oh, don't worry, it won't harm him. Our Nickolas has plenty of fat on his body to sustain him for quite some time, don't you, sweet boy?"

Nickolas let out a soft little moan and swayed on his feet. Sweat darkened the armpits of his too-tight uniform. "Y-es...yes, ma'am."

My gaze swung from Nick to the tray and back again, before finally landing on the headmistress's wife. "I don't mean to be disrespectful, ma'am, but I don't understand why I'm here?"

Her green-gold eyes narrowed, and this time when she grinned, she showed her teeth.

All the better to eat you with, *was the wild thought that flew through my head.*

"Why, Mr. Kingsley, you're here to learn, of course."

The warm, honeyed tones of her voice faded along with the office, leaving me standing in the walk-in closet, clutching the sleeve of my old uniform. I released the fabric and pivoted away, irritated by my unwanted jaunt down memory lane. As much as I'd detested that boarding school, I'd learned a few very necessary lessons back then.

The most important one being the one Mrs. Wiggins had mentioned that day—the value of control.

But I could clearly use a refresher, since I'd just demonstrated a lapse of control by allowing my mind to drag me back to those years without my conscious consent.

Not now, though. Now, I had other lessons to teach.

I worked my way back through the garments, considering and discarding a gray pin-striped suit by Burberry, and a navy one by Paul Smith. Hangers screeched as I slid suit after suit to the side, rejecting each one in turn. My appearance tonight had to be perfect.

I finally settled on a gray micro-checked number by Ermenegildo Zegna. The ultrafine wool was light and airy, and the slim fit would showcase my lean build.

After selecting a button-down in the palest of blues to go with it, I chose a brown belt, tie, and a pair of brown Gucci lace-ups and began getting dressed in front of the full-length mirror that graced the outside of a mahogany armoire.

I shrugged into the jacket, which was the tiniest bit loose, but the blue shirt set off my new bronze skin tone. All in all, the final effect pleased me. This was a special occasion, and I needed to look just right.

"You do realize that studies show women are taught about interpersonal relationships at much younger ages than men. In a marriage, it's the woman's job to nurture. If the marriage fails, that's the wife's fault. After all, she's the one with the superior relationship skills."

I looped the end of my tie through the hole, adjusting the knot before turning to my captive audience. Valerie glared at me from the wingback chair I'd bound her to, but any argument was muffled, courtesy of the gag I'd stuffed into her mouth.

After checking my cuffs and brushing off the lapels, I decided I was ready.

"I imagine you're wondering why I brought you up here." I bent over and tested the gag. Plenty tight. "I'm afraid I have some business to attend to over the next few days, and it would be unwise to leave you in your room."

I slid a knife from the top drawer of the antique dresser

and tapped the flat side against her forehead. "If you make your presence known, I will kill you. Do you understand?"

Valerie's eyes practically snarled at me. She tried to talk, but the thick white cloth absorbed the sound. Along with sparks of anger, I glimpsed resignation in her expression. An understanding that she expected to die either way.

Still feisty, even after days in my basement. All the better. I couldn't wait to bend that fiery spirit, pushing at her until she snapped.

Personally, I'd never understood the appeal of sports. Not when people were so much fun to play with.

I clucked my tongue before a vicious smile peeled my lips back. "You know, Valerie, there are times like today when I wish I'd had the foresight to keep Ben for myself."

Her dead boyfriend's name rolled off my tongue so casually that the reference took a bit to have the desired effect. Valerie's brow wrinkled at first. I witnessed the delicious moment when understanding clicked, widening her dark eyes and triggering her to recoil until her spine fused to the back of the chair.

As if the mere act of putting a meager few extra inches between us might save her.

The rapid rise and fall of her chest delighted me. I sniffed, almost believing I could detect the tantalizing scent of her desperation. Oh, to possess a dog's nose! The ability to detect the fine reek of fear was wasted on our furry friends.

Still. I could appreciate the art of provoking terror in a manner no dog ever could. Watching Valerie cower before me was an exercise in joy. An ebullient sort of power that expanded my very cells and rushed straight to my head.

Forget wine, or Scotch, or any type of hard spirit. If I had my choice, I'd gladly eschew alcohol for life and bottle this feeling instead.

"Yes, Ben would have been oh-so-beautiful to break, wouldn't you agree?"

Valerie watched me, and as I moved closer, began thrashing against the restraints. I smiled down at her, soaking up each tasty morsel of terror that flickered across her face.

Her brown eyes narrowed. My only warning. Her foot shot out, catching the edge of my shin. I dodged quickly enough that her toe only dealt me a glancing blow, but the rage her insubordinate act triggered was full throttle.

Stupid little bitch.

My palm whipped out and connected with her cheek. The force behind the blow cracked like a whip, propelling her head to the side with a vicious snap.

After bending over to inspect the trouser leg that her grimy little foot had touched and reassuring myself there was no mark, I straightened and tapped the knife against my palm.

"The reason you're still with us is because live bait is preferable, but it's not a necessity." I stroked a finger down the wicked silver blade, pleased when her dark eyes followed the motion. "You'd do well to remember that little tidbit, if you'd prefer to remain intact."

21

Nothing stirred on the quiet road nestled along the dense parade of trees, all in the shadow of the Grand Teton Mountains. As Katarina waited behind the wheel of the car parked just off the side of the road, the last of the daylight ebbed from the sky. Without a big city nearby to provide light pollution, the street darkened quickly, even though the green numbers on the dashboard clock hadn't yet hit six p.m.

Leather crackled beneath her fingers. With a sigh, Katarina eased up on the steering wheel that she'd been clutching too hard. She'd spent the last hour sitting here, twiddling her thumbs in her head-to-toe black ensemble. Fretting that the carefully chosen outfit would do her little good if this asshole never showed.

Where the hell was he, anyway?

She wiggled her fingers, but nothing could shake the icy sensation slithering over her skin. Every minute that ticked by upped her fear. Stuck in this car, waiting on her target to show up.

That was all she'd accomplished these last few hours.

Waiting. Sitting around with her thumb up her ass, while all of her plans slipped farther and farther out of reach.

She felt like she was trapped inside a never-ending nightmare, with the worst of her fears come to life.

Bethany was gone. Taken. Kidnapped. And that stumpy little bitch with the blonde bob in the school office had the nerve to smile at Katarina as she'd informed her that Bethany had already been picked up for a doctor's appointment. Too idiotic to comprehend the colossal mistake she'd made, or to realize that Katarina's life had just crumbled to pieces.

Inbred, country hicks, she hissed into the silence. Who the hell had entrusted that stupid, flannel-shirt wearing moron to work at a school and care for kids? Being that damn stupid should be considered a crime.

Katarina dug her nails into the leather sheath in the center console, picturing the razor-sharp blade resting inside. Soothing herself with the promise that soon, very soon, she'd inflict the proper punishment. On the way out of town, she'd take a detour to the school and hack all of the idiot employees into tiny pieces, starting with the bubbly blonde who'd handed Bethany off to a perfect stranger without checking with Katarina first. Bethany's *mother*.

Once she finished carving them up, she'd douse the entire place in gasoline and flick a lit match over her shoulder before driving away. The fire spectacle would be doing Wyoming a public service. Both by rescuing the locals from at least one day of complete, utter boredom, and by preventing the school morons from endangering someone else's child. Hell, she wouldn't be surprised if the locals awarded her a medal as a thank you for the gift.

Or she wouldn't be if most of them weren't such complete dumbasses.

Katarina buried her face in the thick black sweatshirt and

screamed. How? How had Kingsley found them? How long had he been watching them in their little house? Because Katarina suspected, with only a flicker of doubt, that Kingsley was the person responsible for Bethany's disappearance. No one else possessed the motive to track them down in Wyoming, or the means to penetrate the names in the federal WITSEC program.

That left Katarina with a single option. She had to turn the tables on Kingsley and track her own papa down. After spending a panicked hour driving all the streets around Bethany's school and racking her brain for ideas, she'd only come up with one viable option.

A rumble in the distance made her go still. The noise grew louder, and she held her breath as headlights appeared on the road. The vehicle slowed, pulling off the road about twenty yards ahead of where Katarina was parked and into a dirt spot in front of the rent-by-the-week log cabin, all clearly visible from her windshield.

Mick Fortner emerged from the driver's seat of a dark pickup truck. From the light shining off the cabin's porch, Katarina noticed that he was taller than she remembered from the New Year's Eve party at Clayne's. Bigger, too, with broad shoulders that filled a dark sweatshirt and thick thighs beneath his jeans.

Mick walked with a swagger that probably convinced most people to buy his drug-dealer act, but Katarina wasn't fooled. He might be able to slip into a few criminal mannerisms, but he'd never fully managed to shake that outer cop skin.

Under the cover of darkness, Katarina tracked him as he bounded up the single porch step and disappeared inside. She applied a fresh coat of red lipstick, finger-tousled her hair, and grabbed her knife before opening the door.

Blackmail. Pain. Pleading. One way or another, Mick

Fortner was going to help her find Bethany. The method made no difference to her.

She eased the car door shut, fondling the blade before sliding the weapon into her pocket. It felt like years since she'd last drawn blood or experienced the thrill of sinking the metal deep into someone's flesh, even though only a few weeks had passed since she'd wielded a knife on one of Clayne's warehouse workers. Still. She'd funneled a ton of energy into bettering herself, attempting to live the lie of a normal mom in a small town for so long that she'd almost bought into the fantasy.

Almost.

Katarina gave the knife one last pat. On second thought, maybe she'd start with pain first.

She crept toward the cabin, guided by the faint light spilling from a window. Careful in picking out each step. A sprained ankle would be catastrophic.

Crunch!

Too late, the sound alerted Katarina to another presence behind her. A hand clamped over her mouth, and she was yanked backward until her back slammed into a hard surface. A body.

For a single moment, panic seized her, insisting that she struggle and kick as much as possible. Anything to escape the thick arms clamped around her like chains.

Instinct kicked in. Instead of flailing, she grabbed for the knife. Her fingers curled around the handle, and in a flash, the blade was free. She whipped her hand back, slashing behind her and feeling the knife tear through fabric.

"Son of a bitch! You ripped my shirt!"

At the muffled curse, Katarina faltered, freezing before the knife made contact again. Her shock provided the assailant with an opening. He whipped around and shoved her in the chest until she slammed into the car, hard. The knife fell to the ground as searing pain lanced her back, but it had nothing on the fire that burned her lungs when she attempted to draw a breath. She doubled over, wheezing.

"What the fuck were you doing following a man to his place?"

Clayne towered over her, large and furious. It was on the tip of her tongue to snap back that where she went was none of his business, but he'd just have to wait. She was too busy sucking oxygen into her cramping lungs to speak.

"I can tell you've been pulling away lately, but I'm not going to lose you like this, do you hear me? Not to that piece of shit in there. I'll kill him first."

Katarina inhaled one last time before straightening. She studied his face. *He really means it,* she thought. A little dazed by the realization but also…happy? Because even in the dim lighting, she recognized that bloodthirsty expression.

She should. It was the same one she'd seen reflected back at her in the mirror so many times.

Despite the throbbing ribs he'd caused, Clayne's loyalty triggered a rush of warmth inside Katarina. "I promise, it's not what you think."

"Bullshit! You think I'm an idiot? That's what every woman says when they're cheating."

She wanted to argue, but his hands whipped out. Curled around her throat. *Squeezed.*

This time, Katarina didn't hesitate. She slammed her knee up toward his nuts. He shifted to the side, and she connected with his inner thigh instead, but she was already attacking again, with an undercut that caught him right in the gut. He gasped, slackening his grip.

She used the momentary advantage to yank free, but he was on her before she could strike again.

They circled each other like two angry dogs. Katarina kicked out, missing the vulnerable spot inside the knee by an inch. He lunged, but she darted beyond his reach. Blood flowed hot through her veins, humming like an electric pulse and reminding her of how it felt to be alive.

"Bitch," he growled.

"Asshole."

Panting now, she spied an opening and kicked out again. Clayne's hands wrapped around her foot midair and yanked.

Shit. Katarina's hands flew up to protect her head as she tumbled to the ground, twisting on her way down to minimize the impact. She landed in the dirt, on the back side of her hip first. She gasped but kept moving, allowing experience to guide her actions.

Roll out of the way, then jump to your feet.

No chance. Clayne was on her too fast, slamming his chest into hers and pinning her with the weight of his body.

Katarina's muscles tensed, preparing her to attempt one of multiple escape techniques. Instead, she remained still, with her heart thundering in her ears. High on adrenaline and the smell of sweat, and the warm body plastered to hers.

She grabbed the back of Clayne's head and pulled his mouth to hers, digging her teeth into his lower lip until their kiss tasted like blood.

"Witch." He lashed out and pinned her free hand to the ground. His grip tightened, crushing her carpal bones together with an angry squeeze.

The pain exploded through her like a livewire. The most real thing she'd felt since Bethany went missing.

Bethany.

The reminder showered ice water on her excitement, shocking her back to reality. *How could she have been distracted from her purpose so easily?*

Katarina shoved him off, rolling away and jumping to her feet before he could stop her. "Like I said before, it's not like that."

Clayne climbed to his feet, brushed the dirt off his jeans, and faced her with his big hands curled into fists. "Yeah? Then tell me what it's like?"

The sneer in his words warned Katarina that she had a decision to make. Either tell him the truth or accept that he'd never believe that she hadn't driven out to the middle of nowhere for a booty call.

Again, the temptation to tell him to go to hell hovered on her tongue, so no one was more surprised than Katarina by what came tumbling out of her mouth next.

"Someone took Bethany."

Katarina shuddered as reaction set in. Uttering the statement out loud was both terrifying and cathartic. She breathed hard but otherwise didn't move as Clayne leaned in and cupped her cheeks, his calloused palms rough against her skin. He tilted her face back, searching her eyes, she suspected, to find any trace of a lie.

She met his gaze without backing down, and whatever he found in her eyes turned his hands gentle even as his nostrils flared.

"Just tell me who I have to kill to get her back."

22

The white clapboard house squatted at the end of a driveway suffocated by overgrown weeds. Ellie hopped out of the SUV and headed toward a pair of two elderly men who sat on a crumbling cement step, bickering back and forth beneath a sagging awning that looked one strong breeze away from collapsing.

The bald man wearing a faded Dallas Cowboys t-shirt elbowed his buddy as she approached, whistling. "Please, Benny, tell me this is the new nurse."

Ellie offered them a friendly smile and flashed her badge. "Sorry, afraid not. I'm Detective Kline with the Charleston PD."

The bald man went to elbow Benny again, but Benny swatted his friend's hand away. "Stop it, Silas."

Silas's gummy lips peeled back, revealing two missing top teeth. He extended his wrinkled hands toward Ellie. "I've been a bad boy, Officer, would you like to cuff me?"

In an effort not to laugh, Ellie bit her cheek.

"Christ, Silas, would you shut the hell up?" Benny dragged a hand through his shock of white hair and shot his friend a glare for good measure before nodding at her. "Evening, Detective, and ignore this idiot next to me, please. What can we do for you?"

"I'm hoping you can help me find someone. Is Pat O'Rierdon around by chance?"

Benny and Silas exchanged a long, uneasy look. Benny plucked at his cotton sweatpants, and neither man appeared in a hurry to reply.

That was okay. She could wait them out. Ellie folded her arms, watching their uneasy fidgeting grow when she didn't turn around and leave.

Silas hacked, angling to the side to spit a wad of yellow phlegm into the dirt that bordered the porch. "You sure you don't want to find someone else? Cuz if it were up to me, that's what I'd recommend." The earlier teasing note was gone.

"Sorry, but I'm afraid Mr. O'Rierdon is the only name on my list."

The two men shared another glance, and whatever silent communication occurred prompted Silas to scratch his gray-stubbled chin, then jerk his thumb over his shoulder. "He's inside, in the TV room. Don't say we didn't warn you."

"Thank you, gentlemen." Ellie stepped around them on her way to the front entrance. She found the door unlocked and ajar, so she eased it open, her gaze sliding over the splintered frame before assessing the interior.

Good Lord.

Instead of an entryway or living room furniture, the space was crammed with beds. Or more specifically, mattresses. The dirty rectangles lay all over the floor, like some kind of flophouse for the elderly.

Ellie stepped inside, and the stench hit her next. Rancid and ripe, like a mixture of rotting trash, body odor, and feces. Probably partly due to the dirty plates strewn all over the room, crusty with old food remnants that had been sitting out for God knew how long.

Forget that time she'd rushed into the meth trailer without a proper mask. The reek in here was probably ten times worse. Ellie paused, giving her gag reflex time to settle before she pushed ahead, making sure to breathe through her mouth.

Picking her way through the maze of mattresses, discarded dishes, clothes, and trash, Ellie followed the booming laugh track of a sitcom to another room. Along one water-stained wall, an old television sat on a pile of cinder blocks. A few beat-up chairs that looked rescued from the junkyard were scattered around the room, along with a beige couch. She counted a total of three men.

"Is one of you Pat O'Rierdon?"

A man sitting in the closest chair with a walker on one side and a bottle of whiskey in his lap wrenched his gaze away from the screen. "Who the hell are you, and what are you doing in my house?"

When Ellie locked eyes with Pat O'Rierdon, a shiver skated across her skin. The man's pale blue eyes were colder than a mountain lake. In her line of work, she'd stared into plenty of cruel faces, but this was the first time one of them belonged to a man old enough to be her grandfather.

Something about those mean eyes set in such a creased face struck Ellie as wrong. "I'm Detective Kline, Charleston PD, and from the looks of things, you have quite a few people living in your house."

O'Rierdon lifted the bottle to his lips and swigged some of the whiskey. Once finished, he wiped his mouth on a ratty shirt sleeve and belched. "So what if I have some friends and fella retirees staying here too? Don't see that it's any of your damned business."

More than a few, just based on the mattresses in that one room alone.

But Ellie hadn't driven out here to bust his balls over a geriatric flophouse, even if her roiling stomach preferred she did just that.

She fished the photo of Lucas from her blazer pocket and handed it to him. "This kid is my business."

O'Rierdon scoffed, which set off a violent coughing spasm. He doubled over, thumping his chest with his fist. When he finished, the man scowled at her like she was to blame for whatever disease festered in his crappy lungs. "You know I worked twenty-three years at the factory. Every damn day, I sucked down paint fumes and chemical cleaners, breathed all that toxic shit in and never once complained. Didn't miss a single day of work the whole time I was married. Not until my hands started breaking down."

He grimaced at the appendages in question, raising them so that Ellie could see. His fingers were misshapen like something out of a horror movie, the bones twisted and bent in weird ways like decaying tree branches, the joints doubled in size. Despite her knowledge of the man's abuse, Ellie couldn't help but wince in sympathy. "Ouch."

"You're telling me." He let his hands fall back into his lap. "Arthritis, they said. Genetic, which meant the company didn't have to fork over any money for treatment. Doctor said working the job I did would only make it worse, but I figured, what the hell? I'd been there a long time, I figured I might as well stick it out, hope they'd appreciate my loyalty."

He paused to drain another swallow of whiskey.

"Did they? Appreciate your loyalty?"

"Fuck, no. When my hands finally got so bad I couldn't work no more, those assholes fired me. A couple of years too soon to get full retirement. By then it was too late to get another job anywhere else. Even Walmart wouldn't hire me.

All those years I worked, though, I never complained, not once. I did my job, took care of my wife. Raised my kids, even though those little shits are too good to come visit me now. I did everything right, and I still got screwed."

He hunched into the chair, both hands shaking as they wrapped around the whiskey bottle. Once Ellie was sure he'd finished his bitter tirade, she edged closer. "I'm sorry to hear about your troubles, but none of that tells me anything about Lucas Harrison."

The old man grunted. "That Harrison kid was all my wife's idea. She was too damned soft-hearted for her own good, always wanting to pick up some stray. Pitiful. I stood by her, though. Even when she got cancer, and even when it got real bad and entered her lungs. Even when she was nothing but a burden."

Ellie's jaw ached from her effort to maintain a steady expression. *Did he think he deserved a cookie or something?* The man talked about his wife like she was an unwanted pet someone had dumped into his lap, instead of a partner he'd vowed to honor and cherish *'til death do you part.* "And Lucas?"

"We took the kid because my wife got to the point where she couldn't keep up with the house. It's not like I could afford to hire someone to cook and clean for her, you know."

He held up his hands, and Ellie could tell he was about to go on a rant again and inwardly groaned as she listened to him bitch for another couple minutes.

"And Lucas?" she prompted once again.

The old man spit something nasty into a cup. "Around that time, a friend told us about some orphan who needed a place to stay. We opened up our home to Lucas, kept him around even though he couldn't do a damn thing right. But they gave us a dud cuz that kid was never right in the head, if you ask me."

Easy, Ellie warned herself. *Putting this asshole on blast won't get the information you need.*

To be safe, she waited another beat to reply. "Lucas was autistic."

The man curled his lip at that, revealing a brown front tooth. "No such thing as autism when I was growing up, just more bullshit from parents to excuse their kid's shitty behavior and get them special treatment. That's the problem with younger generations, they get away with murder. No work ethic, no discipline. Sit around all day playing video games while their parents wait on them instead of making them grow up." O'Rierdon wound himself up, slapping the chair arm. "All that education these days, and for what? Most of them never do a single worthwhile thing their entire spoiled lives. They—"

"I'm afraid I don't have time to listen to what *they* do or don't do, Mr. O'Rierdon." Even to her own ears, Ellie's voice sounded icy. "I asked you specifically about Lucas Harrison. What happened to him?"

"You mean, once that little shit ran away? Hell if I know, and to tell the truth, I don't care much, either. More trouble than he was worth." O'Rierdon plucked the photo from where it had slipped into his chair, pausing to glare at the image before shoving the picture in Ellie's direction.

She tucked the photo back into her pocket. "I don't believe you."

A laugh rattled from the old man's chest, shaking his feeble body from head to toe. When he lifted his head, Ellie was taken aback again by the cruel glint in those pale blue eyes. "Yeah? What you gonna do about it, *Detective.* Lock me in the pokey because some stupid kid ran away? Good luck with that."

23

When Ellie pulled into an empty space in Roper St. Francis Hospital's visitor parking, her expectations were low. Further prodding of Pat O'Rierdon hadn't yielded any additional information and tempting as it would have been to call the old jerk's bluff and haul his miserable ass into a station, Ellie had no real cause to do so.

She dug the heels of her palms into her eye sockets, sighed, and then hopped out of the Explorer. The hospital was like a beacon of hope in the darkness, the sturdy three-story brick building awash with synthetic light. A gust of wind lifted the loose strands of Ellie's hair, carrying the earthy scent of rain.

Huddling her shoulders beneath her wool blazer, Ellie scurried across the parking lot and followed a sign that promised *Admissions* to a pair of sliding glass doors. Since Pat O'Rierdon hadn't given her a name, the hospital stop was based solely on the facility's proximity to the retirement center, along with a healthy dash of hope.

Not too much, though. HIPAA guidelines restricted the

amount of patient information that even the most coopera-
tive of administrators or health care professionals could
share. Without a court order, Ellie couldn't be too optimistic.

That didn't mean she couldn't try.

The sliding doors whirred open, and soft music filtered to
Ellie's ears as she slipped inside, along with that antiseptic
smell innate to most medical centers. Ellie did a quick scan
of the room before making her way toward the circular desk
in the middle of the lobby, where two women sat behind
monitors.

The woman who spotted Ellie first was young, maybe
early twenties, with an infectious grin and that kind of pixie
hair cut that Ellie loved but could never pull off with her
own wild curls.

Despite the welcoming grin, Ellie discarded the pixie cut
volunteer as too young for her purposes and focused on the
other woman instead. The second volunteer was much older,
probably mid-sixties at least. Prim expression, less approach-
able looking by far.

Ellie uttered an internal groan. Of course. Because
nothing in this investigation could possibly come easy.

"Hi," Ellie squinted at the name tag on the woman's high-
necked blouse, "Molly. I'm Detective Kline with CPD." Ellie
held up the badge. "Can I ask how long you've worked here
at this hospital?"

"May I see that, please?" Molly pointed at the badge.

"Of course." Ellie handed over the thin leather wallet
containing the shield. Molly took her time inspecting the
gold emblem before passing it back.

"Well, Detective Kline, I worked as a nurse here for
thirty-five years. Retired for going on three years now, but I
came back as a volunteer. Is there a particular reason why
you're asking?"

Thirty-five years. Plenty long.

Ellie tried and failed to squash the sudden burst of excitement in her chest. "I'm looking for information about a boy who may have been brought into this facility sixteen years ago."

Molly's expression grew shuttered. "I'm sorry, but I'm afraid that even if I could remember back that far, I'm not allowed to share information about any patients, past or present."

Pretty much the exact spiel she'd expected, but Ellie refused to give up that easily. "I'm looking for a boy. Well, he would be a man now, but he would have been twelve at the time. Big for his age. So pretty he could have been a model, and on the autism spectrum. He would have come in with a broken arm, and I'm guessing other bruises as well."

Because Ellie was watching Molly so intently, she caught the signs of recognition that flitted across the older woman's face. The slight widening of her eyes. The way her right hand flinched up toward her mouth before she snatched it back into her lap.

Molly knew something. Ellie could feel the certainty of it in her bones.

The woman's prim mouth puckered. "I'm sorry, but like I said before, I'm not allowed to discuss patients. Now, if you'll excuse me." The woman turned her attention to the monitor and started typing.

Dammit!

Ellie's previous excitement began to fizzle. "This is really important, or I wouldn't be asking."

No response.

"Please. There are lives at stake here."

The clicking of Molly's fingers on the keyboard ceased. Ellie held her breath, staring at the top of the woman's gray head and willing her to look up.

The clicking started again. A clear signal by Molly that any more pleas were a waste of time.

In what she knew would be a futile effort, Ellie left her business card on the desk. "Please call if you remember anything that could help me find the young man."

Feeling the curious gaze of the younger worker following her, Ellie turned and slinked away, frustration bitter on her tongue.

Now what?

She spied the administration office, but after performing a drive-by and overhearing the dour-faced man with a military buzz cut yell at someone on the phone for not following a protocol, she rejected that avenue as futile. Hospital administrators were notoriously tight-lipped regarding the protection of patient data anyway, and that guy seemed like the poster boy for following proper procedure. In this case, proper procedure would require a warrant, and Ellie didn't think she had a prayer's chance of getting a judge to sign one without more than a hunch for her to go on.

She poked into the gift shop next, but the woman behind the register was too young to be of any help. When the elderly male volunteer she intercepted just outside the store threatened to call hospital security, Ellie figured it was time to throw in the towel and leave.

Ellie exited the same sliding glass doors she'd entered. During her short foray inside, gray clouds had drowned out the stars, and a light drizzle was falling. Huddling under the protective awning in a vain effort to prevent her hair from frizzing everywhere, Ellie fished her phone from her pocket. The call she made rang five times, then went to voice mail.

She waited for the beep. "Clay, it's Ellie. I was just checking in to see if you had any updates yet. Hope you're okay. Call me back when you get a chance."

She ended the call and bit her lip, wondering where to go next.

Fat raindrops splattered the concrete outside the protection of the awning. Great. Like an idiot, she'd left her umbrella in the SUV. Ellie peered up at the stormy sky. Maybe she'd wait a minute and hope this was one of those quick South Carolina showers. The kind that finished before you had a chance to find your raincoat.

As she shifted her weight from foot to foot, the phone in her hand started ringing.

Clay. She lifted the phone to her ear without even looking at the screen.

"Hey, Clay, thanks for—"

A loud, delighted gasp cut Ellie off. "Sorry, dear, it's not Clay, but I'm glad to know that you two are still talking. Does this mean things are getting serious?"

Ellie covered the speaker with one hand and groaned. Seriously? She'd been so certain that it was Clay returning her call that she'd given her mother false hope.

She banged her forehead into her open palm. See? This was what she got for not checking the caller ID.

"Sorry, Mom, but Clay is a work partner, nothing else."

Helen Kline's sigh conveyed years of disappointment. Her mom had finally come around to Ellie's job, but the Kline matriarch had never once given up on the fantasy of her only daughter settling down and providing grandchildren. "Well, isn't that a shame. You two sure seemed to get along at Sunday dinner."

Ugh. And *this* was what she got for thinking she could bring a man home to Sunday dinner without her family jumping to wild conclusions. "Sunday dinners aren't exactly a betrothal."

Her mother interjected with an elegant little noise of protest, which Ellie ignored. "I'm assuming there's a reason that you called that doesn't involve poking at my dating life, or lack thereof. *Again.*"

"No need to get snippy, but yes, I was calling to see if you're free this Sunday evening. Your father was supposed to accompany me to a dinner party that's being hosted on behalf of a wealthy new businessman, but you know how he gets. He was moaning so much that I let him off the hook, but I'd really prefer not to go alone."

Oh, yay. A dinner party full of wealthy snobs, how tempting. "Can't you just skip this one?"

"I would, but I promised that I'd try to sway the guest of honor into opening up his checkbook for a fundraiser." Helen Kline heaved a dramatic sigh, as if attending was such a burden when she and Ellie both knew that her mother lived for such events. "Please? I thought it might be nice for the two of us to spend some time together."

Ellie rolled her eyes. Right. Just her and her mom…plus a roomful of rich socialites. Not her idea of a fun night, but she couldn't tell her mom that. She needed a better excuse. Work, or maybe a pre-existing commitment.

"I don't—"

Ellie broke off when the sliding doors whooshed open and Molly stepped out. The gray-haired woman glanced over her shoulder into the hospital lobby before turning back toward Ellie.

"I'm sorry, dear, I think you cut out. Was that a yes?"

Molly took a step in Ellie's direction, hesitated, then checked behind her again before taking another. Halfway there, she faltered.

Ellie sensed that every passing second brought the ex-nurse closer to bolting. No time to argue with Helen Kline now. "Sure, Mom, but I've got to go. I'll call you later."

She hung up on her mother's cry of delight and nodded at

Molly. "Is there somewhere nearby where I can buy you a cup of coffee?"

LESS THAN TEN MINUTES LATER, Ellie arrived at a cute little café called Cuppa Joe tucked into a strip mall located a couple miles away from the hospital. Molly had given Ellie the name and told her to meet her there, saying she didn't feel comfortable talking at a closer spot where hospital personnel were bound to hang out.

The entire drive to the café, Ellie had been kicking herself, convinced that the nurse would bail, but when she pushed open the bright blue door decorated with a logo that featured a steaming red cup, Molly hovered just inside.

The tension in Ellie's neck eased. "Thanks for meeting me here. What can I get for you?"

"Hot green tea, please. Coffee upsets my stomach. I'll grab us a table while you wait."

While she stood in the short line, Ellie inhaled the fragrant aroma of coffee beans and appraised the interior. Based on the colorful array of cups dangling from the ceiling and painted on the walls, the café took the *cuppa* in its name seriously.

Within a few minutes, Ellie carried two steaming mugs over to the little round table Molly had chosen, nestled beneath an abstract mural of smiling purple and yellow coffee cups by the back wall. Along the way, she passed a few writers huddled over their laptops and a small group of women dressed in yoga pants and sweatshirts. No one was dressed in scrubs or sported a hospital lanyard.

She hoped that was enough to assuage Molly's fears and help the ex-employee to open up.

"Here you go." Ellie set the oversized red mug within Molly's reach before slipping into the empty chair.

Molly sipped the hot beverage and exhaled. "Thank you, this hits the spot."

Ellie sampled her own latte, poured into a teal mug with yellow stripes. Delicious, but then again, she rarely met a coffee she didn't like. After giving the other woman a chance to settle, Ellie pushed the photo of Lucas across the table.

With a shaky hand, Molly reached for the picture and lifted it closer to her face. Moisture filled her gray eyes. "That poor boy. How much pain should one child be called upon to bear?"

"You do remember him."

Molly bobbed her head. "Yes. I almost never worked the emergency ward, but the night he came in was just one of those days. Lots of nurses were out sick, so we were short-staffed and there'd been a multi-car accident. We needed extra hands on deck. That's why I was there in the ER when she brought him in."

Progress, at last. Ellie leaned forward. "Who brought him in?"

"An old woman. I remember because she was too old to be his mother, and very feeble. The whole time she was there, she kept coughing and gasping for air. And the boy, well, he'd broken his arm, so he needed x-rays and a cast, but he was freaked out and not handling being in the hospital very well. You mentioned he's autistic?"

"Yes."

Molly studied the photo, nodding. "It fits. Back when I went to nursing school, they didn't teach us about autism, but growing up, my youngest brother had quirks that fit. That's who I kept picturing when I talked to Lucas. My little brother, Bobby. Maybe that's the reason Lucas responded to me better than the other staff, because I had experience working with kids like that. I'm the one who ended up filling out his chart and helped to calm him down enough to get situated while we waited for the doctor to come examine him."

"Do you remember anything that Lucas said?"

The woman's thin lips curved up. "Yes. He taught me all sorts of facts about camping and surviving in the woods. I remember with Bobby growing up, it was baseball statistics. He was obsessed with them as a kid."

Ellie swallowed a sip of her latte, even more excited now. The camping detail all but confirmed that the boy that Molly remembered was Lucas. "I've heard that Lucas loved camping from multiple sources now. What about his living situation, or the broken arm?"

Molly's mouth flattened as she swirled tea in the mug. "He refused to talk about either of those two things, his guardians, or how he injured his arm. When the doctor came in to reset the bone, he asked too, but Lucas wouldn't tell him either. I mean, the type of fracture he had, along with all those old bruises, made it pretty clear that the break was no accident. But we never heard that directly from him."

Ellie hid her disappointment with another sip of her latte. If this proved to be a dead end too, she had no idea where to go next. "Did he talk to anyone else during that visit?"

"Well, he saw a social worker, but apparently he really didn't want to talk to her, because next thing I heard, he'd run away." Molly wrapped her hands around the mug, as if taking comfort from the warmth. "The old woman who brought him in didn't seem too torn up about his disappearance. She told us 'that happens sometimes.' Not that any of us believed her, but what could we do?"

Ellie gaped, unable to process what she'd heard. "Wait, hold up. Are you saying that a twelve-year-old boy ran away from the hospital, and no one thought to call the police?"

Molly sighed. "He was thirteen, working on fourteen at the time, but trust me, I suggested it, but the psychiatrist shot me down. He said between the social worker and him, they had the situation under control, and that the police would find Lucas and lock him up in some seedy juvenile detention center." She shook her head. "All I could think was how awful that would have been for Bobby, to be stuck in a place like that."

While the woman's chin wobbled at the memory, the nerve endings in Ellie's skin tingled a warning. *Psychiatrist.* She scrolled through her phone until she located the correct photo.

"You mentioned a psychiatrist. By any chance, do you remember if he looked like this?"

Molly took her time examining the pre-surgery image of Dr. Kingsley. "It's been so long, I can't be one-hundred percent sure, but yes, the man in that photo looks familiar."

By now, Ellie couldn't even pretend to feel surprised that yet another case led back to Kingsley.

She ground her molars together, glaring at that hateful face in the photo. Earlier, Molly had wondered aloud how much pain one child should have to endure. The question that haunted Ellie was, *how much pain could a single man inflict?*

Left to his own devices, Kingsley's capacity to hurt others appeared to know no limits.

All the more reason to shut him down. As soon as possible.

Ellie drained the remainder of her latte and pushed back her chair. "Well, thank you so much for speaking with me, Molly. I appreciate your honesty."

"Wait."

The single word reached Ellie as she pushed to her feet. "What is it?"

"The cabin. Did you try hunting for any clues from that cabin where they found the boy?"

Ellie's butt hit the seat hard. She stared at Molly, pulse climbing. "What cabin?"

Molly's gray eyes rounded. "Oh, I, uh...it's nothing. I must have gotten confused there for a second. Happens when you reach my age." She waved her hand and exhaled a shaky laugh in an attempt to cover her blunder.

Ellie leaned her elbows on the table and narrowed her eyes. "Maybe so, but we both know that a senior moment isn't the reason you brought up a cabin. Please, Molly. You agreed to meet me here, and already shared so much. I know you want to help. Why hold back now?" The woman wrung her hands together, so Ellie applied more pressure. "Especially if this might be the one thing that helps me save other kids like Lucas."

Molly folded. "A few years after Lucas ran away, a boy was found in the Croatian National Forest in North Carolina. I could've sworn it was the same Lucas, even though the last name was different. I remember feeling so happy that he'd escaped those terrible people who'd hurt him."

"Did you say anything to the authorities?"

Molly shook her head. "No. I was too afraid that the psychiatrist was right about juvenile hall, or worse, that they'd return him to the family who'd been beating on him. I figured he was better off in the mental institution than either of those other options."

The sudden revelations of the past two minutes were making Ellie dizzy. She pressed her forearms into the table. "I'm sorry, but did you just say mental institution?"

The color evaporated from Molly's cheeks. "I...you should talk to someone who works for the Croatian National Forest. They can tell you more."

When no amount of Ellie's prodding or pleading worked to loosen Molly's tongue further, she said her goodbyes and hurried out of the café.

As drizzle kissed her cheeks on the way to the Explorer, Ellie repeated the name in her mind.

Croatian National Forest.

She unlocked the Explorer and hopped inside. "Don't worry, Molly. Talking to someone at the forest is next on my list."

24

"Here, try this."

Slouched in the passenger seat of Katarina's car, Clayne fished a flask from his jacket pocket. Liquid sloshed inside as he shook the silver container in her direction.

What the hell?

Katarina accepted the flask, unscrewing the top and tilting it to her mouth. The aroma bit her nose an instant before the alcohol burned a trail down her throat. She shivered, relishing the burn.

After one more swig, she passed the whiskey back to Clayne, who chugged for an impressive amount of time before wiping his mouth. "So, what's the plan?"

She stared out the window at the cabin that Mick had disappeared into less than an hour ago and asked herself the same question. What was her plan? On the drive out to the remote rental, she'd been all set to go. She would sneak inside, subdue Mick, and force him to help her find her baby. Then Clayne had shown up, and uncertainty now niggled at her.

From the corner of her eye, Katarina watched Clayne

screw the lid back on the flask before slipping it into his pocket. No doubt about it, a partner would make her plan easier to execute. Especially a man of Clayne's size and strength. But could she trust him? That was the uncertainty holding her back.

"Babe?" He headbutted her in the shoulder like a teenage boy.

"Hold on, I'm thinking."

She drummed her fingers on the steering wheel. For Katarina's entire life, she'd never been able to trust anyone. Not fully. Even the people who'd shown her kindness along the way had expected payment in return, sometimes in the form of Katarina serving a specific role in their lives, or more often, through completion of a job or task.

Now that she was an adult and on her own, Katarina had no interest in dancing to someone else's tune.

Yet, for all his faults, Clayne had never given Katarina that user vibe. She believed that the brawny, small-town drug dealer really did care about her. As much as he could in his messed-up way.

Clayne patted her thigh with his big hand, and that small gesture was what ended up tipping the scales.

"I think that Mick is an undercover cop who was sent out to Wyoming to keep tabs on me."

The reassuring pressure on her leg turned into a tight band before Clayne released her. "Why would a cop want to watch you, I wonder? I think someone hasn't told me everything about her past."

If Katarina brought up Kingsley now, and why she thought the bloodthirsty psychiatrist who'd raised her for over half of her life would send a henchman to spy on her, they'd be trapped in this car all night.

"I figured if Mick has been following me, then he might have an idea of who snatched Bethany." Katarina bunched her hands in his shirt. "Are you man enough to help me go in there and find out?"

Not particularly subtle, but the manipulation did its job, as she'd known it would. Clayne downed another swig of whiskey as he reached for the door. "Damn right, I'm man enough. You just watch."

With a low growl, he jumped out and stormed through the trees toward the cabin. Katarina pocketed the knife she dropped earlier and scrambled after him, jogging to catch up. Her original plan had involved tricking her way inside, but Clayne put an end to that the second he pounded up the single porch step and kicked in the door.

"What the...*Clayne?*"

Mick shot to his feet from the small couch in front of a fireplace, his forehead rumpled in confusion when he recognized the intruders.

Katarina capitalized on his momentary surprise by darting forward while he was still in a state of shock. More importantly, before he remembered to reach for a gun.

"The fuck do you think you're doing?" Mick blinked off the last of his surprise when Clayne rushed forward, driving his forehead into the other man's chest. The momentum pushed Mick back. He staggered but somehow kept his feet.

"That's it, you prick." With a roar, Mick leapt at Clayne.

The two men traded blows. Mick ignored Katarina, leaving her with the perfect opening. While his focus centered on his opponent, Katarina lashed out and swept his legs out from under him.

Mick hit the floor hard, and they managed to restrain him and tie him up with the rope Katarina provided without too much hassle.

At Katarina's bidding, Clayne lifted the other man beneath the armpits and dropped him into a chair. Clayne held him in place while Katarina tied his bound wrists to the chair back's railing. She secured his ankles next before rising and looming over him.

Mick's eye was already swelling shut and turning a spectacular shade of purple, courtesy of Clayne's right hook. His uninjured eye was wide and afraid, though, as he tried to speak through the duct tape Katarina had slapped on his mouth.

She tapped a finger against the gray tape. "Shh, don't worry, you'll get your chance to speak soon enough. First, I want you to listen very carefully. I'm in a hurry, so no jacking around. Let's start from the beginning. How long have you been following me, and who put you up to it?"

Using her fingernails, Katarina grabbed an edge of the tape and ripped the strip off Mick's mouth. He flinched but didn't yelp. "Lady, I have no idea what you're talking about. Why would I be following you?"

"I guess you missed the part where I said I was in a hurry and in no mood for games, huh?"

"Look, I don't know wha—" He screamed when Katarina cut him off with a vicious backhand to his bruised cheek.

"Answer my questions and save us all the hassle. Who hired you to follow me?"

"You're out of your mind." Mick craned his head to appeal to Clayne. "You gonna do something about this chick of yours? She's psycho."

Clayne's hands shot out and wrapped around Mick's neck, only releasing their hold when the other man turned a blazing red color. "I suggest you watch your manners and answer her questions, or your family's going to be picking you up in pieces."

The other man's Adam's apple bobbed. "I have no idea what's happening here, but I'm not lying. I wasn't following her and have no idea why someone else would."

Ten minutes passed, with Katarina's frustration spiraling

to the breaking point. Fresh blood trickled from Mick's nose, but the damn man refused to break, stubbornly insisting that he knew nothing. Even after Clayne punched him a few more times to loosen his tongue.

Katarina glared at his battered face, and her patience snapped. Katarina stalked into the tiny kitchen, snatched a knife off the counter, and returned to the captive. The second the thick wooden handle filled her hand, a numbing sense of calm descended. The knife felt good. Familiar. Just the tool to inspire a man to talk.

And better than using Katarina's own knife, since this one couldn't be traced back to her.

"I'll ask again, who sent you to spy on me?"

Mick's eyes followed the silver blade as Katarina twirled it a few inches from his nose. "The answer's same as before, no one."

"Liar!" Her hand flashed forward, and a thin, red streak appeared on Mick's cheek.

He jerked away, air hissing between his teeth while Clayne placed a cautionary hand on her forearm. "Easy, babe. Don't get too carried away."

Don't get too carried away? Katarina's indignant gaze flew to his, but then he winked and she caught on. Good cop, bad cop. She could play along.

As long as she got to be the bad cop.

They made a good team, her and Clayne. For all the good it did. No matter how hard they pushed him, Mick answered the same way.

He had no idea who or why someone was following her, but it wasn't him.

This time, after Clayne's fist caught him across the jaw, Mick's chin sagged toward his lap, and he didn't move.

Bullshit. She didn't have time for this. Growling, Katarina

yanked on his hair, pulling his head up. "Wake up, you big wuss."

Mick's eyelids fluttered but remained shut. Katarina let go of his hair, and his chin fell back to his chest. Useless. So far, this entire plan was a massive waste of time. And Bethany didn't have time to spare.

Bethany. Where are you?

By refusing to tell the truth, this asshole might as well be the monster who'd ripped her daughter away from her. Always men, taking from her. Never believing they'd have to pay.

Pain tore at Katarina's soul, propelled her hand overhead. The blade hovered there like a promise. *Finish him. He deserves no less.*

Her hand squeezed the handle as memories flashed behind her eyes. Images of other lives she'd snuffed out. So many people. Dead by her hand. What was one more?

Then she saw Bethany's face. Heard her daughter's giggle as she tucked her into bed.

You promised that you'd try to do better. Be better. For her sake. Clayne was only ever meant to be a means to an end, a way to get money so that you and Bethany could escape to an island, remember?

The white beach. Bethany, splashing in the clear blue water.

Just the two of them, living a better life.

Katarina's grip loosened, and the knife dropped to the floor. She retreated a step, chest heaving.

"Why'd you stop?" Clayne stooped down to retrieve the knife.

"Killing a cop puts too much heat on us. I don't want you to be looking over your shoulder for the rest of your life because I lost my cool." A half-truth. No one but Katarina needed to know about her vow to be a better person for her daughter's sake.

"So, what's next?"

Katarina studied the dozing man with a sigh. "We wait for him to wake up. Cops might think they're big and tough, but trust me, he won't last another round with the dream team."

She prayed that she was right.

Clayne snorted. "Dream team, huh?"

But Katarina could tell he secretly liked the fact that she'd called the two of them a team.

Mick moaned. Good. They could get on with it soon. She grabbed his hair to check his eyes again. Her phone rang first, so she let go and retrieved the device from her pocket.

"Seriously? Who could be calling right now that's more important than this?"

"Wouldn't you like to know?" Katarina had no clue, but she'd given the school her number. Maybe they'd gotten a lead, or better yet, this was all some big mix-up, and that irritating office lady was calling to tell her that Bethany was back, safe and sound.

The fantasy died once the screen came into focus. Katarina's fingers went numb while the blood rushed to her ears. *No. Please, no.* She shook her head back and forth and the frenzied motion made the room spin, causing her to lose her balance and stagger.

"You okay? Let me see that, what the hell's going on?"

Clayne tried to wrench the phone from her hand, but she evaded him, stalking over to Mick.

Slap!

Katarina's palm connected with his cheek...again and again. She didn't stop until her skin burned, and Mick finally cracked open his swollen eyes.

"When was the last time you were in Charleston? Did Kingsley pay you?"

Still disoriented, Mick blinked up at her, and Katarina's heart froze. The confusion on his battered face was real.

"Kingsley? I don't know who that is. I'm here for work, from Savannah."

This time, Katarina believed him. *Dammit*. Mick had no idea who Kingsley was. She had the wrong guy.

With a howl of rage, she grabbed the knife off the table. Air whizzed as the blade somersaulted before burying itself in the wall.

"Dammit, Katrina, what's going on? Who was that on the phone, and who the fuck is Kingsley?"

Wordlessly, Katarina pulled up the picture, holding the screen up so Clayne could see too. And even though this was her second time viewing the image, Katarina's heart plummeted to the floor.

Bethany sat bound to a chair with a wide strip of duct tape strapped across her mouth. Dark circles formed beneath her reddened eyes, but it was the glassy expression in them that filled Katarina with helpless fury. Her little girl looked scared.

The worst part, though, was the yellow square of construction paper stuck to her chest that read, *Fun Charleston vacation with Papa.*

There was no more room for doubt.

Kingsley had taken her baby.

25

Bethany scrunched down in the chair, making herself as small as possible as the man walked back and forth with a black cell phone pressed to his ear. One of those weird, grandpa types of phones that folded in half and didn't even have YouTube.

Except the stranger looked too scary to be someone's grandpa.

The man passed by again, giving Bethany a clear view of his profile, and goose bumps erupted on her arms. His face was weird. All sharp and bony with eyeballs that sank into his head. He reminded Bethany of a Halloween skeleton, or maybe a zombie.

The man glanced her way, and she shivered. She didn't like the way he looked at her. Or like being here at all. Wherever here was.

Bethany tugged at her wrists, but they were still tied way too tight. Same with her feet. Her chest started to hurt again, but her whimper was trapped by the tape the skeleton man had slapped over her mouth the first time she'd woken up in the trunk of a car. The skeleton man had lifted her out and carried her up the steps and through the door of a tiny airplane.

When Bethany had looked around inside the little compartment full of couches and leather seats and big TV screens and couldn't find her mama sitting anywhere, Bethany had panicked for real. She'd shrieked into the tape and kicked her legs, wiggling until the man ripped the tape off her face, raised a glass full of orange soda to her lips, and pinched her nose until she choked it down.

The next time she woke up, it was dark outside, and she was in the back seat of a car. Bethany would've tried to jump out the back door, but with her hands all tied up, she was afraid she'd hurt herself.

When the car stopped, the man climbed out and opened Bethany's door. One time at school, a policewoman had visited their class to talk to them about self-defense. The woman told them to run if anyone ever tried to grab them while they were walking down the street or shove them into a strange car, and either yell "Stranger danger!" or "Fire!" and head for the nearest woman or adult with a kid.

Bethany had never really understood why they were supposed to yell fire if there wasn't actually a fire, but the woman had made them promise. Right now, though, Bethany would yell just about anything if it meant someone would come save her. But even if her hands and feet weren't all tied up and her mouth wasn't covered, who would she run to out here? There was no one else. Just the tiny little cabin the man had carried her inside, just so he could tie her to a wooden chair.

She peeked around the cabin again. This place was all dark, with beat-up, dusty old furniture and holes in the walls, and everything smelled gross and stinky, like the inside of her friend Sarah's car when her mom smoked cigarettes out the window.

Bethany had stayed in hotels before. She liked those. Especially the ones that came with a little breakfast room down the hall. Sometimes, they only had bagels and bananas and cereal, but that was okay because she liked Fruit Loops, and they almost always had those.

A couple of times, though, the hotels had a long row full of different hot food too. Bethany didn't care much about the eggs and bacon and potato things, but the waffle bar, yum. That was the best thing ever.

Mama had let her help scoop the batter in the little cup and pour it into the waffle iron. Bethany watched for the light to flash, telling them it was time to flip the waffle over.

When the timer went off, Bethany had been so excited that she'd grabbed the waffle and burned the tip of her finger. She'd yelped and looked up at Katrina. She'd been worried that her mother would yell at her to be safer next time or embarrass her by treating her like a baby.

Not her mama, though. Her real mama had shaken her head, squatted down, put a finger under Bethany's chin, and gave her a serious look. "Be smarter than that next time."

Without giving her more of a lecture, she'd helped Bethany pour blueberry syrup all over her waffle and topped the whole thing off with whipped cream. She'd skipped back to their room, and together, they'd laid on the bed and watched a show about witches on the Disney channel.

That was the best kind of morning, in the best kind of hotel, with the best mama. Nothing like this place.

Bethany bit her lip as she searched the tiny kitchen. She didn't even see a microwave. She doubted there would be any waffles with blueberry syrup here. And whatever was playing on the old TV that sat near a crack in the wall, Bethany was sure it wasn't on the Disney channel.

She scowled at the rectangular screen. The TV was thick and had these weird sticks poking out the top, shaped like a

V, and the show was all in black and white. The people were dressed in strange clothes, like farmers or something, and when the people laughed, it sounded fake and way too loud.

Her throat started to feel all thick and scratchy, like it did before she was about to cry. She fought the urge. *Be strong*, her mama told her all the time. Like Wonder Woman.

Bethany tried to be strong like a superhero, but it was hard. This place was terrible, and the skeleton man scared her. He kept staring at her with this freaky smile, like one of the evil witches from a movie Bethany had once watched.

Right before the witch gobbled up a puppy.

Bethany wanted to go home. Her real home, with her real mommy, Katrina. The one who'd grown Bethany inside her belly.

"Did you know that, when you were in here," Katrina had put Bethany's hand on her stomach, "you used to kick me so hard that I would pee myself just a little?"

Bethany had giggled. "Did you wet the bed?"

"Almost! I swear, I sometimes thought you were trying out for the soccer team in there."

Bethany loved those stories about when she was just a tiny baby curled up inside her mama's tummy. So, so much. Not the later stories, though. She didn't like those at all when Katrina told them. The stories about how a bad man had stolen Bethany away from Katrina as a baby, before her mama ever got to see her even one time.

Until then, Bethany thought that Timmy Michaels was the meanest person in the entire world. He'd stolen her lunch once and dumped it all out in the trash. Another time, he'd made fun of her dress in front of the entire class.

That one lady she'd lived with for a little while when she was younger had yelled a lot too. Martha. Bethany remembered her as more crabby than mean, though.

But a person who stole a baby from their mama in the hospital? That had to be the worst kind of mean ever.

Bethany's other families had been pretty nice. The Jacksons, and then later, Kayla and Jake. Jake had turned out to be crabby Martha's son, which she thought was really weird, but at least he wasn't grumpy like his mom.

They'd been really happy to have Bethany, and Bethany thought she could have learned to be happy with them too. But then her real mama had come back, and she'd felt like the luckiest girl alive.

"How do I know you're not lying?"

The voice was loud, jerking Bethany back to the stinky cabin and the creepy man. He was still on the phone, but now his boots smacked the floor even harder, like her mama did sometimes when she was upset.

"You're just going to keep her for yourself!"

The skeleton stabbed his screen with one of his bony fingers and mumbled angry words under his breath while he stomped back and forth, back and forth. Bethany wondered what the other person on the phone had said to make him so mad.

For the next minute, she sat very still. Afraid that if she moved or made noise or interrupted his call, he'd be mad at her too. Every time he got close to the front window, he'd stop for a second and look outside. Bethany thought that was stupid. What was he even looking at? It was too dark to see much of anything.

Unless maybe he was searching for car lights.

After a while, Bethany grew tired of watching him. All he did was that same thing, over and over again. Wasn't he bored by now? Because she was. She was also scared, plus her hands were falling asleep from being tied to this stupid chair, and she was hungry and thirsty.

Her stomach clenched at the thought of food. She'd only

taken a few bites of her lunch today because she'd wanted to go play with her friends. Mama usually fixed Bethany a snack as soon as she came home from school. Ritz crackers with peanut butter, or string cheese and apple slices, or sometimes, if she was really lucky, Oreos. Then they ate dinner together at the little dining room table, and Bethany usually had another snack an hour before bed.

The stranger hadn't given her even one cracker since he'd picked her up from school.

Bethany's stomach growled. She tried to think about something besides crackers or cheese. But once Bethany started dreaming of food, she couldn't seem to stop. Anything sounded good right now. Even raisins, which she usually traded for her friend's banana at recess.

The skeleton man wasn't stomping as much now. Maybe if she asked him nicely, he'd give her something to eat? Bethany moved her lips, but the tape on her mouth stayed put. Next, she puffed her cheeks a bunch of times. Wiggled them back and forth. That didn't work either.

She blew air out her nose. There had to be a way. Maybe she could rub the tape off somehow? Bethany glanced around and slumped. The chair was stuck in the middle of the room, with nothing nearby to use.

Her ear started to itch, so she shrugged her shoulder up to scratch it. Then she went still. *Wait a second...*

Bethany tilted her head a little more to the side, to test out her idea. There! Now her shoulder was touching her cheek. Right where the tape started.

She rubbed her shoulder against the edge. After a few times, she felt the tape catch and start to unroll. Excitement made her move faster. She was doing it! She was—

"Stop that!"

Bethany jerked back so hard, the chair tipped. The skeleton man saved her from falling by grabbing her knees and shoving them toward the floor. The wooden chair legs hit with a bang.

He shook his head at her and started to turn away.

No! Bethany rocked her weight back again, carefully this time. Just hard enough to make that banging noise.

"What do you want?"

Bethany yelled with all her might. The tape turned the sound into a mumble but at least it was something. She yelled again and again while the man stared at her with that same expression her mama got just before she told Bethany she was being a pain in the butt.

The man threw his hands in the air. "This had better be good." He leaned over and ripped the tape off Bethany's mouth, blowing on her with his icky breath.

"Ouch!" Bethany flinched at the stinging sensation. Her throat clogged up, and her eyes burned.

Be brave, don't cry, she told herself, but some tears leaked out anyway. She couldn't help it. Her lips still burned from the tape, and now her tummy wouldn't stop growling. "I'm thirsty and hungry." *And scared and sad*. But she knew better than to say those out loud.

At first, the man didn't answer. He just stared at her with that creepy I-want-to-devour-a-puppy look on his face.

Bethany decided to try her best manners and ask a different way. "Can you please get me some water and a snack? I really like Oreos."

"My mother used to say that junk food rotted people from the inside out, and that's why we have so much sin in our country. If food didn't come from God, then we shouldn't pollute our God-given bodies with it, and that sometimes, we should go without any food at all." He rubbed his cheek the way Bethany did when she had a bruise. "She said suffering was the only way to build character. Sparing the rod spoils the child."

What did spare the rod mean? Bethany wrinkled her nose and blurted, "Not to be rude, but your mommy sounds weird."

The man stopped touching his cheek. He got really still, the way old Martha used to before she'd yell at Bethany for playing too loud or running through the house in muddy shoes. Bethany shivered, but to her surprise, Skeleton Man cackled. "My mother was a little weird, no doubt about that."

Even his laugh was creepy and sent shivers all over Bethany's skin. Even so, Bethany forced her mouth to smile back. Not because she cared about making Skeleton Man laugh, but because of something Katrina had taught her.

Mama had said that boys might have bigger muscles then girls, but girls were smarter. They just needed to learn to use the tools they had, and then they could usually beat the boys at just about any game.

"Like what?" Bethany remembered asking, picturing the look on stupid Ethan's face if she beat him at tetherball.

"Like smiling."

At the time, Bethany had frowned. "Smiling? That's not a tool. Are you teasing me, Mama?"

Her mama had poked her nose, making Bethany laugh. "No, I'm serious. When you smile at someone, they think you're interested in what they have to say and don't see you as a threat. It's easier to beat someone when they don't think you can."

Bethany had tilted her head, considering that for a second. "So, it's kind of like tricking them?"

"Exactly! Only it's their own fault if they're tricked, so there's no reason to feel bad. After all, no one told them that a smile should mean anything other than a smile, right?"

That made sense. Sort of.

"You'd be surprised at how helpful it can be, so can getting people to talk about themselves. Especially men. The more you get them to talk, the more likely they are to mess up and tell you something useful."

At that point, Bethany had yawned. She was eight. She didn't care much about men.

But she'd remembered.

Be smart, her mama had said. Too many times to count.

So, Bethany kept the smile on her face and sat up straight. *Be smart. Be strong. Get them to talk.*

But what could she possibly talk to this strange man about?

Another burst of fake laughter came from the boxy television, giving Bethany an idea. "What's that show you're watching on TV?"

The man turned his head to glance at the black and white characters in their weird farmer clothes. "It's called *Green Acres*."

Bethany's nose wrinkled. Even the name sounded dumb. Then she remembered that she was supposed to be smiling and gave the man another one of her fake smiles. Like the ones they made you do at school when the man came to take their class pictures. "I've never heard of that one before. Do you like it a lot?"

The man tapped his chin. "You know, I'm not really sure. It's the only show my mother allowed me to watch when I was your age. She was really strict about the television. She called a lot of the programs the work of Satan."

Okay, now *that* was super creepy. His mother sounded even scarier than him. But Bethany was good at pretend games. All she had to do was pretend he was a normal person and keep talking. "What's *Green Acres* about?"

He talked for a long time about the show, so long that Bethany's eyelids started to droop. She had to pinch her finger to keep herself awake. When he finished, she searched for a new topic. "What about…" Bethany looked down at her favorite caped crusader on her shirt. "Do you like her? She's one of my favorites."

He scoffed. "That's pornographic. Heathen characters made to tempt men into sin."

Um. She didn't understand that "p" word, but the intense way he was staring at her now with lips a little open freaked her out.

No more superhero women, but then what could she ask him next? When he reached for the roll of gray tape on the counter, Bethany knew she was running out of time. In desperation, she blurted the first thing that popped into her head. "What's going on? Why am I here?"

He whirled, his eyebrows pinched together. "Good little girls don't ask questions. My mother taught me that."

"Well, my mama told me that the only way you'll learn what you want to know is by asking questions, because other people can't read your mind."

That shut the man up for a long time. Bethany worried that she'd made him mad, but to her surprise, he didn't grab the tape. When he finally spoke, he surprised her even more. "What kind of food do you want to eat?"

Bethany didn't hesitate. "Pizza."

He stared at her just long enough that Bethany decided he was going to say no, but then he nodded and headed into the tiny kitchen. He popped open the yellow freezer and pulled one out. From the chair, she could tell it was pepperoni. Her favorite.

After he slid the pizza into the oven, he pulled a chair out and sat down, facing Bethany. Now that he was making her pizza, she felt a little braver. Even though he still watched her sometimes with that creepy look in his eye.

She asked him about his favorite animals, and if he liked sports. If he had any brothers or sisters, and what flavor of ice cream he liked the best.

The ice cream question made him mention his mother again, and how he'd never gotten to taste ice cream as a kid, but he liked it now.

The way he talked about his mother made Bethany sad inside. Even scary men deserved to have nice mamas who loved them and gave them ice cream. Maybe if his mama had let him eat ice cream and blueberry syrup as a kid, he wouldn't have grown up to be so scary.

"I'm sorry your mama wouldn't let you eat yummy things or watch other TV shows when you were little. That doesn't sound very fair."

This time when the man looked at her, there was an odd shimmer in his eyes. He cleared his throat, and in that instant, his face changed. It turned hard and mean. "Oh, yeah? Well, you sound like a nosy little girl, and maybe that means you don't need a nose anymore."

He jumped to his feet and lunged closer, pulling a knife from his pocket to wave near her nose. Bethany whimpered, her eyes glued to the shiny silver that whistled so close to her skin.

"I like the way blood looks on the end of a knife. So red and pure."

The black part of his eyes—the pupils, Bethany had learned in class—were so big now. Like he was about to change into a werewolf. She cringed back, but the chair wouldn't let her get away.

Be strong. Be strong.

She squeezed her eyes shut and trembled, waiting for the knife to bite into her nose. A buzzer dinged, but when nothing else happened, Bethany opened them again.

The man had stepped back, and his pupils were back to normal. He slid the knife into his pocket, walked over to the oven, and used a dish towel to pull the pizza out.

The smell of cheese and pepperoni drifted to Bethany,

and her mouth watered. Hunger replaced the fear that had gnawed at her...for now.

"It's all done. You can have one slice."

Bethany was so hungry, she could have easily eaten two or three, but she wasn't about to argue.

Be smart, her mama had told her.

And that's exactly what Bethany planned to do.

26

"Hi, you have reached National Forests in North Carolina..."

Ellie groaned and rocked back in her chair as she waited for the beep at the end of the pre-recorded message. She'd spent the past hour alone on the second floor of the Charleston Police Department, parked behind her desk while she scoured the internet for every article she could find on the boy who'd been discovered in the Croatian National Forest during that time frame.

Could the boy they'd rescued all those years ago really have been Lucas Harrison? So far, she wasn't any closer to proving or disproving Molly's claim. None of the articles mentioned a name, and her phone calls had all hit a dead end too. She'd hoped to talk to the forest ranger who'd rescued the boy, but his name made locating him without assistance outside of the forest service a real challenge.

Joel Matthews. Like there weren't thousands of those in the state, and that was assuming the ranger still lived nearby. For all Ellie knew, the man had retired to become a surf bum in Los Angeles or moved to Norway for the free health care.

Beep.

Ellie rattled off her information and why she was calling, ending by asking someone to call her back as soon as possible. Which, based on the recording, wouldn't happen until tomorrow after eight a.m. at the earliest.

After she hung up, Ellie drummed her fingers across the keyboard. Thinking. The ranger angle was a no-go after hours, but what about the mental institution? Those types of facilities were staffed around the clock.

She figured it was worth a shot.

Ellie clicked on the tab where a Google map was already displayed on the page. After plugging the term *mental hospital* into the "search nearby" prompt, the service pulled up the facility closest to the Croatian Forest. She tapped the number into her phone and waited.

The staff member who answered informed Ellie that the medical director had already gone home for the evening and wasn't expected back into the office until the following Monday morning.

"Can you give me his home number? This is regarding an important investigation."

The receptionist's voice dialed down, from lukewarm to frosty. "I'm sorry, but we aren't allowed to share that information without a warrant."

Dammit.

Through gritted teeth, Ellie asked to be transferred to the medical director's voice mail, just in case he checked his messages on the weekend. Once she was finished leaving a detailed message, she dropped the phone back in its cradle and looked around.

The entire bull pen was empty.

"Figures," she muttered.

The steady throb behind her eyes intensified into a full-on blaze of pain. She rubbed her temples as she debated what to do next. No doubt home was the smart choice. Pop a couple of acetaminophen and crawl into bed. Attempt to sleep more than five hours at a time for once.

But her mind was too full to switch off just yet. Names and faces and questions cycled through at a dizzying rate, like the final fifteen minutes of a spin class.

Lucas. Kingsley. Valerie. Plus all the other young, innocent victims from the giant stack of cases splashed across her desk.

Ellie snapped Lucas's file shut, pushing the folder to the side before dragging the next one toward her. She'd hit the wall with Lucas for now, so what? The other missing children deserved her attention too.

A knock jerked her head toward the hall. Clay leaned against the doorjamb, his knuckles resting against the wall. "You're working late."

"Yeah. My mind's racing too much to sleep anyway, so I figured I might as well keep plugging away. Any news on Val?"

He ambled into the room with that easy, loose gait she admired, stopping to snag her neighbor's chair. He spun the back to face her before straddling the seat and folding his arms along the top. "Not yet, though not from lack of trying. Charlotte Cross is handling the case."

Ellie tilted her head, analyzing his expression. "You like her."

Clay nodded. "I do. She's smart and determined. I get a good vibe."

"Me too. I just wish Valerie had been located already. I'm really worried."

"We'll find her."

Ellie believed him. Clay was good at his job, the best. And Charlotte Cross had a fire inside her that reassured Ellie that the Savannah cop wouldn't rest until she tracked Valerie down.

The part that worried Ellie was...*when?* Before Kingsley had a chance to torture another brave woman to death? Or after?

"What about you, anything interesting happen today?"

Wow, where to start? Ellie thought back over the past twelve hours and couldn't believe the events hadn't spanned an entire week.

"Lots. Starting this morning with Vasquez. A couple of days ago, he was in my face, practically victim shaming me for having survived Kingsley. Today, he saunters in and drops a social services report on my desk." She tapped the file folder.

Clay picked it up. "Summerville?"

"Yeah. It's an internal investigation into a small retirement community in Summerville where they were buying children to serve as free labor for the elderly. One day he's all but accusing me of being in league with Kingsley, the next, he's acting cagey and helping me with my current cases." Ellie wished she could put a finger on why she disliked the man so much, but instinct was all she had. "I don't trust that man at all, and his Jekyll and Hyde routine just increases my doubt."

"He's probably just passionate about the work and gets a little overzealous sometimes, same as you and me. I wouldn't sweat it."

Easy for him to say. Clay hadn't been there when Vasquez snarled at her over Kingsley like a rabid wolf. Ellie debated pressing the issue, but when she opened her mouth, a yawn came out instead. Clay tossed the folder onto her desk.

"Look at the time. It's after midnight, which means you've been going nonstop since whenever you got up this morning, five? Six? You look exhausted, so why don't you let me drive you home?"

As quick as pushing a button, Clay's quiet declaration killed the adrenaline buzz flowing through Ellie. She *was* exhausted. "What about you? You look like you could use a good night's sleep yourself." Dark shadows smudged the area beneath Clay's eyes.

"I can sleep when I'm dead."

Ellie hated that expression, hated the way her skin chilled at the thought of death's eager hands reaching out for Clay.

Forcing her mind from that morbid path, she gathered her things but allowed Clay to herd her out of the building and into the passenger seat of her SUV. The bodyguard on duty followed behind them as Clay drove to her apartment complex, accompanied by music from a smooth jazz station.

Inside, the apartment was dark, so Ellie flipped on the lights as she headed for the kitchen. A flash of bright orange on the counter caught her eye. A note from Jillian.

Ellie,

There's half a pizza in the fridge. See you tomorrow, catching up on lost time with Jacob tonight.

xo your roomie

Ellie passed Clay the note. "The two of them are so cute it's kind of sickening, don't you think?"

Instead of laughing or agreeing, Clay's expression turned serious. "What I think is that Jacob's a lucky man."

Something deep inside Ellie's stomach twisted in response to his intense gaze, but instead of leaning into the feeling, she snorted. "Sure he is. For now. But what happens over time, when he's away for too long, or too wrapped up in a case to pay enough attention to her, or she's worried all the time for his safety, and they start fighting? Sooner or later, it's bound to end badly. All the statistics agree that cops make terrible romantic partners."

Several seconds of silence passed before Clay lifted a shoulder. "Sometimes the payoff is worth the risk."

His steady gaze never wavered from her face when he spoke, and the intense gleam in those golden eyes stole the air from Ellie's lungs. Only an idiot wouldn't realize that this conversation had somehow shifted away from Jacob and Jillian.

She drew in a stilted breath, mesmerized by the hunger emanating from the rugged agent in waves. "I-I'm not always that great with risks."

Heart pounding, Ellie moistened her lips with her tongue. Clay's gaze tracked the motion and remained stuck on her mouth even once she finished, full of the same yearning that a heroin addict shows a needle. It was like his naked desire unlocked Ellie's own, because heat surged low in her belly, filling her with a sense of urgency.

They reached for each other at the same time. Lips locking together. Hands everywhere, in a frantic rush to touch and be touched, to stroke warm skin. After so many weeks of locking her feelings for Clay up into a tiny box and shoving the entire thing into a trap door in her mind, Ellie had almost convinced herself that those longings had disappeared. Or at least, dwindled.

Now, she realized how much she'd been deluding herself. If anything, the force with which her body throbbed and her heart sang suggested her feelings for the agent had bred and multiplied.

As one, they stumbled in the direction of the couch. Ellie pulled her lips away from his only long enough to unbutton her blouse and rip it off. Clay used the pause to yank his own shirt over his head. Then they were kissing again, warm skin melding together, but soon, even that wasn't enough.

Ellie felt like she might implode if she didn't have all of him and fumbled with the belt looped through his pants, moaning with frustration when the accessory refused to cooperate quickly enough.

Afterward, with her body satiated and limp and Clay nestled beside her, Ellie drifted off right there on the couch, falling into the deepest sleep she'd experienced in weeks.

27

Clay opened his eyes to sunlight striking the gold threads laced throughout the comforter, courtesy of a gap in the curtains. When he stretched his arms overhead, the material moved, glimmering in that thin sliver of warmth.

Wait. His bedroom didn't have any curtains. Just those cheap plastic blinds that kept breaking off whenever he touched them.

Alarm burst through him, mobilizing his legs to spring out of bed a millisecond before his memory kicked in. Last night, he'd visited Ellie at the office. They'd ridden home together. Talked about Jacob and Jillian. A single kiss had quickly blazed into more, snapping the thin restraints that held the last of his self-control.

After that first round, they'd passed out on the couch together. Then, in the early hours of the morning, they'd stumbled their way to Ellie's bedroom for a repeat session, indulging in a more leisurely performance before sacking out again.

A soft snore emitted from the prone figure beside him.

Ellie was sprawled on her stomach with both hands flung over her head, still out cold. Even snoring, with half her face plastered to the sheet and her red hair tangled and wild, she was breathtaking. And she smelled delicious. Like sugar and spice and sex, all rolled into one.

Desire stirred in his loins, tempting Clay to wake her up for a third round, but he stopped short of touching her cheek to rouse her. Last night when he'd arrived at the office, she'd been teetering on the edge of exhaustion. She could use the extra sleep.

Clay eased off the bed and padded into the living room to collect his clothes. The discarded shirt and pants were no problem to locate, but his boxers proved more difficult. After turning in a few circles, he finally spotted them dangling behind a potted plant in the corner.

Damn. Guess he'd been a little too distracted by that point to worry about his aim.

Chuckling to himself in the quiet apartment, he dressed and headed for the kitchen, peeking inside the fridge to see what he had to work with in terms of breakfast. Eggs, cheese, ham, green peppers. Good enough to whip up a decent omelet.

As he cracked eggs into a bowl and heated a burner, he daydreamed about the events that had just transpired. When he'd offered to drive Ellie home, Clay's intentions had been pure. Sleep had been the only thing on his mind.

Clay shook his head, watching the egg mixture sizzle in the hot skillet. Who was he kidding? Sure, rest may very well have been the main goal at first, but when it came to Ellie, Clay's feelings were always lurking just beneath the surface. Biding their time until an opportunity presented itself.

The way one did last night.

He sprinkled cheese, diced ham, and bell pepper on top of the eggs, humming beneath his breath. Planned or not, he had no regrets. Ever since Ellie had backed away from the intimacy between them, Clay had fought to keep his attraction less blatant in order to minimize distress on her part. Plus, he didn't want to put their work relationship at risk.

But no matter how cool his outward appearance, Clay had never once lied to himself. He'd stubbornly clung to the dream that, one day in the not-too-distant future, Ellie would ditch her fears and open her heart to him. And yeah... that he'd end up back in her bed had been part of that fantasy too.

Clay shook the skillet, smiling as he hummed. He'd never fully believed that his fantasy would become reality.

Now that it had, he planned to savor the moment. And pray that the fact the sky had yet to fall in would convince Ellie of a truth he already understood. The two of them could have everything—the job and the relationship. The obstacle blocking their route to happiness was Ellie's reluctance to jump back in.

She wandered into the kitchen as he flipped the second omelet for the last time.

"Breakfast is served." Clay brandished the plate high on his hand like a suited waiter in a five-star restaurant before sliding the meal across the counter with a flourish.

His spirits waned when Ellie slumped into a chair and refused to look him in the eye, twirling a red curl around a slender finger.

"Thank you." She didn't move to take a bite.

Sirens wailed in his head. Had he miscalculated? Been so caught up in his own needs that he'd somehow neglected hers? No, last night had been great, for both of them. Clay had never been surer of anything in his life. But it didn't take an FBI agent's instincts to spot Ellie's discomfort.

A pit opened up in his gut. "Everything okay?"

She pushed the omelet around the plate without tasting it. "We need to talk."

Shit.

The pit deepened, becoming a bottomless well. The eggs, which had tasted delicious a few seconds ago, turned to a nauseating lump in his mouth. Clay guzzled water to force them down his throat, wishing he'd bolted out the front door as soon as he'd woken up. Anything to delay whatever doom Ellie was planning to drop on their relationship next.

A shrill ring disrupted his downward spiral.

"I need to grab this." Clay held up a finger while shooting a silent *thank you* to his caller for the temporary reprieve. "Special Agent Clay Lockwood."

"Agent Lockwood, I'm glad I reached you. This is Agent Dillon Moore with the DEA."

Clay frowned. The name was drawing a blank. "Hello, Agent Moore, what can I do for you?"

"We've never met, but I've been working undercover under the alias Mick Fortner to infiltrate a Midwestern drug operation that led me to a small town in Wyoming and a woman that I think you're acquainted with. Katrina Becker, or as you probably know her, Katarina Volkov."

Agent Moore's announcement propelled Clay to his feet. Hell. Katarina and drug dealer in the same sentence did not bode well. "You ran into Katarina?" When he repeated her name, Ellie's head jerked up.

"I did, last night. Or more like, she ran into me." The gruff voice paused for a beat. "She and her boyfriend—a low level guy trying to climb his way up in the business—showed up at my rental cabin out of nowhere. Fuckers tied me up, beat the shit out of me, even used a knife to try to get me to talk."

Clay swore. *Dammit, Katarina. What the hell were you thinking?* And why was he surprised?

"Are you okay?"

"Yeah, I'm fine, plus or minus a few dozen bruises and some fresh stitches. Guess she thought the old scars needed an update."

Under different circumstances, Clay would have chuckled at the man's self-deprecating humor. Not now, though. Every nerve was stretched taut, and he was too on edge to do much beyond grind his teeth while he stood by for further information.

"Look, I would've called sooner, but they drugged me, and once I came to, the damn knots they tied were a bitch to get out. The whole time they were working me over, I listened to their conversation, even when they thought I was unconscious."

Clay gripped the counter until his knuckles turned white. As sure as the sun rose every morning, he knew the news would be bad. From across the way, Ellie sat rigid, watching him with growing concern.

"And?"

"Sounds like Katarina's daughter was snatched by Kingsley. That's the reason they were interrogating me. She somehow got it stuck in her head that I was in on Kingsley's plan, and he'd sent me to spy on her. She believed that right up until she got a message on her phone. From their conversation, I'm pretty sure someone sent proof of life. Now, Katarina's on the way to Charleston to track her kid down, and damn, is she pissed."

Not just pissed...terrified.

The one person Katarina cared about besides herself was her little girl. "Thanks for calling. If you remember anything else..."

"Yeah, yeah, I know where to reach you."

Ellie pounced on Clay while he was still in the process of ending the call. "What is it? What's going on with Katarina?"

Clay braced his elbows on the counter while his mind

reeled. Whiplash from the rapid-fire mood swings of the past fifteen minutes. He'd kicked off the morning happy and hopeful about the status of his and Ellie's relationship, an optimism that morphed into anxiety the instant Ellie announced that they needed to talk. Moore called before Clay had a chance to process that emotion, switching him over to anger when he learned of Katarina's assault on a federal agent. Then he learned about Katarina's daughter and fear took the lead.

Christ. This was bad. Really bad.

He relayed the information to Ellie, noting how her green eyes grew wider and wider. She gasped when he reached the end, and her hands started to shake. "Dear god, Harmony is in danger again?"

The *again* echoed in his skull, reminding Clay of the story about the first time Ellie met Harmony. She'd run into the little girl and a woman leaving a store, and her gut instinct kicked in, warning her that something was amiss. Closer inspection confirmed to Ellie that the little girl's body language was off.

Suspecting that the girl was being kidnapped, Ellie had given chase to the woman. When the choice came down to the kid or her own skin, the abductor had chosen herself, tossing the little girl into the water so that Ellie would have no option but to dive in after her while the would-be-kidnapper zoomed away on a speed boat.

Clay grimaced. The would-be-kidnapper in that scenario had been Katarina, in the first of her wild attempts to reclaim the daughter who'd been stolen from her at sixteen.

In retrospect, that incident seemed quaint. The stakes now were so much higher.

"Everything we did to protect Harmony, and she still ended up in that monster's hands. That poor girl, she must be terrified."

The fear lacing Ellie's voice triggered Clay to snap a leash on his own. Her eyes glistened when he skirted the counter and enveloped her trembling hands in his. "Hey now. Don't forget who rescued that child those other times. You saved her before, and there's not a doubt in my mind that you'll do it again. And I'll be right by your side helping. Okay?"

A tremor wracked her body before she lifted her chin in that defiant manner that Clay loved so much. "Okay. Let's start planning. Before we do anything else, you need to check in with Katarina's marshal and see if she and Harmony are really gone."

Despite the situation's urgency, Clay allowed himself a moment to marvel at the woman before him. Deep wells of compassion combined with brains and fierce strength. Those were the traits that made Ellie Kline so remarkable. Even now, she was already whirling into action.

"While you call him, I'll try Frank," she named the marshal they'd worked with when Gabe disappeared, "see if he can help."

"Okay." Clay placed the call to the U.S. Marshal Service. After getting the runaround and being redirected twice, he finally convinced the person on the other end of the line of the gravity of the matter and got passed up the chain of command, to someone who promised to send Katrina's marshal out to perform a well check and get back to him ASAP.

When he finished, Ellie was tapping a pen against a list of phone numbers. "My call to Frank went to voice mail, so I started tackling airlines. We can call and see if passengers using the name Katrina Becker purchased a ticket to Charleston over the past twelve hours, see if we can intercept her at the airport. If she booked a red eye, though…"

Clay's jaw tightened. "Then she's already here, leaving us

swinging in the wind. Yeah, I know. But for now, that's our best play."

"Okay. Let me throw on some clean clothes and we'll head out. I'll call Fortis on the way, persuade him to round up as much manpower as possible to send to the airport."

Clay watched her disappear into the bedroom before collecting their plates and scraping the untouched meals into the trash. He was leaning against the front door, keys in hand, when she reemerged, dressed in a fresh pair of gray pants and a teal blouse, with her red hair scraped back into a hasty ponytail.

He straightened. "Ready?"

"Don't have much of a choice."

Clay moved to open the door for her, but Ellie rushed forward and beat him to the punch, all business as she swept out of the apartment ahead of him. Clay trailed a couple of feet behind, snatching one last glimpse of the couch before the door shut and cut off his view. As he retraced their steps from the previous night, he sighed.

What a difference twelve hours could make.

With that final thought, he shoved his personal life to the side where it belonged and focused all his energy on locating Katarina Volkov. If they got lucky, she'd lead them straight to Harmony and the madman who took her.

And if not...

Clay shrugged off the morbid sensation that shivered across his skin and lengthened his stride.

If not, well, they'd just have to make their own luck.

A little girl's life depended on it.

28

Through the hidden camera I'd set up in the bathroom, I watched the woman hurry through a shower, tsking when her jerky movements made the bar of soap slip from her grasp yet again as she attempted to lather up her legs.

"Dammit!"

She kicked the wall, yelping when she stubbed her toe.

I chuckled at her little temper tantrum from behind the monitor. "Oh, Valerie, you have no idea how much your distress delights me."

Her distress, and her obliviousness. Because I was confident that poor, sweet Valerie didn't suspect for one second that I was privy to all her grooming rituals via my handy technological devices. If she did, she never would have shed her dirty clothes and climbed under the rain shower spray in the first place.

The shower shut off, and I steepled my fingers. Ah, now we were getting to the good part. As Valerie climbed out and wrapped a towel around her body, I leaned closer to the screen, hungry to devour every nuance of her expression when she spotted my gift in the attached bedroom. Oh, her naked, glistening skin was attractive enough, but true satisfaction wasn't achieved through carnal lust.

Rather, it was earned through the art of toying with one's prey.

Common men spent the majority of their lives salivating over the promise of female flesh. Captives to their base instincts. No better, for the most part, than mindless, rutting beasts.

Only an erudite like myself—no, an *artist*—rose above such pedestrian pursuits to seek out elevated fulfillment instead. Nothing compared to the exquisite experience of stripping humans of their dignity. Of torturing fragile bodies and minds until survival—in all its resplendent, vicious glory —became their singular motivation.

I clicked a button to split the picture on the monitor into four quarters, warmed by Valerie's antics as she ran to the window, clutching the towel to her breast. After rattling the lock to no avail and peering down at the jagged rocks waiting below, she banged the glass one last time for good before giving up and retreating to the small pile of clothing I'd arranged near the footboard of a magnificent four-poster bed.

The additional three cameras in the bedroom were positioned to record this next reaction. I held my breath, anticipation dancing across my skin. My lovely guest didn't disappoint.

When she lifted the frilly, lace-trimmed pink panties with the bright pink bow in the center, confusion rumpled her forehead at first. She glanced down at the bed to where a pair of white ankle socks and a tiny, matching pink t-shirt waited. Fitted and cropped to reveal her belly button.

When the significance clicked, her lips pinched together, and she dropped the panties like they burned to the touch.

"You son of a bitch! You think you're funny, trying to dress me like that sick pathetic asshole you sold me to?"

Truth be told? I did find it rather amusing to give Valerie the exact same outfit she'd been forced to wear every day for months while old, feeble Arthur Fink with his little girl fetish leered at her from the safety of his bedroom.

"I'm not wearing any of this filthy stuff, do you hear me? Screw! You!"

She snatched up the clothing and flung them at the wall. Once they hit the floor, she ran over to stomp on the garments with so much adorable vigor that her sopping hair sprayed water droplets.

I flipped a switch on the console. "My, my, someone is rather testy this evening, aren't they? I won't force you to wear them but do know this. You won't be leaving that room until you're dressed in the outfit I so graciously provided."

Satisfied by the way she jumped when the speaker transmitted my voice, I sat back and grinned while my mind wandered.

A scrawny boy with the protruding sternum of a plucked pigeon stood naked and trembling in the middle of the cafeteria. The headmaster prowled a wide circle around him, smacking a leather strap into his palm with every slow, considered step

"This unnecessarily vulgar display is on your head. I gave you ample warning that school uniforms were either to be worn properly or else you'd lose the privilege of wearing one at all. You made your choice by thwarting the dress code, which is why we are here now being forced to witness this grotesque display."

From my spot at a nearby table, I watched the vignette play out in the hushed room. Horrified yet also intrigued. Until that very moment, I'd never considered the power of clothing, or lack thereof. Or the way it could be used to exert control over someone.

My phone pealed with an alert, a notification that Milos had arrived with Katarina's brat in tow. I leapt to my feet and all but danced my way down the stairs. After an aggravating number of setbacks, the pieces of my plan were finally falling into place. So perfectly that I wanted to throw my head back and shout my glee up to vaulted ceilings that had served as silent witness over years of stilted family vacations.

But I had too much control to fall prey to such an impulsive gesture, so I limited myself to a measured smile.

One that doubled in size when I opened the door to admit Katarina's offspring and Milos. "Come in, come in." I swept the door open wide with a flourish, stepping aside to make space.

The little girl ushered inside by Milos was thin without being gawky, with the same blonde hair and splash of freckles across her nose and cheeks that I recognized from photos. As she scurried by, I detected a hint of strawberries and sweat of the sweet, prepubescent variety exuded by children before they ripened into adults.

The thing I hadn't been expecting, though, was the impact of the wide brown eyes when they landed on me. So similar in shape and size to her mother's that I was struck silent for a moment.

Had my Katarina ever looked so innocent? I considered the question as an odd sensation thrummed through my vessels.

"Well, hello there, Harmony. You won't remember me, but I've met you before, a long time ago."

I even squatted down to her level to show that I was no threat. A lie, of course, but she'd learn the truth soon enough.

The little girl's chin trembled before she scurried back to Milos, plastering herself to his side and clinging to his hand. It was rather shocking. She acted as if I was the one with the ugly, cadaverous face, and he was the one sporting Hollywood-level good looks, courtesy of a skilled plastic surgeon.

Milos's jaw gaped as he stared at the girl clutching him

like he was a human teddy bear, but I could see the predatory look in his eyes. He would soon be disappointed.

My good mood soured a little as I straightened to my full height. Harmony peeped out from behind Milos, sneaking glances when she thought I was distracted. The notion that Katarina's daughter might prefer Milos, of all people, to me was absurd to the point of shock.

"I still get to keep her, right? As payment once this is all over?"

Those were the first words that Milos uttered. My eye twitched over his lack of decorum, but I controlled the pulse of anger, keeping my tone mild. "And good evening to you too, Milos. I hope your trip went smoothly. Can I offer you something to eat or drink?"

I dodged his question with one of my own. No need to upset the poor man until I was sure of my intentions.

After Katarina, I'd never expected to want another daughter, but now that Harmony was here, only two years shy of the age her mother had been when I'd removed her from those dreadful adoptive parents, I couldn't help but imagine all the fun we'd have together.

The horror that me raising Bethany would inflict on my former protégé was, of course, a prime part of the appeal.

"That's not an answer. You're not thinking of going back on our deal, are you? About the girl?"

Milos looked a little like a horse that had just scented a coyote, shifting his weight around and checking out the door behind him. My annoyance flared at his antics.

If the cretin craved reassurance, he'd better resign himself to a tedious wait, because I could hardly cave to his demands now. He'd only lose respect for me, and that simply wouldn't do.

The hired help needed to know their place.

"You'll be the first one to know when I make my decision.

Later." I stared at him and was rewarded when he looked away. "Now, take our young guest to the kitchen and feed her. But be sure to pick up your mess."

I turned on my heel, checking my watch as I strode away. Dismissing him in favor of more pressing matters. Almost time now.

Tap tap.

With a flick of my finger, an app on my watch screen popped to life. The map materialized, complete with the little blinking dot. "Why, hello there, Katarina," I crooned at the device. "I can't wait for the family reunion."

Too bad she had no idea that the picture of Bethany I'd had Milos send her contained a Trojan. Once she'd clicked on the image, presto! Her every key stroke and movement were revealed.

I sat in the chair at the head of the dining table, content to watch that little dot move away from the Charleston airport for thirty minutes before pulling out my phone and allowing myself to dial.

"Who's this?" Katarina's greeting was no-nonsense, clipped. Very much the adoptive daughter I remembered.

I sighed into the receiver. "Ah, Katarina, whatever should I say? You've filled me both with heartfelt pride and a profound sense of disappointment. Yes, I trained you to be lethal, but I'd hoped to instill a certain loyalty in you as well, at least to me. Imagine my dismay when you turned on me like a starving jackal, the second I became wounded."

A pause. "Well, I guess it's a good thing I don't give two fucks about your dismay then, or your disappointment. I don't need your pride, either, old man. I've been surviving just fine without it."

The *old man* rankled. "I'm afraid I disagree with your assessment, but that's okay. After all, fathers and daughters often don't see eye to eye."

A choked noise at my characterization of our relationship restored my smile. People never ceased to amaze me with how easy they were to manipulate. Even the superior specimens like Katarina fell victim to my machinations.

"Stop wasting time and just tell me what you want."

"Why, daughter dearest, you should know by now...it's a surprise." I repeated the words I'd shared with her when she was only ten years old.

Minutes before I'd slaughtered her adoptive parents.

The lengthening silence told me that Katarina remembered that moment too, and my veins pulsed pure joy at the victory. This bullseye was far sweeter than most because the target wasn't just anyone. She was my progeny, by intention if not by blood.

Over the years, I'd bent scores of humans to my will, but Katarina's capitulation would be the most delicious by far.

"Where's Bethany? I need to hear her voice, know that she's o-okay."

Though my tough, talented daughter performed a valiant effort to hide her emotions, that faint crack revealed all I needed to know. As long as I held Bethany, Katarina was mine. To manipulate as whim dictated.

"Because I understand the sacred bonds that tether parent to child, I'll grant your wish."

I entered the kitchen, pausing to select a knife from the nearby drawer before strolling over to the sleek glass table. At my approach, Harmony lifted her head from a plate of cheese and crackers and leaned toward Milos, who'd positioned himself a scarce foot away.

A quick tap switched the phone to speaker. Smiling, I set the device on the table. "Your mother is on the phone. Can you say hello so she knows you're here?"

The little girl's dark eyes latched onto mine, but beyond that, she didn't behave at all as expected. No shrieking, no crying, no begging for her mom to take her home. Instead, she nodded, her freckles stark on her pale face but otherwise not showing outward signs of the distress I knew she must be feeling.

"Hello, Mama."

I marveled yet again at the little carbon copy who sat brave and dry-eyed before me. So much more like Katarina than I'd dreamed possible. Yet another child who'd experienced enough upheaval in her short life to infuse her with a capability and poise far beyond her tender years.

"Baby, it's me. Are you okay?"

"Yes, Mama."

During the exchange, I checked my watch again and smiled. "There, you see? Your daughter is safe and sound here with me. But where are you right now, dear Katarina?"

A telling hesitation as my protégé prepared the story. "What do you mean, where am I? I'm in Wyoming. You know, the place where you stole my daughter from school."

At her bald lie, my grin widened. I clicked my tongue before expelling an exaggerated sigh. "Yet again I find myself disappointed by you. Have you really forgotten so much already in my absence?"

Another pause. "Forgotten what?"

"Why, that I know everything, of course. Silly girl." I clucked my tongue again in mock disapproval. "I'm afraid since you're not here, I'll be forced to exact my punishment on your precious girl. Another lie like that will cost her a pretty eye."

With a flick of my wrist, the steak knife flashed in my hand. I lunged across the table and grabbed a handful of Harmony's blonde hair, pushing the knife closer until the metal blade kissed her cheek.

She screamed, but smart thing that she was, didn't

struggle in my grasp. Likely realizing that such a reaction could cause the knife to slip and cut her delicate flesh.

"Stop, please, don't touch her! I'm sorry, I won't lie anymore, I swear. I'm in Charleston. Oh god, please, just leave her alone."

The jumbled rush of Katarina's panic seeped into the empty places inside me, filling the voids, at least temporarily.

Alas, the feeling never lasted. Never satisfied me for long. But I still relished the sensation whenever I could, all the more precious due to its fleeting nature.

"Much better. See, that wasn't so hard. Now, listen closely. I'm going to give you directions, and I'll expect you to follow them as soon as we hang up the line. Oh, and make sure you show up alone. Otherwise, I'm afraid I'll have no choice but to transform your lovely daughter into a cyclops."

Nary so much as a peep from little Harmony when I made the threat. The sight of her stiff little shoulders and stoic little face flooded me with a burst of pride.

My attention returned to the map and my anticipation grew as the dot began to move, blinking its way down the highway that led straight to us.

Soon, my Katarina. Soon we'll be together again.

29

Tucked away in his room, Luke scratched the charcoal across the white page. Some people might think his room was too small, but he liked it here.

He had a bed and a bookcase full of his favorite outdoor magazine and survival themed books, all arranged in order from his most to least favorite. Elysium let him tape up as many of his pictures as he wanted, and the walls were covered with them. Drawings of squirrels, birds, and other forest animals, paintings of rivers, trees, and the woods. Even a couple where he'd sketched the cabin in a back corner.

The pictures helped Luke remember, and even though remembering always created a tight ache in his chest, he sketched and drew anyway. He wanted the reminders of the time he'd spent in the wilderness, because those were the days when he'd felt the most alive. Free.

Someday, Luke vowed to return to that cabin for longer than a single two-hour visit once a year. For now, at least he could draw, and remember.

Charcoal flew across the page as he sketched out more of the buck, so absorbed in the process that the double knock on his door barely registered. When two orderlies barged into his room, Luke shot them a distracted glance before returning to the dark shape emerging beneath his fingers.

"Freddy, this is Luke. He's considered one of the low-risk patients, even though he's been here longer than just about anyone else."

The familiar orderly—Jeff was his name—lounged against Luke's dresser while he talked to the new person. Luke didn't love strangers, but after ten years in Elysium, he'd started to become used to them. Employees were always coming and going here.

Scratch, scratch, scratch.

The buck's antlers started to take shape.

"What's wrong with him that he's been here so long?"

Jeff held up both hands. "Whoa, whoa, hold up. We can't run around asking what's wrong with the patients, Freddy. That's not the right word to use. Try again."

"Sorry. I should have said, what's his diagnosis?"

The antlers finished, Luke turned to the buck's face. He bit his lip in concentration. Eyes were always the hardest for him. They were also the most important. Mess up the eyes, and the animal ended up looking like a cartoon character.

"Much better. Luke here has been diagnosed with autism, PTSD, and an unspecified form of delusional disorder. Speaking of..." Jeff clapped his hands twice. "Hey, Luke, my man. It's that time of the day again, you ready?"

Luke had learned early on in his stay that no one cared if he was ready. He took the pills on his own or they were forced down his throat, but either way, the pills ended up in the same spot.

People thought he was weird, but at least he didn't go around pretending to offer people choices that didn't exist.

Luke sighed and set his charcoal on the desk. "Sure."

He turned to the two men dressed in matching gray

scrubs and smiled politely, the way Dr. Eddington had taught him.

Jeff offered Luke the tiny plastic cup that held his daily pills. "So, with low-risk patients like Luke here, our procedure looks like this. Give them the pills and water, and make sure to watch them swallow."

Luke accepted the blue and white pills, sliding them into his mouth first, and washing them down with the cup of water. After swallowing, he opened his mouth and lifted his tongue for inspection.

Jeff barely glanced his way. "And then they do that, so you can look and make sure the pills went down, and they aren't hiding them to spit out the second you leave the room. Any questions?"

"Naw, that sounds easy enough. Check these out, though."

Luke bounced his leg as the new orderly strolled along his wall and examined Luke's pictures. He didn't like when people breathed on his art, it made him feel itchy all over.

The itchiness grew more unpleasant when the man leaned in near Luke's favorite, so close his nose almost touched. Then the orderly reached for the edges as if to yank the paper from the wall.

"Don't!" Luke jumped to his feet and darted over, whisking the drawing to safety before pushing the orderly away from his treasures. "Leave my pictures alone."

"Hey, settle down, buddy, or I'll have to report you." Jeff wagged his finger near Luke's face. "You know you aren't allowed to shove people."

Luke retreated, his treasured drawing clutched to his chest while the other orderly waved his hand. "Don't report him, that was nothing. My little sister shoves harder than that, and she's ten." Freddy swept a lock of hair across his forehead and flashed Luke a smile. "Sorry, man, I got carried away. Your pictures are really good."

Luke didn't bother to reply. The new orderly's opinion of his artistic capabilities was of no consequence to him.

Jeff nodded. "Yeah, they're part of his delusion. Luke believes he spent three years in the forest, stranded in a cabin with some girl."

"No shit. I mean, uh, crap. Sorry." Freddy squinted at Luke's art again, and then shook his head. "You know, I think I had that fantasy once when I was a teenager too."

"Oh yeah? Then your fantasies must have been a lot more G-rated than mine."

Luke frowned, not sure what G-rated meant, but the two men laughed as they headed back out the door.

"Bye, Luke," Jeff called over his shoulder.

"Bye."

Once the door clicked shut behind them, Luke returned to his drawing. A close-up sketch of the cabin had appeared on one side, next to the outline of the buck. He still remembered the very first day he'd started building the cabin.

Luke had escaped from the terrible hospital where they kept him locked up inside with all the loud noises, bright lights, and terrible smells, and had run as far away as he could go. He kept running until his legs got too tired to run any more. He didn't know exactly where he wanted to go, only that he needed to end up in the mountains. Luke felt safe there, living among the animals and the trees. Far, far away from people.

People like the old man and his wife.

He'd kept going until there were more trees than roads, and farther still, until the roads all but disappeared completely.

It hadn't been easy building a shelter, but Luke didn't mind. Not when the fresh smell of earth and pine surrounded him, and the babble of running water. The leaves blowing in the wind and the chirping of birds.

And not a single person to yell at him to help with the bathroom or calling him a freak and telling him to stop obsessing over camping.

The first structure he'd built had been a hut. Primitive and basic, just enough to protect him from the rain and sun and help hold at least a little heat in at night. But every day, he'd kept working. Gathering wood, collecting materials, shaping tools. The special watch with all its little gadgets that his stepdad had given him helped him survive, but so had all the skills that Aaron taught him, along with the hundreds of videos he'd watched and books he'd read.

Each day, he worked, not stopping until his cabin was complete.

That morning, Luke rose when dawn first peaked in through the window before the sun ever showed on the eastern horizon, same as he did every day since he'd slept beneath the roof of the cabin he'd built with his own hands. He gathered the fishing gear he'd crafted through the use of a knife rescued from the river and through scavenging other people's litter—an activity that had also provided the two big plastic soda bottles he used to collect water—and headed out to the river to fish.

His trek to the river included zigzagging down a narrow path he'd created through groves of trees and bushes. Mornings were the best because of the animals rustling around as they scurried in search of food. Luke much preferred the caws of the jays perched on the branches over human conversations, and the fresh, earthy scent over the overpowering stink of perfumes and colognes.

He was just about to pop out in the small clearing that marked only a half-mile to the river when the voices reached his ears. Luke ducked behind the closest tree, his heart racing. People never wandered out this far. Luke had made sure of that before picking the place to build his home.

"See anyone yet?"

"No, keep looking!"

Luke knew that sound traveled, especially near water, but the voices sounded closer now. Downstream. Probably no more than *one-hundred yards away. There were two men at least, and they were searching for someone.*

Luke's body started shaking. What if they were looking for him?

For the first time in months, the fire ants reappeared, stinging as they crawled over his skin. Luke wanted to drop his gear, curl into a ball, and rock until the bad men left, but if he did that, they might find him.

He couldn't let that happen. He needed to hide.

Luke turned and hurried a few yards back up the path. The thick section of brush was right where he remembered, next to a set of giant boulders that he sometimes climbed to sun-warm his skin on chilly days. Luke darted into the bush, the sharp branches tugging at his shirt and scratching his arms, even though he tried to push them out of the way.

Their leaves hid the girl from view until he reached a hollowed-out spot in the middle.

Luke froze as a pair of huge blue eyes regarded him from a pale face with an ugly, purple bruise on one cheek. The girl was crouching in a ball, and when Luke stepped closer, she cowered like she was afraid he might hurt her.

He remembered how bad that felt. How getting bruises on his face had hurt, both on his skin and bone and on the inside too. The girl was a stranger, but Luke already knew he didn't want her to be scared of him.

In the distance, one of the men shouted again, but Luke couldn't make out his words. The girl flinched like she'd been hit.

What Luke did understand was that if they wanted to stay safe, they needed to leave.

He put a finger to his lips. "Shhh."

The girl nodded once, her eyes still wide and spooked.

Luke held out his hand. At first, all the girl did was stare at it, for so long that Luke worried she wouldn't come with him. Right when he'd almost given up hope, the girl placed her damp, trem-

bling hand in his. Practicing the quiet steps he used when he hunted small animals, Luke led the girl up the path, through the forest he knew like it was his own backyard.

The girl was quiet too, and quick to learn. He didn't even have to remind her to avoid stomping on pine cones. As they weaved deeper into the forest, away from Luke's home just in case, the men's voices faded, and finally disappeared.

When he was sure the men were gone, Luke doubled back and took the girl to his cabin.

"We should be safe now. No one comes this deep into the woods except me."

The girl nodded. "Thanks."

Until she spoke that first word, Luke had worried that the newcomer would be loud like the other kids he'd met, or talk all the time and disrupt his peace and quiet. But her voice was soft, almost like a whisper, and held a musical tone that reminded Luke of a bird.

He liked birds. Maybe the girl would be okay after all. Maybe she wouldn't make the fire ants come out before her bruises healed and she left.

Except, days passed by and the bruises faded, but the girl never left. The two of them fell into a happy, quiet routine.

As months and years came and went, he grew taller and stronger. So did she.

She was good at fishing, as good as him, and even better at some things. She fixed the holes in the blankets that Luke had created from discarded clothing he collected on his hikes, and weaved mats out of plants that she stacked on top of each other to build beds. Unlike other kids Luke had known, the girl never took up too much space. She brought warmth to his cabin. That warmth was partly because of the homemade beds, but Luke also thought some of the warmth came from her presence too.

With a long exhale of breath, Luke tugged the stack of pictures on the far corner of his desk closer and began flipping through them. Each one represented a memory he wanted to preserve. Like this one, of the stream where he'd spent so much time fishing. And this one, of those boulders he used to climb on to soak up the sun.

He continued leafing through the drawings, smiling at the pregnant squirrel he used to share berries with, and another of a fallen tree with a beautiful doe peering over the top. Here was one of his first hut, really only a pile of plant leaves he'd bound together with a roll of fishing string he'd found.

When Luke flipped to the last picture, he stopped. The ache in his chest grew.

With the river rushing by, Luke hopped onto the first rock that crossed the bend. The fish traps he set up waited to be checked on the other side, wedged into crevices in the shallows.

The thick gray clouds overhead were drifting away, uncovering the sun for the first time that day, but the morning's rain hadn't evaporated yet, turning the rocks slicker than usual. Luke didn't have any problems on the first two, but when he leapt to the third rock, his left foot slid on the slippery surface.

He tried to lunge forward, but then his other foot slipped, and the momentum toppled him over. He yelped, his arms circling as he plunged backward. Panic struck an instant before a snap caused pain to explode in his left arm. His skull snapped next and everything went dark as he plunged into the water.

At first, the icy cold deflated his lungs. Luke sank, too shocked to react. The blaze of agony when he moved his arm jolted him awake.

Move, or you'll drown.

Kicking his legs, he propelled himself toward where light streamed in from the surface, gasping when he broke free.

The current was strong, yanking Luke along like he was no heavier than a leaf. His arm hurt, was probably broken, and he didn't think he could swim to the bank with one arm, even if he went in a diagonal direction, like the survival books told him.

He choked on a mouthful of water, remembering another instruction in one of the books:

If you can't get to shore, roll onto your back with your feet facing downstream. This method will conserve energy and allow you to protect your head by spotting dangerous hazards in the river as they approach.

Luke paddled his right arm, fighting the current and the pain to turn. He screamed when a branch smacked into his broken arm but kept working. By the time his feet faced the right way, he was panting and so drained, all he could do was float. When the pain in his arm faded, somewhere in Luke's mind, he understood that it wasn't a good thing. That the numbness likely meant hypothermia was close to setting in.

But he was tired, so tired. Too tired to care as the water rushed in his ears, dragging him farther and farther away from the fishing traps and his little cabin where the girl waited for him to return.

When Luke woke up, he was in the back of a Jeep, with two men in uniforms sitting in the front. He was confused as to how he got there. All he knew was that his body hurt all over, and he was exhausted. Worse even than after those first few days when he'd escaped from the old man and woman, running and hiking miles and miles because he'd been too scared to stop. At least this was his left arm. Not like the right arm he broke back then. He hadn't been able to write or anything until the horrible cast came off.

Then he remembered. The fish traps. Slipping on the rocks into the river.

The girl, waiting for him. Probably worrying by now.

Luke bolted upright in the back seat. A wave of dizziness hit him, and pain exploded in the back of his head. His vision started to fade, but he fought hard.

You can't pass out again. The girl needs you.

He scooted to the edge of the large opening in the back, studying the terrain. The ranger drove the Jeep at a fast clip down a dirt path, but Luke spied a sharp curve up ahead.

That was his chance.

Luke braced himself for the jump. The ground was hard and would hurt, even with the Jeep slowing down, but he could take the pain. He'd had just as bad, or worse, living with the old man and his wife.

What Luke couldn't take was leaving his cabin and the girl.

Luke dangled his legs over the edge and drew a deep breath. Before he could leap, the ranger in the passenger seat yelled, "Stop the car, he's gonna jump!" and something grabbed his shirt, yanking him back into the seat.

After that, there were no more chances to run. The second ranger climbed into the back seat next to Luke. Someone was always by him, right up to when they took him to the ER, put a cast on his arm, and then transported him to this place.

Luke blinked down at the half-finished portrait. The gentle curve of the girl's cheek, the rounded chin. The wild waves of her hair, especially after she took a dip in the river. Her delicate nose. He'd replicated most of her features on paper, all except the eyes. Her big, blue eyes had been his favorite feature, and Luke could never seem to get them just right from memory.

He traced the charcoal curl with a finger, and the motion caused a white plastic rectangle to slip from his sleeve and hit the desk.

Elysium Psychiatric Center, Freddy Reece, employee

Luke flipped the security card he'd swiped from the new orderly when he'd pushed him away from his drawing. He ran his thumb over the magnetic strip and smiled.

30

T hat evening, the conference room on the second floor of the Charleston Police Department was packed full of law enforcement for an emergency meeting. Tempers all around the table flared, Ellie's included.

When Clay and Ellie had finished filling in Valdez, Fortis, and the five other officers Fortis had rounded up on the Katarina and Harmony situation, a blissful silence had descended on the room. But that quiet only lasted the length of time it took for the occupants to absorb the information, which turned out to be less than ten seconds.

After that, everyone wanted to talk first. Round and round they'd gone, sharing plenty of opinions but coming no closer to a concrete plan of attack. Ellie fidgeted in her chair, checking the door behind her every minute or so.

See? This was why she hated team meetings. Achieving consensus with so many big egos involved was too much like herding cats. In the end, a lot of effort was expended to get nowhere fast.

All this meeting had done so far was to convince Ellie

that her usual impulse to jump into an investigation on her own without first seeking a rubber stamp was the right one.

Fortis banged his fist on the table, cutting off a heated argument from a sandy-haired detective named Marty who wanted to rally all the troops and swoop in. Her gray-haired boss shook his head. "I understand the drive to nail this guy, but we can't rush this. Not with Kingsley. We've tried that method in the past, without success. That bastard is too slick by far and has endless resources available to help him stay under the radar. We need to all take a deep damn breath and plan this out thoroughly before we make our move this time."

Ellie shot upright in the chair, her knuckles white on the armrests. "We don't have time to plot out a master plan. There's a kid at stake this time. An eight-year-old girl."

Fortis scowled at her. "As I'm well aware, Detective Kline, since you told me less than fifteen minutes ago. I might have a few years on you, but I'm not quite out to pasture yet. I haven't forgotten about the girl."

A few snickers broke out, but Ellie ignored them. There was too much at stake to care about such trivial crap at the moment. "Okay, then you understand why we need to scour every single inch of Charleston until we find him, or at least a sign. Kingsley is out there, somewhere. He—"

"You can't know that for sure, Kline. Hell, you shouldn't even be here." Valdez crossed his arms as he glared across the table. "Any defense attorney worth his salt could get Kingsley's whole case thrown out if they spot your name on any part of the investigation, so why do you continue to jeopardize it by inserting yourself where you don't belong?"

Fire raced up Ellie's neck. "I don't give a damn about having my name on any papers, and yes, I agree, keeping it off is the smart move. As for the rest, did you stop to consider that, if we lose Katarina, we won't have any Kingsley case left to lose?"

Murmurs kicked up while Valdez raked his hands through his short hair, clearly just as frustrated as Ellie. "Katarina is definitely the key witness in our case against Kingsley's criminal enterprise, but I'm starting to wonder if that woman was ever on our side in the first place."

From the seat to Ellie's left, Clay leaned forward to address Valdez. "I'm not sure where you came across the notion that Katarina was ever on our side, but I can tell you right now that it's a load of bull. The only side Katarina has ever been on is the side that favors her survival, and that of her daughter. And like it or not, she's never pretended otherwise."

"Yeah?" Valdez's dark eyes flashed as he shifted his ire to Clay. "I guess you'd know, seeing that you're the one who cut that sweet WITSEC deal for Katarina." He grimaced, like he'd smelled a rotten egg. "Which I will never claim to under-stand. What judge in their right mind grants custody of an eight-year-old to a woman like Volkov?"

For once, Ellie agreed with Valdez. She recalled her own horror when she'd first learned that not only would Katarina skate free of her heinous crimes, but that the judge had granted custodial rights for Harmony too. The fact that Clay had been the person to facilitate the deal had been one of the reasons Ellie had initially slammed the brakes on their relationship.

With time, though, she'd learned more about the foster system. After investigating horror stories where children ended up in temporary homes with parents who didn't give a damn about them, she had a better grasp on both sides of the argument.

Yes, Katarina had committed heinous acts and put inno-cent lives at stake. That didn't negate the fact that she'd been victimized from an early age, or that she loved her daughter. Enough to risk her own capture and even death to track the girl down multiple times.

Ellie often thought that police work would be cake if life really was as black and white as depicted on TV.

Distracted by her own thoughts, Ellie missed the first part of Clay's response, focusing back in as he finished up. "...and if you have a problem with the court's decision, I suggest you take it up with the Attorney General. He's the one who gave the order, not a judge."

Score one for Lockwood.

Valdez didn't have a snappy comeback for that. He sank back in his chair with a huff. Ellie thought she'd done a stellar job hiding her smirk, but when the detective scanned the other faces in the room, his eyes narrowed on hers. "Fine, but none of you except Kline here disagreed when I said she shouldn't even be in this meeting discussing Kingsley's case. So, why are you still here? Do you secretly want to jeopardize the case?"

Other heated discussions broke out all around, but Ellie only had eyes for Valdez. She leapt to her feet, her chair squealing across the floor from the force of her shove. Spitting mad, she stalked around the table.

He stood up before she reached him, so that when she stopped less than an arm's length away, she had to tilt her head back to glower in his face. "Out with it. Right now."

"Out with what?" He crossed his arms again and glowered right back.

"The reason why you hate me so much."

Valdez flinched. A tiny movement but perceptible nonetheless. Ellie interpreted that to mean her question had surprised him. "Don't bring personal feelings into this, Kline. Tell me something, though. Have you been one-hundred-percent honest when you say you've shared everything you know about Kingsley?"

Even after cycling through this before with Valdez, the accusation that laced his question stung. Ellie reared back. "Yes, I have! And where is this even coming from? I haven't done anything to earn this kind of distrust."

The detective studied her, his aggressive, puffed-chest posture unchanged. "Maybe not you specifically, but this department, yeah. You all had a dirty cop and shrink with ties to Kingsley right here in this department, operating under your noses. A fact that went unrecognized for years."

"And as I've told you before, that dirty cop predated me by decades, and I'm the one who figured out he was dirty in the first place! The shrink too." Ellie rocked back on her heels, sucking down a deep breath to keep a tight lid on her rising fury. "What about you? How do I know that the reason you keep attacking me isn't because you're a squeaky wheel?"

Valdez's mouth fell open at the suggestion that maybe he was the type of crooked cop who accused his fellow officers of being dirty in order to deflect suspicion. He slapped a hand over his temple and rubbed his eye. "I'm sorry, did you just accuse me of being a crooked cop?"

"Yes! Maybe! Although, what the...are you *laughing* at me?" Ellie frowned at the other detective. Nope, no doubt about it. His mouth had started to twitch. "That wasn't meant as a joke."

The detective covered his mouth with his hand, but now Ellie could hear the smile in his voice. "I know you didn't. I'm sorry, I think—"

Whatever Valdez was about to say was drowned out by a barrage of shouting.

Ellie blinked and turned a half-circle, startled by the sight. Maybe her squabble with Valdez had been contagious because all but one officer was locked in a heated argument now, over logistics. The noise level continued to rise, to the point that Ellie crammed her hands over her ears.

The door to the meeting room slammed shut, cutting through the voices like a gunshot. Police Captain Gil Browning capitalized on the distraction by snarling into the temporary lull. "All of you! Shut! The! Hell! Up!"

Quiet descended. All heads swiveled toward the captain as he prowled to the center of the room and splayed his feet shoulder-width apart. His gaze raked over every single one of them, and when it was Ellie's turn to bear the brunt of that angry glare, she wanted to shrink into the floor.

"Remind me again, is everyone in this room an officer… or a LEO of some kind?" Browning tacked the last part on with a curt nod at Clay.

Ellie and Valdez mumbled their agreement, along with the rest of the room's sheepish occupants.

Browning cupped a hand to his ear. "I'm sorry, I didn't quite catch that. I said, are we all law enforcement officers in this room?"

This time, a chorus of yeses replied.

"Damn right we are." He propped his hands on his hips. "That means we're all on the same side. The right side. The side of the law. And I'll tell you what, there's nothing criminals like Kingsley would like better than to know we're at each other's throats over him. In fact, I bet if he overheard the same thing I did outside this door a minute ago, he'd be giving himself a mighty pat on the back right about now."

Ellie's chin dipped toward her chest, and a lot of the others did the same. Because Browning was right. Not only that, but he shouldn't have needed to remind them.

"Now, stop playing into this monster's hands by fighting with each other and get your sorry asses back to work. Valdez, Kline, Fortis, and Agent Lockwood, I need you to stick around for a few minutes."

Officers shuffled out of the room, hanging their heads and skirting Browning's eye. Once everyone but the four he'd asked to stay left, the captain pushed the door shut before turning and leaning against it.

His shrewd gaze settled on Ellie, making her cheeks flame. She shifted her weight from foot to foot, feeling like a little kid who just got busted fighting over a swing on the jungle gym.

She closed her eyes. Opened them. Time to own her part of the foolishness. "I'm sorry, I—"

Browning held up a hand. "Tell her."

Ellie blinked. Tell her what? She craned her neck, trying to figure out who Browning had barked at. *Valdez.*

The other detective slid a glance her way. He opened his mouth, then shut it again while scratching the back of his neck. "Captain?"

His hesitancy made it clear that Valdez wasn't sold on Browning's idea of sharing just yet.

Browning groaned. "Detective Valdez, do you believe that I would ask you to share such confidential information if I doubted the trustworthiness of anyone standing in this room for even one second?"

Valdez shook his head. "No, sir."

"Then what are you waiting for? Come clean and put an end to your and Kline's squabbling once and for all."

Valdez's shoulders drooped in defeat. With a sigh, he reached into his pocket and withdrew a leather wallet. He flipped to a tear-away compartment and lifted the badge hidden inside until it hovered at Ellie's eye level.

Internal Affairs

Ellie reeled as she read the words. "You're with IA?"

"Yeah. The Kingsley investigation caught the attention of some higher-ups in the department. They were concerned about the possibility of other dirty cops after

Jones, so IA sent me here to make sure that wasn't the case."

Ellie couldn't believe what she was hearing, not after all the horrors she'd endured at Kingsley's hands. Her hands rounded into fists. "You mean, like me? They specifically thought I might be a dirty cop?"

"I get how this must feel weird to you, but come on, Kline. You know better than most how often Kingsley's victims don't come out the other side with squeaky clean souls intact."

As much as she wanted to argue, Ellie couldn't. Valdez was right, and for once, she suspected he wasn't trying to ruffle her feathers. Still, he was also correct in that it did suck to be a suspect. Especially after she'd spent so many sleepless nights and hours plotting how to put Kingsley behind bars.

She nodded, swallowing the bitter lump in her throat. "I understand, but I'm a detective because of what happened to me, not in spite of it. And I know I won't have any rest, this life or the next, unless Kingsley is brought to justice and pays for his crimes." Ellie locked eyes with Valdez. "We're on the same team."

The detective inclined his head. "I believe you. Now. And I'm sorry for any distress my questions might have caused, but I had to know for sure."

Valdez extended his hand. After a flicker of hesitation, Ellie fitted her palm to his and shook. Because if their situations had been reversed, Ellie would have been just as suspicious about Valdez. She could hardly cling to a grudge over the man doing his job.

At least she hoped so.

"Good, good, but let's skip past the kumbayas and have everyone take a seat."

Ellie and Valdez exchanged a quick grin over Browning's grumpy order before sliding into a chair. Once everyone was settled, Browning led a discussion on Kingsley, urging each of them to share any fact or bit of information about the murderer, no matter how small.

After twenty minutes, their output dwindled, so Browning moved the meeting along. "All right, now that we're all on the same page with Kingsley's background, let's talk about how safe we think Harmony Volkov, otherwise known as Bethany, is in Kingsley's hands."

When no one else chimed in right away, Ellie spoke up. "I've been fretting over this exact question ever since the undercover agent called Clay to tell him that Kingsley had taken Harmony."

She paused and bit her lip, surprised when Valdez ended up being the one who prodded her to continue. "What conclusion did you reach?"

Her jaw clenched. She hated to have to say what she'd been thinking. "I think that Kingsley might end up using Harmony as a replacement for Katarina."

Valdez frowned, and as she searched the other faces in the room, Ellie noticed that Browning's eyebrows were raised. Even Clay looked surprised. But the longer Ellie had thought about it, the more convinced she'd become.

She just needed to convince the rest of them too. "When Katarina turned on Kingsley, he not only lost his protégé, but a daughter figure as well. The one person he could always count on to look up to him, or so he thought. Katarina's defection had to be a huge blow to his ego. He'll want to punish her, probably kill her, but that doesn't mean he doesn't care about her still, in his own, twisted way. Replacing her with Harmony would fill two needs at once. Revenge, and companionship. I think—"

Music bleated from her cell phone, cutting her off.

"One second, let me check this." Ellie accepted the call

and pressed the phone to her ear. "Detective Ellie Kline, CPD."

"Hi, this is Ranger Joel Matthews with National Forests in South Carolina. I got your message, and yeah, I remember that boy you were asking about."

Ellie clutched the phone as she jumped to her feet, breathless with sudden hope. "That's great. Do you happen to know where he is now, so I can speak with him? It's part of an ongoing investigation into child trafficking."

"Um…" The ranger cleared his throat, hesitating while Ellie sped from the meeting room amid curious stares and escaped into the hallway. "I'd bet my pension that he's still in the same place we dropped him off back then. Elysium Psychiatric Hospital. That's where he was a couple years ago, I reckon."

The news zapped the strength from Ellie's legs, and she sagged against the wall. *Lucas Harrison was alive and well. Safe in a mental hospital, just like the nurse had suggested.* "Thank you so much, you don't know how happy this makes me."

After obtaining the ranger's cell number and promising to schedule a time for a longer follow-up interview, Ellie hung up, reeling. That was how Clay found her when he poked his head out of the meeting. Leaning on the wall for support and grinning like a doofus.

His eyebrows hiked up as he eased the door shut behind him, muting the ongoing murmur of conversation within. "I was coming out to make sure you didn't get bad news, but going off your expression, looks like I didn't need to worry."

Ellie offered him a dazed smile. "Lucas Harrison is alive. Safe. Apparently, he's spent the last several years in Elysium." She tested the words out loud and wondered if they sounded as foreign to him as they did to her. "I need to go and arrange a visit, so I can close his case. At least it's a way I can be productive right now."

Unlike with the Kingsley case.

"Excuse me." Eager to return to her desk and bury herself in the happier distraction of closing Lucas's case, Ellie pushed off the wall and brushed past Clay on her way to the bullpen. Before she made it far, light pressure on her shoulders stopped her.

Using his hands as gentle guidance, Clay rotated Ellie back to face him. "Hey, that's great news about Lucas, but we're also going to find Harmony, okay?"

His thumbs rubbed circles on her shoulders, as if he hoped the soothing motion could infuse her with a dose of confidence. Ellie sighed. If only life were that simple.

But as seconds passed with their gazes locked together, Ellie noticed her lungs filled a little easier, and her head lifted a little higher. The odds stacked against finding Lucas safe after so long had been dismal and look how that had ended up.

"Thanks." Ellie shut her eyes, allowing herself another few heartbeats to relax into his touch and absorb the comfort he offered before sidestepping out of reach. "Talk later?"

"Definitely."

When Ellie reached her desk, she dropped into the chair and rubbed her temples. Too many surprises in a short time had her brain spiraling in all different directions.

Dragging her water bottle across the desk, she unscrewed the lid and guzzled down several deep gulps, praying the cool liquid would clear her head. First the terrible news with Harmony, then the great news concerning Lucas, with Valdez's little surprise tossed in the middle, because why not? No wonder her mind was like a wobbly blob of mush.

She flexed her fingers and sighed. Well, too bad, because she still had work to do. First off, confirming that Lucas Harrison was indeed a patient at Elysium and typing up her report. Finalizing his case would free her up to focus on the other kids.

Ellie dug in, making calls and typing. When she finally came up for air, the bullpen had emptied out. She yawned and stretched her arms, then her neck. Time for a sugar or caffeine break. Stifling another yawn, she wandered out to the vending machines in search of a temporary fix for her lagging energy.

She returned to her desk two minutes later armed with both a gooey treat and coffee. As she ripped open the candy wrapper and prepared to dig in, her phone rang.

She bit off a hunk, anyway, chewing as she checked the Caller ID. *Unlisted.* Great, always super promising when the bozo calling her hid their information.

She answered with her mouth full. "H-wello, Detective Kwine." Served them right for dialing a cop from an unregistered number.

"H-hello? Is this the police?"

The voice sounded female. Young, like a child. Ellie swallowed the bite of chocolate and peanuts.

If this was some kid making a prank call, so help her...

"This is the police. I'm Detective Kline. Do you need help?"

Ellie sat down and waited for a ridiculous punchline. One time, a boy had called her to report a missing person. She'd taken him seriously and asked for the name. Seymour Butts. That's what the little turd had said with a giggle before hanging up.

"Yes, please, help me! This strange man kidnapped me and took me to a cabin, and now I'm at this house, and they made me call my mama and almost cut me with a big knife, and I'm scared. Please, please, come get me."

The little girl's words tumbled out one on top of the

other, high-pitched and scared. A fist squeezed Ellie's lungs. *If this was a joke, it was in really poor taste.*

"Slow down, it's going to be okay. We'll try to get you safe, but first, can you tell me your name?"

"My name's Bethany, and please, I don't like it here, come get me, please. I want—"

The girl cut out. A scraping noise followed, like someone was fumbling with the phone.

Bethany...as in Katarina's daughter?

Shock stole Ellie's voice, but only for a moment. "Bethany? Are you still there? Hello?"

Another scrape. "If you want the girl, you need to come get her now. You have thirty seconds to come outside. I'll give you additional instructions once you're out of the building."

The new voice was deep and gravelly. Definitely an adult male, but not Kingsley.

Ellie's hands turned to ice. "But—"

"No buts. No arguments. No second chances. Thirty seconds to be outside, or you'll never see the girl again." The calm, even manner in which the man spoke convinced Ellie more than anything that he wasn't bluffing. And even if he was, well...that wasn't a gamble she was willing to take.

"Where do you want me to go?"

"Outside, and don't try to warn anyone. Your bodyguard is, um, indisposed so don't attempt to contact him either."

Oh god.

"Where?" Her voice was steadier than she felt as she whirled around, wildly searching for someone to help her. A murder-suicide and a home invasion had emptied the bull pen of any detective who would normally be there this late. Of course.

"Thirty seconds, starting now."

Hyper-aware that the countdown had started, Ellie

squandered the first few seconds considering her next move. She wanted to break things and scream but that wouldn't help anyone. Especially not Bethany.

"Twenty-five..."

As the vile man's countdown rang in her ear, Ellie grabbed the first thing she could find—a file folder—and scribbled a note.

Track my Apple watch!

Finished, she flung the pen across the desk and yanked open her desk drawer, scrabbling through the contents until she found what she needed.

"Nineteen...you better hurry, Detective."

She shoved pepper-spray in one blazer pocket and the taser in the other.

"Fourteen..."

With thirteen seconds left, Ellie whirled and sprinted for the stairs.

31

After checking her rearview mirror one more time for a tail, Katarina made the last right turn. The rental car's navigation system directed her to the address Kingsley had provided, which turned out to be a large house on an enormous lot in a quiet, wealthy neighborhood.

The driveway was set back from the street and empty, but she cruised by before pulling a U-turn and parking the beige rental near the curb, a good thirty yards away. In the distance, thunder rumbled, followed a few seconds later by the sky illuminating as lightning zigzagged to the ground. She cut across the yard, her boots sinking into the thick, damp grass. No outdoor lights winked against the moonless night sky, and the windows on the home were dark.

If Katarina didn't know any better, she'd guess the occupants were away on vacation, or maybe sound asleep. But she did know better.

Kingsley had always loved games. This time, she guessed the game he wanted to play was possum.

She reached the brick walkway and prowled up to the

front door. The knob jiggled beneath her hand. The door clicked before swinging open on silent hinges.

Katarina crept into the entry and paused, straining to detect any signs of life. Nothing. The house was silent as a tomb and almost as dark. A dim glow from deep within the interior suggested that somewhere, at least one light was on. Katarina wondered if it was a trap and decided to search that area last, just in case.

Edging forward, she led with the flashlight feature on her back-up phone, sweeping a semi-circle to illuminate the surroundings. She didn't delude herself. The man who'd raised her had likely known she was here the second her shoe touched his grass, even though she'd hidden the bugged cell phone behind a fire hydrant a couple blocks away.

That still didn't make barging inside, flipping on every light switch, and yelling, "Papa, I'm home!" a good idea.

The glow fanned out, catching on large, furniture shapes draped in white sheets like ghosts. Her boot creaked on a wooden floorboard, and she froze, her heartbeat ratcheting higher.

After fifteen beats, Katarina started creeping again. No one stirred, and as her light shined on the walls, she noticed that even the paintings were covered. Door after door in the hallway opened to more of the same, so she doubled back toward the main rooms while the fury she'd worked so hard to cage on the drive over rattled its chains.

Maybe she'd been wrong, and Kingsley wasn't here. Maybe sending her to a deserted house *was* the game. Or possibly a warm-up round.

She moved deeper into the house, past a large living area with still more sheets, and debated calling Clayne. They'd split up at the airport. It was her idea to approach the house from two different sides. When she'd called from the burner phone after talking to Kingsley, Clayne was already a good ten miles ahead and had promised to do recon and position himself before she arrived.

Her finger fell away from the phone icon. If Clayne hadn't announced his presence when she'd arrived, that likely meant he was well hidden. Best to leave him that way, until the right moment.

Outside, a cannon boomed, cracking through the night air like a whip. Katarina dropped into a crouch until she realized that it was more thunder and continued with her search.

The phone light swept over a chandelier, making the crystal shimmer. Positioned beneath the fixture was the first uncovered piece of furniture—a large, rectangular dining table. Beneath the light beam, the wood emitted an eerie glow, but the oddity that stopped Katarina in her tracks was the elaborate place settings.

She traced the gold leafing on the closest plate and frowned at the faceted crystal goblets. Why bother with china dishes and fancy silverware when the rest of the house looked abandoned for the winter?

Uneasy, she skirted one end of the table and headed toward an arched opening, freezing when she spotted shadows flickering on the wall. A quick assessment revealed the cause to be one of those lanterns with LED lights made to masquerade as flames resting atop a wooden buffet. She understood the placement when her gaze fell on the white card folded beside it.

Welcome, Katarina.

We await you upstairs.

As she stared at the familiar, flowing script, fear crawled across her neck. The sudden instinct to turn and walk right back out the door, jump into the rental and drive somewhere that Kingsley could never find her was strong. So powerful that Katarina took a reflexive two steps back before ever realizing that she'd moved.

She swung the phone to the right, illuminating the hardwood steps that twined up to the second floor. The darkness beyond her light's beam appeared sinister in the weak light. A stairway straight to the devil.

Or Kingsley.

Katarina wasn't sure which option would be worse.

Her breathing grew shallow. If it weren't for Bethany, she'd leave this place now and never look back.

But because of Bethany, she had no choice. Katarina would roll the dice in whatever game Kingsley had masterminded. She'd just gotten her daughter back. She wasn't about to abandon her now.

Katarina double-checked the arsenal she'd strapped to her body before starting the climb. Like the rest of the house, all the pictures hung on the walls were shielded by strips of white cloth. At first. Until she reached the middle landing.

When she reached the uncovered painting, Katarina paused, lips parting as she recognized the subjects. The elaborate gilt frame held a portrait of Kingsley and Katarina as a young girl. His hand rested on her shoulder while she clutched a knife in her small fist.

Katarina's stomach clenched, but she pressed on as more uncovered images came into view. The first three were paintings of the first people she'd ever killed. The next was of the shaggy-haired boy who she'd fancied herself in love with once, back when she was only fifteen. The boy had worked at a little convenience store near where she and Kingsley had lived, and Katarina admired his surfer good looks whenever they'd stopped in to grab a pack of gum or soda.

At the time, she'd thought she'd kept her crush hidden from Kingsley, but those shrewd eyes picked up everything. After blushing her way through paying for a Twix, Kingsley had turned to her in the car. "He might be pretty, but he's not worthy of you, my sweet. You were made for greater things than an empty-headed, minimum-wage cashier in a dead-end job."

After that visit, Katarina never saw the boy again. The next cashier had shrugged when she mustered her courage to ask if her crush had quit. "Dunno. I heard he just stopped showing up one day. You know how it is."

And even back then, Katarina suspected that she did know how it was, but she'd never asked. She hadn't wanted to know for certain.

The next one was a photograph of her smiling in front of the scariest roller coaster at Six Flags, the one Kingsley had insisted she ride until she stopped screaming during the spirals and sudden drops. Another showed her decked out in camouflage in front of a forest with her hand propped on a rifle, fresh from her sniper training. There was yet another photo of Katarina wearing her gray jiu jitsu gi right after she'd earned her black belt.

Memory after memory, splattered across the wall. The bullseye that she'd practiced on every day with her favorite set of throwing knives all stuck in the middle circle. A newspaper clipping about the man she'd killed in that hotel room on her road trip down the coast with Eden.

As she scanned the pieces of her past, the frightened whispers in her head ceased. Quieted by an icy resolve.

Katarina had fought to contort herself into the identity of a single mom living in a quiet mountain town, but despite her efforts, she'd never quite fit. Why?

She traced a finger down a photo and smiled. Because deep in her bones, her organs, the blood that flowed in her veins, Katarina was a killer.

Then. And now.

Katarina prowled down the upstairs hallway, following the pictures to the only closed door at the far end of the corridor. She twisted the knob and eased the door open just a crack.

Nothing stirred, so she shouldered the door open farther and slipped inside, halting when her gaze landed on the man tied to a chair.

Between her phone and another battery-operated lantern on the dresser, there was just enough light for her to recognize the plaid flannel shirt and the face.

Clayne.

Shit.

She should have known their plan would never work.

After a quick perimeter scan, Katarina scurried over. His hands were bound to the chair's arms in Kingsley's preferred method, and his eyes were glazed, like he was stoned. Drugged, more likely, courtesy of one of Kingsley's special blends.

She shook his arm, but he didn't react. An unpleasant sensation kicked her in the gut. Guilt, maybe, since she'd dragged him into this mess. But she didn't have time for that now.

A muffled mewl from the shadows made Katarina stop cold. A feminine sound.

"Bethany?" she whispered.

She whirled toward the noise, rushing over toward a second chair. As she drew closer and her vision sharpened, the hope flowering in her chest wilted again.

Not Bethany, but a grown woman dressed like a little girl in pink lacy underwear and a matching pink cropped shirt.

Frowning, Katarina peered at the woman's features above the metallic strip of duct tape. Something about the woman niggled at her brain. That face. She could have sworn she'd seen it before.

Her gaze swung past the woman and landed on a third

chair. Empty, save for the unoccupied restraints draped across the arms. Like a lover, waiting for an embrace.

The sight triggered a silent alarm in Katarina's head. Every sense screamed in unison—*trap*.

She slowly backed away. One step. Then two. Before she could take a third, Kingsley's voice echoed through the flickering shadows.

"Katarina, thank you for coming. Please take a seat in the empty chair and we can get started."

Katarina whirled, swinging the phone's light in a wild arc around the room.

Where is he? Where?

She spotted a tiny speaker up near the ceiling at the same time that his deep, mocking laughter surrounded her.

"Did you really believe I'd be foolish enough to allow you to find me first? Come now, my sweet daughter. You know me better than that. Sit, please. I find that my patience is wearing thin."

Katarina flipped off the speaker, even as she sensed the trap doors slamming into place all around her. "Fuck your patience! If you like that chair so much, how about you sit in it? Where's Bethany?"

"Your daughter is safer than you are right now, I can assure you of that. Now sit, put on the restraints, and tighten them. If you force me to ask again, I'm afraid dear little Bethany will be the one who pays."

Katarina swore under her breath as sweat dampened her shirt. Even though there were three chairs this time, she'd grown up with Kingsley and understood what that meant.

This room was a setup for his favorite game. *Die, bitch! Die*. And Katarina didn't want to play. Three people would sit down, but only one would get up.

Katarina turned in a slow circle. "No matter who you put in these chairs, I'll always choose my baby. Even if it's a choice between Bethany and me, I will always pick my daughter. So why don't we skip all the drama and cut to the chase?"

More laughter flowed into the room, snaking across Katarina's skin. "Who said anything about you being the one who gets to make the choice?"

Too late, Katarina realized her miscalculation. Either Clayne or the woman in pink would be deciding who lived or died, not her. Kingsley had placed her on the menu for execution.

Fear clamped down on her heart, and she whirled, sprinting for the door.

The harsh sizzle reached her first, and an instant later, her body exploded in agony.

The taser crackled as it pulsed even more electricity into her nervous system, buckling her legs from beneath her. Fire burned white-hot everywhere. Convulsing, she collapsed to the floor, while one thought broke through the pain.

Bethany, baby, please forgive me for failing.

32

M ilos hunched behind the steering wheel while the windshield wipers swished and swatted away the first sprinkle of raindrops and grew increasingly restless as the seconds ticked by. Despite the late hour, he felt like a sitting duck, swimming alone near the edge of a pond during the middle of hunting season, just begging to be shot with a rifle. Only, the pond in this case was the parking lot of the Charleston Police Department, where he idled in a spot with a clear view of the lobby doors.

Abducting a police officer right in front of a building crammed with cops struck Milos as a really bad idea, yet here he was. Taking on all the risks, even when Mr. Abel wouldn't even commit to giving him the girl as they'd originally agreed.

That slow, controlled burn inside him flamed up his neck, down his arms. His legs. The way it had just before he'd exploded on his mother that first time.

The girl was his. *His.*

They had a connection. Mr. Abel had noticed it too. The way the girl had clung to Milos at the house. Milos could tell by the other man's facial expressions that the knowledge displeased him.

He sneered into the quiet lot. He bet his boss was jealous. Well, too bad. Milos wasn't giving up the girl without a fight.

But for now, he'd carry out Mr. Abel's orders, even if that meant taking on all the risk. Milos peered at the unmoving doors, drumming his fingers on the wheel while he waited and spoke the countdown into the phone.

Mr. Abel thought he was tough, but Milos was the one with balls of steel. No, scratch that. After this job, his family jewels qualified as diamond coated.

Either brave, or a complete fool.

Fool. Idiot. Moron.

His mother's insults paraded through his head and soured his stomach. In her eyes, Milos could do nothing right. Like the day he'd brought a stray cat home, or when he'd gotten a C in math. That time when he'd wanted to surprise his mom with dinner, but he'd filled the pot too high and the water had boiled over and spilled on the stove.

Or once when a little girl in his class had invited him over to play. That time, his mother had added new barbs to her arsenal.

Pervert. Jezebel. Slut.

Motion in his peripheral vision jerked Milos out of the trance. The redhead was scurrying from the lobby to the sidewalk, craning her head every which way.

He smiled into the phone. "Five…"

When she neared the curb, Milos shifted the car into drive and tapped on the gas. Her head swiveled in his direction as the car eased alongside her. The locks clicked open, but she didn't reach for the door, instead squinting into the interior.

"Three," he said, watching her hands. She would be armed, he knew. "Two."

His drumbeat on the steering wheel sped up, but the lady cop just stood there. Staring at him.

"One."

Dropping the phone, Milos tapped the gas again, and the car rolled forward at a crawl. He was confident that the woman wouldn't shoot him yet. The redhead was too inquisitive and brave. She'd be determined to find his little girl.

Sure enough, the redhead lurched after him. The passenger door flew open, and she jumped in. With a flash of movement, a gun appeared at her side.

Anticipating her doing something so foolish, Milos didn't hesitate. He attacked, pressing the stun gun against her thigh. Her entire body seized, but the detective didn't drop the gun. Even as she cried in pain, her eyes nearly bugging out of her face, the weapon lifted…lifted…lifted.

"I like your spirit," he said as he ripped the gun from her grip just before jamming a syringe into her thigh. He pressed the plunger. "Go to sleep now, little bird."

"No…" But her protest was weak from the effects of the electricity and the sedative already pumping through her system.

"Yes, that's right." He knew he had to hurry, but he took advantage of their closeness and kissed her cheek and the tip of her nose. "Sleep, baby bird."

She fought it. She struggled. She spat in his face.

But in the end, her eyelids fluttered, and his little bird slumped into a deep sleep.

Too easy. In fact, taking the redhead was so easy that, as Milos drove away from the building, he experienced a pang of regret that there hadn't been more opportunity for the lady cop to put up a fight. It was more fun that way.

But no, he had his little girl to think of now. Milos needed to remain disciplined because nothing could get in the way of his plan to keep her.

Because she's mine.

Milos cruised down the darkened roads, obeying all the speed limits and traffic laws. After checking at a stoplight to make sure no one else was watching, he unsnapped his seat belt so that he could lean far enough over to secure the redhead's. A traffic stop over the most trivial infraction could ruin all his careful plans. He allowed himself a quick sniff of her hair—it smelled fruity—before settling back behind the wheel.

When he reached the back entrance of an old grocery store that he'd scouted for cameras on the ride over, he pulled into the darkened lot behind the store and shifted into park.

Patting the cop down took less than a minute. Milos relieved her of the Glock 22 along with a taser in one blazer pocket, a can of mace in the other, and a six-inch serrated knife tucked into her left boot.

During his final scan, his gaze lingered on the watch strapped to her right wrist. He pulled it closer and whistled a high-pitched chirp when he tapped the screen. "Tricky little bird, wearing your smartwatch, but not tricky enough."

Once he'd scooped up the cop and deposited her in the trunk, Milos steered the car back to the road. While waiting on Mr. Abel's next text, Milos headed a few miles west, away from his final destination, and buried the watch in a dumpster in front of a home remodel. When he returned, Milos cruised the streets aimlessly, waiting on Mr. Abel's text.

The ping alerted him three minutes later.

It's time.

Milos drove straight to the house in the wealthy neighborhood with the sort of exorbitant lots and expensive cars that would have set his mother off on a rant about sin. If she'd known what Milos was up to right now, she would have screamed until her throat gave out.

Lucky for him she was dead.

Milos pulled into the driveway and hurried to the trunk, wiping his moist palms on his pants. Not long now before the little girl was finally his.

In his eagerness, he fumbled the second syringe, but he caught the plastic dispenser before it hit the ground. Milos steadied his hands before opening the trunk. He was too close to the prize to mess up now.

As Mr. Abel had predicted, the drugs from the first shot still held the detective immobile.

Not for long.

"Time to wake up, little bird." Lightning cracked the sky as Milos stabbed the second syringe into the detective's thigh. Within a few moments, her eyelids twitched, then blinked. With a gasp, she bolted upright. The crack of her skull on the trunk lid tickled Milos's funny bone, and he snickered.

The redhead stopped rubbing her head to glare at him… then lunged. Her fingernails scraped his face, but she was still too weak from the medication to do much damage. Still, she tried, and for fun, Milos let her.

"You think this is funny, kidnapping a police officer? Trust me, you're not going to be laughing when my colleagues arrest you and throw you in a cell for the rest of your fucking life."

Milos's head pulsed at the curse, and he wrapped one hand around the woman's throat while securing her wrists with the other. "You shouldn't yell at me or talk like that. Only dirty women use those kinds of words. Women like Eve, the original temptress."

Her eyes widened, then narrowed. "Fuck. You. You misogynistic fuck."

She lunged to the side, but Milos caught her by the red ponytail and yanked her back down. "You're no little bird, you're a slut. Just like the apple and the serpent responsible for man being ejected from the Garden of Eden."

He slapped duct tape over her mouth before she could taint him with any more of her foul profanities. This was why Milos preferred little girls to women. Women were already corrupted, whereas little girls were still pure. Like his Bethany.

His pulse quickened. He pictured the little girl's reaction when he introduced her to pain. Her body would sing, and she would sob, but eventually, his little chick would learn the same lesson that Milos had mastered at his mother's knee.

After dragging the detective out of the trunk, Milos nudged the nose of the confiscated gun into her back. "Walk."

He marched the redheaded whore into the house, his muscles quivering from the knowledge that soon, he'd be enlightening the little girl on the appreciation of pain.

33

The instructions coming from the monster's mouth sounded like they were being spoken underwater. As Valerie sat bound to the uncomfortable chair, she wondered if Kingsley had drugged her food somewhere during the course of the day, or if the sound effect signified that she was in shock.

A muffled noise drew her attention to the right. The strange man was fighting his restraints, thrashing around like a fish out of water. If Valerie's mouth hadn't been covered, she would have warned him to save his strength. Kingsley had too much practice to mess up an important detail like their bindings.

But her mouth was taped, and ultimately, it didn't matter if the man worked himself ragged or not. The only path to freedom was through winning Kingsley's game.

He droned on with the rules to *Die, Bitch! Die* while Val waited in numb silence and wondered if this was repayment for a past life sin. What else but karma could explain her ending up in the clutches of the same serial killer twice? That went beyond bad luck.

The woman strapped to a chair between Val and the struggling man gazed at Kingsley in utter stillness. Val only had a view of her profile, but that was enough to register the sheer hatred the stranger aimed at their tormentor.

"We're here!"

The new male voice carried into the room from a distance. Faint, but clear. Valerie's heart skipped a beat before rebounding with a quicker tempo, rousing her from her detached little cocoon. More people meant they might have a chance.

Kingsley held up a finger, like they were at a tea party. If Val hadn't been so terrified, she might have giggled. "Excuse me one moment." He crossed the room to the doorway. "Bring her upstairs!"

Her? Her who? Not another contestant for his demented game?

"No, I need you to come downstairs first!" The man's voice was louder this time. Insistent.

Kingsley shook his head, stepped out of the room, and then seemed to change his mind. He turned and stalked over to Valerie, muttering something that sounded like, "The help need to learn their place."

The last of Valerie's numbness vanished when he released the straps that held her hostage with angry jerks of his hands. Her muscles tingled with adrenaline, igniting a dormant ember of hope. Kingsley was upset, which meant that something was wrong or not proceeding according to plan.

This was likely her one—and only—shot to escape.

She bided her time, plodding along in front of him like a pliant, hopeless puppet as he fisted one hand in her hair and jammed a gun to her ribs with the other. Out the door and into the hallway. Toward the staircase.

As she stumbled forward, she pep-talked herself, reminding her terrified brain that she was much stronger now. All she needed was a single moment of distraction. A chance to break free.

As she plotted, tears clogged her throat. Perspective was a bitch.

Before that fateful night when she'd agreed to meet a stranger on a dating app, she'd been feeling dejected. From her crummy apartment to her annoying roommate, she'd been too busy lamenting all the ways in which her life hadn't turned out exactly as she'd hoped.

So, so stupid. She'd give anything for a do-over.

She'd already loved and lost Ben, who'd been brutally murdered thanks to Kingsley. Her second chance with Flynn, she'd blown over PTSD mood swings. If Valerie escaped this mess, she vowed to give up dating completely and make her peace as a single woman. And promise never to feel sorry for herself again.

Her scalp shrieked when Kingsley yanked her hair, halting her progress a little shy of the top step, where the shadows deepened.

"Milos, I'm tired of this nonsense. Quit testing me and get up here, *now.*"

Milos. Val rolled the name around, but it didn't strike a bell.

"No! Keep your promise first. Send Bethany down to me as a trade!"

Valerie winced when the hand holding her hair twisted. "I'm afraid that's not possible. Bethany has an important role to play, one that cannot be altered."

"No!" A crash followed. A slam. Several bangs in a row. "I knew it!" The screaming had taken on an almost hysterical note this time. "I knew you were going to do this. You told me at the beginning the girl was mine, and now you're trying to go back on our deal. You want her for yourself, but she's not yours. She's mine! Give her to me!" More banging carried up the stairs. Val realized the noises were part of an adult temper tantrum.

Kingsley's breath brushed her ear as he laughed. "She's not yours until you earn her, Milos, and unfortunately, you haven't accomplished that yet. Perhaps you never will."

An enraged roar echoed from the lower level. "I'll kill your redheaded detective, I swear! I'll kill her right now, and what happens to your plan then?"

Val's stomach plummeted. *Oh no. Oh no oh no oh no.* But even as she breathed the silent chant, Milos shoved a woman into the soft glow at the foot of the stairs. The red curls and pale face confirmed Valerie's fears.

Ellie.

The gun pushed harder into Valerie's back, making her ribs protest in pain. The cruel fingers laced throughout her hair tightened so much that tears sprang to her eyes before easing again.

When Kingsley clucked his tongue, not a trace of the anger showed. "Milos, here I thought you were a professional when, all this time, your mother was right. You really can't be trusted to do anything right, can you?" He heaved a disappointed sigh. "I suppose that's to be expected, though, when you're raised by an ignorant, small-minded fool who lived her life based on made-up words in a book dictated by an imaginary man in the sky."

He's provoking him. A hysterical laugh bubbled up Valerie's throat. She'd found herself in this madman's web twice, and now she'd somehow managed to get trapped in the middle of a psychotic pissing match.

"Don't you talk about my mother!" the man named Milos screamed, sounding beside himself while Valerie shook the last of the cobwebs free from her head. This was it. There was no one else to save her this time, no clever detective swooping in to rescue her at the final hour.

Valerie had a single chance to rescue herself, and hopefully Ellie. She planned to make it count.

Her muscles tensed, ready to spring at just the right moment.

Not paying her any attention, Kingsley continued on in his conversational tone. "I think your mother would be very disappointed to learn what a failure you are, don't you? Generally speaking, but also as a man. That's why you like torturing little girls, isn't it, Milos? Because you're afraid of grown women? After all, you weren't even brave enough to come to the house without a woman to hide behind."

"I'm not afraid!" With an ear-splintering howl, Milos shoved Ellie to the side.

Before Ellie even hit the floor, the pressure on Val's rib cage vanished as Kingsley repositioned the gun to aim at the angry man.

Now!

Val lunged forward, yanking herself free. Agony tore at her scalp, but it didn't stop her from throwing her body to one side. As she braced for the fall, she watched Milos lock the gun on his target.

What was he waiting for? Shoot him n—!

Before the thought was complete, the stairway cracked multiple times in a row as bullets exploded all around her. She tried to remember what she'd been taught in her self-defense classes...tuck and roll.

By the time she'd rolled down the first few steps, Milo's body convulsed and collapsed to the floor. Over the roaring in her ears, Valerie swore she heard a thud from behind.

She prayed that noise was Kingsley taking a bullet, but she wasn't about to waste time finding out. Ears still ringing, Val stumbled down the next step toward freedom.

Ellie appeared, a gun raised high, her mouth open to scream something Valerie couldn't understand.

I'm coming, Ellie. We're free.

On the next step, Valerie's legs buckled as pain exploded through her back and chest. She reached out, grabbing the railing. She missed and began a plummet she couldn't control.

It was okay, though.

The fall didn't even hurt that much.

Everything happened so fast.

One moment, Milos's long arm was locked around Ellie's chest, and the next, she was stumbling away from a vicious shove to the back.

She was still recovering her balance when the gunshots rang out. Three.

As Ellie ducked for cover behind the banister, Milos fell backward, slamming into the hardwood floor skull-first. She sprinted over to grab the gun he'd dropped, and the second the cold steel was in her hands, she whirled and aimed at the second floor just as Valerie's body jerked.

"Val!"

The other woman hit the landing, but movement at the top of the stairs snatched Ellie's attention.

She squeezed the trigger and fired two rounds at Kingsley's retreating back. When he disappeared from sight, she kept her gun up but turned her attention to Valerie. The other woman's hand shook as she reached for the railing, lost her balance, and tumbled down the remainder of the steps.

Ellie raced to Valerie's side, and relief blanketed her when the other woman moaned. Moaning was good. Moaning meant she was still alive.

But when Valerie removed the hand clutching her chest,

Ellie's own heart went still. Bright red blood poured down the pink t-shirt, gushing from a single bullet wound.

"Ellie?" Already, Val's voice sounded weak to Ellie's ears.

Stop. She's going to be okay.

Ellie sank to the floor and pressed her palms to Valerie's chest. "I'm right here. You're going to be fine, you hear me? Just hold on."

Valerie gazed up at her through dreamy eyes. "It doesn't even hurt anymore. That's weird, right?"

Dammit.

"Hold on, Val! Please." But no matter how hard Ellie pressed, warm liquid continued to flow between her shaking fingers.

"Is he dead? K-Kingsley?"

Ellie snuck a peak up to the top, knowing she was a sitting duck where she was. "Not yet, but don't worry, I'll take him down. All you need to do is hold on, and you'll see for yourself."

"Th—" Valerie broke off with a wet cough.

Tears stung Ellie's eyes. "Shh, save your breath."

"N-no…" Valerie's hand fluttered to Ellie's arm. "Have to s-say, th-th-thank you. For always c-coming to save me…g-get him for me."

The first tear fell, sliding down Ellie's cheek like lava. "You don't need to thank me, got it?"

Valerie's harsh inhale was her only answer.

Ellie pressed harder, desperate to hold back the blood. "Val, you hold on now." The words were thin as they were forced to move past the clog in her throat.

This time, the exhale was more like a rattle.

She needed help…a phone…something.

Please, God. Help us. Help.

Valerie's breaths grew farther and farther apart, and the young woman's gaze fixed on something on the ceiling. The hand on Ellie's arm lifted, reaching toward something Ellie couldn't see.

"Ben…"

Tears poured from Ellie's eyes as silence washed over the room.

Valerie Price died with a small smile on her face.

34

W ith one hand clutched to my ear, I ran for the bedroom where my victims waited, reeling over Milos's betrayal. How had I misjudged the situation so badly? There were no excuses. I was a highly trained psychiatrist and should have noticed the signs of Milos's unraveling long before he reached the breaking point.

Ellie had nicked my ear with a bullet, and blood trickled down my neck as I hurried down the hall. Valerie's fall had saved me from an almost certain death by distracting my little detective, and I wasn't about to squander my advantage.

None of this was happening according to my vision. I'd wanted them all. Each of the women who'd escaped me. I was the one who was in control, not them. How could they not understand that by now?

My plan was in shambles. That bullet I'd delivered to Valerie's back would end her soon, if it hadn't already. She was supposed to play my game!

Gray edged my vision as my breathing turned harsh and uncontrolled, but I comforted myself with a reminder of the remaining hostages. Bethany in the safe room, and these two in—

I skidded to a stop just inside the bedroom where my players waited, stunned to find Katarina crouched by her boyfriend's chair, tugging at his bonds. So unworthy of her to waste precious time attempting to free that cretin.

She had, however, managed to free herself from my bonds. I had to give her credit for that.

A quick survey of her chair showed me how. The wooden arms lay on the floor, detached from the rest of the structure. Clever girl, but that came as no surprise. Not when I'd been the one to mold her into the remarkable woman she'd become.

My eyes narrowed at her frantic attempts to free the man. But, no, this type of behavior was unbecoming. My daughter, risking her life to save a man who wasn't even worthy to lick her boots?

Unacceptable.

Rage spilled over, blocking out the pain from my injured ear. Time was limited with Ellie here, so I had to be quick.

She still hadn't seen me, and as I approached, I extracted a knife from my pocket and tossed it at the kneeling woman. She jumped when the weapon clattered near her feet, and I smiled, leveling the gun at her chest when her dark gaze finally landed on me.

Our eyes met, and a fresh spark rekindled beneath my skin at this start of a new game. One where she didn't realize that I only had a single bullet left in the chamber.

"Remember our very first surprise together, back on that day I showed up at your house? How I killed those vile people who adopted you?"

A delicate shudder shot through me as Katarina nodded... slowly. Crouching on the floor, she watched me like a wild animal wary of a hunter's trap.

"It's your turn to do the same. It's my condition. If you ever want to see your daughter again, you'll replicate those efforts from so long ago."

Katarina was shaking her head and mouthing *no* before I could finish, so I raised my voice and cut her off.

"If you don't, I will never reveal where sweet little Bethany is, and I promise you that she will never be found. Your daughter will die...cold, alone, and starving. His life or your daughter's, the choice is yours."

"What the..." Clayne yelled, yanking hard at his restraints. "There's no way she's going to do that, you crazy son of a bitch!"

While he continued to curse, my attention remained on Katarina.

Partway through my speech, she'd started shaking, but as she stood, I recognized the resolve in her tense shoulders. She knew what was expected of her. Before she ever reached for the knife, my pride threatened to bubble over.

"Yes, that's my girl. Go on, make your papa proud."

Clayne thrashed his head back and forth. "No, don't listen to that sick fuck! I swear, we can find Bethany together! Then we'll get away from all this!"

The man's rounded eyes were glued to the weapon clenched in his lover's fist, and a sob escaped his parted lips. The room soured with an ammonia-like stench, and I sneered at his show of weakness. Just as I'd thought...this pathetic worm wasn't remotely worthy of my girl.

Do it.

Snot bubbled from the man's nose as Katarina pulled her arm back. When she hesitated, her body as taut as an arrow about to be launched, I egged her on with silent encouragement.

End this blubbering fool of a man and reestablish yourself as worthy of me rescuing you from your miserable existence all those years ago.

Clayne was sobbing openly now. "Come on, babe! It's me. Please don't do this! Please. We can—"

The knife swung.

The man screamed.

Goose bumps launched across my skin as my Katarina buried the blade deep into his worthless heart. Watching closely, I savored Clayne Miller's death throes, satisfaction roaring in my ears when I spotted the knife hilt perfectly angled between his ribs.

A fitting end to what, given time, would have proved to be a disappointing relationship. If nothing else, I'd spared my daughter that pain...just like I'd saved her from that cashier with more hair than brains back when she was still only a teen.

Even the sight of Katarina sinking to her knees beside her murdered lover with her head bowed couldn't dim my joy. Because when the chips were all on the table, she'd gone all in, with nary more than a moment of hesitation.

I beamed at the top of her downcast head.

That's my girl.

35

E llie pounded her laced hands into her friend's chest, willing her heart to restart. "Come on, Val."

A minute passed. Then two. Ellie's shoulders ached from the force of the compressions, but she would have administered CPR until her arms fell off if there was any hope at all. The realist in her had to admit defeat, though.

Feeling detached from her own body, Ellie slipped her right fingers up to check Val's carotid again. After fifteen seconds with no pulse, she had to accept the truth. Val had lost too much blood, and that gunshot had almost certainly struck her heart.

No ambulance in the world could save her now.

A hole tore open in Ellie's soul, and a whimper pierced the stillness. Hers. Shock held her frozen over the still, wet body. This brave, strong woman who'd successfully fought to free herself from a murderer was gone. Killed by the sadist who'd been responsible for putting her in harm's way in the first place.

Ellie's wounded moan transformed into an animal-like growl. She launched to her feet and hit the nearest light switch. When nothing happened, she grabbed the lantern off the buffet and looped the handle through her belt before scrabbling over to search Milos for any other weapons. Anything she could use to get Kingsley. That monster fled the moment his own life was in peril like the coward he was, but unless he'd sprouted wings, he was still upstairs.

Grabbing her Glock from the floor, Ellie lunged to her feet and bounded up the stairs while the lantern rattled against her thigh. Halfway up, she spared a glance for some photos of Katarina on the walls but didn't slow her pace.

A hallway full of closed doors beckoned at the top of the stairs, and Ellie wasted no time kicking the first one in. Her boot cracked against the wood three times before she burst inside, gun pointed and swinging in a wide arc. "Come on out, Kingsley, and say hello. I'm the one who got away, remember?"

A desk and chair covered in billowy white fabric were the sole occupants, so after a quick scan, Ellie moved on.

"Don't tell me you're okay with the living proof of your failure walking free? I'm here for the taking, come and get me!"

The first time she slammed her foot on the next door, shock reverberated up her leg, but the structure held. Another kick, and it sprang open with a crash.

Ellie performed a quick check of the bedroom, once again with the furniture covered in sheets. Empty. Her mouth tightened as she returned to the hall and repeated the process on the third door.

While she was checking that room's closet, a sharp crack whipped her head around.

Gunshot.

A bestial howl of pain and rage followed, and Ellie froze with her gun pointed at the door. Creeping back to the hallway, she turned the weapon toward the last room. Heart thundering, she sprinted down the narrow corridor, using momentum to smash the door in on the first try before going in low.

As she swept the space, she faltered because her first impression was blood...everywhere. It looked like some eccentric creative had splattered a gallon of red paint in an artistic fit of rage.

She spotted the man right as the sharp scent of urine bit her nose. He was slumped, chest perfectly still. Based on the blood pooled under his feet and the big black knife protruding from between his ribs, she didn't need any medical experience to suspect that he was dead.

Ellie crept closer and swore. With those restraints locking his arms in place, the poor bastard hadn't even had a chance. The setup reeked of Kingsley.

The hairs on her arms rose as she performed a slow turn. A small gold object glinted from beneath the bed, but before Ellie could reach for it, she spotted more red droplets on the floor.

Her fingers tightened on the trigger as she followed the red trail to a body deep within the shadows. A woman dressed in black army-type pants and a black t-shirt was sprawled on her back. Athletic build. Dark Hair. Also unmoving.

After clearing the room and finding no other bodies, living or dead, Ellie hurried over to the motionless figure. Dark lashes fanned pale cheeks and hid her eyes from view, but those sharp cheekbones and full lips were forever etched into Ellie's memory.

"Katarina, what the hell happened here?" she whispered.

Ellie sank to her knees and reached a shaky finger toward Katarina's neck, dizzied by the sense of déjà vu. First Val, now Katarina. Two of Kingsley's escapees murdered in one night.

Ellie had her issues with the latter woman, but she'd never wanted her to end up like this.

When she touched the clammy skin, she didn't expect to find a pulse. She *really* didn't expect the body to jump. Ellie shrieked and stumbled to her feet, gun raised and ready as she scoured the room with a frantic gaze while her nerves kicked into overdrive.

Trap, trap, this was all a trap.

But no one jumped out at her. Nothing stirred, except the injured woman on the floor.

"He shot me."

At Katarina's hoarse snarl, Ellie swung the gun in her direction. Kingsley's former protégé clasped a hand to her chest, just below her collarbone.

Still leery, Ellie motioned with the gun. "Show me the damage."

Katarina winced as she tugged her shirt collar down with the opposite hand. Beneath the blood staining her skin, a small round hole was visible. "Happy now?"

Unbelievable. Even now, bleeding from a gunshot wound, the woman was snarky. Ellie took that as a sign that Katarina would make a full recovery. "Not by a mile. Where's Kingsley?"

"No idea. He killed my boyfriend and promised to take me to see Bethany but shot me instead. Fucker!" She shouted the last word, then yelped and pressed her hand tighter to the wound, squeezing her eyes shut against the pain.

Ellie's hands slipped on the gun. "Bethany isn't here?"

Katarina's eyes flew open. "What? You mean you don't have her yet?" Using her good arm, the woman shoved herself into a sitting position. "What are you doing then? Get the hell out of here and find my daughter! Go! Now!"

Cursing loud enough to wake the dead, Katarina dragged herself to her feet and stumbled for the door. She paused in the threshold just long enough to tuck the arm on her injured side into the hole of her shirt in a modified sling with the aid of some colorful curse words.

"Which way did Kingsley go?"

Katarina turned in a circle, her eyes wild. "I don't know. I didn't see."

Ellie had been in the third room when the final gunshot had gone off, so she couldn't be totally sure of where Kingsley could have gone. She ran to a window, which was locked from the inside, before throwing open the door of a closet. Nothing.

Shit.

"Why are you just standing there?" Katarina screamed from the hallway. "Help me search! If that man gets away with my daught—"

Shuddering, she broke off and turned her back on Ellie.

Her cop instincts shouted an internal warning, reminding Ellie that the other woman was a dangerous criminal. But Ellie only hovered there for an instant before heading into one of the other bedrooms to hunt for Bethany behind a sheet-draped dresser. In her injured state and without a gun, Katarina wasn't as much of a threat, and there was no doubting that her panic over her missing child was genuine.

Plus, she was right. The two of them could make much quicker work of clearing these rooms if they teamed up.

Still, as they performed a thorough inspection of each nook and cranny big enough to hide an eight-year-old girl, Ellie kept one eye on the other woman. Old habits died hard, and she trusted Katarina only marginally more than she did the man who raised her.

With teamwork, they made quick work of the first room, then the second, with no signs of a little girl.

While peering inside an armoire in the third room, a

rumble outside made Ellie pause. From across the room, Katarina's head whipped up. "Is that a car engine?"

Without replying, Ellie raced to the nearby window. A nondescript black SUV skidded out of sight around the corner.

"Dammit!" She smacked her palms and rattled the glass as a helpless storm raged inside her. How? After all of this, after everything, how was Kingsley getting away again?

From somewhere deep within, a scream formed, but she trapped the noise inside her. Afraid to set Katarina off. Scared of setting herself off too.

Instead, Ellie hurried back into the room with Clayne's dead body and swept the lantern across the floor. Blood, chair leg, shoes...*there.* Peeking out beneath the sheet-covered bed was half of a golden rectangle. Ellie squatted and retrieved a discarded cell phone.

Please don't be dead.

Without the security code, Ellie couldn't dial the precinct, but emergency services still worked. She raced down the hall as she dialed, relieved to find Katarina where she'd left her.

"This is 911, what's your emergency?" a female voice answered.

"Hi, yes, this is Detective Ellie Kline. I'm at the scene of a multiple homicide and one of the perps is driving away."

A keening wail escaped Katarina at the news. Ellie plugged her non-phone ear and turned away, crossing the room to hear better. "Can you connect me to Charleston PD?"

After the 911 operator's initial confusion, her call got redirected. Ellie explained the situation to the officer who answered at the station, and before the call was disconnected, he assured her that CPD was on the way.

"He's really gone? With my baby?" The plaintive question drew Ellie's attention back to where Katarina slumped against the wall, her eyes bloodshot and tear tracks snaking down her cheeks.

Ellie stared at her former enemy's agonized face and couldn't help but feel for her. Not much in this world could rival the horror of knowing a man like Kingsley had your child. "I'm sorry."

The longer Ellie gazed into those haunted eyes, the more she wondered if there truly was a glimmer of shared understanding lurking within their brown depths. Or if the connection was all in her imagination, conjured by the sympathy wrenching at her heart.

After a jagged breath, Katarina's wounded expression shifted into something sharp and determined. "What are we going to do about it?"

Ellie's jaw hardened, and her chest swelled with her own determination. "We're going to find her."

36

Outside the interior set of double doors that guarded access to Elysium Psychiatric Center, Ellie toyed with the white visitor's pass clipped to her shirt, rocked on her heels, and counted down the seconds until the receptionist buzzed them in. "Here we go. Let's hope this visit leads to more kids being found."

The buzz sounded, and the lock clicked. Clay pulled the door open and let Ellie enter the bright corridor first. "Here's hoping. At the very least, you'll finally get closure on Lucas's case."

Ellie smiled at a young bald man in scrubs who hurried by them before pausing to peer into her bag. The DNA kit was there, nestled against Lucas's file and another file containing photos of the other missing children.

"Well, has anything jumped out of your bag and run away since the last time you checked?"

She rolled her eyes at Clay as they followed the receptionist's directions and turned left past a tree-filled atrium. The sun-dappled greenery provided a welcome break from the artificial lighting. Compared to most hospitals, this one at least smelled pleasant enough. The soft citrus aroma was much better than the usual antiseptic stench of bleach.

"Very funny. I just want to make sure we can confirm this boy's identity as Lucas Harrison once and for all. I need this one thing to go right."

The echo of their footsteps almost drowned out Clay's soft reply. "I'm sorry about Val."

Ellie flinched. Hearing her name still hurt. "I know you are. I'm sorry too."

After an intensive manhunt that ended in a cold trail of frustration and rage, it was becoming clear that Kingsley had found yet another hole to hide in. The pain that had continued to surge through Ellie since he got away had only grown sharper when she'd taken time off to attend Valerie's funeral the day before.

Ellie had insisted on paying for the service, but nothing could erase her guilt over the woman's death, or her grief. To fight that hard only to wind up dead by Kingsley's hand… well, the reality was almost too painful to bear.

Ellie had made sure that Valerie was buried next to her parents. Before she'd left the gravesite, she'd crouched down and whispered a promise over the freshly churned dirt.

"I won't stop until I get him, Val."

Ever since that moment, Ellie had felt combustible. Her body vibrated with feverish energy, the kind that rattled her bones and burned. Sometimes, the feeling grew so strong that Ellie feared the force might rip her apart.

She could only pray that she found Kingsley first.

"Did you check in on Katarina this morning?" Clay led them down another hallway.

"Yeah. Based on the amount of screaming she was doing at any nurse or hospital employee who had the misfortune to check in on her, I feel confident saying that Katarina will be completely recovered from surgery in no time."

They traded a brief smile before the amusement died, leaving Ellie feeling volatile again. She jiggled her hands in her pockets to soothe the fire beneath her skin. From the first time she set foot in the hospital, Katarina had been yelling at anyone who would listen to help find her daughter.

Back at the precinct, Ellie had cornered Valdez and smacked him on the chest. "Get your ass moving and *find* them."

Valdez must have sensed Ellie's internal frenzied state, or read wildness in her expression, because the detective's eyes had widened for a fraction of a second and he'd retreated a step. "I'm all over it, I promise."

He'd darted away right after that, like the new, post-Valerie Ellie Kline scared him.

She clenched and unclenched her hands. Good. Valdez should be scared.

Ellie would hound him and everyone else involved in the case until Kingsley was in custody and Bethany was safely recovered. She still couldn't believe she'd been so close to getting him...again.

The murderer had escaped through an undetected door in the master closet, an old servant's staircase that led to the kitchen. She'd been just inches from the hidden door. If she'd taken the time to find it, she would have been right behind him instead of watching him drive away from an upstairs window.

He'd never get away again, she promised herself.

Ellie veered toward the wall to allow a young couple sporting visitor tags to pass. A petite woman sobbed while the man rubbed her shoulder as his own eyes leaked. She waited until they were out of earshot. "Do you think the artist sketches will help find him?"

"I do. Remember, ever since his cosmetic surgery, we've been operating at a huge disadvantage. We know what he looks like now thanks to the details you and Katarina shared with the sketch artist, plus we have a name."

Abel del Rey. Thanks to Milos's phone, they'd found the alias Kingsley had been using. Not much else, unfortunately, but it was something.

"We'll find him this time, Ellie."

The quiet confidence in Clay's voice was like mist to her fire, helping tame the flames before they burst into an inferno. Where her moods were mercurial and volatile, he was a rock, and despite the often bumpy road of their relationship, she'd never appreciated his solid presence more.

To their left, a window revealed a glimpse of a rectangular table surrounded by plastic chairs, one of which was occupied by a dark-haired woman in glasses and a white lab coat. After double checking that the plate on the door read *Conference Room*, Ellie rapped on the wood and peered inside. "Dr. Eddington?"

The woman glanced up from a laptop with a smile that reached her eyes. "That's me, and you must be Detective Kline and Agent Lockwood. Please, come inside."

Ellie entered the room. When she reached for a chair opposite the psychiatrist, her attention fell to the man at the far end of the table. He stared into his lap, and his chair rattled with his fidgeting.

Ellie could relate.

She settled behind the table and pulled the files from her bag while Clay folded his body into the seat to her left. After arranging the folders in a neat stack, Ellie turned back to the man. "Lucas?"

When she called his name, the man's shoulders stiffened, but he didn't lift his head.

Dr. Eddington pushed her laptop to the side. "Luke?" She spoke in a soft, soothing tone. "These are the people we talked about. Detective Kline and Agent Lockwood. Can you say hello?"

Ellie held her breath as the man lifted his head. When his blue eyes met with hers, she wanted to shout in relief. Those eyes, the bone structure, the full mouth. They'd still need to perform the DNA test for confirmation, but based on the age progression photos, there was no doubt in Ellie's mind that the man known as Lucas Coleman and the missing boy named Lucas Harrison were one and the same.

"Hello." His gaze fell away quickly, and his teeth flashed as he raked them over his lower lip.

"Hi...Lucas? Do you prefer to go by Luke?"

The man shrugged in reply, so Ellie glanced at Dr. Eddington for input. The psychiatrist nodded, so she angled her face toward Lucas and smiled.

"So, Luke, Agent Lockwood and I are here on an investigation. We're trying to locate children who were stolen from their families many years ago by bad people who didn't treat them well, and we have good reason to believe that you were one of those missing kids. Did your name used to be Lucas Harrison?"

Another shrug, but the chair rattling grew louder.

Once again, Dr. Eddington interceded. "Luke, these people are trying to help you. Wouldn't it be nice to find your family again?"

A long pause. "Aaron is dead."

Dr. Eddington frowned. "Aaron?"

When Luke didn't answer, Ellie interjected. "I think he means his stepfather, Aaron. He was in the army, and he died overseas just before Luke went missing."

Ellie watched the young man closely as she spoke and didn't miss the increased tempo of his bouncing leg when she mentioned his stepfather, or when Dr. Eddington had suggested reuniting him with his mother. "You're an adult now, Luke. No one can make you go back to your mother if you don't want to."

His leg paused, and he glanced at Dr. Eddington for confirmation. "Really?"

She nodded. "Really. If you're released from here one day, you'll be free to go where you choose."

Luke appeared to think about that for a moment, and for an instant, a smile lit up his face. "Good."

The sunny expression that showcased his model-like features twisted Ellie's heart. To think that predators like Kingsley and Burton and the Bird and the Brute preyed on such innocent beauty was sickening.

She drew a steadying breath and rubbed her fingers along the folder. "We'd like to start by showing you photos of some of the people we think were responsible for taking children away from their families. Is that okay?"

Luke's nod was barely perceptible.

"Thank you. Would you mind coming over here to sit? It will be easier to look at the pictures that way." Ellie patted the empty chair to her right. "Or I could come down there and sit by you, if that's better."

In response, Luke's chair squealed across the floor as he rose and shuffled over to the empty chair. He scooted himself in, keeping his head down the entire time.

"Thank you."

Ellie opened the top folder and showed Luke a photo of Burton followed by the couple who'd forced him into taking photos before returning him like an ill-fitting coat.

He replied to each photo with a single nod but refused to answer any of Ellie's questions about them, or about whether or not any other adults were involved.

Questions about the retirement community met the same fate. Disappointing, but Dr. Eddington had prepared them ahead of time for this type of result. She'd informed them over the phone that Luke didn't like to open up about his past, which, in her opinion, was the result of severe trauma.

Up to this point, Clay had remained quiet, but now he spoke up. "Time to move on to the missing kids?"

"I think so."

As Ellie stuffed the first folder back into her bag, a phone rang.

Clay checked his screen and rose. "Excuse me for a moment."

When the door snicked shut behind him, Ellie turned to the man bouncing his leg in the chair next to her and softened her voice. "Luke, I know these next questions might be difficult, but it could really help us find other victims like you. Can you tell me if someone ever took photos of you with other children, or if you roomed with any?"

Luke's neck sank into his shoulders as he hunched deeper in the chair. His posture reminded Ellie a little of that famous Victor Hugo novel, and her heart twinged at his obvious discomfort. She understood better than most how difficult it was to open up about abuse, but the job was the job. If detectives eased up every time the questioning turned tough, the majority of cases would go unsolved. Every victim deserved one hundred percent.

That was the thought that helped Ellie open the folder and pull out photos. "Here, let's try this. I'll show you some photos, and just let me know if one of the children looks familiar, okay?"

After a long hesitation, Luke gave the faintest of nods.

Ellie released a quiet, relieved breath. "Thank you. I promise I wouldn't put you through this if it wasn't really important."

She slid the first photo onto the table. Luke glanced at the image of the eleven-year-old girl with stick-straight brown hair and freckles for a couple seconds before shaking his head.

Four photos in, Luke stopped jiggling his leg and straightened. "He stayed in the house for a while and then went away."

Ellie squeezed her hands together in her lap before relaxing them again. An excited gesture or outburst right now could send Luke into shutdown mode. "Do you happen to remember his name, or anything else about him?"

"No."

His reply dampened Ellie's excitement a little, but she mentally shrugged and moved on. "Okay, how about this boy?"

The next several pictures all received a quick head shake and dismissal, with Ellie's shoulders drooping more with each rejection. Finally, Luke paused on a photo. She held her breath while he chewed on his lower lip, studying the blonde girl for a good fifteen seconds.

At the end, he pushed the photo away with a decisive jerk of his head. "No."

The next series of photos all met the same fate. So did the ones that followed. No. No. No. By the time Ellie pushed the picture of another blonde girl in front of him, she was ready to throw in the towel. By now, it seemed obvious that he hadn't run into many of these kids or didn't remember them if he had, and either way, she needed to start from scratch and brainstorm a new avenue of investigation.

Ellie sighed and started to drag the little girl's photo back toward her.

"Wait!"

At the abrupt command, Ellie froze and stared at the young man. He'd sprung upright with his back now stiff as a board, and his wide eyes were glued to the girl's face.

This one. This one he knows for sure.

Luke confirmed her conclusion by snatching the photo and hugging it to his chest.

Ellie traded glances with Dr. Eddington before the doctor turned back to Luke and cleared her throat. "It seems as though that girl was someone special to you. Can you tell us who she is?"

When Luke raised his head, his eyes were shining. "It's her! The *girl*!"

Ellie didn't understand. The girl? What girl? Behind her glasses, Dr. Eddington's wide eyes now resembled an owl's, and Ellie's pulse picked up speed.

Whoever she was, this girl clearly wasn't news to the psychiatrist.

Dr. Eddington mouthed *wow* before turning to Ellie to explain. "When Lucas first arrived, he shared many stories about the time he spent living in the woods. The girl, as he has always called her, was often a prominent feature in those stories. You have to understand that at the time, he'd been through a lot, and was recovering from some pretty severe trauma. The way he talked about her, the fact that no one had ever spotted another person out in those woods, well… we chalked this girl he insisted had lived in his cabin with him up to imagination. A fantasy created by his brain to help alleviate the loneliness of living on his own at such a young age."

Ellie waited as the psychiatrist angled her face away and brushed her fingers beneath one eye. After inflating her chest and releasing the air, the doctor turned back, composed once again.

"I'm sorry, it's just…all this time, he's insisted that she was real, and I didn't…I even added delusion disorder to his diagnoses, along with the ASD. There just wasn't any evidence of her existence, and given his history with imaginary friends and PTSD…"

Dr. Eddington shook her head, her gaze a little watery as it landed on her patient.

"I'm sure it was hard." There was more that Ellie wanted to add, such as: *why couldn't you take him more seriously, especially when he never gave the fantasy girl up?* Instead, she bit her cheek. If Dr. Eddington's reaction was anything to go by, Ellie doubted the woman would be so quick to dismiss a child's stories as fiction in the future, no matter how wild they sounded. "What happened to the girl?"

Behind her lenses, the doctor blinked. "That's a good question. I guess...I guess nobody knows. When Luke was fished from the river with a broken arm, the rangers took him to the ER, and then he wound up here. That must be why he's always so eager to return to the cabin every year. He's hoping she'll be there, waiting."

"Who'll be there waiting?"

Until Clay's baritone came from behind her, Ellie hadn't realized he'd reentered the room.

"Luke's mystery girl. Her." Ellie nodded at the photo Luke had finally released and was arranging on the table with care. "She's—"

A strangled cry interrupted her, and Ellie's chair began to shake.

"Clay?" With fears of heart attacks and strokes gripping her chest, Ellie twisted in her seat. Clay's ashen face didn't soothe her alarm, nor did the strong fingers that curled around her chair back. Without the support, she feared he'd collapse to his knees.

"Clay, what's wrong? Can you talk?" Ellie said as Dr. Eddington pushed to her feet.

"Mr. Lockwood, do we need to get you to the ER?"

"No." The agent lifted a trembling hand from the chair to point at the photo. "That...that's Caraleigh."

Stunned, Ellie turned back to the picture of the pretty blonde preteen staring up from the table.

Oh my god. Caraleigh.

Ellie's hand flew up to cover her mouth as she stared at that image in disbelief. The mysterious girl from Lucas's past, the one he'd lived with in the woods all those years ago?

That girl was Caraleigh.

Clay's missing sister.

The End
To be continued...

Thank you for reading.
All of the Ellie Kline Series books can be found on Amazon.

ACKNOWLEDGMENTS

How does one properly thank everyone involved in taking a dream and making it a reality? Here goes.

In addition to our families, whose unending support provided the foundation for us to find the time and energy to put these thoughts on paper, we want to thank the editors who polished our words and made them shine.

Many thanks to our publisher for risking taking on two newbies and giving us the confidence to become bona fide authors.

More than anyone, we want to thank you, our readers, for clicking on a couple of nobodies and sharing your most important asset, your time, with this book. We hope with all our hearts we made it worthwhile.

Much love,
Mary & Donna

ABOUT THE AUTHOR

Mary Stone lives among the majestic Blue Ridge Mountains of East Tennessee with her two dogs, four cats, a couple of energetic boys, and a very patient husband.

As a young girl, she would go to bed every night, wondering what type of creature might be lurking underneath. It wasn't until she was older that she learned that the creatures she needed to most fear were human.

Today, she creates vivid stories with courageous, strong heroines and dastardly villains. She invites you to enter her world of serial killers, FBI agents but never damsels in distress. Her female characters can handle themselves, going toe-to-toe with any male character, protagonist or antagonist.

Discover more about Mary Stone on her website.
www.authormarystone.com

Donna Berdel

Raised as an Army brat, Donna has lived all over the world, but no place has given her as much peace as the home she lives in with her husband near Myrtle Beach. But while she now keeps her feet planted firmly in the sand, her mind goes back to those cities and the people she met and said goodbye to so many times.

With her two adopted cats fighting for lap space, she brings those she loved (and those she didn't) back as characters in her books. And yes, it's kind of fun to kill off anyone who was mean to her in the past. Mean clerk at the grocery store...beware!

Connect with Mary Online

facebook.com/authormarystone

goodreads.com/AuthorMaryStone

bookbub.com/profile/3378576590

pinterest.com/MaryStoneAuthor

instagram.com/marystone_author

Made in United States
North Haven, CT
02 January 2023

30497390R00183

The Author

Stanley Duane Kauffman was born near the village of Mattawana in Mifflin County, Pennsylvania. After graduation from Belleville Mennonite School (1954), Kauffman attended Eastern Mennonite College (now University) in Harrisonburg, Virginia where he received a B.S. in Secondary Education (1958). After obtaining a M.A. in History from Temple University (1963) his further graduate study included a year at St. Andrews University in Scotland (1968–'69).

In August 1958 he joined the faculty of Christopher Dock Mennonite High School at Lansdale, Pennsylvania, where he taught until his retirement in June 2003. In addition to his role as a social studies instructor, he chaired the Social Studies Department, served on the Administrative Council and Curriculum Committee, and was a faculty representative on the Campus Senate. He is presently on the Board of Trustees of the Historians of Eastern Pennsylvania at Harleysville, Pennsylvania, and a member of the Franconia-Lancaster Choral Singers.

Kauffman's interest in genealogy and Mifflin County Amish and Mennonite history led him to publish *Christian Kauffman: His Descendants and His People* in 1980 and *The Mifflin County Amish and Mennonite Story* in 1991. Duane and his wife Naomi (Hoover) Kauffman live near Perkasie in Bucks County, Pennsylvania where they are active in the Perkasie Mennonite congregation.